YOU BETRAYED ME

Books by Lisa Jackson

Stand-Alones
SEE HOW SHE DIES
FINAL SCREAM
RUNNING SCARED
WHISPERS
TWICE KISSED
UNSPOKEN
DEEP FREEZE
FATAL BURN
MOST LIKELY TO DIE
WICKED GAME
WICKED LIES
SOMETHING WICKED
WICKED WAYS
SINISTER
WITHOUT MERCY
YOU DON'T WANT TO KNOW
CLOSE TO HOME
AFTER SHE'S GONE
REVENGE
YOU WILL PAY
OMINOUS
RUTHLESS
ONE LAST BREATH
LIAR, LIAR
PARANOID
ENVIOUS
LAST GIRL STANDING

Anthony Paterno/Cahill Family Novels
IF SHE ONLY KNEW
ALMOST DEAD
YOU BETRAYED ME

Rick Bentz/Reuben Montoya Novels
HOT BLOODED
COLD BLOODED
SHIVER
ABSOLUTE FEAR
LOST SOULS
MALICE
DEVIOUS
NEVER DIE ALONE

Pierce Reed/Nikki Gillette Novels
THE NIGHT BEFORE
THE MORNING AFTER
TELL ME

Selena Alvarez/Regan Pescoli Novels
LEFT TO DIE
CHOSEN TO DIE
BORN TO DIE
AFRAID TO DIE
READY TO DIE
DESERVES TO DIE
EXPECTING TO DIE
WILLING TO DIE

Published by Kensington Publishing Corporation

LISA JACKSON

YOU BETRAYED ME

KENSINGTON BOOKS
www.kensingtonbooks.com

This book is a work of fiction. Names, characters, places, events, and incidents either are the products of the author's imagination or are used fictitiously. Any resemblance to actual persons, living or dead, events, or locales is entirely coincidental.

KENSINGTON BOOKS are published by

Kensington Publishing Corp.
119 West 40th Street
New York, NY 10018

All Kensington titles, imprints, and distributed lines are available at special quantity discounts for bulk purchases for sales promotion, premiums, fund-raising, educational, or institutional use.

Special book excerpts or customized printings can also be created to fit specific needs. For details, write or phone the office of the Kensington Special Sales Manager: Attn. Special Sales Department. Kensington Publishing Corp., 119 West 40th Street, New York, NY 10018. Phone: 1-800-221-2647.

Library of Congress Card Catalogue Number: 2020931279

ISBN-13: 978-1-4967-2222-5
ISBN-10: 1-4967-2222-1
First Kensington Hardcover Edition: November 2020

ISBN-13: 978-1-4967-2223-2 (ebook)
ISBN-10: 1-4967-2223-X (ebook)

10 9 8 7 6 5 4 3 2 1

Printed in the United States of America

CHAPTER 1

The Isolated Cabin
Cascade Mountains
Washington State
December 10

Alive!

I'm still alive!

I blink. Disbelieving. Stare up at the ceiling that seems to dance and spin above me.

My body trembles on the floor.

Twitching.

Flailing.

Sputtering.

But I wasn't killed.

At least not yet.

The twin burn marks on my neck are painful. They remind me that I could well be dead, that if the nose of a pistol had been pressed to my skin, rather than the cold metal tips of a stun gun, I'd be lying in a pool of my own blood, dead to the world.

It's only a matter of time, my mind warns.

I try to focus, blinking as I moan and twitch uncontrollably, feeling the hardwood of the tiny house against the back of my head. The vaulted ceiling seems higher than usual as it stretches over a small living area. It reels as my eyes try to focus, but they still jiggle in their sockets, my vision fragmented.

I stare at the built-in couch with its vibrant throw pillows, then spy the ladder leading to the loft, but everything in my vision pitches and weaves, refuses to stay steady. I try to focus on one item: the door leading outside, my only chance of escape, but it's closed down and appears to shift and sway.

God help me.

For just a second, I close my eyes, try to stop the shaking, but I fail to gain control of my body again.

Click, click, click.

Footsteps! The floorboards vibrate. Boot heels striking the hardwood remind me I'm not alone.

With effort, I twist my trembling neck and roll my head to one side to see my captor slipping something into the small refrigerator.

"Why?" I try to say, but nothing but a garbled groan slips past my lips. "Why?" I try again, but the person who's trapped me doesn't respond, just slams the refrigerator door shut and, with a disparaging glance at my shaking body, steps over me to the single door of the cabin and throws it open.

A blast of wintry air rushes inside, a few flakes of snow following. No, I try to scream. "Nnnnnneeeeeooo." Again, the sound is a cry of despair, the single word unclear.

But my captor understands.

Pauses for the briefest of seconds.

Then steps through the door and yanks it shut.

Thud!

I try to crawl toward it.

Click!

The lock's engaged.

Don't leave me, *I silently scream, my mouth opening and shutting like a just-landed bass gasping for air.* How can you do this? You, who swore you loved me? How can you leave me?

The betrayal is gut-wrenching, sitting sour in my stomach as I make another attempt to stop my muscles from shaking. Pull yourself together! Do it!

I try to stand, manage to get my feet under me, but the soles of my shoes slide, and my body flops to the floor again. All I can do is scoot, limbs palsied as I push my way to the door.

Over the frantic beating of my heart, I hear boots crunching on icy snow and the inevitable beep of a vehicle's keyless lock responding to a push of a button on a remote.

Don't do this!

I reach up, take a swipe at the door handle, and fail to clutch it.

With all the effort I can muster, I try again, this time connecting, my muscles finally responding. Groaning, I haul myself to my feet, and I slump against the door frame.

An engine revs as I reach for the door handle again, grasp it, and find it locked. Unmoving. As it always is. Locked tight.

Damn it.

Tears spring to my eyes as I hurl my body to the ladder and teeter for a second. My muscles quiver, and I grit my teeth, make a false start, and slide a bit. Locking my jaw against my chattering teeth, I grip harder, then slowly, rung by rung, climb until I can just peer over the windowsill of one of the five twelve-inch-square windows strung near the ceiling of the wall with the door.

Through the glass I see outside. The snowy landscape is stark in the small clearing, rimmed by tall firs, branches heavy and laden with ice and snow. In the clearing, I see the car, headlights glowing, cones of light illuminating the lane as it drives away.

My heart sinks.

Don't let it! The person who did this doesn't deserve your sadness. Get mad, damn it.

As the trembling in my body eases, I feel a swell of anger slowly rising. My fingers grip the upper rung on the ladder so hard my knuckles show bone white. The sound of the engine fades.

As it has before.

"I'll get you," I vow, my words hoarse but at least intelligible as I glare at the retreating vehicle, its taillights blinking red through the trees, reflecting blood-like on the snow. "You'll never get away with this."

I'll make sure of it.

CHAPTER 2

Cascade Mountains
December 1

"You prick!" Fighting tears, Megan pounded the steering wheel of her Toyota, then hit the gas. The tires spun, snow and gravel spraying as she backed up, threw the car into gear, then, the beams of her headlights splashing on snowy landscape, tore down the long lane leading away from James Fucking Cahill's farmhouse. And then, as if he were seated in the passenger seat, she kept ranting. "How could you? How the hell could you?"

She shouldn't have been surprised.

Once a cheater, always a cheater.

So why had she expected him to be her boyfriend, the man she thought was the love of her life, her soul mate, the goddamned "one," if you believe that rot? Of course, he'd shown his true colors and had turned out to be a two-timing dick.

She blinked hard, tears beginning to slide down her cheeks as she reached the county road, cut in front of a snowplow clearing the roadway, and sped through the night toward town. Angrily, she dashed the offensive tears away, while fence posts and fields of white passed by in a blur. At the stop sign, she slowed, then cranked the wheel and headed west, circumventing the heart of Riggs Crossing and speeding through the near-empty side streets of this little backwater town that purported itself to be an honest-to-God, year-round Christmas village. But then she knew as well as anyone how appearances could be deceiving, didn't she?

Out of the corner of her eye, she spied an elderly woman walking a little black Scottie dog in a sweater. Gray curls poking out from a red beret, the woman, in the glow of a streetlamp, shook her head and wagged a finger before making a "slow down" gesture by patting the air.

Megan didn't care. It was all she could do not to make her own gesture by flipping the woman off. But she didn't.

No reason.

Other than her heart was broken, her mind mush.

Why, why, why had she been such an idiot as to fall in love with James Cahill? She should have known better. "Crap." She *had* known better. In her rearview, she saw the old lady now on her cell phone, probably dialing 9-1-1 and reporting an erratic driver terrorizing the usually serene, almost bucolic streets of this little town tucked into the mountains of Washington State.

Too bad.

But she eased off the accelerator.

Didn't want or need a ticket.

It wasn't as if she was blind, for God's sake. She'd seen how James had been looking at that new girl in the restaurant, the way he'd once looked at her. But what had she expected? Didn't she know from personal experience how easily James's head had been turned? And women were always throwing themselves at him, a tall, handsome man with a cowboy attitude and a get-ready-for-the-ride-of-your-life smile that could turn even the most wary heart. They didn't even have to know that he was rich, or would be, to fall for him.

Hadn't she?

"You're an idiot," she said, not for the first time.

Oh, she couldn't wait to get to Seattle and her sister! Once in Rebecca's condo, she'd pour herself into a bottle of vodka and forget the bastard.

"Lying, cheating prick," she grumbled.

He belonged to her!

Didn't he get that?

Probably not now.

But he would. She'd see to it.

You know what?

She should just disappear on him.

Make him miss her.

Make him regret ever cheating on her to the depths of his soul!

Yeah, that's what she'd do.

Sniffing, she brushed the tears from her eyes with a gloved hand, then gripped the wheel so hard her fingers ached as she headed out of town and into the surrounding mountains. Then, as the snowfall increased, she flipped on her wipers.

Rebecca was expecting her.

Her sister. God. It was almost impossible to accept that James had been interested in Rebecca first. And, damn it, Rebecca, the ice queen, had fallen for him too! Well, nearly. As much as Rebecca would allow herself to fall for a man like James—a sexy bad boy with a reputation . . .

That was the trouble with James! He was handsome as hell and enough of a cad—yes, a cad!—that women found him attractive *without* even realizing he was rich. Or . . . would be, once he inherited the rest of his share of the Cahill fortune. Even without that knowledge, women were continually flinging themselves at him, and he, prick that he was, didn't exactly discourage them.

Fortunately, in Rebecca's case, she'd put all that behind her.

Her sister was long over James.

Right?

Didn't matter, Megan told herself, chin jutting as she squinted through the windshield, snowflakes swirling and dancing in the glow of her headlights.

Rebecca would know what to do.

She always did. Rock-steady, determined Rebecca Travers would help Megan set things right. Despite any latent feelings Rebecca might harbor toward James.

Megan's conscience twinged a bit. How many times had she relied on her sister? How often had she run crying back to her older sibling, who always helped? Even when . . . ?

She felt a small stab of guilt, which probably should have been sharper. Deeper. She glanced at her reflection in the rearview mirror.

The blue eyes in the reflection were red-rimmed, but not because of remorse. If she had the chance to do it all over again, to right that wrong . . . she bit her lip and pushed the thought out of her mind as her car struggled against the incline. She *wasn't* a bad person. Not really. And James . . . Oh, dear God, James . . .

A lump filled her throat as the Corolla nosed upward, snow now covering the pavement and piling along the sides of the road where the plow had come through earlier. She fiddled with the defrost knob, as the windshield was beginning to fog, and cranked the temperature to the highest level.

Nothing.

The fan was broken. Had been for weeks.

"Shit." She grabbed a used napkin from the coffee shop, which had been wedged into a cup holder. Lump in her throat, she swiped away the film as best she could, then she squinted through the windshield.

What little traffic there had been had thinned, and finally, as the car climbed, engine whining, she found herself alone on this stretch of road winding through the night-dark peaks of the Cascades. She pressed harder on the gas. "Come on. Come on." Visibility was hampered by the ever-increasing snowfall and, of course, the useless defroster. Once more, she wiped a spot clear above her steering wheel to see that now, in the mountains, the snowstorm was nearly a whiteout.

"Great."

She thought of James, and her heart crumbled. A wash of memories slipped through her mind, and tears threatened again. She hit the gas at the next sharp turn.

Her wheels shifted.

Spun.

She eased off. "Get a grip," she told herself as the car straightened out, the beams of her headlights reflecting in a million swirling flakes, the engine lugging down with the steep incline.

Their last fight had been their worst. Never before had anger and nasty words turned physical, but tonight her rage had been mercurial.

More tears.

Blinding her, just as rage had blinded her earlier.

Shaking her head against the memory, she floored the accelerator, snagged the wet, wadded napkin, and took another swipe at the fogged windshield as the road dipped suddenly.

"Crap!"

Her heart froze.

Another corner loomed, this one hairpin sharp.

Automatically, she hit the brakes.

The back tires spun as she turned the steering wheel with her free hand.

The Corolla hit ice and began a slow, steady swirl.

"No . . . no, no, no!" She was high in the mountains, the tops of eighty-foot fir trees level with the road, their icy branches laden with snow, the canyon below invisible. "Oh, God." She took her foot off both the brake and the gas . . . that was what she was supposed to do. Right? Drive into the spin or some such thing? Her heart pounded in her ears.

In slow motion, she saw the edge of the road, the piles of snow hiding the guard rail, if there was one, and beyond, the darkness.

Fear crystallized her blood.

Don't panic, Megan! Do NOT panic!

But a scream started to form in her throat.

Suddenly all four wheels found traction, and she had control again.

Oh . . . hallelujah . . .

Heart thudding, nerves jangled, she licked her lips. That was close. So damn close. She let out her breath slowly, concentrated on what she had to do, pushed the fight with James far from her mind and drove ever upward, meeting no cars, which seemed weird even with the blizzard-like conditions here, near the summit. A few more miles and she'd be heading downward.

To Seattle.

To Rebecca.

To sanity.

Over the summit, the car sped up.

She eased on the brakes, hands holding the steering wheel in a death grip. Around one corner. Faster and faster.

Slow it down!

But the car raced forward, gravity pulling her downward, the foggy windshield nearly opaque.

She tapped the brakes a little harder, the back end of the car sliding around a corner, her breath tight in her lungs. She swallowed as she guided the car down the narrowing road, snow piled high on either side.

Just a few miles and—*Oh, shit, what's that? Something in the middle of the road? At the next turn? No!*

Her heart a jackhammer, she squinted through a thin patch of clear glass.

On the road ahead something moved.

Something tall and dark against the white.

A deer? Elk? Some other creature?

The steady snow masked its shape as it darted to the side.

Two legs?

"Fuck!"

A man? Woman? Goddamned Sasquatch?

The shadowy image stepped into the middle of the damned road.

A person. Definitely a person.

What the hell?

"Hey!" she yelled, slamming on the brakes. "You idiot!"

The car shuddered.

No!

It began to rotate.

Faster and faster.

She rammed the gearshift into LOW.

But it was too late. The Toyota slipped sideways, spinning out of control. Through the windshield, she caught glimpses of the sheer cliff face on one side of the road and the steep canyon on the other. In the middle of it all, a person. A brainless, idiotic freak. "Shit, shit, shit!" She tried to steer, failed, the Toyota careening wildly to the mountainous side of the road, her bumper shearing ice off the cliff, only to send the little car back across the lanes, rushing toward the ravine, the scenery a snowy blur.

It was all over.

She knew it.

Through the foggy glass, she caught a glimpse of the snowy treetops in the thin beams of the headlights and, beyond the treeline, the vast darkness of the canyon.

This was how she would die, her car hurtling over the edge, crashing through the trees in the yawning darkness, plummeting hundreds of feet to the nearly frozen, snaking river far below.

God, no!

She stood on the brakes.

The crevasse beyond the treetops loomed.

One wheel found pavement.

Caught.

The back end of the Toyota shimmied.

Heart hammering, adrenaline firing her blood, she ignored everything she'd ever heard and cranked hard on the steering wheel, away from the ravine.

The car twisted. The Corolla's hood pointed directly at the massive wall of stone.

No person on the road between.

What had happened to that shadowy image?

She didn't have time to think about it. Just tried like hell to right the car, turning the wheel gently, her heart pounding wildly, her mind swirling.

She bit her lip.

The front wheels found traction, and she touched the gas, propelling the car forward, away from the canyon.

And straight at the wall of ice and stone.

She stood on the brakes.

Wheels locked, the car skated faster.

Megan braced herself.

Bam!

The Toyota collided with the mountain.

Her seat belt jerked tight.

Her eyes squeezed shut.

The car's front bumper crumpled, the hood damaged in a horrific groan of twisting metal and shattered plastic. The windshield cracked.

Something flew forward, launched straight into the mirror, shattering the reflective glass.

She expected the impact from the airbag as it burst out of the steering wheel.

Steeled herself.

Her car jolted to a stop.

No sudden burst of pressure or mass of air shot at her; no balloon trapped her against her seat.

Instead, there was silence.

Sudden and deafening.

And she was alive.

Miraculously unhurt.

Disbelieving, she stared at her gloved fingers, clenched in a death grip over the wheel. She slowly released them as she let out her breath. Her hands were trembling, her entire body quivering.

Get hold of yourself. You're okay.

Glancing through the cracked window, she tried to calm her wildly racing heartbeat, to focus.

The car. Can you drive it?

Could she get that lucky?

What were the chances?

She twisted the key, heard the starter grind. "Come on. Come on." If she could just get the car going, she would back up so that it wasn't crosswise in the road. She could put the car in NEUTRAL, if she had to, and aim downhill, riding the brakes, right? Until she was in civilization . . . or until she could call . . .

Her thoughts were interrupted. Her phone? Where the hell was her phone? She searched the interior quickly, then remembered something flying into the rearview mirror. Was that her cell? Desperately, she patted the seat next to her, wet from her spilled coffee and loaded with books and her backpack, anything she could just toss into the car.

Nothing.

Quickly, she scoured the floor of the passenger area, but it had a trash basket and two pairs of shoes and . . .

Oh, screw it!

It doesn't matter! Just get the car out of the road so you don't get T-boned.

She twisted on the ignition. The starter scraped, but nothing happened.

"Oh, come on!"

Another try, and the engine turned over, but . . . a movement caught her attention. Something dark in the shards of glass in the rearview.

From the corner of her eye, she saw something move, a dark and skittering image in the spiderweb of the rearview mirror.

The back of her throat went bone dry.

Oh, God. The person she'd seen moments before.

The cause of the accident.

She glared into the mirror, tried to make out the idiot who had caused this wreck. The damned moron was behind her car, barely visible, but definitely there. And now moving to the center of the road.

As if to block her path again.

Still risking both their lives.

Megan's temper spiked. What kind of a cretin would—

She threw open the door just as a cautionary *Be careful* cut through her mind. "Are you out of your mind?" she screamed, craning her neck for a better view. "Get out of the way! What the hell's wrong with you?"

No movement.

Nothing but bitter cold air.

And the silent whiteout.

No person.

Just the eerie quiet, broken only by the rasp of the Corolla's engine.

The warning hairs on the back of her neck raised.

Had it all been her imagination?

No, of course not.

She pulled the door shut and was about to back up when she saw the figure again. Right in the middle of the road . . . *again.* Almost taunting her.

What the hell was this?

It doesn't matter what it is. It's weird as hell. Not good. Get out. Get out now!

She swallowed back her rising fear.

What if the person needs a ride? What if they're stranded?

"Who cares?" she muttered. It wasn't as if the jerk-wad was waving her down, trying to get help. No, this was something else.

Something very wrong.

Something evil.

She touched her toe to the gas again.

Her damaged car struggled, wheels spinning.

"Don't do this," she whispered, her panic rising. She had to get out of here now. Her phone, where the hell was her phone? No time to search for it. "Let's go," she said to the car as the engine ground, the wheels spun, and she went nowhere. "Let's go, let's—"

Out of the corner of her eye, she saw movement in the side-view mirror.

The person in black was approaching!

Now she trod on the accelerator. "Come on!"

Closer. Through the curtain of snow, a figure dressed in ski gear from head to toe—mask and hat to boots—made his or her way along the side of the whining car.

Megan let up on the gas, then hit it hard. The back end of the car shifted a bit, but the tires found no traction.

The person was right outside the door, and Megan was ready to yell at the cretin, to read the brain-dead idiot the riot act, when she noticed the gun, a black pistol in one gloved hand.

Oh. God.

She began shaking her head, still trying to drive off until the barrel of the gun was level with her head.

Megan's heart dropped.

Fear curdled through her blood.

Panic jettisoned through her, and she started to turn. To run.

Leave here. Now!

"Get out!" the attacker growled.

Megan froze.

That voice!

Did she know this person? This nutcase?

She couldn't tell. All she could focus on was the barrel of the gun.

Black.

Deadly.

Aimed straight at her heart.

CHAPTER 3

Valley General Hospital
Riggs Crossing, Washington
December 4

"I have to leave." James Cahill gazed hard at the nurse adjusting his IV. Lying in bed, doing nothing, was getting to him. The hospital walls were closing in on him. And the not remembering? That was killing him.

"In due time," she said pleasantly, offering him a sympathetic smile. Sonja Rictor, RN, according to the name tag that swung from a lanyard at her neck. In her forties, a knowing smile on her face, her curly red hair clipped away from her face, a sprinkling of freckles sprayed across a slightly upturned nose, she was slim and attractive. And, he guessed, blessed with a will of iron behind that empathetic grin.

"The time is now." It was all he could do not to grab her wrist and give it a shake, to emphasize that he was serious. He'd always been a little claustrophobic, blessed or cursed with a lot of energy. That much he did remember. Being confined in a hospital was definitely not his thing.

"I understand."

"Do you?"

She gave him an "I've heard it all before" look that, he supposed, was meant to shut him up. It didn't.

"Mr. Cahill—"

"James. It's James," he said, not interested in any kind of formality.

"I'll talk to the doctor, *James.*"

He felt a sharp prick as she adjusted the needle, but he didn't wince, didn't want to appear to be a damned wuss.

"He'll get you out of here as soon as he thinks you're ready." She shook her head. "Trust me, these days we don't keep patients a second longer than absolutely necessary." Stepping away from the bed, she asked, "So, how's your pain?"

"It's fine."

"On a register of one to ten, ten being the highest-intensity pain?" She motioned toward the wall, where a chart had been tacked. The chart was a display of cartoon faces, everything from a pleasant, pain-free grin under the number 0 to a contorted, red-faced grimace at 10. "When you say you're 'fine,' is it fine as in here?" She indicated a calm, happy-looking face under the number 2. "Or?" She moved along the row of ever-increasing unhappy faces. "Here?" She tapped a gloved finger at a sweating, frowning image at 8.

Shifting on the bed, he felt a sharp jab in his shoulder. *Blast.* "I'm okay."

"Uh-huh." Disbelief.

"I said, 'I'm okay.' "

"That might be up for debate." Her eyebrows elevated. "So? Your pain level?"

"Maybe a five. Or . . . a seven. Yeah, a seven." It actually was much higher, but he couldn't bear looking as weak as he felt. He always struggled when he wasn't in control.

"Mmm." She wasn't buying it, had probably seen it all before. "No reason to be a hero."

"That, I'm not," he assured her. No lie there. It was one of the things he did know about himself, one bit of insight he recalled. And about the only thing. At least as far as recent history went.

"I'll get you something to make it a little more tolerable," she promised as she stripped her gloves at the door and tossed them into a wastebasket.

"Wait," he said as she started to leave. "What day is it?"

"The date? The fourth." When he didn't respond, she clarified, "Of December."

He squeezed his eyes shut, tried to do the math, but had no real starting point. "So I've been here . . . what? Two days?"

"It's Sunday. You were brought in Thursday night."

"The first." *He'd been here three damned days?* And in that time, he remembered only glimpses of people coming in and out of the room, bothering him, not allowing him to sleep, always asking how he was feeling or poking or prodding him; he'd had no awareness of time passing.

Until today. A digital clock mounted over the door told him it was a little after two in the afternoon, the gray sky outside confirming that dusk was still a few hours off.

"I'll talk to Dr. Monroe," the nurse said. "He's on duty this weekend." She stepped out of the room.

Two and a half days of his life gone. Lost in the black hole of his memory. How had it happened? James had no inkling why he was here, though he was sure he'd been told. In the haze of the last few days, he recalled seeing the doctor, though it was vague, and he couldn't call up the guy's name or what the doc had said was wrong with him. If they'd even had that conversation. If so, he couldn't call it up.

Obviously, he'd screwed up his shoulder. It hurt like hell, no matter what he'd told the nurse. And his chest ached, sharp pain cutting through it when he shifted—bruised or broken ribs, he figured. Then there was that ominous bandage over half his head. And when he rubbed his jaw, it hurt.

He glanced around.

The hospital room was small, with only the bed, a TV mounted on the wall, and a vinyl chair placed near the heat register that was tucked beneath a single window. The view wasn't that great; it overlooked a parking lot a story or two below. A few cars were scattered throughout the lot, all collecting snow that was continuing to fall, the asphalt covered with a white blanket showing few tire tracks.

Had he been in a car wreck? A bar fight? Fallen? What? He moved on the bed, winced, trying to remember. But it was a no go. Whatever information had been imparted had floated away on a wave of pain and/or medication, which, right now, wasn't working.

Didn't really matter.

He needed to get out of here. Get back home. He had a ranch and a hotel on the property, along with a Christmas-tree farm and a tiny-house construction business, all on acres outside of town.

He rubbed his eyes.

Felt as if he were clear-headed since . . . since . . . God, why couldn't he remember? Pushing a button on the bed frame, he raised his bed high enough that he caught a glimpse of himself in a mirror mounted over the sink. "Jesus," he whispered, barely recognizing himself in the reflection. His usual tan had faded, and he appeared gaunt beneath at least a three days' growth of beard shadow. His eyes were sunken deep in their sockets, his brown hair unruly where it was visible, the bandage wrapped over his crown. Down the left side of his face, deep gouges—like claw marks—were visible. As if he'd been on the losing side of a takedown with a cougar.

The old punch line *You should see the other guy* swept through his mind, but he didn't so much as crack a smile. Because he knew there was no other guy. In James's experience, those who usually scratched and clawed were female. That didn't bode well. Well, hell, none of this did.

"Not good, Cahill," he said and fell back against the pillows.

He was in a fight with a *woman?*

He squeezed his eyes shut. Tried to recall.

A memory, hot and dark, started to surface: a woman's distorted, furious face bloomed, then withered away again.

This was so wrong.

He started to rise again, threw off the scant covers just as the door swept open and a bald man on the north side of forty stepped into the room. His name tag read: GRANT P. MONROE, MD. A trimmed goatee that had started to gray covered his chin, and behind rimless glasses, his gaze met James's. He introduced himself and added, "We met earlier."

Did we?

"You may not remember."

"I don't."

"Hmm." Noncommittal. But his eyes narrowed a fraction.

"In fact, I don't even remember how I got here."

"Results of a concussion." He was using a penlight to stare into James's eyes. "Should clear up in a few days."

"Should?"

"Could be longer. Might come all of a sudden, seemingly out of nowhere, but more likely in bits and pieces as something you see or hear creates a connection. As time passes, as your brain heals, hopefully you'll piece it all together." He shone his light in the other eye.

"Hopefully?"

"No one can be certain."

"How comforting."

The barest hint of a smile at the sarcasm. "Give it time."

"What choice do I have?" James grumbled.

The doc didn't react, nor answer, but explained that not only did James have the concussion, but he had suffered three cracked ribs and torn ligaments in his right shoulder, along with some abrasions and contusions.

"You're lucky," the doctor concluded.

"Lucky?"

"Could've been much worse."

"How?"

"Well, the blow to your head could have killed you."

"I was hit?"

"You fell."

"I fell?" he said, thinking of all the damage.

"Or were pushed," Nurse Rictor said as she returned, sweeping around the doc to insert something in his IV as Monroe examined his shoulder.

"Pushed?" James repeated.

Monroe lifted James's right arm, rotating it slightly, and James felt the color drain from his face as he sucked in his breath. "Bad?" Monroe asked.

"I'll live."

"Good." Monroe returned James's arm to its sling. "Bruised and lacerated shoulder," he explained. "Nothing broken. As I said, 'lucky.'"

James snorted his disbelief, then said, "So back to what happened—?"

Before the nurse could answer, the doctor said, "The police want to talk to you about that. We were instructed to not answer your questions."

"What? Why not?" James asked and, despite a warning glance, Nurse Rictor responded, "Because of the investigation."

"What investigation?" This was beginning to sound ominous.

"You'll have to ask them. They want to speak to you."

"Great." James couldn't remember all that much, at least not concerning recent events, but he knew he had an instinctive aversion to the cops.

"How did I even get here?" James asked.

"Some kind of fight or altercation," the nurse said. When she received the hard look from Monroe, she added, "He has the right to know."

"Fight?" James repeated. God, he thought he was long over bar fights and the like, had years before learned to contain his mercurial temper.

"Domestic dispute," she offered.

She had to be kidding. "With whom?"

"We don't know that," Monroe interjected, and the nurse rolled her eyes, obviously as tired of the red tape as James was.

"That's what we heard from the police," said Rictor. Still ignoring the doctor's grim expression, she barreled on. "It happened at your house. Nine-one-one was called, and the paramedics found you there. You had fallen or were pushed and hit your head against the corner of a hearth."

He sat up a little straighter, trying to remember. In his mind's eye, James saw himself backing away, stumbling, falling as he avoided . . . who? what?

Fireplace? He saw the raised brick hearth at his farmhouse, recalled stumbling backward, trying to avoid . . . what? *who?*

A woman.

He touched his cheek again.

A blistering memory teased at him . . .

You'll never see me again!

The words stabbed through his mind.

Who had spat them out so viciously?

He should know.

But he didn't.

Now he asked the nurse, "Who made the emergency call?"

"Don't know," she admitted.

"So who was I fighting with?" he demanded again.

He saw a shadow flicker across Dr. Monroe's face. "No one's really sure. The police want to talk to you, hear your side of the story."

"The person who I was fighting with. He—she's not here? Wasn't admitted?" James asked, thinking the person might be injured as well.

"Not that I know of."

The nurse interceded. "She could have been taken somewhere else."

"She?" he said, his worst fears confirmed. "Who?"

Rictor shook her head. "No one knows what really happened. Yet."

"But I was in a fight with a woman and ended up here?" he clarified, agitated. "Is she all right?" He was sitting up now, ignoring the pain.

"The police think it was with your girlfriend."

Something deep in James's gut tightened, and he felt there was a grain of truth to the story.

"My girlfriend?" he repeated, faces of women he'd seen in the past flitting through his brain, faces he couldn't name . . .

"Megan Travers."

"Megan." He said the word as if tasting it, felt Monroe's hard gaze and Rictor's curious one studying him as he tried to bring up a face to match the name. An image teased at his brain, but it was shadowy and vague, the features indistinguishable. Slowly, he shook his head, and a dark thought burned through him. What if she hadn't made it? What if the reason they were being so coy and the police so adamant about wanting to talk to him was that she was dead, that he . . . oh, God, that he'd killed her? An accident. Surely. "But she—Megan—she's all right?" he asked, his heart thudding, a deep fear clutching his soul.

"I don't know anything about it." Monroe avoided his eyes. A bad liar. "You'll have to ask the detective."

Detective? Not just a cop called for a disturbance. The nurse had said "investigation," hadn't she? So it only made sense that detectives would be involved.

"But she didn't die," James said, his voice tight. God, what had happened?

The nurse started to say something, but the look the doctor sent her shut her up.

James grabbed her arm.

"I have to know," he said, his voice a rough whisper. She gazed pointedly at his gripping fingers, and he dropped his hand.

Monroe's face was hard, cut in stone. "The police will tell you—"

"Screw the police! I need to know!" He pushed upright, swung his legs over the edge of the bed as a bolt of pain shot through his chest.

"Mr. Cahill," Monroe said firmly, "I'd advise you to take it easy." His manner had gone stiff. "And don't touch Nurse Rictor or any of us again. The police will tell you what you want to know."

"Call them," James ordered.

The doctor nodded. "Already done."

Dread stirred inside James, and his jaw clenched at the thought of facing the police. He'd never liked cops; he remembered that, and he never would. He'd had more than one run-in with the law, back in his hellion-of-a-teenager days, when he was a hot-headed youth who'd rebelled against his parents, his scandal-cursed, wealthy family, and the whole damned world.

So why all the trouble now?

What had landed him here? He fought to recall, but came up empty. Whatever had happened, it had been bad. Very bad. He forced his thoughts to earlier in the week, what he could remember of it: the snow that was still falling outside the hospital windows, the coming of the busy season with the approaching holidays.

He'd been brought here Thursday, the nurse had said. What had he been doing? The last thing he recalled was that he'd been working on an order for one of the tiny houses . . . right? And there had been some kind of glitch, but he couldn't remember what. He'd gone from the shed, where the house was being constructed, to the inn . . . like always . . . right? Picked up dinner at the restaurant and . . . and . . . and driven home. He remembered stepping inside, his dog greeting him, and then headlights in the driveway. Then?

Damn if he could recall.

Monroe was speaking again, bringing him back to the here and now. "—a call in to Detective Rivers."

"He's the cop I need to talk to?" James asked.

"Yes."

So be it. No one here was going to give him any answers. He read it in Monroe's staunch professionalism. James was being stonewalled. Either the doctor didn't have any answers or had been instructed to keep his mouth shut. And Sonja Rictor had clammed up. Grabbing her had been a mistake. She was now as tight-lipped as Dr. Monroe, saying only, "I'm sure you'll sort it all out once you remember." She injected something into his IV. "This should help take the edge off."

"I need to get out of here," he said.

"Not tonight." Monroe was firm, and James had trouble concentrating, probably from whatever it was that had been slipped into his IV.

"If you don't let me out of here—"

The doctor cocked his head in unspoken question: *Then what? Where do you think you'll go? What do you think you'll do?*

"At least give me my phone."

"We don't have it," the doctor said, looking at the nurse for confirmation. She gave a quick shake of her head.

Blinking to stay awake, James said, "It must be at home . . ."

"I'll check on you tomorrow," Monroe was saying, and James watched him leave the room, the nurse at his heels.

James lay back on the pillows, his eyelids heavy as the meds kicked in, and he suddenly didn't care that he was being held here in the hospital or that his cell wasn't with him. He thought he heard the swoosh of the door to his room opening, and he tried to waken, but his eyelids were so heavy. He managed to crack one eye and caught a movement, then the back of someone he didn't know, someone in scrubs scuttling away, a rope of jet-black hair falling between her shoulders as she hurried out of the room. He blinked, and she was gone.

If she'd ever really been there.

His mind was playing tricks on him, and the person quickly exiting the room could well be just a wayward image his mind had created.

But had he caught a waft of some perfume?

It didn't matter. Not now. Not when he was so damned tired, grateful for the sleep pulling him under.

As he slipped away, a woman's face floated for a second before his eyes—a beautiful woman with even features, a quick, wry smile, dark auburn hair, and a suspicious glint in her gold eyes—but he didn't know if she was real or a figment of his imagination. Someone he knew or had just seen in passing. Her name—did he even know it? It eluded him, and he remembered the nurse's assertion that his girlfriend had been Megan. But that didn't seem right. He felt his eyebrows slam together as he tried to conjure her to the surface of his faulty memory, only to fail. Who the hell was she? he wondered, before drifting away on a soft, welcome cloud of relief.

CHAPTER 4

"Amnesia? Can you believe that?" Detective Brett Rivers didn't. Not for a second. He shot a skeptical look at his partner over the snow-covered hood of his Jeep Cherokee before climbing inside. He'd woken up in a bad mood hours before, and as the day had worn on, it hadn't improved much.

Wynonna Mendoza slid into the passenger seat and buckled up. A petite woman in her mid-twenties, she was whip smart, smooth-skinned, and not afraid to speak her mind. Her usually unruly black hair was pulled into a knot at the back of her head, and large hoop earrings dangled at the sides of a face that was devoid of makeup. Her eyes were light green and sparked with intelligence, and her humor was sarcastic. Like his. She sent him a look. "The doc says it's possible."

"Possible or probable?"

"Possible," she said as her phone beeped. She pulled it from her jacket pocket.

"Pretty damned convenient, if you ask me." He reversed out of the parking space, then wheeled through the lot. Snow was still falling steadily, and he flipped on his wipers as he reached the first intersection. "I'm not buying it."

"Head trauma. Concussion."

"Yeah, yeah."

They were passing by the storefronts at the center of town, hundred-year-old buildings tucked tightly together, most with Western façades and awnings, pedestrians bundled in thick jackets with hoods or warm stocking caps as they hurried from one shop to the other. Mendoza was buried in her cell phone, answering a text, but said, "It happens."

"If you say so."

"I don't. The doc does." A pause. Then, "You really want to do this?" She looked up from the small screen.

"Uh-huh." He felt as if he was spinning his wheels. Already stuck, with no new answers, and even though he'd been to the hospital twice, he hadn't had a chance to interview Cahill. Each time, he'd been asleep, and the doc in charge didn't want the patient disturbed.

Fuck that.

"It's your show."

"Case," he reminded her. "My case."

"Whatever." She sounded bored, but she slid him a quick sideways glance, and he knew she was needling him. A little nervy for a newbie. But it helped lighten things up.

Besides, he wasn't exactly a senior with the department himself, he thought as the town stretched out, tightly packed storefronts morphing into strip malls, gas stations, and parking lots. He'd spent years with the San Francisco PD before a change in leadership coincided with his divorce, and he'd decided to chuck it all, move anywhere out of state, far from the bustle of the city and a clog of humanity.

He'd envisioned this middle-of-nowhere county in western Washington as just the spot to land, far from Astrid and her new husband, away from the noise, headaches, and crowds of an overpopulated city.

He thought he'd left serious crime behind him.

But, hey, guess what? People are people, and now he was staring at a missing person, possible kidnapping, and potential homicide all rolled into one case.

Centering around James Cahill. Mr. No Memory.

Forever sleeping and probably in a haze of drugs anyway.

Rivers glowered through the icy windshield of his Jeep as the remnants of town gave way to a few houses bordering the river whose snowy banks lay white against the dark, fast-moving water, the bridge spanning its chasm icy with the cold. On the far side, all evidence of the town disappeared, the landscape a white blanket over acres of farmland rimmed by stands of evergreens and broken into sections by fences. A few farmhouses were visible, long lanes plowed, lights in windows against the gray day, eaves mustachioed with ice and snow.

He barely noticed as he drove, his wipers scraping snowflakes from the windshield, Mendoza again into whatever was so fascinating on her cell. The engine hummed, the interior warming, and Rivers's thoughts were centered, as they had been for a couple of days, on James Cahill.

When Rivers had been a cop in San Francisco, he'd heard about the Cahill family. The Cahills' wealth, philanthropy, and scandals had been legendary, always cropping up in the news and forever a headache for the department. There had been a little—no, make that *a lot*—of crazy running through the Cahill generations, and James, even living up here in Bumblefuck, Washington, was heir to a fortune that had existed for a century, or perhaps longer.

Old San Francisco money.

And now, lo and behold, the golden boy was up to his eyeballs in trouble.

Go figure.

Rivers's fingers tightened over the steering wheel.

"Pretty out here." Mendoza had glanced up, her gaze straying to the passenger window, where she was watching a couple of horses running through the drifts, manes flying, tails streaming like banners as they kicked up sprays of snow.

He didn't argue. "Sure."

She threw him a glance. "Come on, Rivers, even you can stop long enough to smell the roses."

"Horses. You mean smell the horses."

"Lighten up."

He didn't. His thoughts were dark as the encroaching night as he drove through the ever-rising hills to the Cahill estate, a massive piece of property of nearly four hundred acres that included a working ranch, a Christmas-tree farm complete with inn and restaurant, and a grouping of newer, linked, barn-like structures where Cahill designed and assembled some of those ridiculous, high-end tiny houses. Homes on wheels you could barely turn around in, the kind that made a New York apartment seem spacious. But as small and unique as those little mobile houses were, they were constructed on a vast parcel of land in the Cascade foothills, much of it forest.

Finding a body in that area would be like looking for a needle in a haystack. And the all-points bulletin for Megan Travers's car had turned up nothing. Then again, the police might not even be looking for her except for the missing person's report from Travers's sister, Rebecca, and her statement that Megan had been upset and called her, told her she'd had a fight with James Cahill and was driving through a near-blizzard to reach Rebecca's condo in Seattle.

But she hadn't arrived.

That had been two days ago, with Megan Travers already missing nearly twenty-four hours at that time.

Coincidentally, James Cahill had been discovered unconscious and wounded, a struggle evident in his home, a note from someone, presumably the missing Megan, declaring she was leaving him on the very night she had called her sister to say she was on her way.

"We've already got Knowlton's statement," Mendoza reminded him as she fiddled with a knob on the dash, adjusting the vehicle's temperature.

Robert "Bobby" Knowlton was the person who had found Cahill and called 9-1-1.

"He might have forgotten something."

"Okay." She wasn't buying it, but she quit messing with the controls for the heater.

"And I like to see the scene when it's not crawling with techs and deputies and EMTs tromping all over the place." He didn't know why he was explaining it, as it was, as she'd said, his case. He slowed for a curve just as an oncoming pickup drifted across the middle of the road.

"Watch out!" she yelled.

Rivers jerked on the wheel, his SUV swerving, a tire skimming the edge of a snow-covered ditch.

The truck, fishtailing, missed them by inches.

The Jeep slid and caught as, beside Rivers, Mendoza braced herself. "Holy—"

"Idiot," he muttered under his breath.

Mendoza was twisted in her seat, aiming her phone through the back window as she attempted to snap pictures through the glass. "You should go after that guy! He could've killed us!"

"I should."

"I'm serious, Rivers! That prick is dangerous! I'm calling it in."

Rivers checked his rearview, but the truck was already out of sight, having disappeared around the curve and into the curtain of snow.

Mendoza had her phone pressed to her ear and was already describing the pickup to a dispatcher. "I don't know . . . Chevy, older model."

"Ford," he corrected. She shot him a look.

"Rivers says it was a Ford. White, I think."

"Silver."

Another dark glance was sent his way. "Silver. With . . . Washington plates, I think. I couldn't really see. And no, I didn't get the plate numbers."

This time he didn't interject as she told the dispatcher the location; but it was an effort in futility, just a chance for Mendoza to let off steam. She clicked off.

"He probably just hit ice and slid into our lane."

She frowned. "Doesn't matter. No excuses! Either you know how to drive in the damned snow, or you stay the hell home." Craning her neck again, she peered through the back window as if she expected the pickup to reappear. It didn't. "Anyway," she said, letting out her breath as she settled into her seat again. "Road deputies will be on the lookout. I hope they nail that moron."

"They could get lucky."

She let out a huff of air. "You don't even care."

"Got my mind on other things."

"Bigger problems than getting killed and meeting St. Peter today?" There was still an edge to her voice.

"Right."

"We're here anyway," she said just as he spied the rustic inn set back from the county road. "And we're not alone." They'd caught up with a line of traffic, many cars peeling into the parking lot of the Cahill Inn. Like most of the commercial buildings in Riggs Crossing, the two-storied hotel was complete with a Western façade of weathered cedar siding, a covered porch running the length of the building, and, to add authenticity, hitching posts and watering troughs flanking the two wide steps leading to the front doors.

"Straight off a Hollywood set," Mendoza observed, as Rivers spied the turnoff to the Cahill house. "Y'know, for an old Western show like

Gunsmoke. Or *The Rifleman*." Then, as if she anticipated a question, "My grandpa's a big fan. There's a Western channel on cable, and whenever he's not watching sports, he's tuned into reruns of old black-and-white shoot-'em-ups. *Maverick*. That's his fave. It still holds up."

He wasn't paying too much attention to the conversation as he peeled off the main road, just before the hotel, leaving other vehicles to vie for limited parking space in the lot that separated the hotel from the lane to James Cahill's home. A border of fir and pine divided the private lane from the commercial property. Through a line of trees, Rivers noted that the back side of the Cahill Inn was visible. There, additional parking separated the inn from a café near an arched entrance to Cahill Christmas Trees. The area was bustling with people in ski coats, puffy jackets, gloves, and hats. Couples pulling kids on sleds. Workers in red jackets strapping trees onto the roofs of vehicles.

The Cherokee jarred as it hit a root hidden by the snow just before the gate posted with a sign that read PRIVATE PROPERTY.

"I'll get it," Mendoza said, already slipping on gloves.

Before Rivers could argue, she was out of the Jeep and unlatching the gate to shove it open, the lower rail scraping a mound of snow behind it. He drove through, and she partially shut the gate again before hopping back into the passenger seat, bringing with her a rush of frigid air.

"Geez, it's cold," she said, shivering.

"Winter."

"I hate it."

"Then you moved to the wrong place."

"Probably." She didn't elaborate, and he didn't pry. The truth was he didn't know much about her, just that she'd transferred from a department in New Mexico, somewhere around Albuquerque, and her record there had been clean, even stellar, and the one time he'd asked about the move, she'd said, "It was time." He hadn't pushed as his own reasons for ending up at Riggs Crossing had been personal.

Well, mostly.

He drove a quarter of a mile farther through copse after copse of fir, pine, and larch before the lane took a wide bend to open into a clearing. A blocky white farmhouse capped by a gabled green roof and skirted by a broad porch sat atop a small rise. Scattered around the back end, he saw, through a veil of snow, several outbuildings. A pump house, barn, and shed were barely visible, and whatever lay beyond, pastures or other buildings, was anyone's guess today.

"Looks the same as it did the other night," Mendoza observed as the engine idled. She was eyeing the house and grounds, now empty, seeming almost desolate.

"Except there aren't a dozen deputies, paramedics, firefighters, and crime-scene techs climbing over the property. The news crew is gone, and the neighboring lookie-loos have disappeared."

"Along with all of the evidence."

"Yeah, maybe."

"What was here was collected."

He wasn't arguing that fact, but he needed to see the place for himself without the distractions of other cops. What the hell had really gone on here? Why had James Cahill landed in the hospital, his girlfriend gone missing?

Rivers would never admit it because it sounded crazy, but whenever he stepped into the scene, he could imagine what had happened, roll a video in his mind, "see" the crime unfold. At least in his mind's eye.

It wasn't ESP.

It wasn't his cop's "gut" feeling.

It was more of an intuitive re-creation, something innate in him. He'd only told one person, his ex-wife, Astrid, when they'd been married. And she, true to her nature, had laughed in his face.

"Oh, God, Brett, so now you're, like, a psychic?" she'd said, her eyes dancing as she sat across from him at the kitchen table. "Or is it psychotic? Give me a break." She'd taken a swallow of wine and then shaken her head. "I wouldn't be telling too many people about that, not at the department. They could think you've gone 'round the bend, you know."

That was the one piece of advice she'd given him that he'd taken. He knew his method of using his innate senses sounded a little nuts, so from the time of that one slip of the tongue with his then-wife, he'd kept his thoughts on the matter to himself.

Mendoza was already climbing out of the Cherokee as Rivers cut the engine. Pocketing his keys, he stepped outside into ankle-deep snow, an icy gust of wind slapping him in the face.

She flipped up the hood of her jacket and headed for the house. "Knowlton's supposed to meet us here, right?"

"Yeah."

"Even though he already gave his statement."

"Maybe he remembered something else since he gave it."

"Fat chance." She seemed irritated.

"Hey, I know you think this is a waste of time, but it's something I have to do," he said as they walked to the house.

"I'm here, aren't I?"

He stepped up the slick steps to the front door, where crime-scene tape that had been stretched across the frame now flapped in the wind. Over the noise of gusts rattling the branches of the surrounding trees, he heard the rumble of an approaching engine.

"Here we go," Mendoza said, nodding to the lane.

He spied a battered old pickup, wipers scraping against the falling snow, visible through the trees.

Bobby Knowlton.

Foreman and friend of James Cahill.

The person who'd made the emergency call to 9-1-1.

Right on time.

CHAPTER 5

"James? Can you hear me? James?"

The voice sounded far away. Soft. Female.

James opened an eye and blinked. For a second, he was disoriented, then remembered he was still lying in a hospital bed in a private room, snow still falling beyond the window. A woman—a gorgeous woman—was standing at his bedside and looking down at him through worried blue eyes.

He was light-headed and realized it must be the meds that made it seem this was almost an out-of-body experience.

"It's me," she whispered, sliding a worried glance to the door. "Sophia."

Not a nurse.

Wispy blond bangs poked out from beneath a hood that was trimmed in some kind of fur or maybe faux fur—he couldn't tell. A thick scarf was twisted around her neck. Her nose was short and straight, her cheeks flushed as if she'd just come in from the cold, and she was dressed in a long black coat.

He blinked again and focused. *Sophia?*

Her gaze searched his. Hopeful. "Remember?"

He didn't.

"Thank God, you're okay," she said, and the corners of her lips teased upward. She had a great smile. Full lips shiny from a pink gloss opened slightly to show a glimpse of straight white teeth.

"Yeah," he said, trying to place her.

Not the woman who had pierced his memory. Not the woman

with the dark hair and suspicious eyes that had resurrected in his dulled mind.

"You do know me?"

"Sure," he lied. But she was familiar. How?

She was too sharp for him. "Right." She rolled those incredible eyes. "I'm Sophia," she repeated, a little more loudly, as if that would help him remember. When he didn't respond, little lines appeared between her eyebrows. "Sophia Russo."

He turned the name over in his mind. Came up with nothing.

She was waiting for his reaction, trying to read his expression.

The name was ringing faint bells, but still he couldn't place her. "Yeah."

She let out a disgusted sigh and again rolled her eyes. "So, it's true. You really don't remember, do you?"

"Not everything."

"But me. You remember me." She was insistent. Almost pleading. Then she cleared her throat. "I mean you should. After everything."

What the hell was "everything"? He knew better than to ask.

"Sort of." He blinked. He was having trouble concentrating. Sleep seemed determined to pull him back under.

"You are such a liar!" But she didn't seem mad. Not really. Her gaze moved to his lips, and for the briefest of seconds, he thought she might lean over and kiss him. She didn't. Instead, she sighed, and he caught the hint of a fragrance, a perfume that was slightly familiar. "I'm your girlfriend."

That didn't sound right. He looked at her. Gorgeous and maybe . . . but nothing. And didn't the nurse say something about Megan being his girlfriend? He was groggy, but he was sure he had that right.

She read his mind. "Wow. I just hope this . . . amnesia? I hope it's temporary."

"You and me both."

She sent a hasty, almost secretive glance around the room. "Listen, I'm not supposed to be here. Nobody knows I came, and no one can find out."

"Why?" He tried to push himself into a sitting position but was only able to lever himself onto the elbow of his good arm.

"You're not supposed to have visitors." She glanced at the door, which was slightly ajar, almost but not quite closed. "I had to sneak in, wait until there was a change in the nursing shift and some kind of emergency down the hall." Her gaze swept the room. "As it is, I'm sure I'm on camera, but I tried to disguise myself."

"Why can't I have visitors?"

"Not sure. Either doctor's orders, or it comes from the police."

The cops. Again. His insides clenched. Despite the pain, he pushed himself into a sitting position.

"I just wanted to see that you were all right." She turned, as if to leave.

He reached out, grabbed her wrist like he had the nurse's. "Why would the cops keep me from seeing anyone?" he asked, trying to keep his mind on the conversation. It seemed important. It *was* important.

"You know."

"I don't."

She glanced at his hand, wrapped firmly over her wrist. He let go.

"Oh. Maybe you don't. It's because of Megan."

A fleeting image sizzled through his brain, a split-second recollection of a woman, her face twisted in anger, her hair damp with snow, her pale eyes sparking with hatred. And then she was gone, the mental picture dissipating as quickly as it had appeared.

His gut twisted.

That angry woman was Megan. He didn't know how he knew, but he was sure of it. "What about her?"

"She's missing."

"Missing?" So that was what the nurse was going to tell him when the doctor cut her off.

"Yeah, like in vanished." Sophia threw up her hand. "No one's seen her since the night you were brought in here. Everyone says you two got into a huge fight, and then she disappeared."

Again, a face appeared behind his eyes, the angry countenance of a woman yelling at him, accusing him of cheating . . .

"According to the news, no one's seen or heard from her, and even her car is gone, can't be located."

This wasn't making any sense. And yet bits and pieces of that night were poking at his brain, little shards of memory cutting through the fog.

"I figured the fight was about me," Sophia whispered. "I mean, that's what everybody thinks."

"Who's everybody?" he asked, trying to keep up while the memory of the woman, so furious she was nearly spitting, began again only to wither away. What had happened? What had he done?

"Well, you know. Everyone at the inn and the Christmas tree farm, they're sure she'd found out about us and was pissed."

He held up a hand, then winced with the effort. Damn it all. "How would you know?"

"You know."

He didn't.

With a disbelieving smack of her tongue, she said, "Because I work there."

"You work for me?"

"Duh." She flashed him that smile again, then added, "Okay, okay, I get it. So, technically, I work for Cahill Industries, but who are we kidding? You are Cahill Industries, so yeah, I work for you and have for the last six months." She was nodding, encouraging him to remember. "And we were like . . ." She bit her lip. "We were an item, I guess."

"We were seeing each other?" This wasn't making a lot of sense.

"If that's what you want to call it." Her eyes twinkled with a naughty little spark, and she showed a dimple, her nose wrinkling. "I knew you'd remember."

He didn't, but let it pass as he tried like hell to piece his life, or at least his love life, together. "And Megan?"

"Oh. Well . . ." She pulled a face, then tilted her flattened hand from side to side. "You hadn't quite broken it off with her."

That had a ring of truth to it.

And spelled trouble.

Sophia admitted, "But she might have found out about us and . . ."

The implication was hard to miss. ". . . and she didn't like it."

A shrug, as if one thing would automatically lead to another. "So she found out about me, I think, and got pissed off. The way I figure it, she drove over to your house, and you got into a fight, and you ended up here."

Again, the flash of a woman advancing upon him, tears burning her eyes, rage flushing her face, anger radiating from her in waves appeared behind his eyes. "And that's when Megan went missing."

She bit her lip as she studied him, as if she couldn't quite trust him. "You don't remember the fight?"

An inner voice cautioned him to sidestep that one. "No."

"Nothing?" She seemed skeptical.

"That's what's weird," he admitted. "But the doctor said I came in through the ER."

She reached out and touched his hand, her fingers cool. Familiar. "Bobby found you."

"Knowlton?" God, he didn't remember that at all.

"He was the one who called nine-one-one."

"And Megan wasn't there?"

She shook her head, blond hair glinting under the overhead lights. "I asked Bobby, and he said you were alone."

"He say anything else?"

"Not to me."

James's head was pounding, but he was trying like hell to recall anything that would help him make sense of this nightmare.

She lowered her voice even more and squeezed his fingers, only to release them. "Have you talked to the cops?"

"No. Not yet."

"But they've been here?"

"The doctor said so. But I don't remember." And then he thought of something else. "I'm missing my phone. And this one"—he motioned to the old-fashioned phone on the bedside tray—"is useless as I can't remember anyone's number."

"I'll see if I can find it," she said, but didn't sound too sure of herself. She leaned in closer. "I think you should know that the police were at your house. They searched the place and took stuff."

"What?"

She shrugged. "That's just what I heard. Bobby said they were hauling stuff out of there."

"My phone?"

"Maybe. Like computers and stuff."

"Can they just do that?"

"They're the cops. They can do what they want."

"But there are limits." He was trying to think. Why would the cops confiscate his belongings? Did they really think he was some kind of criminal? Wasn't that the kind of thing they did on a drug bust? Or a murder case? His insides turned to water. Was Megan dead? Is that why the doctor wouldn't say anything?

Footsteps sounded in the hallway outside, and Sophia froze. Eyes wide, she held a finger to her lips and slipped to the side of the room, to the spot where the door would hide her should it be flung open.

It wasn't.

The footsteps faded as whoever was in the hallway passed.

Sophia let out her breath. "I better go. But I love you," she said. "Remember that." Her smile was shy, her cheeks suddenly pink with the admission.

Love?

That seemed wrong. "Wait," he said.

He needed more information, but she was already peeking through the opening of the cracked door, scouting out the corridor. Turning, she mouthed, "I'll be back," then pulled her scarf up over her nose and walked quickly but noiselessly out of the room.

James watched her leave.

He'd been dating Sophia *and* Megan? Not just dating, but involved. Sexually, she'd implied. And emotionally. Hence the word "love."

Deep inside, he sensed that whatever had happened to Megan wasn't good and that somehow, someway he could be blamed. The scratches on his face seemed to pulse, and he caught another glimmer of memory, of nails bearing down on him, ready to tear into him. She—Megan, he presumed—had been furious. Enraged. Ready to rip him apart.

He tried and failed to remember the argument, the fight, but it teased at him, images struggling to surface only to disappear again.

And now Sophia claimed she loved him.

No wonder the cops wanted to have a chat.

Or possibly more than just a chat.

What had he gotten himself into?

Holding on to his ribs, he swung his feet over the side of the bed. Pain shot through his torso, and his head pounded, but he ignored the throbbing ache and, using the bed to steady himself, walked to its foot to stare up at the television, stretching his IV tube to the max. The flat screen appeared to be plugged into the wall socket overhead. Then he made his way back to the bed and tried the remote again. Nothing. He flipped the remote over and opened the back to find that the batteries had been removed.

Not good.

He studied the controls on the bed itself, the buttons that were marked clearly for calling the nurse or raising and lowering the head of the bed, even the foot. No button for the television.

With an effort, he hoisted himself back onto the bed and fought sleep.

Somehow, some way, he had to find a way to remember.

Maybe you don't want to, a nagging voice in his head suggested. *Maybe you won't like what you'll find.*

Tough.

Anything was better than this, he thought, starting to drift off again.

Not knowing was killing him.

CHAPTER 6

Bobby Knowlton climbed out of his truck—an aging, beat-up Chevy—then tossed the butt of a cigarette into the snow, its red ember fizzling as he half-jogged to the house. "God, it's cold," he said with a mock shiver as he approached Rivers and Mendoza.

Knowlton was pushing sixty, wiry, his features sharp as a razor's edge. His leathery skin was permanently tanned from working outside, and he hadn't bothered to shave for a day or two, silvery stubble covering his chin.

"You're the detectives, right?" He was wearing a jean jacket, battered Levis, and a baseball cap pulled tight over his head.

"Brett Rivers, Riggs County Sheriff's Department." Rivers offered up his ID, but Knowlton waved it away, stuck out his hand, and shook Rivers's palm. "My partner, Wynonna Mendoza."

"I'd like to say 'a pleasure,'" Knowlton said, glancing at the badge Mendoza had flashed, "but under the circumstances? Not so much." He shook her hand as well, then added, "I go by Bobby. Christened Robert, but my folks called me Bobby as a kid, and the name just stuck. Look, I don't know why I'm here. I mean, I already gave my statement to some deputy, and I just don't know what more I can tell ya." He was nervously searching the pockets of his battered jacket. He pulled out a crumpled box of Marlboros, then changed his mind and shoved the pack back inside. "As I said, I gave my statement two days ago to a deputy."

"Kate Mercado," Mendoza said.

Bobby gave a quick nod. "That's her."

Rivers met the questions in the foreman's eyes. "I'd just like to go over it one more time."

"Oookay." Knowlton paused. "You're not thinkin' I had somethin' to do with all this," he said, suddenly suspicious. "'Cuz that's just plain crazy talk. You know?"

Rivers hadn't gone there, but he let the foreman run his mouth just to see what he had to say. "I was down at the Brass Bullet. Kinda my thing after work. I was there for two, maybe two and a half hours, waitin' on a feed delivery that was held up 'cuz of the weather, s'posed to come in later, after hours. Y'know?" His bushy eyebrows rose beneath his cap. When Rivers didn't respond, he frowned and held up a hand. "Well, hey. If you don't believe me talk to Mike, the bartender, Mike—oh, what's his name—Mike . . . Mike." He snapped his fingers. "Mike McGillicuddy. Yeah, that's it. Talk to him. He'll tell ya."

Rivers said, "I just wanted to hear it myself."

Knowlton took a second to size him up, seemed satisfied with what he saw, and said, "Well, okay, then. Let's go inside. Freezin' our asses out here."

That was the first statement the foreman uttered that Rivers accepted as fact. As Knowlton began unlocking the front door, a dog began to put up a ruckus, barking and scratching on the other side of the thick oak door. "That's Ralph," Knowlton explained, then yelled through the panels as he let himself in. "Ralph! Hush! Geez, hold your horses, will ya? I'm comin'." To the detectives, he half-apologized. "The deal is that I said I'd take care of Ralph, didn't want him to be taken by animal control or whatever. He's fine."

He didn't sound fine. It sounded as if the dog intended to shred the door to pieces while barking his fool head off.

"Is he dangerous?" Rivers asked and saw that Mendoza had backed up a step.

"Ralph? Nah. It's the whole 'bark is worse than his bite' thing, y'know?"

Rivers wasn't so sure, and as Knowlton swung the door open, the dog shot out, a black-and-brown streak that leapt across the porch and down the few steps to start running in wide circles through the snow in the front yard. Yipping excitedly, snow clumps flying, the shepherd tore from one end of the yard to the other.

"Guess he's got a little energy to burn off," Bobby remarked as they stepped inside. "I shoulda taken him home with me. I kept thinkin' James would be released any time and would want the dog here." He snapped on some of the interior lights, and in the wash of illumination, Rivers eyed the room again.

The front of the home was split by a staircase, living room on one side, dining room on the other. The living area was filled with a mismatch of comfortable furniture in no particular style: leather recliner, short sofa, two easy chairs now toppled over; they had been, it seemed, situated around a fireplace with a raised hearth, one corner of which was still stained with blood.

Cahill's blood, he presumed.

Lab tests would prove it out.

The house was just the way the police had left it, swept by the crime-scene team, fingerprints taken, electronics removed, trace evidence collected, digital photos snapped, blood samples already sent to the lab and currently being checked for DNA. A faint odor of ash from the last fire hung in the air.

"Man, you guys really know how to trash a place," Bobby said, surveying the disheveled shelves and layer of fine fingerprint dust. "Don't you all ever clean up after yourselves? James is gonna be pissed."

A messy house was the least of James Cahill's problems.

Knowlton adjusted his hat on his balding head. "Isn't all this overkill? I mean it's not like anyone's dead, right?"

"We hope not." But Rivers had learned long ago to be thorough. No one was known dead, that was true, but this had been their one chance, before Cahill returned from the hospital, to search his house top to bottom. Better safe than sorry.

"I kinda feel like I'm steppin' on someone's grave. I mean, I know nobody's dead—er, we think not—but still, seems a little weird, if ya know what I mean." Knowlton glanced back through the open door, and Rivers followed his gaze to the yard. The shepherd was still racing through the snow, tail tucked, tongue lolling. "He's just showin' off. Probably lonely. I'll take him back to my place till James gets back."

Rivers turned back to the mess that was the living room. "Let's go over what happened again."

"All right." Then in a louder voice over his shoulder, "Come on in, Ralph! The party's over!"

Rivers and Mendoza stepped away from the entry as the dog bolted back inside and Knowlton slammed the door shut, sealing out the cold.

"It was just like I said in my statement," he said. "After a beer or two, I'd picked up the feed and was on my way over here to look in on the livestock; that's my job here, y'know. I'm like the foreman of the ranch, though I don't have no official title. I worked here before Cahill bought the place five—no, six—years ago, and he kept me on. Good of him." He yanked off his gloves and glanced out the window. "I was about a quarter of a mile north, headin' this way—south, y'know—when I saw a car pull out of the lane." He pointed through the window to the snow-covered drive. "Whoever was behind the wheel was driving like a bat outta hell, nearly hit the damned snowplow that was taking care of the snow in front of me, and let me tell ya, you don't want to be messin' with a rig that size. But that's what happened; the car tore out and swung around in front of the plow, then headed north, toward town." He hitched a thumb in the general direction.

"You recognize the vehicle?" Mendoza asked.

"I can't be sure. It was snowing hard, a near blizzard, and already dark. All I can say for sure was that the car was dark. Blue. Or black. Maybe charcoal gray."

"Megan Travers's car."

"I'd guess. Wouldn't swear to it, though, and I didn't see the driver. The windows were fogged, and I was too busy trying to get out of the way and not hit the damned plow that had put on his brakes to avoid a collision." He shook his head and whistled softly. "It was close. The driver swerved like a son of a bitch, then hit the gas and passed me on the fly. For a second, I thought we might hit head-on."

"You're sure it was a car, though, not an SUV or truck?" Mendoza said.

"Oh, yeah." Knowlton, bushy eyebrows slammed together, shook his head. "Crazy shit. Anyway, I followed the plow until I got to the drive leading up here, drove to the house, came in, and found James right over there." He pointed to the corner of the fireplace hearth. "He was out cold. Had a pulse—I checked—and was breathing, but there was a lot of blood, and I thought . . . well, hell, I didn't really think, y'know, just called nine-one-one, and the ambulance came and the fire department, and all you all, and . . . and that's it. All I know."

"What time was that?"

"Hard to say. But maybe seven or so. Seven-thirty? Yeah, around then. Everything was real late that day, real late, on account of the storm. That's why I stopped in for a brewskie or two."

Mendoza changed the subject. "Did James have any enemies?"

"Oh, sure." Then he heard himself and amended. "Well, not the kind that would want to kill ya."

"Who?"

"Well, mainly girlfriends, I guess." Knowlton glanced again at the fireplace and the brownish-red stain.

"More than one?" Rivers asked.

"Oh, yeah." He was nodding, rubbing the gray stubble on his chin, his eyebrows elevated a fraction. "Trouble is, y'know, women, they don't like to share."

Mendoza said, "So he might have more than one girlfriend at a time?"

"Sure."

She pressed. "And his girlfriends didn't like each other?"

"I'm guessin'. I mean it's not like that sister-wife thing on TV. You know the one where several wives all get along." He rolled his eyes. "Yeah, like that would ever happen."

"Did James say as much?"

"Not to me." He looked from one cop to the other. "But it's a problem, ya know, not breaking it off with one before taking up with another. Women—they tend to not like that."

"Men, either," Mendoza observed, and Rivers wondered if her comment was a generality or from personal experience.

Knowlton's gaze drifted to an antique rifle mounted over the mantel. "He's probably lucky he didn't get shot."

"His girlfriends have tempers?" asked Mendoza.

"Isn't that what they say?" Knowlton mused. " 'Ain't no force of evil as bad as a woman scorned' or something?"

"Something," Mendoza said, and to her credit, she didn't correct him. "Do you have any of the girlfriends' names?"

"The recent ones," he said as Ralph returned and Knowlton bent over to scratch the dog behind his ears. "James was dating Megan Travers. The one that's missing. She and James, they had a thing going for a couple of months, maybe more. I'm not sure on that."

Mendoza asked, "You know anything about her?"

"Nah. Not much."

"Family? Friends?" Mendoza pushed.

"Sorry." He seemed sincere. "Didn't pay all that much attention. As I said, they came and went."

Mendoza asked, "Who else?"

"Well, lemme see." He screwed up his face in concentration. "There was a schoolteacher who lived in . . . Marysville or Everett, someplace north of Seattle, I think."

"Her name?"

"Janice or Jenny? Somethin' or other. But they'd broken it off. A while back. Probably over a year or more."

"That's two," Mendoza said. "Anyone else?"

He looked thoughtful. "There is the blonde who works at the inn. First as a waitress, then in the office. She's had her eye on James for a while, and I've seen 'em together a few times. Her name's Sophie, er, Sophia . . . but, sorry, I don't know any more about her."

"But she was seeing James?" Rivers pressed.

"I think so . . . but don't quote me on that. Just 'cuz I ran into them alone a couple of times don't mean a whole helluva lot. Coulda been talkin' business, y'know, as she works for him, but hell . . . well, there's just something about how a woman looks at a man she's interested in. It's different. And she was always around, y'know? *Always.* Like she really wanted James to notice her."

"This was recent?"

He nodded. "James didn't say anything, but it seemed that they were together a lot. But as I said, women, they were always fawnin' over him. Willow, she works at the hotel, she had her eye on him too, at least I think so." He scowled. "Not that anything was goin' on between the two of them, at least not that I know . . . but I caught her lookin' at him a time or two, and she was watchin', y'know. Like a cat starin' at a hole in the ground, waitin' for a mole to stick out his little head before she pounced. That's what it was like with her . . ." Then, as if he realized he'd said too much, he added, "Well, what the hell do I know? Look, you'll have to ask him when he wakes up. I didn't really keep tabs on his love life." Running a hand around the back of his neck, he said, "That's about all I know. Just what I said before. Now I need to see to the stock." Knowlton scrabbled in his pocket again, retrieved his pack of Marlboros, and this time didn't bother shoving it back. He pulled out a cigarette and pointed the filter tip at Rivers. "Talk to James."

"We will," Mendoza said.

Knowlton jabbed the cigarette into the corner of his mouth. "Let's go, boy," he said to the dog. "Guess you may as well come home with me tonight." To Rivers, he added, "Listen, I've got chores to finish, so if you all have any more questions, just follow along. I'll answer what I can, but I got nothing more to say. It's all in my statement."

"Wait," Mendoza said, but Knowlton was already walking. He led them through the kitchen, which smelled faintly of chili that had hardened in a takeout container left on the table. They followed him out the back door and through a narrow, covered back porch that served as a laundry/mudroom and connected to a dark woodshed filled with dusty chunks of oak, fir, and cedar, the dirt floor packed by a hundred years of footfalls.

At the far end of the shed, the door opened to the yard between the house and outbuildings. Knowlton paused to light up just as he stepped outside, the lighter clicking and the smell of smoke tinging the air. The dog took off, scaring up two crows who cawed their indignation as they fluttered to the high skeletal branches of an apple tree, knocking off clumps of snow and a few stubborn leaves.

Outside, Knowlton shot a glance at them. "You have somethin' more to ask?"

"Yes." Mendoza was a little irritated; it showed in the tight corners of her mouth. "Other than the women, did Cahill have anyone he didn't get along with? Coworkers? Employees? Boyfriends of the women he dated?"

"It's not like we're all one big happy family," Knowlton admitted, "but no, I don't know anyone who was out to get him." He squinted through the falling snow. "Anything else?"

Rivers shook his head. "Not now."

"Good." He held up both hands, almost in surrender, then turned and strode through unbroken snow to the barn.

"You gonna let him walk off like that?" asked Mendoza.

"You got any more questions?"

"No. Yes. Like none that come to mind, but a million."

"Then we'll catch him later."

Mendoza scowled as she watched Knowlton and the dog disappear into the barn.

"Well, that was sure worth our time." Her breath came out in a fog.

"Maybe."

"And maybe not."

"I'll meet you in the Jeep." Rivers tossed Mendoza his keys. "I'll just be a second."

"Whatever." She was already opening the gate leading to the parking area.

Rivers went back through the woodshed, taking in the dust and disuse of a place where he suspected rats and squirrels and whatever could get inside had nested. An axe had been left in a battle-scarred stump that was obviously used as a splitting block.

Rivers walked through the long back porch as he retraced his steps, and in the mud/laundry room he noted the work boots beneath a bench and ski jackets hung on hooks. Nothing out of place.

At least not where the cops had left well enough alone.

One of the jackets was stained and frayed. Well worn. Rivers walked to it, found a pair of work gloves that were nearly worn through stuffed in the pockets. Favorites. Stiff with sweat. Without a second thought, he slipped the pair into a pocket of his own coat and headed back inside.

He made his way through the kitchen and dining area that Cahill had obviously used as an office, then walked into the living room, where he stared at the cold fireplace, the blackened bits of logs, and the thick ashes in the firebox, the smell of burnt wood barely discernable. His gaze focused on the corner of the hearth, on the stained bricks and discolored mortar.

Just what the hell had happened? He knew there had been a fight; somehow, Cahill had fallen and cracked his skull, along with a few ribs, and the Travers woman and her car were missing. But what had been the impetus to start the altercation? How had it escalated? How had a grown, strapping man let a smaller woman get the better of him? And where the hell was Megan?

Christ, was she even alive?

Rivers let his mind imagine James Cahill as he'd seen him that night. The Cahill heir had been unconscious but was being tended to by two EMTs, a man and a woman, who had hoisted him onto a stretcher. There had been two deputies called to the scene to begin with, then he and Mendoza followed shortly. By then, the crime-scene techs were there, one of whom had discovered the wadded note on the floor near one of the side chairs by the window. The missive had been short and to the point:

J—
I'm leaving you.
This time forever.
You'll never see me again!
M

The assumption had been that the note had come from Megan Travers. It was fairly dramatic and old school in this era of text messages, e-mail, and instant communication.

And why come here with the note? To leave it? Had she thought he'd been gone? Who had wadded it up? Had it even been recent? Was it from Megan? Or another woman? According to Knowlton, James Cahill had more than a few women interested in him. Thc note was in a woman's handwriting, it seemed, but it could be fake. Possibly planted.

It just seemed out of place.

The lab would provide answers if there were any fingerprints or DNA left on the scrap of unlined paper. Why leave a note when you were face-to-face? Had she left the note earlier? Or, again, was it someone else?

He thought of the car speeding out of the driveway that Knowlton had spied. Presumably Megan's. Presumably with her at the wheel.

Then again, he couldn't presume anything.

"Where are you?" he asked under his breath.

Was she hiding?

Or dead?

Examining the room, he imagined the fight. Had it occurred right before the speeding car had left, or earlier? Had whoever was behind the wheel been involved? Certainly. That he would assume. Over a woman—or make that *another* woman, as Knowlton had suggested?

Was it possible that James Cahill had staged his own injuries?

That seemed too far-fetched. Too dangerous. He studied the hearth again . . . Anyone who had slammed his head against those bricks had to have been suicidal.

Or desperate.

Closing his eyes, he reached into his pocket, felt the gloves, and conjured up the vision of a woman coming at James. She is angry, her features twisted in fury, her hands swinging, nails sharp enough to gouge deep ruts in his flesh.

Screaming, she attacks, pushing him and slicing his left cheek as she swipes at him. He steps backward to avoid the attack, stumbles, and hits his head on the hearth? Knocks himself out? Cracks his ribs in the fall?

Or had he been the aggressor?

He considered the scene from a different angle, even physically turning, though his eyes were still closed. Was that a dark figure lurking on the staircase? An accomplice waiting to attack? If so, in league with whom? James? Megan? Someone else?

Had there been another player here? A third party, either by design or, no— His brows knit together as he concentrated. That wasn't quite right. Not exactly lurking in the shadows. But pulling the strings, taking advantage, and—

"Rivers?" Mendoza's voice cut into his vision.

His eyes flew open.

Embarrassed, he glanced over his shoulder to find Mendoza standing at the foot of the stairs.

"You okay?" she asked, watching him closely.

He hadn't even heard the door open, nor felt the rush of wintry wind racing through the entryway.

"Fine. Just wanted another look."

"What were you doing?"

"Thinking."

"Huh." Disbelief. "You find anything?" She was eyeing him skeptically from beneath the hood of her jacket.

"Nah." He gave a quick shake of his head. He was irritated that he'd been disturbed, but he hid it. "Let's go."

"Ohhh . . . kay," she said as they walked outside to the porch. He pulled the door closed and heard the latch click into place.

In silence, they headed to the Cherokee.

She was already strapped in by the time he climbed inside. "What is it with you?" she asked, turning to face him. "It was like you were in some kind of trance or something."

"I told you, I was thinking." He started the engine and backed around the Silverado, giving the Jeep a little too much gas. "Just getting the feel of the place."

"That was it?" she asked.

"That was it."

"And what did you feel?"

He slid a glance her way and put the Jeep into DRIVE. "Nothing," he replied, remembering Astrid's laughter when he'd confided about his methodology to her. "Absolutely nothing."

CHAPTER 7

James opened a bleary eye.

Night had fallen.

But he guessed only a few hours had passed, that he hadn't lost another day. God, he hoped not. He remembered Nurse Rictor coming in to check on him again and adjust his IV, but he'd been half asleep when she'd stepped into his room, and whatever had been added to his bloodstream had knocked him out.

Now he stared through the window to the darkness beyond. Security lamps cast a vaporous blue glow over a mostly deserted parking area. Snow was still falling and had piled up on the shrubbery, asphalt, and a few scattered vehicles.

He started to rub his chin with his right hand, but a stab of pain stopped him, so he used his left, felt the beard stubble of more than twenty-four hours. How long had he been here again? He checked the clock, mounted high over the television. 8:26. Still Sunday, he presumed. He blinked, decided his pain wasn't quite as severe as it had been earlier.

But a woman had visited.

The blonde. Sophia.

He'd fallen asleep after she'd left and almost thought he'd dreamed that she'd been in his room, had hallucinated with the head injury and drugs.

But he knew better.

She was real. Had been here. And some of what she'd said rang true. He did know her, and yeah, she probably did work at the inn, but had he been involved with her? Slept with her? Surely, he'd remember that.

But no . . .

Still, he didn't believe she was lying.

He shifted in the bed and again rubbed the stubble on his chin.

And flinched.

More pain.

Damn. Whatever meds he'd been given to make him more comfortable had definitely worn off. His head was clearer, despite the dull ache that pounded behind his eyes.

He needed to get out of here. He had a life. A business. And a small ranch with some cattle and horses. And a dog . . . Ralph. Damn. He couldn't just lie around in the hospital. He pushed himself upright and twisted the kinks from his neck. His mind was still fuzzy, but he had to get out of this bed and hospital and . . . His eyes searched the room for his clothes, even though he was still hooked up to the IV.

The door to his room was ajar, and his throat was dry as cotton. As he reached for his water glass on the bedside table, he heard a soft ding announcing the arrival of an elevator car. Lifting the glass, he felt another sharp jab in his rib cage, and with it came some clarity.

Megan.

Her name floated through his consciousness.

Sophia had mentioned her, hadn't she? But he hadn't been able to put the name with a face. Now, however, he remembered. Early twenties. Pale blue eyes that twinkled mischievously. Freckles over a short nose, a deep dimple in one cheek, and straight hair, somewhere between blond and brown, that brushed her shoulders.

Yes!

His heartbeat increased.

The memories teased, but he couldn't quite grab them and hold on.

Then a quick, intense image flashed—her pretty face twisted in rage, her hair damp with snow, her lips curled angrily, her eyes bright with hatred.

"I swear, James," she'd breathed, "you'll never see me again. You're going to regret this for as long as you live!"

"Fuck," he whispered under his breath.

It was true.

There had been a fight. In his house. She'd been furious with him and swinging some kind of long weapon with one hand, maybe a machete or a bat, all the while swiping bare-handed at him with the other. She'd found out about something . . . Oh, God, had it been about Sophia? Isn't that what Sophia had said earlier? That she'd suspected they'd been fighting over her? He yanked at the hair in front of his bandage. *Think, Cahill, think!*

He remembered backing up in his living room, trying to calm her down, trying to grab at what she'd been flailing. But she'd been furious. Outraged. Intent on doing serious harm.

The weapon—a *poker.* Yeah, the fireplace poker. Not a machete. Not a baseball bat. She'd scratched him, he'd turned for a second, and she'd landed a blow to his head, and he'd tripped, and—

"I really don't think it would be a good idea! He's sleeping now." A woman's sharp voice interrupted his train of thought. "Did you hear me!" She sounded irritated. The image in James's mind faded as he glanced to the partially open door. "Please. Don't." The voice was firm, punctuated by the staccato beat of quick footsteps heading his way.

"This will only take a minute." A different woman's authoritative voice.

Familiar?

Maybe. But he couldn't place it.

The door to his room flew open, nearly hitting the wall.

"Now, wait a minute—" The nurse called from somewhere down the hallway. "You can't just barge in there!"

But she had.

This tall woman hesitated for just a second, then marched over to his bed.

Did he know her?

"James." She spit out his name as if the very sound of it burned her tongue. And she sure looked like she knew him. And probably hated him. "Where is she?"

"What? Who're you?"

She hesitated, but her dark eyes sparked. "Are you for real?" She glared at him. "You're not seriously going to play that game with me."

"Do I know you?" He pushed on the button to raise the head of his bed.

She made a sound of disbelief. "Do you know me?" she repeated with more than a little contempt. "Save it, okay? Don't try any of that amnesia BS on me. It won't work."

"Look, lady—"

"Lady?" She rolled those expressive eyes, and her lips tightened. And in that second, he had a flash of memory. He did know her. He remembered her face, the glint of intelligence in her eyes, the crest of her cheekbones, and her quick dimple when she smiled. And then there was the anger . . .

"What did you do to her?" Her lips were flat against her teeth. "If you did anything to hurt her, I swear I'll—"

"Stop!" Nurse Rictor swept into the room. "You need to leave," she ordered in a take-no-prisoners voice. "Now."

"You'll do what?" James demanded of the visitor, his head finally level with hers.

"You can't threaten a patient," the nurse said, but the woman didn't budge. Her dark hair was wound into a messy bun at the base of her neck, her face slightly flushed, skin taut over high cheekbones. In jeans and a coat cinched tightly around her waist, she was mad as hell. But there was something in her expression, an emotion that didn't quite match her fury.

Fear?

Complicity?

Something wasn't right here, he sensed. His memory might be elusive, but he'd always prided himself on his ability to read people, and with this woman, something was definitely off. "Who are you, and why the hell are you threatening me?"

"Ms. Travers." Rictor interjected her voice a little more calmly as she attempted to take control. "If you'll just wait until Mr. Cahill has seen the doctor—"

"I want to hear what she has to say," James cut in. *Ms. Travers?* But not the woman he remembered attacking him.

"Where's Megan?" she demanded.

"Who are you?"

Something dark crossed behind her eyes, an emotion beyond her anger. "You seriously don't remember me."

"I'm sorry—"

"Save it. And I don't think you've been sorry in your life."

The nurse let out a frustrated sigh. "Ms. Travers—"

"Rebecca," he said. Her name came to him in an instant.

"Ah, you do remember." Her eyes narrowed, silently daring him to confess. When he didn't react, she said, "You know, I heard about your supposed amnesia, and let me tell you, I don't believe it for a second. So you just tell me what happened to Megan."

He shook his head, felt a jab of pain. He *knew* this woman, and it was more than just because she was Megan's sister. He had a flash of her on a beach somewhere. The sun was shining, and she was running toward the water, the ocean stretching wide, the foamy tide lapping on pale sand. Laughing over the roar of the ocean, she turned her head, her wild hair catching in the wind, her arms and long legs slim and tanned . . . a red-and-white-striped bikini barely covering her butt . . .

Oh, yeah, he'd known Rebecca.

Intimately.

"Right," she said. Gone was any sense of laughter or frivolity that he'd caught a glimpse of in his quicksilver memory. The woman who currently met his gaze was stern to the point of severity.

"Ms. Travers, it's time for you to leave." Rictor was firm.

"I will leave. Once I hear what happened to Megan."

James said, "I already told you—"

"I know what you said," she snapped. "But I don't believe you."

"Then why don't you tell me what you think happened to her?"

"God, I wish I knew. Would I be here if I did?" Rebecca glared at him. "I haven't heard from her since she called me from the road, crying hysterically, saying she was coming back to my place. She hung up and never showed. No calls, no texts, no nothing!" Her color was high, her expression scathing. And yet there was something underneath, another emotion.

She hates me, he thought. *And that hatred runs deep.*

Rebecca wasn't finished. "The news is reporting that you and she got into a fight the other night, and I can confirm that. She went on and on about it being over with you, that you'd had a horrible fight, and that she would tell me all about it when she got to Seattle."

"And—?"

"And, obviously, she didn't make it. I've tried and tried to reach her. As I said, phone calls and texts, but nothing . . . not since that night." Beneath her hard veneer there was a hint of fear. For Megan? Or something else? "I've called the police and her friends and the hospitals and . . . and . . . oh, God." She expelled a slow breath, and for a second, he thought she might break down. Instead, she set her jaw. "She's just disappeared."

"And you think I had something to do with it?"

"The whole world does, James." Rebecca's mouth tightened. "Me, personally?" she bit out. "I wouldn't put anything past you. She said you were seeing some other woman, a blonde she said. Suzi. No—Sophie. That's it. Dating her while you were still involved with Megan. She called you a man-whore. No surprise there, though, right?"

Before he could reply, she went on, "She said you two got into a huge fight, and that it was over. She didn't tell me all the details, she couldn't. She was too upset, so she was going to fill me in when she got to my place. But she never made it." Rebecca's loathing of him was barely concealed. "So, come on, James. Tell me. Where the hell is she?"

"All right, miss." This time Nurse Rictor had had enough. She stepped closer to Rebecca, trying to separate the visitor from her patient. "If you won't leave right now, I'm calling security."

Her gaze never leaving James's, Rebecca said, "Call them. But I want answers." She jabbed a finger at James's hospital bed.

James didn't flinch, but his irritation was mounting. The lie slipped easily over his tongue. "I don't remember what happened that night. Or much more before it. I'm having a helluva time piecing together what my life was right before all this came down, so maybe, if you were in contact with your sister, you could shed some light on it."

Rictor had retrieved a cell phone from the pocket of her scrubs. "Mr. Cahill isn't supposed to have visitors."

"Too late," James pointed out.

"You both can sort all this out once he's released."

"Fine," James said, "I'm getting out of here."

The nurse shook her head. "Not before you're released; not without the doctor's permission."

"With or without. I don't care." He was sick of all the bull.

"That's it." The RN started punching buttons on her cell phone, but Rebecca was already heading for the door and sending James a final scathing glance over her shoulder.

"This isn't over," she said.

"You're right about that." He swung his legs over the edge of the bed and sucked in his breath as the pain in his chest jolted through him.

"This time, James, you're not going to get away with it." Then she was gone, her footsteps fading in the hallway, her threat still ringing in his already pounding head.

This time?

Jesus-God, what had he done?

Rictor stepped closer to his bed, but sent a scathing look at the still-open door. From the hallway, the elevator call button dinged. "She should never have gotten in here."

"It's all right," he said, though nothing was right. He doubted it ever would be. But his memory was returning, in frustrating bits and pieces, and he was encouraged. "Where are my clothes?"

"You need to talk to the doctor."

"Then call him."

Her lips pursed for a second. "I'll talk to Dr. Monroe and let him know that you're insisting on being released, and we'll get the paperwork in order. But until then, just wait." Her eyebrows lifted over the tops of her rimless glasses.

"How long?"

"I don't know." At least she was being honest. More than he could say about himself. "But I'll do what I can to speed up the process since you're so gung ho to leave. Now, please, just lie back. I'll put in the call, check your vitals again, and see how you're managing your pain."

"I'm managing it just fine."

She pulled a face suggesting she didn't believe him.

He pushed himself a little more upright. "And if you don't mind, can you get the TV to work?"

She hesitated.

"I'll turn it on the second I'm outta here."

"Doctor Monroe thought it would be best if . . ." Her voice faded.

"We're past that now, aren't we?"

She hesitated, then said, "Okay, give me a sec." She left for about three minutes and came back with two batteries, which she slid into the remote. Once they were installed, she pushed the largest button on the face of the remote. The television blinked to life, the flat screen offering a commercial for a local mattress shop. She handed him the remote.

As he switched channels, searching for the local news, she left again, then returned to unhook his IV.

"I've put a call in to Dr. Monroe. It shouldn't be long now."

"Good." He accepted a cup of small pills that, she assured him, would "take the edge off."

She wasn't lying.

Within ten minutes, his headache and pain in his shoulder quit throbbing quite so hard, and he finally found a news station. He was starting to feel groggy when a report on the mystery surrounding the missing Megan Travers appeared on a split screen. A news studio with a man and woman anchor team filled half the viewing area. On the other side, a woman reporter in a blue ski jacket, her red hair catching snowflakes, stood in front of a large sign that read CAHILL FARMS.

James's stomach knotted as she spoke into a microphone: ". . . still in the hospital and under a doctor's care. Cahill is the owner of several businesses, including this Christmas tree farm and the attached café and inn."

"Great," he murmured.

"And what about Megan Travers?" the woman in the studio asked seriously.

"According to police, James Cahill was dating Megan Travers, who is currently missing." The studio side of the split screen flashed a picture of a woman with light hair, an oval face, and light blue eyes.

Megan.

The woman who had snarled, "You'll never see me again," as she'd brandished a poker at him.

But now there were other mental pictures as well. In his mind's eye, he glimpsed her laughing and sipping wine on a verandah overlooking Puget Sound, and then another image of her tossing a snowball at him as he turned . . . and many, many more, all coming to life suddenly. His throat tightened as he thought of waking up next to her and kissing her and . . .

He closed his eyes for a second and tried like hell to remember that night. Before the rage. What had happened? He remembered eating takeout, letting Ralph have a little bit of cornbread, and leaving the remains in the sink. The dog had barked, and he'd looked out the window to see headlights cutting through the falling snow.

And then?

And then . . .

Had the doorbell rung? Had she let herself in with her key?

". . . worked as a receptionist at the McEwen Clinic in Riggs Crossing and hasn't been seen since she left the office last Thursday," the TV reporter was saying, breaking into his thoughts. "Allegedly, there had been a fight at Cahill's house, located just north of here. James Cahill was found by someone who worked for him. That individual called nine-one-one. Once help arrived, Cahill was transported to the hospital, where he is currently recovering from wounds he appears to have received during an altercation."

"But Megan Travers wasn't there?" the female studio anchor asked.

"No, Beth. Megan Travers and her vehicle were missing. And still are. A witness, the driver of a snowplow in the vicinity Thursday night, saw a black car drive away from the scene after nearly running into the plow, and it's thought the driver was most likely Megan Travers, who was supposed to be heading to her sister's home in Seattle. She never arrived. Police are asking anyone who's seen or heard from Megan Travers to call them at the number on the screen." As she spoke, a telephone number scrolled across the bottom of the screen. "She was driving a black twenty-ten Toyota Corolla." The reporter rattled off the Washington license plate number of the car before she signed off, and the double image changed into a studio shot; the anchors smiled and went to commercial.

Switching off the television, he glanced at the clock, decided to give the doc one hour.

Then, come hell, high water, or hospital red tape, he was out of here.

CHAPTER 8

Rivers stared at the computer monitor in his office. On the screen was the driver's-license photo of Megan Travers—not a great picture, more like a mug shot of a serious woman in her twenties with layered brown hair and deep-set blue eyes. High cheekbones and freckles. He knew her stats by heart: height, weight, birth date. She'd grown up in Yakima and gone to college at Evergreen State College in Olympia before dropping out for an unknown reason. She'd done office work in a car dealership and several medical offices, had never been married, and less than a year earlier, had moved to Riggs Crossing, where she'd taken a job with a local clinic. Somewhere along the way, she'd met James Cahill, more than likely before moving from the city to a town of less than three thousand. She'd rented a one-bedroom unit at the Abernathy Apartments on Cedar Street.

"Our boy's awake," Mendoza said as she appeared at the doorway of their shared office.

"Cahill?" Rivers glanced up from his computer.

"One and the same. I just phoned the hospital."

Rivers was irritated. "The doctor was supposed to call me."

"Probably still will."

He was already rolling back his chair, away from the clutter of his desk, and reaching for his jacket. "I thought you went home."

"I did. Even took in a kickboxing class, picked up takeout, showered, and called the hospital. According to the nurse on duty, James Cahill woke up about twenty minutes ago and had a visitor. Megan Travers's sister, Rebecca Travers."

Rivers's brows lifted.

"It wasn't a social call. According to the nurse, Rebecca Travers was aggressive and argumentative and wouldn't leave when asked to. Had to nearly be thrown out of the hospital."

"Have you spoken to her?" He was on his feet, stuffing an arm down one sleeve of his jacket.

"No. She called in to Missing Persons. Filed the original report. But she lives out of town. Seattle."

He remembered that.

Mendoza went on, "She answered some questions on the phone with a deputy, but is scheduled to come in on Monday."

"Good." Maybe then they would make some progress. He had several people he wanted to interview again, plus he wanted to talk to someone at the state police about Megan Travers's Toyota. So far the BOLO hadn't turned up anything on the Corolla. "Why didn't the hospital call us and let us know he was awake?"

"Don't know."

He checked his pocket, jangled his keys, felt for and found his wallet.

Mendoza stepped out of the way and started for the exterior door, following half a step behind him. "The nurse, Sonja Rictor, had already spoken to Dr. Monroe, and he gave us the green light to talk to his patient."

"Good of him," Rivers said sarcastically.

"We all have rules."

"And some don't make sense."

"So you end up bending them, right?" she asked.

He didn't answer, didn't want to go there. "I'll drive."

"Have you had dinner?"

"No."

"Then I'll drive. I brought along half of a veggie sandwich from Jerry's Deli for you."

"Veggie?" he repeated as he pushed open the back door and Mendoza stepped through. The bitter cold wind slapped his face.

"It's got two kinds of cheese—Havarti and cheddar—so not really vegan." She shot him a glance. "And you know what they say about beggars not being choosers."

"Yeah. I heard."

They crossed the lot to the spot where she'd parked her Prius, and he slid into the passenger seat. Once inside, Mendoza reached behind him to the back seat and retrieved a white sack. "You can eat on the way. Hopefully it's not frozen."

"Thanks."

The sandwich wasn't, and was better than he expected. He munched away, wishing he had a beer as she drove through the streets, where Christmas lights had been strung and were now dancing in the wind. "So tell me about Rebecca Travers," he said around a final bite.

"Don't know a lot. She's unmarried—not sure if she's divorced or single; no kids and a couple of years older than Megan. As I said, she lives in Seattle, Queen Anne district, a condo she bought a few years back, and does some kind of marketing, I think. Not sure about that. Something with computers, though." She slowed for a light.

"She tight with her sister?"

"Tight enough that Megan called her last Thursday after the fight with Cahill."

"Alleged fight," he cut in.

"Phone records concur. And I caught a glimpse of him when I stopped by earlier. He does look like he went two rounds with a bobcat."

"Nothing's been proved. Yet."

"I know. Oh, and I called the snowplow driver who was working the road in front of the Cahill lane that night, the same dude Deputy Mercado interviewed. His story hasn't budged. Dark car, maybe an import, pulled out in front of him. He didn't notice the plates, but thought they were from Washington." She pulled into the parking lot, which had been plowed earlier but was now covered with snow. He wadded up the white sack, and she said, "Just toss that into the back. I'll get it later."

Mendoza parked, and they headed into the hospital and to the second floor, where they found James Cahill sitting up on the edge of his bed and arguing with a nurse about being released. He was dressed in jeans and socks, a hospital gown still covering his torso. Bandages were visible on his shoulder and head, but his eyes were clear.

"James Cahill?" Rivers asked, though, of course, he recognized the man.

"That's right." Wary, lips flat, eyes suspicious.

Rivers offered up his ID. "Detective Brett Rivers, Riggs County Sheriff's Department. This is my partner, Detective Mendoza." She too held out her ID wallet.

Cahill slid a glance at the outstretched identifications, then met Rivers's gaze without flinching. "Okay."

The phrase *cocky son of a bitch* flitted through Rivers's mind. "We'd like to ask you some questions about the night you were injured."

"I don't remember much of it."

Rivers felt the back of his neck tighten. "Well, maybe you can tell us what you do remember."

"Just a sec. Do you mind?" He indicated a wrinkled shirt on the bed beside him—one he'd been told Bobby Knowlton had left for him as the police had confiscated the clothing he'd been wearing on the night he'd arrived. Before Rivers could say anything, he let the hospital gown fall and, with difficulty, slid into the shirt, his jaw tightening, his skin blanching beneath his beard as he forced his right arm down the sleeve. "You aren't the only ones who want to know what happened that night."

"Were you alone?"

"I just said I don't know." He grimaced as he ran a hand over the tuft of brown hair on his head that wasn't swathed in a bandage. "Why don't we just cut the bull? I've seen the news and know that Megan Travers is missing, that the rumor is that she and I got into some kind of fight at my place, but I don't remember it."

"None of it?" Mendoza asked.

A beat . . . and Rivers got the impression Cahill was going to lie, or at least stretch the truth a bit.

"I don't recall anything about that night. At least, nothing concrete."

"Do you remember being with Megan?" Mendoza asked.

He shook his head.

"She was at your house that night."

"Everyone says so, and yeah, it's obvious something happened, and I ended up here busted up, but . . ." He met Rivers's gaze, his eyes slightly defiant. "I just don't remember."

Mendoza was clearly skeptical.

"What's the last thing you do remember?" Rivers asked.

He looked down, appeared to concentrate. An act? To hide his actions? Or a confused man searching the reaches of his memory? "I know that I worked in the shop that day; there's a home we're building for a couple in . . . in Oregon. Welches, Oregon. It's gonna be a ski cabin. Anyway, they wanted it for the holidays, and there was a holdup; the tile she picked out is on back order." He drew a long breath, wincing. "I called the tile company, and it was too late to reach anyone as they're on the East Coast, so I hung up, left the office—the office in the main building, where we assemble the houses—then drove to the inn, where I picked up some chili and cornbread to go and headed to the house. After that . . ." He shook his head slowly. "I went out with Ralph, my dog, to look at the horses. I fed Ralph, heated up some chili, and ate it while watching the news."

"Time?"

"Around six-thirty or seven, maybe. It was the national news, but I always tape it. And then . . ." His eyebrows slammed together, and staring at the floor, he muttered, "Damn it," under his breath. "And then I don't know."

Rivers asked, "Was anyone with you?"

"No. At least not that I can recall." From the corner of his eye, Rivers saw a nurse slip into the room.

"Did anyone come by?" Mendoza asked. "While you were watching TV?"

"I don't think . . . oh, hell, I just don't know, but I feel pretty certain that no one was there when I got home. Just the dog."

Mendoza asked, "Did you see Megan Travers that day?"

"No . . . well . . . maybe." He rubbed the stubble on his chin, just under the scratch marks on his cheek. "Was that the day she came to the office?" He thought. "I don't know."

"Would anyone else have seen her?"

"Yeah. Well, I think so." Cahill let out an angry, frustrated huff and glanced out the window. "I really don't know." He turned back to Mendoza. "And I don't want to guess."

Unfazed, she asked, "When was the last time you do remember seeing Megan Travers?"

"I don't know! That's what I've been trying to tell you." He scowled. If he was putting on an act, it was a good one. Rivers almost bought it. But not quite. "Look, Detectives," Cahill finally said, "I barely remember Megan, and as for the last time I saw her"—he shrugged—"I just . . . I just don't have any idea. I—I just have a feeling . . . that . . . that I didn't know her all that well."

"But you do remember her?" Rivers persisted.

He nodded slowly. "It's all kind of jumbled and disjointed. I remember what she looks like, and that we . . . were involved."

"Sexually," Mendoza said. It wasn't really a question.

Cahill paused. "I assume so." But something flickered in his eyes. Yeah, he was lying.

"You don't recall that?" she asked, skeptically.

Glaring at her, Cahill asked, "Do I need an attorney?"

Rivers said, "No one's saying that you should contact a lawyer."

"I don't think you would." Cahill's lips tightened. "You know what? I'm not talking to you anymore. Not without representation."

"This isn't an episode of *Law & Order*," Mendoza pointed out.

"Doesn't matter. And by the way, do you have my phone? And my computers?"

"We do."

"Fu—" Cahill started to say, but changed his mind. "I want them back."

"As soon as we're done with them."

"I want them now!" he bit out, temper flaring. "ASAP! I don't know what legal authority you have, but I want my things!"

"I'll see what I can do," Rivers said, knowing that the computer techs were searching through Cahill's phone records and computer files and would be doing so for a while. But it was interesting to see how quickly James Cahill could lose his cool.

"In the meantime, I'm contacting my attorney."

Rivers nodded curtly.

"Are we done here?" A vein in Cahill's temple was throbbing, and one of his hands had fisted.

"Yes, that's enough," the nurse answered for them. "Now, please. Let him be."

Rivers wanted to keep baiting Cahill, just keep nudging him with questions, really delve into this supposed amnesia, but judging from the determined set of Cahill's jaw, it was doubtful he would answer any further questions.

Mendoza, though, wasn't ready to throw in the towel. "Just a few more questions."

"No," Cahill and the nurse responded in unison. Cahill added, "We're done."

"If you change your mind," Rivers suggested.

"I know where to find you."

"Good," Mendoza clipped out, barely hiding the fact that she was irritated.

With the nurse giving them the evil eye, he and Mendoza walked out of the room, but not before Rivers heard Cahill say to Nurse Rictor, "Look, I'm leaving. Now. With or without the doctor's say-so."

For the first time since stepping into the hospital room, Rivers believed James Cahill was actually telling the truth.

And if he were actually being released, then Rivers was going to make certain he was followed.

Maybe then this case would break wide open.

CHAPTER 9

Sometimes you just get lucky.

Sometimes a story falls in your lap.

Sometimes it just screams to be written.

Today was Charity Spritz's lucky day.

And about damned time.

She was thirty-three, for God's sake, and not getting any younger. A glance in her rearview mirror confirmed it. Frowning, driving through this cold-as-an-iceberg town, she thought of her life.

Unmarried.

No children.

A dead-end job.

Until today.

Because she'd gotten lucky.

She actually allowed herself a smile.

All the hard work and sacrifice had been worth it. Finally. She even noticed the sparkling Christmas lights strung across the streets, the painted snowmen and women on storefront windows, the Salvation Army volunteer, all bundled up and ringing his bell as shoppers in heavy coats, gloves, boots, and caps hurried past.

Maybe Riggs Crossing wasn't so bad after all, because it was going to give her the biggest story of her life. "Thank you, James Cahill," she said to the empty car as the town in its fake Christmas glory became a sparkle of lights in her rearview. She had to concentrate on the road ahead. Her fourteen-year-old Hyundai minivan slid a bit; it was not an ideal snow vehicle—well, not an ideal vehicle for her, period. But she'd bought it for a song from her older half-sister, whose kids had basically lived in it. The stains on the carpet and an ancient nest of forgotten french fries she'd recently discovered under the passenger seat only gave testament to the fact that this vehicle was *not* for her. Not for the long game. She was definitely more of a Cadillac or Mercedes or BMW girl. Someday. But for now, the paid-for van was like her mobile office, complete with computer, cameras, Wi-Fi, sleeping bag, and change of clothes—just in case she needed them.

Or in case she couldn't make the rent.

She shuddered at the thought and remembered that today her luck had changed.

And a good thing. She was sick to her back teeth of being assigned to some stupid-ass local-interest story. Who gave a rat's ass about the new agenda for the school board, or what new taxes were about to be levied, or who won the best pie contest at the local fair, or, God help us all, who was voted the sexiest bachelor in Riggs Crossing?

Save me!

She'd been pushed from one boring story to another, though once in a while she was actually on television, when statewide news developed near Riggs Crossing. There was a chance that she'd be able to parlay this story into something on camera, and she was ready. Unlike Seamus O'Day, the lead reporter on the missing-woman story. She let out a disgusted snort. O'Day should be put out to pasture. Over sixty and once a sports reporter for the *Seattle Times*, he'd been shit-canned from that position. Instead of working the Megan Travers story, O'Day would rather be watching a ball game, any effin' game, while sitting on a bar stool at the local watering hole, the Brass Bullet.

Not Charity.

Uh-uh.

She was on this one.

She smelled a mystery and a scandal, the kind of story that could garner statewide, if not national, attention and just could land her, if not on the television news cycle, then on her own videotaped version. This was just the kind of racy article that could catapult her out of this podunk Nothingsville town with its tiny rag of a newspaper and into something much, much bigger.

If not the *New York Times* or *Washington Post* or *Chicago Tri-*

bune, then one of the national tabloids, anything to get out of Riggs Crossing, Washington!

This story could be her ticket out.

She'd make sure of it.

She drove past snowy fields with sagging fences and stands of fir trees until she spied the inn, an old hotel that James Cahill had brought back to life. Oh, he'd had a vision, she thought, pulling into the gravel-strewn lot and waiting for an elderly couple to back s-l-o-w-l-y out of a parking spot.

But then he was a Cahill.

Growing up with the proverbial silver spoon stuck firmly between his teeth.

The rich get richer.

"Ain't it the truth?" she said to herself as she zipped into the parking slot. She was already working on the story behind her editor's and sports nut O'Day's backs, and she'd done some digging on the Cahill family in San Francisco. If she were lucky—and she was today—she'd be able to wangle herself a ticket to the City by the Bay and get some backstory and dirt on the Cahill family.

Wouldn't that just be the best?

Smiling, she cut the engine, checked her look in the mirror, and added a touch of lip gloss to her naturally pink lips. Dark bangs poked out of her red ski hat; her eyes, smoky gray, were bright, and her skin was a little rosier than usual, but she looked good, and she knew it. She woke up looking good. Lucky that way.

There was that word again.

She locked the minivan before heading inside the quaint building with its stained cedar siding and thick plank-covered porch. God, enough with the Western motif! She half-expected to be greeted by a saloon girl straight off a Hollywood set, but inside, the hotel looked like it belonged in the twenty-first century.

She'd tried to talk to James Cahill earlier, but she'd been thwarted by a nurse built like a fullback who had blocked her entrance to Cahill's room. Since Charity had learned that Cahill was finally awake, but amnesic—didn't that beat all?—it might be better to gather information from other sources, have her facts down, before she went face-to-face with him. She had a gut feeling he might not want to be all that forthcoming.

She eyed the surroundings, including a long front desk manned by a woman in her fifties who was helping a customer. To one side was a single elevator and an open staircase, near a tall Christmas tree glistening with white lights and red ribbon. The opposite side of the desk area opened to a wide dining area and a bar where several patrons were nursing drinks and staring at a flat screen mounted on one end.

Twinkling Christmas lights had been strung over the archway to the bar area, and Charity couldn't help but think the yuletide festivities were a bit overdone. But then James Cahill made the bulk of his money at this time of year, didn't he? He profited from all the goodwill and big bucks that were a part of the holiday spirit.

A real prince of a guy.

She headed into the bar, where she slid onto an open stool next to a fortyish man in a Mariners ball cap sporting a trimmed goatee that was just starting to show hints of gray. A half-drunk glass of beer sat in front of him, and he was watching some basketball game on the muted TV. He turned away from the television long enough to check her out, his gaze lingering a second longer than necessary; then he picked up his drink and turned his attention back to the game.

The barmaid was dropping a slice of lime into a glass and flicked a glance Charity's way. "I'll be with you in a sec," the blonde said and placed the drink in front of a woman three stools down. Then it was Charity's turn. "What can I get for you?" Blondie asked. She was pretty, Charity thought, with her blue eyes, cute little nose, and easy smile. Her name tag read SOPHIA. Charity felt she'd hit pay dirt. This woman—Sophia Russo—was the woman James Cahill had been rumored to be seeing while still involved with Megan Travers.

Perfect.

"I'll have a whiskey. Straight up."

"Any particular kind?"

She eyed bottles displayed on lighted shelves in front of a mirror mounted behind the bar. "Jack. Black Label."

"You got it."

Though he didn't cast a glance her way, Goatee-man's eyebrows inched upward a fraction. Good. She pulled off her hat and shook out her hair, then dropped the hat on the vacant stool next to her clutch.

And that got his attention. He actually gave her an appraising stare.

"What?" she asked him. "You expected I'd order a cosmo? Or a lemon drop? Or maybe a piña colada?"

"Maybe," he admitted and took a long swallow from his glass, draining his beer.

That was the problem, she thought. Everyone, including this clod in the Mariners cap, underestimated her.

But not for long.

"Well," she said as the bartender slid the drink in front of her. She picked it up, held it close to her lips, and said to him, "You were wrong." She smiled, just enough to let him know that yeah, she was hot, and he wasn't getting any of it.

James under his breath. Unless he wanted to hitchhike home, he'd have to wait until someone brought him his pickup; otherwise, he was stuck here.

Riggs Crossing, unfortunately, didn't have much in the way of Uber, Lyft, or even a damned taxi service.

But it shouldn't take long for his ride to get here.

Despite the doctor's orders, he was leaving, and he'd called Bobby to bring him some clothes, then haul him back home. "You'll still be without wheels," Knowlton had confided. "The cops, they took your Explorer."

"Then I'll use the company pickup."

"They got that too."

He'd clipped out, "Fine. I'll deal with them. Just come and fetch me."

"You sure about this?"

"Do I sound unsure?"

"Fine. Fine. I'm on my way."

So he just had to wait. A half hour or so. He'd already called for the paperwork to sign himself out, been transferred to a different department twice, then gotten the runaround from someone in "admin." Something about waivers for going against medical advice or some such rot. He didn't care. If the doctor didn't sign him out, or if the paperwork didn't arrive before Knowlton, he'd just leave and deal with the fallout later.

He swung his legs over the bed.

Felt a twinge in his side and ignored it.

He'd have to give up the pain pills, he supposed. Probably couldn't get a prescription from the doctor when he was hell-bent on disobeying the man's advice. Fine. He'd deal. It wasn't as if he hadn't before.

That much he remembered.

More than one bar fight.

But that had been a while back. High school? College? Some other time? He didn't know. Couldn't call it up. But it was there, buried and not that deep. Slowly, bit by bit, his injured brain was beginning to remember a bit. Maybe when he got home, settled back in, he would recall more about Megan, how involved they were, why they'd been fighting, what had happened. He raked a hand through his hair, touched the edge of his bandage, and felt a slice of pain. He glanced at the clock.

Twenty more minutes, possibly twenty-five.

Along with the rattling of a cart in the hallway, he heard footsteps, and suddenly Doctor Monroe was back. "I hear you want to get out of here."

"You heard right," James said.

Monroe frowned. "It wouldn't hurt to stay another night."

"I need to get home."

If the doctor thought about arguing, he kept it to himself. "If that's the way you want it."

"I do."

With a nod, Monroe said, "Then I'll leave you with some prescriptions and talk to admin about your discharge papers. You'll probably have to jump through a few hoops. Insurance and all that."

"All right."

"No driving for a few weeks, until I give you the green light," he added, and James wanted to argue, but didn't. It wasn't as if he had a vehicle at his disposal anyway. "And I want to see you this coming week. Make an appointment. If anything doesn't seem right, call immediately."

"Fine."

"All right, then," he said reluctantly. "You should be out of here within a couple of hours."

When James started to argue for a quicker release, the doctor was already stepping to the door. He held up a hand to cut off any complaints. "Paperwork."

"More like red tape."

"Whatever you want to call it." And Monroe was gone.

Could he wait for the grinding wheels of hospital administration to spew out dozens of sheets of paper that he wouldn't read anyway? Already, he was climbing the walls. And he wasn't a patient man; that much he knew about himself.

He considered. Maybe he'd just have to up and go, and to hell with all their protocol.

CHAPTER 10

In the mirror over the bar, Sophia watched the newcomer, a pretty woman who'd taken off her hat and dropped it, along with a small bag, onto an empty stool after ordering a whiskey.

There was something familiar about her, but Sophia couldn't quite put her finger on it. The newcomer was making small talk with Marshall, a regular who occupied the stool next to her. Sophia had known Marshall for a while as he worked for James in the shop as a carpenter. He was a good enough guy, but was always hopping from one girlfriend to the next.

Like James.

She ignored that thought. From the body language of the woman seated next to him, it seemed that Marshall was more interested in her than she was in him. And then there was the fact that the woman continually looked through the windows to the property at the side of the hotel where, beyond the trees, the lane to James's house ran.

What was that all about?

Not that Sophia cared.

She was marking time.

Until James got out of the hospital.

James was pretty beaten up, but he was tough, she thought, tucking a slice of lime onto the side of a martini glass, then placing it, along with a bottle of Bud, on a tray for the waitress to scoop up and take to table three, where a couple sat cuddled together on the same side of the booth.

As she reached for the bottle of Jack Daniel's behind the bar, she wondered about James's fight with Megan, but not too much. The important thing was that he was going to be okay and Megan was out of the picture.

Good.

That bitch had been making him crazy. What a nutcase!

Sophia dropped ice into a metal tumbler and poured the whiskey over it. She usually didn't bartend, but she'd reluctantly taken this shift after receiving a panicked call from Donna, the night manager, when Sophia had been driving home from the hospital after sneaking in and seeing James. Donna had practically begged her to take over for Zena, one of the regular bartenders, who was ill again. Big surprise. Zena was about three months pregnant and milking it with her morning sickness, which weirdly happened to occur just about the time she should be arriving for her shift here at the hotel. Zena swore the mere smell of booze caused her to upchuck.

Really?

Sophia doubted it, but tonight, as Donna was desperate to find someone to fill in and Sophia desperately wanted to be seen as dependable, a "team player," she'd accepted the job.

Again.

Besides, the whole place was owned by James, and the more she could curry favor . . .

She caught the woman on the stool observing her; their gazes clashed in the mirror's reflection, and there was something more than just a casual look, something deeper. Even worrisome.

No doubt, she had recognized Sophia as the "other woman" in the Megan Travers disappearance mystery.

Fine.

Sophia had gotten used to the stares, even the questions.

"Aren't you the one?" a particularly nosy busybody had asked when she'd worked in the café across the parking lot. The woman, with curly red hair, small glasses, and a disapproving smirk, had been in the gift shop, waiting to be seated and fingering a Christmas ornament on display, one of the faux fir trees that were part of the seasonal decorations.

"Pardon me?" Sophia had said, picking up menus as she was ready to seat a party of four.

"You know, the girl James Cahill was seeing on the side." Her pointy little chin had elevated a notch.

Sophia had felt herself blush as she'd squired the other guests, a couple with two small children, into the eating area.

When she'd returned to the station, ready to seat the next couple, the woman who'd made the comment was standing in line, ready to purchase an ornament—an angel with folded wings. Along with her payment, she'd left a note:

1 Corinthians 6:18

Later Sophia had made the mistake of checking the verse online:

Flee from sexual immorality. All other sins a person commits are outside the body, but whoever sins sexually, sins against their own body.

There had been a few other under-the-breath remarks and tons of questioning glances, all of which she had ignored.

So the woman on the bar stool meeting her gaze in the mirror didn't particularly bother her, except that she felt they'd met somewhere.

That was the trouble with working here.

She was too visible.

As she strained the cold whiskey into a glass, she silently hoped Zena's not-so-morning sickness would soon abate. Not likely. Zena was a bit of a slacker. And acted as if she were the first person on this damned earth who had ever ended up pregnant. Sophia imagined she'd be called in to "sub" a lot more in the future.

She'd have to find a way to say no. And that would be easier when James was out of the hospital.

The sooner, the better!

From her position she could see in the reflection that the Jack Daniel's Straight Up woman really wasn't interested in Marshall. She flirted a bit, just to keep the conversation going, but Sophia could tell she was just shining him on. Sophia should know. Hadn't she played that same game a million times?

Until James.

James Cahill had changed everything.

Even now, just at the thought of him, her breath caught in her throat, and she mentally berated herself for falling so hard.

She caught a signal from a couple at the far end of the bar and pinned a smile on her face, dropping off the whiskey on her way to take their order. This couple had been bickering from the moment they walked in, but after one drink had appeared to chill out a bit.

Not that alcohol usually helped. In most cases she'd observed, liquor tended to fuel the fire. But as she watched, the man reached over to take the woman's hand and rub the back of his thumb over her knuckle line, and the woman smiled into her apple martini.

Ah, bliss.

As people came and went, laughing and ordering drinks, or picking at the nuts and pretzels, Sophia caught snatches of conversation. Just bits and pieces, but a lot more of it swirling around James Cahill. Actually, since Megan Travers had gone missing, business in all of James's enterprises, including the hotel and bar, had picked up. Which was kind of sick, when you thought about it.

Fame or infamy—both always got people's attention.

Two thirtysomething guys took seats at the bar: Gus Jardine, the taller one, and Bruce Porter, shorter and stockier in his ever-present Yankees baseball cap. Both worked for James. Sophia knew who they were, just not a lot about them. They both smelled of smoke, and Jardine kept fiddling with his lighter. Over shots of tequila, they were not only discussing the national basketball rankings and their latest hunting trip; they'd also figured out what happened to Megan.

". . . he did her and then he did her, if ya know what I mean." Unshaven, his black hair long and curly, Gus confided to Bruce as Willow, that stealthy kitchen assistant, hurried in with fresh ice. She poured it into the refrigerated tub near the soda machine, and it rattled so loudly Sophia had a hard time catching the end of the conversation. She thought Gus said, "Something went wrong."

"Well, duh. Of course it did," Bruce agreed. "The fucker was doin' two chicks at once."

Sophia's back stiffened, and she glanced in the mirror, to see if he had figured out she was one of the "chicks."

Apparently not, because Bruce didn't catch her eye. Instead, his gaze followed after Willow as the thin woman, her black braid swinging behind her, hurried back through the swinging door to the kitchen. Good riddance, Sophia thought. Willow, barely out of her teens, hung out with unreliable Zena. Worse yet, Sophia had caught Willow staring at James with a quiet fascination that bothered her, that had really gotten under her skin, which she'd forced herself to get used to. Even pregnant Zena had followed James with her eyes from time to time.

It was exhausting. And irritating.

The problem was Sophia recognized that look, knew what it felt like to want something so badly, so out of reach that you ached inside.

Well, too damned bad.

James was off limits!

"The double-chick thing isn't a bad gig if you can get away with it," Gus was saying, still musing aloud about seeing two women at once and finally stuffing his lighter into his pocket.

"But not many guys can." Bruce's attention was back to his drinking/hunting buddy.

"Unless the chicks are dumb as shit." Gus threw back his drink, wiped his mouth with his sleeve, and slammed his shot glass. His buddy followed suit.

They both laughed. Ugly, guttural snickers. Then signaled for another round.

Sophia, inwardly burning, considered cutting them off . . . or doing something worse, but she had to keep her cool and hope they didn't read the papers, see her name tag, and put two and two together.

She saw the woman who'd nursed her Jack Daniel's quickly gather up her things, fling a bill on the bar, and abruptly leave.

For a second, Sophia thought Marshall had said something offensive. Or maybe it was Gus or Bruce. Then, through the window, she saw the headlights through the trees separating the hotel property from the lane to James's home. Her heart soared. He was home! She caught a glimpse of the woman with the red hat hurrying out the front doors.

She'd been waiting for James.

As Sophia had suspected.

A quick flash of jealousy cut through her—and then a deeper emotion as she finally remembered where she'd seen the woman. *On TV.*

"Crap," she whispered under her breath.

Ms. Whiskey Straight Up was really Charity . . . Charity Spitz, no,

Spritz, like wine spritzer. She was occasionally on TV as a local reporter whenever a station in the tri-cities to the east, or Seattle and Tacoma in the west, needed local talent to report on a story, usually weather.

Sophia had only seen her a couple of times, but she recognized that face and, more importantly, the questions lurking in her eyes. Maybe the men in their thirties hadn't recognized her, but Charity Spritz certainly had.

And now she was going to talk to James.

"Hey! How 'bout another?" Bruce asked. "We're getting thirsty."

"Right away," Sophia said automatically and pinned her for-the-customer smile on her face. "The same?"

"*Si, si*," he said. "Another shot of Jose for me and my *amigo!*"

They both laughed uproariously, and it was all she could do not to spit in their drinks.

This was crazy, Rebecca thought, shivering in the night. Certifiably crazy.

And illegal.

And possibly emotional suicide.

Nonetheless, Rebecca trudged through the snow along the lane to James Cahill's house and managed to keep her footsteps in the already packed-down trail, her breath a cloud. As the drive opened to a clearing, with a rise upon which the farmhouse had been built, she still kept to the deep ruts that had already been broken by the footsteps of cops and rescue workers, reporters and curious neighbors who had wandered over before the place had been cordoned off. With any luck, the new snowfall would cover her tracks, and she wouldn't be exposed. Inside the pocket of her jacket, she crossed her fingers, then glanced over her shoulder for the umpteenth time to assure herself that she wasn't being followed.

In the dark of the night, with snow everywhere, she imagined she saw a figure hiding behind a tree or lurking just on the other side of an outbuilding, but no one appeared, and she told herself she was just letting her nerves get to her. Despite all her mental berating, her heart was beating crazily, her pulse pounding in her ears.

Just keep going!

She plowed forward and wondered if anyone would spot her vehicle, hidden within the crowded parking lot at the hotel. If someone checked license plates against those guests registered . . .

Don't think about that. You'll be fine. This shouldn't take too long. Just in and out.

She picked up her pace, her own doubts chasing her through the night. This was probably a wild goose chase, but she had to do something.

James was a liar. And worse.

But a murderer?

That seemed a little—well, make it a lot—far-fetched. But who knew? At the clearing where vehicles were usually parked, she cut to the back gate and, following a previously broken path, made her way to the woodshed, out through the dark, dusty-smelling room and to the attached back porch. It was long and broad, with several doors opening off it to what, Megan had told her, were an old root cellar and oversized closet, past a laundry area to the back door. She tried it, but the knob wouldn't turn in her gloved hands. She'd expected as much and, praying that James's dog wasn't on the premises, leaned over and let herself into the kitchen by crawling through the large dog door cut into the lower panels. It was a tight fit, but not impossible, and she squeezed through without too much difficulty. Once standing, she didn't move—and strained to listen.

She heard the hum of the refrigerator over the rumble of air being forced through old heating ducts, but no click of toenails on hardwood, no low growl from the darkened rooms.

No dog.

Good.

She let out her breath, but her heart was pounding, and that stupid little voice in her head was screaming: *What the hell do you think you're doing?* Slowly, using the flashlight app on her phone, she picked her way through the rooms, sweeping the bluish beam over the mess.

When she'd left James at Valley General, he'd been determined to be released, so there was a chance he was already on his way back here. She didn't have much time.

What she expected to find at his home she didn't know, but she couldn't just wait around for James Cahill to "regain his memory" or the police to turn up anything on Megan. Time was ticking away, and her sister—make that her *reckless* sister—was in trouble. Rebecca was sure of it.

Did she really think James had harmed Megan?

As much as she distrusted him, she couldn't quite believe that.

But what did she really know about him?

And then there was his involvement with Sophia Russo. Not a surprise, really, but Sophia worked for him. Rebecca had seen her through the windows of the hotel, serving at the bar, her blond hair shimmering in the dimmed lights as she mixed drinks. Megan had told her about Sophia, about the fact that every time she turned around, she saw the woman.

"I can't seem to get away from her," Megan had said in a phone conversation. "She works at the restaurant and the farms, and she's everywhere in town. I know Riggs Crossing is a small town, but not *that* small."

"Maybe she's following you or checking you out."

"It's weird," Megan had said.

And Rebecca hadn't said what was uppermost in her mind:

Maybe she wants to be you.

At the very least, Sophia had wanted James Cahill.

Now Rebecca eased through James's home. The house was a wreck, the police obviously having searched it thoroughly. Good. But she had to step carefully around debris left on the floor as she made her way from kitchen to dining area to the base of a staircase and the living room, where her phone's light showed a raised hearth, the bricks stained a dark crimson in one corner.

James's blood?

Or Megan's?

Or even someone else's?

Her stomach rolled at the thought as she imagined a body falling against the sharp bricks, head bouncing with a sickening crack. Then she thought of the bandage around James's head, the sling supporting his arm, his supposed amnesia.

Stepping slowly into the room, she felt her skin crawl. She walked to the fireplace and touched the darkened brick with the fingertip of her glove. She tried to imagine the scene, the fight. Megan was mercurial, she knew that, and she was upset; that too was a fact. And she'd left this place on her own; Rebecca knew that as well. But something had happened.

It crossed her mind, not for the first time, that Megan could be hiding somewhere, that she was actually fine and just watching this play out, as a punishment to James. And to her.

But that seemed far-fetched.

Even for overly dramatic Megan.

"No," she said aloud, her voice startling her as she swung the light over the room and then started for the stairs. Old as they were, they creaked as she climbed and reached the second floor. It felt empty, and two of the bedrooms appeared unused. One had only a twin bed, while the other was cluttered with leftover furniture and bags of clothes, books, and odds and ends. Both rooms, like the floor below, had been searched, as had the bathroom at the top of the stairs and the linen closet. She stepped over a pile of towels that had been left on the floor near the railing and moved into the final room on the floor, James Cahill's bedroom.

As she pushed the door open, her stomach knotted. She felt more of a trespasser here than anywhere else in the house. Her muscles clenched as she stared at the huge bed, the mattress askew, the bedding on the floor. This was the room where James and Megan . . .

Stop it!

She forced her mind back to the task at hand. To find anything, any tiny bit of evidence that might tell her where Megan was.

Like you can do better than the police.

Maybe. She knew Megan; they didn't. Tamping down her emotions, she kept her mind on track and searched with only the light from her phone. The battery was winding down, and she'd heard it was better to just turn on lights so neighbors wouldn't be suspicious, but there were no neighbors out here, and if James returned suddenly, she didn't want him to see her silhouette in a window, so she kept her flashlight trained on the room.

She checked the nightstands, but both drawers had been dumped, their contents not holding any clues. She pawed through some of the personal things and paused when she saw a package of condoms.

Unopened.

Reminding her.

Her lips twisted, and she pushed aside a forbidden memory.

Of James Cahill.

And how she had once imagined she loved him.

Stupid, stupid woman.

She straightened and told herself this was nothing more than a wild goose chase. Glancing through the window, she noticed sudden headlights, twin conical beams lighting up the lane as a vehicle pulled into the lot.

What? No!

She shot into the upper hallway, intent on hurrying down the stairs, when she heard a voice on the porch. Then the door rattled and suddenly opened.

Oh, no!

"Ralph! Slow down." James's voice over the frantic, scattering rustle of toenails on the floor.

The dog?

With a click, the lower level was cast in light, fingers of illumination crawling up the stairs. At the base, she made out a pair of jeans-clad legs.

"Jesus H. Christ, it's cold out there." Another man's voice as the front door slammed shut, and noiselessly, her heart beating frantically, she backed into James's room and closed the door so that it was open just a hair, wide enough that if she pressed her face to it, she could get a narrow view of the darkened upper hallway.

Now what?

She let out her breath slowly. Silently.

Think, Rebecca, think. How in the world are you going to get out of here without getting yourself caught?

CHAPTER 11

"What a mess," James muttered as he strode through his kitchen, where he could find a path in the debris. He kicked a box of cornflakes out of his way, and the box burst open, half the contents, hundreds of flakes, adding to the disaster.

Drawers hung open, cupboards had been emptied, pots and pans were scattered across the floor, plates and silverware covered the counters. Wearing the clothes Bobby had brought to the hospital, his head still swathed in a bandage, his arm in a sling, he felt his jaw tighten as he moved into the dining area. His head was pounding, and the house was destroyed. Everything that hadn't been taken by the police had been shuffled through, left, and was covered in a fine black powder of fingerprint dust. "Fuck." His laptop and computer were gone, his vehicles as well, and the house . . . He shook his head and felt the headache beginning to pound again.

"I told ya," Bobby reminded him. He'd picked James up at the hospital, even bringing Ralph, who was now jetting through the rooms and barking wildly, just as he had when James had climbed with effort into Bobby's truck. The shepherd had been beside himself, all over James, licking and whining and wiggling before settling down in the truck. The good news was that Bobby had brought him fresh clothes and the hospital had returned his wallet. The bloodstained shirt and jeans he'd been wearing on the night Megan disappeared were with the police.

Now, the dog was going nuts again, whining and barking, running through the rooms and up the stairs.

"Guess he missed you," Bobby said. He was carrying a plastic bag holding James's meager belongings that he had had with him at the hospital.

Upstairs, Ralph was barking up a storm, as if he'd treed a squirrel. "Ralph! Enough!" James yelled and whistled to the dog. "Come."

Whining, Ralph clambered back to the first floor, where James stood in what had once been his living room and stared at the chaos.

"This is—"

"Pretty damned bad."

"—an effin' nightmare."

"Fuckin' nightmare," Bobby corrected, eyeing the disaster.

James grunted his agreement.

His recliner had been tipped over, the side pockets emptied, the old leather covered in the gritty dark film. Books and magazines were strewn over the floor, the shelves of the bookcase empty, the mantel swept clean, his lantern and lighter that had been upon it now on the floor, along with everything else.

He felt a surge of anger run through his blood.

"It's like they were looking for drugs," he said, and Bobby shook his head. "Then what?"

"A weapon."

"What? My . . . gun?"

"It's missing."

He walked into the dining room and saw the drawer where he'd always stashed his pistol. It was hanging open, the Glock not inside.

They think you killed her.

For the first time, he realized that until Megan was found, he would be a primary target of an investigation looking into her disappearance.

"I told ya, you shouldn't have left the hospital," Bobby reminded him. "I don't know why that doctor let you out."

"And I told you, it was my decision."

"A piss-poor one, if you ask me."

"No one did."

"Look, if you want, you can bunk with me," he said. "The missus won't mind."

James wasn't so sure of that. "The missus" was Bobby's third wife, Cynthia—"Just call me Cyn"—a buxom brunette who had always viewed James with a calculating eye, forever, he thought, measuring him up, her eyes thinning behind the smoke of one of her imported cigarettes. He didn't doubt that "Cyn" had googled him many times.

"You and Ralph can bunk in the second bedroom. Now that Cyn's kid is gone, it's free, and Ralph, I think he likes The Princess."

James didn't believe it. The Princess, Cyn's long-haired cat, whose entire name seemed to be Princess-Baby, wasn't all that likable.

"Thanks, but I'll stay here," he said, feeling his lips twist. "Home sweet home, and all that, y'know."

"More like 'Home sweet disaster,' if ya ask me, but hell, it's your life." He scowled at the stairs. "You able to get up to your room?"

"If I have to." But not tonight. The steps, which he'd always taken two at a time without a second thought, now seemed formidable. And there was no food in the fridge. And the house was filthy, almost unlivable.

Ralph was pacing at the foot of the stairs, looking up to the second floor and whining as if to say, *Come on, let's go to bed.*

"Okay, how 'bout this? I stay at the inn for a few days until I can get this place right." He owned the place, and the hotel had clean rooms, maid service, telephones, working Wi-Fi, and room service connected to the restaurant and bar.

"What about Ralph?"

"One of the dog-friendly rooms."

"Cyn and The Princess will be disappointed."

James snorted. But Bobby was nodding, so he asked, "Would you mind going upstairs and grabbing some of my things? In the closet. Jeans and a couple shirts. I've got a shaving kit in the bathroom."

"Not a problem. I'll be right back down." He started up the stairs, and Ralph, the traitor, was bounding ahead, leading the way.

Rebecca's heart was beating like a drum. With her ear pressed to the door of James Cahill's bedroom, she strained to listen, catching only bits and pieces of the conversation. It sounded like they might be leaving—James and some other man and the dog. God, the dog. It had come galloping up the stairs just as Rebecca was about to leave. She'd been able to slip back into the room, but the dog hadn't been fooled and had whined and barked.

Now, it sounded like someone was coming again. She looked around frantically at the closet and bathroom, then under the bed. No, no, and no! The only hiding spot was a smaller closet, one with a door barely three feet tall, and she shot across the room, ducked down to the point that she was nearly kneeling, and folded herself inside the cold, dark attic space where she suspected insects, bats, and mice had probably nested.

Her skin crawling at the thought, she heard the door to the bedroom swing open, a light snap on, and then the dog barking and lunging at the door to this attic space. Oh, God, no! How could she explain that she'd come here looking for some kind of clue to her sister's whereabouts?

"Ralph! Stop it, ya fool dog! Christ, what's in there? A raccoon?"

She half-expected an angry hiss to come from the dark corners of the space where luggage and boxes and broken furniture had been shoved. The dust was thick, and she had to hold her nose to keep from sneezing.

The dog was still going at it. She heard his sharp barks and saw his shadow in the thin line of light shining beneath the door.

Don't open the door! Don't open it.

But she heard the sound of footfalls closing in. Hardly daring to breathe, she held on to the tiny peg that served as a door handle on this side of the closet and braced herself, intent on holding it shut should whoever was on the other side decide to investigate. Her feet were on the door, her arms outstretched, her fingers beginning to sweat despite the frigid temperature, her weight thrust away from the door.

"You want to see what's in there?" she heard the man say, and her heart sank. His voice was clear now, his shadow having joined the near-frantic whining and barking dog.

Her heart was in her throat. How could she explain herself? She'd have to lie. She couldn't admit that she was here searching for Megan's things, that she'd taken the opportunity of James being in the hospital to look around behind his back. She could envision the charges being brought against her: trespassing, breaking and entering, burglary . . . and God knew what else.

"What the hell's the matter with you!" the guy said, and the dog started scratching wildly. "What's in the damned attic?"

Oh. Dear. God.

Don't open the door!

"I'm not sure I want to know," the guy said. "Come on, Ralph. We don't have time to chase squirrels or rats or whatever. Not now. You can get 'em later. With James. Let's go!"

And then, miracle of miracles, the dog, still barking, left, his toenails clicking on the old hardwood as he scrabbled away.

Rebecca let out her breath and felt her body sag. She had to get out of here. Before anyone came back. She considered her options. She'd entered through the dog door and could retrace her steps and use the dog's exit or even go out the doors if the dead bolts hadn't been engaged, and no one would be the wiser. Before she'd been trapped, she'd considered the option of climbing out an upper-story window. The bedroom across the hall from James's had a window that opened to the roof of the long porch that stretched to the back of the property. Her footprints would show in the snow, but if she was lucky, no one would notice, and the snow would keep piling up.

Definitely her last resort.

Sneaking around wasn't her forte. She'd always preferred the direct approach, and so, like it or not, she'd have to face James again and somehow jog his memory.

But he couldn't find her hiding in his attic like a snoop or a crazy person.

No, she needed an even playing field to earn his trust.

But first, she had to sneak out of this place before the dog came roaring up the stairs again. Swallowing back her fear, she pushed open the door and looked through the slit. The bedroom was dark, aside from a slice of light at the door from the outer hallway, and it seemed empty.

No sign of man or dog.

No sound of voices drifting up the staircase.

Still . . .

Heart knocking, holding her breath, she let herself out of the closet and quietly closed the attic door behind her. Carefully, avoiding the clothes, books, magazines, and personal items on the floor, she picked her way toward the door.

The dog gave a sharp bark again, and she stumbled, nearly tripping. Instead, she fell against the bed and bit her tongue, catching herself so that she wouldn't crash into the floor or let out a cry.

Another sharp bark, and she nearly bolted toward the attic again.

Then she heard the doorbell.

Through the living room window, James saw the headlights of a vehicle as it approached, rounding the final curve of the lane.

Now what?

Behind him, Bobby and Ralph were hurrying down the stairs.

A van pulled up outside, parking near Bobby's pickup, and a woman in a long gray coat and red hat stepped out and started trudging across the lawn. She was wearing knee-high boots and didn't seem to care about stepping through the deep snow to the front porch.

By the time she rang the bell, Ralph had given a warning bark, and James was already at the door.

James opened the door, and the woman under the porch light smiled up at him.

"Hi!" she said. "I'm Charity Spritz with the *Clarion,* and I'd like to ask you some questions about what happened here and about Megan Travers."

"No."

"Do you know what happened to her?"

"I said, 'No,'" he repeated and didn't bother hiding his irritation. Ralph was going bananas again, and he said sharply, "No! Ralph. Sit!"

The shepherd did, ears cocked, eyes focused on James.

Bobby asked, "What's this?"

"I'm Charity Spritz," she said quickly. "With the *Clarion.*"

"I've seen you on TV," Bobby said with a sharp nod of his head.

"Yes. Right. Once in a while I do a spot for KPTD. I just want to ask Mr. Cahill and . . . and you too, some questions. You are?"

Beside him, Bobby straightened to all of his five feet, nine inches. "Robert Knowlton. I'm the ranch manager."

"So you were the person who found Mr. Cahill, last Thursday night? Here," she said, motioning toward the interior of the house.

"That's right," Bobby said with a quick grin.

"Enough!" James cut in. He'd had it with people and their interest in his life. He didn't want to talk to the police, or Megan's sister, or Sophia, and especially anyone from the press. His head ached, his shoulder was throbbing, and he hadn't showered or cleaned up in what seemed like forever. "Please, just leave."

"But I only have a few questions."

"I'm sorry." He really wasn't.

"But I'd like to write your side of the story."

"My side?" That sounded bad. "There are no sides."

"Of course," she said with a smile, though she was craning her neck to peer around him and view the interior of the house, *his* house. "What I meant was, I'd like to publish the truth."

"Talk to the police."

"Again, I'd like to hear what you have to say." She seemed so earnest, her eyes beseeching his. "I went to the hospital but was turned away."

"Look, Ms. Spritz. I just got home, and tonight isn't a good time."

"Tomorrow then?" She seized on the idea.

"No."

"The citizens of Riggs Crossing have questions."

"Don't we all?"

He started to close the door.

"You're Riggs Crossing's golden boy. The man who comes from San Francisco and makes good in this small town."

"I'm *not* from San Francisco."

"But your family is," she reminded. She dug in the pocket of her coat, retrieved a card, and thrust it at him.

Bobby snatched it from her gloved fingers.

"Tomorrow," she said as he shut the door.

"That was rude." Bobby stared down at the business card.

James closed his eyes for a second and thought he heard a floorboard squeak overhead. "What was that?"

"I think you may have unwanted guests upstairs. Ralph went nuts at the attic door. Must be a nest of critters up there."

James frowned, but found he didn't care as he looked through the window and watched Charity Spritz's silver van drive back through the gate and along the lane leading to the main road. Good. "You get my things?" he asked Bobby.

"Right here." Bobby held up the plastic sack from the hospital. It was obviously fuller than it had been when they'd arrived.

"Let's go." He was tired and just wanted to lie down.

"Okay, but I think it'd be in your best interest to talk to that reporter," Bobby advised as they walked back through the destroyed dining room and kitchen. "If Megan doesn't show up, it's only gonna get worse. Wouldn't hurt to have a friend in the press."

"I'll think about it," he promised and watched as Ralph lagged back, whining at the base of the stairs.

"Fool dog," Bobby muttered. "He's been acting strange ever since that night—ever since you've been gone."

James gave a sharp whistle, and Ralph bounded into the kitchen. "Come on, let's get out of here."

CHAPTER 12

Rebecca expelled a long, pent-up breath.

Phew.

She literally almost wiped her brow.

The house was dead quiet and had been for ten minutes. She was alone. No sound of the dog whining or paws clicking, no conversation from downstairs, no longer any strip of light under the door. Just the rumble of air through the heat ducts and the pounding of her own heart.

She'd heard them leave and now peered through a slit in the blinds as the headlights of a van lit up the lane and disappeared around the corner. She waited at the window until the red glow of taillights vanished through the veil of falling snow.

Carefully, mentally crossing her fingers, she inched to the door, then hesitated, her hand on the knob.

What if they'd left the dog?

She thought she'd heard the shepherd commanded to "Come," but wasn't certain what that had meant. Had he taken the dog with him, locked him in a kennel?

But what choice did she have? She couldn't stay here all night. And who knew when James might come back? Slowly and silently, she pushed open the door and stared into the shadowed landing. A bathroom to the right and across the hallway? The bedroom with its window that opened to the wraparound porch roof that connected to the back extension? With an eye to the dark hole that was the staircase, she darted across the landing and into the spare room.

Last resort, she reminded herself and, pushing aside all of her fears, started down the stairs. Though the big old house remained still, she held her breath as she stepped onto the lower level. The interior was cast in a wash of thin gray light, the illumination from a single outdoor security lamp reflecting on the snow. She decided to leave through the front door as there had been a lot of footprints and paw prints disrupting the snow. As for the dead bolt?

Too bad.

Let James wonder if someone had been inside.

Served him right.

Mouth dry, starting to sweat despite the temperature, she pushed back the latch and opened the door, then stepped onto the porch.

All quiet.

Dark sky, falling snow, freezing temperatures, but noiseless.

Still, her skin prickled.

All she had to do was hurry down the lane and, at the road, make her way across the parking lot of the inn to the spot where she'd left her car. Another twenty minutes and she'd be home free—

Scraaape!

She turned toward the sound, a scratch that came from the spot where the porch wrapped toward the back of the house.

And saw nothing.

Just your imagination.

Pulse going wild, she scanned the snowy landscape more carefully, but found no one hiding in the shadows.

Just get out of here.

As softly as possible, she pulled the door shut behind her and started off the porch.

Scraaape!

Louder.

Just the wind, causing a branch to rub against the roof or—

Her heart was a jackhammer as she started across the lawn.

A deep growl rumbled from the porch.

She froze.

Turned.

Saw the dark figures on the porch. A man and a dog with a shaggy coat, pointed ears, eyes reflecting the eerie light.

Her stomach knotted, and she was about to run when an all-too-familiar voice stopped her cold: "Rebecca."

Oh. God. *James.*

"You scared me! What're you doing here—?" she started.

"I forgot something," he said, but she looked to the parking area, where there was no vehicle. His friend must have dropped him off, and he'd returned to catch whoever was inside his house. She hadn't fooled him at all.

"And I live here," he went on. He'd been leaning against the siding but pushed himself away from the house and started slowly toward her. "So the question goes to you. What're *you* doing here?" The dog walked at his side, its hackles up, its eyes focused on her.

"But you . . . I thought you were in the hospital."

"Until I wasn't." He moved slowly down the steps. He was angry: she saw it in the shadowy light. "Why the hell did you break into my house?"

"I didn't break into it."

"It was locked."

She knew she could outrun him. He wasn't that steady on his feet, and he looked like hell, she saw as he got closer, his head still bound as it was, his skin pale in the wintry half-light. But she couldn't outrun the shepherd, and he'd eventually catch her even if he didn't sic the dog on her. The jig, as her father used to say, was up. "The dog door was open."

"You crawled through the dog door? Jesus, Rebecca, what's wrong with you?" Then as if he actually thought she might answer, he held up a hand and asked, "Why?"

In for a penny, in for a pound. "I thought I might find something here that would help me find Megan."

"By breaking into a house that had already been searched by the police?"

Even to her own ears, it sounded ridiculous.

He stared down at her, obviously angry. Not the first time, she reminded herself. "And what did you think you'd find?"

"I'm not really sure. Something. Anything. To help me find Megan."

"In my house?"

"Yes!" she said, her own anger rising. "That's where she told me she was coming from." Rebecca pointed a finger at the house. "She said she'd had a horrible fight with you and that she had to get away. That she was afraid of you."

"Afraid of me?"

"Why do you keep repeating everything? *Yes.* She was out of her mind—hysterical—and so I thought maybe coming here would help me get some idea of what happened. It's not as if you're filling in all the blanks."

"I would if I could, but—"

"Yeah, yeah, I know! You can't effin' remember."

His lips flattened as a gust of wind rattled through the branches of a nearby tree. "Come on, let's go inside, it's freezing." Despite the anger radiating through him, he appeared a little unsteady as he walked up the steps to the front porch.

"I should go."

"Not yet." He was angry. "Where's your car?"

"At the inn." She glanced toward the empty parking area. "Where's yours?"

He snorted. "With the police for now. They, like you, seem to think I did something to your sister."

"Did you?"

"Of course not."

"You remember," she charged and took a step toward him.

"I wish."

"Then how do you know?"

"I just know, okay," he threw back at her. "I'm not violent." But the pulse throbbing near his temple, at the hairline not covered by his bandage, said otherwise. "I would never hurt . . . anyone."

"And this you know. This, you remember."

The dog growled.

She didn't break his angry gaze.

"I wouldn't hurt her."

He seemed convinced, but she knew how easily he could lie. She said, "You left in a van with that other man and then came back because you knew I was inside."

"Ralph knew someone was." He looked at her. "I don't have rats in my attic."

"And then you stood out in the freezing weather after just getting out of the hospital?"

"That's right." Now he pushed open the door and stepped into the vestibule, the dog with him. Just inside the door, he snapped on a light. "Take a look around. A good one. Instead of skulking with a flashlight or whatever. This is how I found my place, trashed by the police."

"And whatever happened before," she said, walking to the living room and staring at the stain on the raised hearth. "Is that blood . . . all yours?"

"Don't know."

"Another memory lapse?"

He glared at her, then looked away. "I figure the police will sort it out." With obvious effort and a grimace of pain, he turned over his recliner and made a gesture for her to sit. "Tell me what *you* know." She hesitated, and he added, "You want to figure this out. Correct?"

Nodding, she tried to rein in her own spiraling temper and added softly, "Of course I do."

"Good. Then tell me."

Glancing around the disheveled room, she considered. She wanted answers, and here was James, ready to talk apparently. What did she have to lose?

"Megan called me on the way from here. After your fight." Standing near an empty bookcase, she explained about Megan's panicked, hysterical call and the next few hours and days of waiting when she didn't arrive. "I didn't worry at first. She has a history . . . well, you know, of . . . overreacting."

He made a sound that could have meant anything. "What was she overreacting to?"

Rebecca leveled her gaze at him. "She thought you two were exclusive. Apparently you didn't." When he didn't respond, she added, "I don't know why it came as such a shock to her. She knew . . . she knew you."

She hoped that remark might jog his memory.

If it did, he didn't show it.

She went on, "I thought, at first, that she'd gotten over her anger and maybe she'd turned around, you two made up, and she just forgot to keep me in the loop." She looked out the window to where snow was still falling. "I didn't even worry all that much when she didn't answer her phone or respond to my texts. I thought she probably felt foolish and didn't want to explain anything, but when she hadn't responded by . . . God, what was it? Friday night, I guess? I began to worry and started calling around to her friends and coworkers, who told me she hadn't shown up for work. One of them . . . Ramon . . . tried to contact her too. Even went to her apartment and called me to report that she wasn't there and her car was missing. So I started checking with everyone I could think of, anyone she mentioned that I could find and, of course, the hospitals."

"And nothing."

"So here we are."

"Leaving you to think I had something to do with it."

"Obviously, her story about the fight was right."

"And it makes sense to you that I was injured badly enough to be taken by ambulance to a hospital where I was in a coma but still had a way of getting rid of your sister?"

"I'm thinking you could have . . . an accomplice," she said. "Megan told me you were seeing someone else."

"So instead of breaking it off with her, I staged an entire fight and hired someone to kidnap her? Seriously, Rebecca?" He walked into the dining room and, wincing a little, knelt near a cabinet with a door hanging open. "Shit," he said upon looking inside, then retrieved a dusty bottle of some kind of liquor. He held it up. "Drink?"

"No, thank you."

He scrounged in another cupboard and returned with a couple of glasses, along with the bottle. "Sure?"

"I don't want a drink." She'd had drinks with him before . . . and that hadn't turned out the way it should've. "This is serious, James."

"Yeah, I got that."

"And, coming out of the hospital, being on painkillers and all, I don't think you're supposed to drink either."

He nodded curtly. "Agreed. But then . . . it's been a helluva couple days, don't you think?" He set the glasses on a small table that hadn't been upended in the police search, poured them each a healthy shot, and left the open bottle between them.

"Maybe you should be more careful," she suggested.

"No 'maybe' about it. But to hell with it." He tossed back the first drink. "And you want to know why? Everyone in this damned town, including you, seems to think I'm, at the very least, a kidnapper and, at the worst . . . God, I don't want to think." He poured himself another shot.

"Wow. Slow down."

"Isn't that why you're here?"

"I just want to find out the truth."

"And nail me to the cross," he said, eyeing her.

She wanted to lie but didn't, and at that moment headlights washed over the windows as a battered old pickup pulled into the lot. More guests?

"Must be the calvary," he said.

"You mean cavalry."

"Either way." He then knocked back the liquor that had been in the second glass just as footsteps sounded on the porch. Ralph shot to his feet and trotted to the front door.

"You're going to kill yourself."

"Hope never dies." He cocked an eyebrow at her. "But I don't think so. Not today. Not from a couple of drinks."

"It's your funeral." Footsteps on the porch. Who? she wondered. Not wanting to get caught in another awkward conversation and explanation about what she was doing here, she hovered to one side. She just needed to get out. "I've got to go."

"We'll take you to your car."

"Who's we? I don't need a ride. It's a short walk."

"That's Bobby. Coming to take me to the inn."

The man who at that moment pushed in the front door was small and wiry, with a cap pulled low over his eyes, the scent of cigarette smoke clinging to him. He gazed hard at Rebecca. "Well, I'll be. Ralph was on to something."

"That he was. This is Rebecca. Megan's sister. My foreman, Bobby."

Bobby asked, "What're you doin' here?"

"She thought she might find something that would help her locate her sister."

"So she broke in?" Bobby asked, scowling. "I locked the place myself."

"Something like that. Long story. The upshot is that she's parked her car at the hotel, so we're giving her a ride back."

He looked about to argue. Instead, he just squared his cap on his head. "All right," he said shortly.

"Look. Really. I can walk," Rebecca declined. "It's not that far. You're hurt, and I doubt there's much room in the truck."

James was heading for the door. "Bobby's truck's got a bench seat."

The thought of being wedged tight between the two men even for a short distance was daunting.

"I don't think—"

"There's no use arguing with him," Bobby said. "Let's just get on with it. Cyn—that's my wife—she's been texting me like crazy. I need to get home."

"Let me grab a hat," James said and disappeared down a hallway to return wearing a black cowboy hat that partially covered his bandaged head. "Let's go."

Rebecca didn't like it, but she was hustled out of the house and to the Silverado and, along with the dog, crammed inside. Bobby was behind the wheel and James against the passenger window, Ralph curled at their feet, his dark eyes never leaving Rebecca's face.

You can get through this, she thought, ignoring the fact that the length of the outside of her leg was pressed tight against James's, that he was so close. Memories of being with him flooded her mind. He might not recall their short time together, but she did—in all too vivid detail. Seattle had never seemed so vibrant, so alive than in the short few months she'd spent with James. Nor, she realized, had she. His betrayal had been bitter.

With her own damned sister.

And then he'd done the same to Megan.

She should have felt some satisfaction in that, she supposed, but didn't. With an effort, she closed her mind to all those ridiculous thoughts and even more ridiculous feelings. The past was the past, and apparently it hadn't made enough of a lasting impression on James that he could feel even a twinge of emotion about it.

They jostled on the ride in the close, warm cabin of the truck, and the smell of smoke and liquor enveloped her. Thankfully, the drive was short, less than five minutes that somehow felt like eons of staring silently through the windshield while watching the wipers slap away the snow.

At the inn, Bobby found a parking slot close to the entrance, pulled in, and cut the engine. Almost before the truck had stopped, James opened the passenger door and climbed out, as if he were as anxious as she was to avoid the close contact.

Good.

She too needed to break the intimacy of the closed space.

Keys in hand, she slid across the bench, stepped outside and into the sharp cold. With a glance to the driver, she said a quick, "Thanks for the ride," to Bobby, then to James, still standing by the open passenger door, "This isn't over."

"She doesn't like you much," Bobby observed as he hauled James's bag up the few steps to the porch of the inn.

"The feeling's mutual."

He shot James a disbelieving look and held the door open, and James eased his way into the familiar surroundings of the hotel. Intimate lobby, bar, and dining room to one side, elevator bank and fourteen-foot Christmas tree to the other.

Walking wasn't as easy as it had been. The booze had been a mistake; Rebecca had been right about that, if not much else. He was a little light-headed, detached from his body, which helped with the pain but not so much with his stability.

Worse yet, the feel of Rebecca's body next to his in the pickup had been a jolt.

Half an hour later, after Bobby had carried up his plastic bag of belongings to one of two executive suites at the hotel, James was finally alone. *Executive* was a bit of a stretch, James thought, as he moved slowly across the room, but the suite had a bedroom, bathroom, French doors, and a desk, along with a fold-out couch in the living area and a compact kitchen, complete with small stove and apartment-sized refrigerator. He was lucky to have it due to a last-minute cancellation, as the inn was booked solid through the new year.

Didn't matter that he owned the damned place. Well, he and First Crossing Bank.

James moved into the bathroom, stripped, and surveyed the damage to his body in the full-length mirror. He looked like hell. Though his legs and lower torso were unscathed, his head was still partially wrapped, his arm in a sling, his ribs bruised. And then there were the scratches down the left side of his face. They'd been cleaned, and there was evidence of antiseptic on his skin. Scabs had formed in his beard, and he supposed he would be okay in a week or so. And if not, a short beard would disguise the marks, but for now . . .

He pointed the shower head to hit him low on the back, then stepped under the spray. He tried to keep his sling and bandages dry, but failed and thought, *tough.* He cleaned himself, shampooed what he could of his exposed hair, and then let the hot water and steam envelop him. He was on the mend; he could feel it. His body was healing.

But he still couldn't remember.

Not clearly.

And the pain was still a dull throb. Despite the scotch, he'd never sleep without the aid of medication. He considered the fact that he should have stayed another day or two in the hospital, then banished the thought.

He thought about Rebecca. Beautiful and angry as hell. Convinced that he had something to do with her sister's disappearance to the point that she broke into his house and skulked around. She didn't trust him. Didn't like him.

But she had.

He didn't clearly remember, but felt that she had cared about him, possibly more than he had cared for her. Though he couldn't recall the details of their relationship, he knew deep in his gut that women had always been his downfall.

Apparently, they still were.

So was she here for Megan?

Or for him?

His ego . . . shit. It had always been a problem. That much he did remember. He found the bottle of pain pills on the counter, shook out a couple, tossed them back, and leaned against the sink. Why could he remember only bits and pieces?

Because you don't want to. You know from some psychology class you took that the mind protects itself, that sometimes areas of your life are too painful to remember, so the mind closes the door to whatever it was that was so brutal.

Face it, you can't remember.

Not now, anyway.

Glancing at his scruffy reflection in the mirror, he considered his lack of memory and decided it might just be for the best.

CHAPTER 13

If James Cahill thought he was going to get off the hook that easy, he had another think coming, Charity decided as she drove to her apartment, a studio cut into what had once been the maid's quarters in a larger home. She pulled into the driveway and eyed the place.

It appeared right smack out of a damned Currier and Ives lithograph: a three-storied Victorian with snow on the roof and even icicles hanging from the eaves. Years before, the grand old home had been sliced into five apartments, including the owner's living quarters on the main floor. Another unit was housed in the basement; two more were on the second floor; and finally the smallest, Charity's studio, was tucked into the third floor.

She knew her neighbors by sight and by their names on the mailboxes, but that was about it. The guy in the basement kept to himself—some kind of computer nerd, she thought and wondered if he was really into porn or something nefarious; she told herself that she had to check that out. The people on the second floor were a couple, and the wife was pregnant. Oh, goody. Soon there would be a screaming baby. Charity could hardly wait. The only semi-normal person in the whole place was a woman of about forty or so in the apartment below hers, neighbor to the pregnant couple on the second floor. And that woman—Maribelle Edwards—just happened to work at Cahill Industries as a cook, which, Charity decided, was a stroke of luck. She reminded herself to cozy up to Maribelle, take over a bottle of wine and loosen her lips about what went on behind the closed doors of the hotel.

She hurried into the foyer and took the stairs to her apartment. It was messy, with a couple of pairs of jeans left on the floor, a comforter sliding off the couch, and an array of glasses left on tables—but compared to the mess she'd caught a glimpse of at James Cahill's place, her home looked shipshape.

Kinda.

As she locked the door behind her, she kicked off her boots, then shrugged out of her coat and adjusted the heat on the thermostat, which had two settings: colder than Antarctica in winter and hotter than hell. She opted for the latter.

Still burned by Cahill, she found an opened bottle of wine in the fridge, poured herself a glass of merlot, and slid up to the table that doubled as her desk. As the space started to warm, she took a couple of long swallows, then fired up her laptop.

Time to find out more about James Cahill. She planned to go into the office in the morning armed with a ton of information and insist the editor hand her the Megan Travers story. It was hers, dammit, and Seamus O'Day, that decrepit old ex-jock, wasn't doing jack shit. It was time someone, namely Charity, took the bull by the horns and exposed Cahill for the fraud that he was.

She felt certain he knew more than what he was saying.

Amnesia?

Ha.

What were the chances?

"Slim to none," she said aloud and started with Google.

She found information on the old scandals involving the Cahill family and felt a warm glow surround her. From the whiskey and wine? Maybe. But probably because she knew she was about to blow the roof off the frickin' James Cahill/Megan Travers story.

"Take that," she said aloud as she skimmed article after article on Marla Cahill and her daughter Cissy and, drum roll, sweet little James.

Not so friggin' innocent.

Sipping from her glass, she read and printed out the stories that caught her eye. The Cahill family was from old San Francisco money and had been wealthy for generations. They'd established Cahill House for pregnant girls who had nowhere to turn. They'd suffered through scandals involving sex, money, lies, and buried secrets that just wouldn't stay hidden. Through it all, the damned family had flourished, even though the matriarch, Eugenia, was now dead, yet another victim of murder.

Homicide and mental disorders ran through the Cahill family history, and now, she wondered, was this current crisis being covered up again, by James, the youngest heir and golden boy? Could he have somehow killed his girlfriend and hidden her body, then stooped so low as to injure himself to cover up his crime?

That seemed unlikely, and there was the rumor that Megan had been on her way to see her sister after their fight. So, if Megan was alive when she left James, was it possible that he had had an accomplice who'd helped him, or had he caught up with her himself and killed her?

She leaned back in her chair and thought it all out.

Somehow, someway she was going to find out all of James Cahill's secrets.

And she was going to dig up all the dirt on his family.

He wasn't the only one who had connections in San Francisco. Her aunt lived in Oakland, just a short drive across the bay, and it was the holiday season. Maybe it was time for Charity to reconnect with family and combine a business trip with pleasure. Merry, merry, and all that crap.

Smiling to herself, Charity walked back to the kitchen, where she topped off her glass, then picked up her phone and scrolled through her contacts to see if she still had Aunt Maureen's phone number.

The dream was so real.

A woman nuzzling up to him, kissing him, her breath hot and warm against his skin as he lay on the bed. James moaned from deep in his throat as she slid her tongue down his chest and lower.

He reacted, his erection hard. Aching.

His blood on fire.

Her mouth slid along the length of him, her tongue slick and hot and persuasive.

Rebecca? He saw her face, though his eyes were closed; her image held for a second, then faded, but the sensations, sexual and thrilling, continued to consume him.

The heat.

The wet.

The need.

Pressure mounted, and just when he thought he could no longer hold back, she was atop him, riding low over his hips, but moving gently . . . so moist . . . so hot . . . moving faster and faster, with the rise in his heartbeat and his breaths . . . Oh, God, oh, God, ooooh . . .

He bucked upward, straining.

A spasm jolted his body.

Then another and another.

He groaned with the release.

His hips dropped against the mattress.

Pain ripped through his rib cage.

What?

His eyes flew open as the woman slid off him.

No dream.

No hallucination from medication.

This woman was in bed with him.

The room was nearly dark, the barest light coming through the partially closed shades, and for a second, he was disoriented. He wasn't home, he wasn't in the hospital, but he was . . . oh, holy shit! He fumbled for the bedside lamp, found a switch, and the dark room was suddenly awash in warm light.

Sophia, naked, was now pressed warm next to him, her blond hair tousled, her eyes glittering with amusement. "Good morning," she whispered and tried to pull the cover back over him.

"What're you doing here?"

He blinked, trying to orient himself. Not home. Not the hospital. Oh, right. The inn.

"Isn't it obvious?" Her smile was beguiling as she stretched her arms over her head and tossed her hair over one shoulder, exposing the back of her neck, where a few freckles usually hid behind her thick blond tresses.

"I mean . . ." He pushed himself away from her, putting distance between them on the bed. "Why are you here?"

"You invited me."

That didn't sound right. "When?"

"Last night. While you were at the front desk checking in . . . I was closing up the bar and looked into the lobby where you were standing with Bobby. You caught my eye and gave me the signal."

"What signal?"

"The nod, which meant I was to come up, so I did."

He didn't remember that. Was she lying?

She arched a coy eyebrow. "Aren't you glad?"

"Yes . . ." Was there any other answer?

Leaning on both elbows, she cocked her head, her hair falling over a naked shoulder to brush the top of one breast.

Her smile faded a bit. "You don't remember?"

He could recall walking into the hotel and still being in a bad mood. His house was a disaster, his computer, laptop, iPad, and phone all missing, compliments of the police; he was under suspicion in Megan Travers's disappearance, and he couldn't recall seriously important pieces of his life. He did remember that he'd found Rebecca Travers in his house, though, that and the fact that he'd consumed two—or was it three?—drinks in quick succession had probably contributed mightily to the headache that was pounding behind his eyes.

"Oh. Well . . ." She eased to the side of the bed and actually blushed. "I'll leave."

"Look, I'm just messed up."

"I was hoping to help with that." She glanced at him but, when she realized he wasn't going to tell her to stay, reached for her clothes. "I thought maybe I could take care of you while you were recuperating." She slid into a skimpy bra, then pulled a thong up over her shapely legs before standing and snapping it into place over a perfectly round rump.

She was beautiful.

Gorgeous.

A fact, he was certain, she was very aware of.

"I would've stayed with you at your house, or you could have bunked at my apartment." She tugged a gray turtleneck over her head, then pulled her hair out of the neckline. "You could use some help, someone to take care of you."

"I'll be okay."

She shimmied into a short black skirt. "If you stay here, I suppose."

"I do have a house."

She was fastening her hair back into a ponytail. "But I heard it's a wreck."

"Nothing that can't be fixed."

She glanced at his sling, left on the side of the bed.

"Well, eventually, I'll be able to handle it," he said.

"And in the meantime? You lucked out that there was an unoccupied room here, but I checked, and the inn is booked up. Solid. Until the week after New Year's. So are you going to throw out paying customers to keep this room?"

"Someone will cancel."

"If you say so. But the invitation's open. You can come to my place, and I'll look after you, and when your house is ready and you're, you know, better, maybe not using a sling for your arm, you can go home. Or any time, for that matter."

The offer made sense, but he didn't want to commit.

She saw his indecision. "Hey, fine. Do what you want." Sitting on the edge of the bed, she slid one foot into a knee-high boot, wincing a little as she forced her foot into the leather. "I was just trying to help." She zipped up the first boot, then did the same with the second, before reaching for a wool coat that she had tossed over the back of the single chair in the bedroom. "But if you don't want it, that's cool." As she wound a red scarf around her neck, she flashed a quick, knowing smile. "I'll see ya," she promised, as she bent over the bed to look him directly in his eyes. "Let me know if you need anything. Anything."

"I will."

She kissed him lightly, then straightened and, without another word, opened the door to the living area and swept past Ralph, who'd been lying on the other side. The dog barely glanced up as James heard the click of the front door close behind her.

He didn't know whether he felt relief or disappointment or a little bit of both.

CHAPTER 14

The Isolated Cabin
Cascade Mountains
Washington State
December 15

There has to be a way out of here. Has to!

This thought careens through my brain for the millionth time as I sit cross-legged on the pull-out bed, a sofa with a sleeping bag tossed over the mattress.

I just need to get outside.

Once there, I might even recognize this spot in the wilderness. Because I really don't know where I am now, and I could have been fooled as to where I am. I was unaware of how long I'd been here after being zapped with a stun gun.

How stupid was I? Never did I think I would be attacked.

"Idiot," I grumble, then turn my attention back to the immediate problem of finding a means of escape.

Assuming I can free myself, then what? Where am I? Am I dozens of miles from civilization, or only a quarter of a mile down a lane to a major road? Are the tall trees I catch glimpses of real mountain firs, or possibly just the most remote part of the Christmas tree farm? I've never heard any traffic other than the sound of an engine whenever my captor returns, but it's possible this cabin isn't as remote as I have been led to think.

Maybe not hours from civilization, but minutes . . .

I wonder if anyone is searching for me.

Surely they are.

I swallow back my fear that no one even knows I'm missing, that lies have been spread about the reason I'm unavailable.

If only I had my phone or a radio or any way to communicate to the outside world!

I eye the small interior of the room again, absently searching for some crack in this jail, something I've overlooked, and as I do, I wonder what is to become of me?

If no one other than my kidnapper knows where I am, then what if something happens to them?

My stomach knots, and I try not to think about how dire my situation is.

"You have to get out of here yourself!" I remind myself as outside the wind howls, mocking me. Involuntarily, I shiver, though, of course, I'm not really cold. Not with heat radiating from a propane fireplace glowing brightly in the corner. I wonder vaguely what will happen when the propane runs out or the generator I hear huffing away goes silent. What if my jailor decides not to come back or is incapacitated? What then?

"For the love of God, stop it!" I push that awful thought aside, but it keeps creeping back, a horrid little worm crawling through my brain, reminding me of how vulnerable I really am. "Go away!" I yell out loud.

Again.

Drawing my knees to my chin, I stare upward and out the windows mounted high overhead. Small, in a neat row, none large enough to slip through, the tops of snow-dusted fir trees visible as night descends. There are two larger windows, but they are now shuttered—"retrofitted" would be the right term—in other words, boarded over. Useless. Immovable.

I know.

I've tried to force them open and have the bloodied fingertips and broken nails to prove it. Of course, they didn't budge. That's one thing about a Cahill Tiny House: It's built solidly.

This model, with its shimmering silver-gray tile backsplash, trendy stone counters, even a small, damned chandelier, is gloriously high end, but still a prison.

At first, I'd thought this was a sick joke.

That my "kidnapping" was all some sort of elaborate, misguided prank.

I should have known better.

I should have realized what I was dealing with. But after the first night, and the second, and the third, I'd come to realize the treacherous truth, that I was being held here, possibly left here to die, and I'd started to panic.

Now, throat dry, muscles tense, I wonder, will I ever be free again? Or will I be trapped here forever?

Oh. God. No. No!

Certainly, if I were going to be killed or hurt, it would have happened already. Right? Why keep me locked in this remote, isolated cabin? Surely, if my death were the ultimate goal, it would have already occurred.

So, what then?

Ransom?

No.

A darker thought begins to filter into my mind, but I block it.

But my heart aches. In the time I've been held here, the only person I've ever seen was my captor.

Someone I trusted.

Someone I'd been waiting for all my life.

But did my jailor have an accomplice?

Maybe.

What if the person who did this told a careful lie, explained away my absence? How long would it take for anyone to realize that I'm really gone, truly missing?

Panic rises again, my heart fluttering, my hands beginning to shake uncontrollably.

"Get a grip!" I order myself over the soft hiss of the fire.

I have to be calm.

Forceful.

My only chance is to keep my wits about me.

"Don't give in!"

I scurry down the ladder and cross to the minuscule bathroom, where I stare at the fixtures, all bolted down tight. I know they're steadfast. I've tried every damned day to pry them off with my bare hands. And failed. But there has to be a way out! I can't believe this box—wooden sides, some Sheetrock, metal, and glass—is impossible to escape from.

I know that there are vents, and holes where plumbing is connected to some kind of water source and septic tank . . . right? And there is electricity from the generator.

Think!

There has to be a way out of this!

Use your brain!

There's a chance I could start a fire with the propane stove, but then I would probably be trapped before anyone saw the blaze. I'm not ready to die yet. Not that way.

And I need to feed my vengeance.

The only visible way out is the door, so the most likely scenario is to distract my keeper the next time I'm visited to replenish my supplies.

If that happens.

There is always the chance that I could be left here alone to die, a slowly painful death from hunger or dehydration should my water give out, or from going psycho completely and utterly bat-shit crazy.

Is that the ultimate plan?

That someone I trusted, someone I held dear would be so cruel?

Rather than dwell on that excruciating thought, I go over the prison again, inch by upscale inch.

For what seems the millionth time, I eye ceiling and walls, loft space and living area, and the ladder that slides like a barn door from one side of the loft to the other. Nothing there.

I've checked every screw, nail, and bolt in the entire house, trying to pry free the tiniest of weapons, anything with which to attack my kidnapper, but every damned thing is screwed down tight, and I have no tools, not even a plastic knife or fork or friggin' spoon to try to pry my way to freedom.

Damn, damn, damn!

Desperate, I study the ladder once more, then slam it to one side with such force that it bounces and returns, seeming to laugh at me. I examine the one step on the ladder that had seemed a little loose, but that was just my imagination. I give it another tug, and it doesn't shift at all.

I rock back on my heels and glare at the beast of a ladder.

It won't help. But there has to be something, one little flaw. I just have to find it.

Once more, I start opening drawers and cupboard doors, searching the insides and . . . then . . . Oh!

Like a bolt of lightning, an idea strikes.

The drawer pulls! Why haven't I thought of it before? If I could loosen the screws . . . but that's the problem, isn't it?

Still . . .

Heart pounding, I check every one.

All fitted tight.

Nothing loose, but if there was anything to wedge in the inside of the drawers . . . My fingernails are broken, and there is nothing, not one damned thing . . . or is there? Adrenaline sliding through my veins, my pulse pounding, I rifle through the trash, something my captor takes away after each visit. Nothing . . . except . . .

The meals that had been provided are prepackaged, the kind from the freezer section of a grocery store—the food frozen in tiny plastic containers.

I find one in the garbage pail, pull it out, and without rinsing it, test it. My heart is beating wildly as I attempt to force the lip of the dish into a screw head behind a kitchen drawer.

No good.

The plastic is too thick. I swear furiously. But I don't give up.

The bottom of the dish is thinner than the sides, I think.

Biting my lip while attempting to tamp down the hope starting to soar, I try to tear the plastic.

No go.

Again.

But it proves impossible.

My grip slips.

I wash the tiny tray and my hands, drying both, then tackle it again.

"Come on," I grit out as I begin to work the small dish between my hands, making a valiant stab at tearing the black plastic.

There's a reason plastic doesn't decompose for upward of a thousand years, something I think I've heard. Tearing it seems im-

possible, and I sure don't have a millennium to do it. But if I can just get an edge started . . .

Twisting the little tray back and forth furiously, I see the black plastic turning gray and start to whiten. "Good. Good." More pressure. More twisting. Faster and faster, until I'm actually sweating. "Come on, come on," I mutter, moving the hard material back and forth, back and forth, trying to break through, create a seam. I just need a slim edge to insert in the screw so I can remove it.

The damned plastic holds fast.

"Shit."

I wipe my brow.

Set my jaw.

Go at it again.

Faster and faster.

Twisting, turning.

Back and forth.

Suddenly the plastic begins to click as I twist.

Yes!

My hands are sweaty.

My fingers are cramping.

I stick with it.

Ignore the pain.

Back and forth.

Back and forth.

You can do this! Don't give up.

"Come on."

Snap!

Suddenly the small plate breaks apart, now in two pieces.

Each with a paper-thin edge.

I can't help but smile and let out a whoop of triumph.

I know where to start. Not here in the living area, where everything is visible, but in the bathroom. I hurry to the small, closet-like room and open the cupboard door under the bathroom sink. It is small, but screwed tight to the back of the door is a slim bar with hooks on it, to be used to hang a washcloth or small towel. Not much of a weapon, but one that can be easily hidden. Now, if I can just unscrew it.

Carefully, holding my breath, I force the piece of plastic into one of the screws and try to twist, to turn the damned thing.

Nothing.

Not the smallest budge.

Damn!

"Oh . . . no, no, no! This is not going to happen," I say aloud and despite a new sense of despair I keep at it, banging my knuckles.

Cursing.

Sweating.

And yes, even praying.

I have to make this work!

I have to save myself!

Because, like it or not, no one else will.

I am on my own.

CHAPTER 15

Riggs Crossing, Washington
December 5

On Monday morning, using the key he'd found hidden on the sill over the door, Rivers let himself into Megan Travers's apartment. It was just before 5:00 A.M., a time he felt he could be in the place alone.

Mendoza wasn't with him.

They'd been there before, complete with all the necessary paperwork, and looked over the place under the watchful eye of the apartment manager.

Today, he needed a few minutes in Megan's home all by himself.

When he and Mendoza had come by the first time, the door had been latched, but not locked. Someone had secured it since.

He made a mental note to check with the manager.

Inside, nothing had changed. The apartment was as they'd left it and was the same cluttered mess as it had been. Dishes and a half-eaten sandwich, along with near-empty glasses of liquid, had been left on the coffee table, while the small dinette table was a catchall for magazines, mail, and coffee cups.

In the bedroom, the bed was unmade, the duvet in a pool on the floor, dresser drawers left open, the closet showing scattered clothes and hangers as if they'd been ripped from the rod.

He stepped into the minuscule bathroom, where cabinet drawers had been opened; Megan's "scrubs," the clothes she'd been wearing at work, according to coworkers, had been stripped off and dropped onto the floor, left alongside a pair of thick-soled shoes. On the bureau top, a scattering of scarves, jewelry, and a pair of socks. A silver necklace was nearly falling into an open drawer, its filigreed cross winking in the half-light.

No purse, laptop, or phone had been located.

All evidence pointed to Megan Travers having left in a hurry.

Alone?

Or with someone?

By choice?

Or forced?

He hesitated just a second, then scooped up the necklace and dropped it into his pocket.

Fingering the tiny links, he walked into the living room again, stared at the nearly drunk bottle of diet soda on a side table, then stood before a bookcase where pictures filled a couple of shelves, all of Megan, all more flattering than her driver's license photograph. There was one shot of her with James Cahill, standing under an arch with lettering that read CAHILL CHRISTMAS TREES. Other photos were of Megan with people he didn't recognize, possibly some of those friends and acquaintances that he had phoned when she'd first gone missing, each and every one of them saying the same thing, that they hadn't heard from Megan "for a while" or that they "had lost touch" with her.

Except, of course, for the people she'd met in Riggs Crossing.

According to the people she worked with at the McEwen Clinic, Megan had left as she normally did and wasn't visibly upset on the day she'd disappeared. Possibly on the way home, a short drive, or after she had arrived here, she'd gotten an upsetting phone call? Or met with someone? The trip from the McEwen Clinic was less than three miles.

Five minutes, tops.

She'd then come into the apartment, stripped out of her work clothes, pulled on others, and stuffed an overnight bag with essentials—makeup, clothes, and electronics. She'd taken the time to scribble a handwritten note. The pad of the same kind of sticky-note stationery had been left on the coffee table, along with near-empty glasses and a stained coffee cup. Then she'd left, not even bothering to lock the door behind her.

She had presumably driven to Cahill's home, confronted him, they'd fought, and she'd left again, nearly colliding with the snowplow and calling her sister from the road in the middle of a winter storm. She'd been heading west, driving erratically, according to at least one witness, presumably to Rebecca Travers's home in Seattle.

Somewhere between here and there Megan had vanished.

He stood in the middle of the messy living room, clutched the chain inside his pocket, and closed his eyes, imagining the scene, sensing Megan's anger. Her fury.

She runs into the apartment.

Upset.

She strips off her clothes and changes, grabs her things from the bathroom and closet, stops at the coffee table to write a note.

Why bother if she were going to face James Cahill?

She rips the sheet from the notepad and is so angry she flies outside, not bothering to lock the door behind her, and—

Click.

His eyes flew open.

"Who the hell are you?" a woman demanded from the open doorway, her hand on the knob. She was poised to step inside but instead kept her distance.

He let go of the necklace, allowing it to fall into the depth of his pocket. "Detective Brett Rivers, Riggs County Sheriff's Department."

"You have ID?" She was wary, dark eyes assessing.

"And you?" he asked, even as he recognized her from one of the pictures on the shelf. He reached into his pocket, and her eyes followed his move. When he found his wallet and opened it, she didn't relax.

"What're you doing in my sister's apartment?" she demanded.

Rebecca Travers. He'd figured as much. Around five nine or ten, with darkish auburn hair pulled back and covered in the hood of a ski jacket, she had little, if any, resemblance to the missing Megan.

"Looking around."

"The manager said the police had come and gone."

"We did. But I wanted another sweep," he said, stating the obvious.

"Why?"

"Just in case I missed something the first time around."

“Does that happen often?” She was still in the doorway, snow falling behind her.

“No.”

“It looked like you were in some kind of trance or calling up the dead or . . . whatever. With no lights on, just an app from your phone. Weird.”

He let that go. “You’re Rebecca.”

She gave a stiff nod. “That’s right.”

“We’re supposed to meet this morning.”

“At the Sheriff’s Department,” she pointed out. “Not here.”

“And you came by, why?”

“It’s my sister’s place. I have a key. Not that I needed it, but I thought . . .” Her voice trailed off, and she frowned. “I don’t know what I thought I’d accomplish, but I was hoping that something here”—her gaze, which had been fastened on Rivers, slid to survey the rest of the untidy room—“might help me figure out what happened.”

“Is there anything?” he asked and thought about the necklace he’d lifted.

She hesitated, took a step inside, and shook her head. “No.” She didn’t bother shutting the door, obviously not trusting him completely, allowing a cold breeze to blow through the small rooms as she snapped on a light.

Her gaze traveled over what, he assumed, were the familiar objects in the living area. Letting her hood fall away, she walked to the bookcase and picked up the picture of Megan and herself in a restaurant, their heads together, big smiles on their faces, colorful drinks on a table in front of them.

A shadow crossed her face as she set the framed photo back on the shelf.

“Is this the way the apartment usually was—how she kept it?”

“Yeah, probably. I’ve only been here a couple of times, and Megan isn’t the neatest person on the planet.”

“So you don’t see anything unusual?”

Stepping through a small dining area to the kitchen alcove, she said, “No, but I’m probably not the best person to ask.”

“Who would be?”

A pause as she eyed a small, drooping poinsettia on the windowsill. "James, I guess. James Cahill." She flicked him a glance, grabbed a glass from the sink, and poured a little water into the soil of the potted plant.

"You know him?"

Another beat. "We've met."

"And?"

"And he's the reason she was so upset and driving to my house." Her lips tightened almost imperceptibly. "And if you believe what you read in the papers, he was the last person to see her alive—to see her." She cleared her throat. "She told me that they'd had a horrid fight and that she was coming to stay with me. She didn't show up, and I came over here, found out that James was in the hospital with injuries from some kind of altercation, which just confirms what Megan told me." She drew a breath. "He did something to her," she said quietly, almost to herself. "I just know it."

"How?"

"Because of what she said. Because she was so upset on the phone."

"What do you think happened to her?"

"God, I don't know! I wish I did. Isn't that your job?"

"It is."

"Then find her."

"We will."

"Good," she said and headed for the bedroom.

Rivers turned to follow her, but stopped when he saw, through the open doorway, the manager of the apartments hurrying across the parking lot. Emma-Mae Frost, pushing seventy, umbrella in one gloved hand, pistol in the other.

Uh-oh.

"What in God's good name is going on in here?" Emma-Mae demanded, her face red with the cold. In the light, he saw she was wearing red pajamas beneath a knee-length puffy coat with a hood, her feet covered in furry-topped ankle boots.

"Detective Rivers. You remember me."

"I do," she declared. "How'd you get in?"

"Put down the gun," he suggested carefully, though Emma-Mae had already let her hand fall to her side and was no longer pointing the weapon at him.

Rebecca stepped out of the bedroom. "Oh, whoa!" Her eyes rounded as she stared at the pistol.

"Put the gun on the table," Rivers said.

"Who're you?" Emma-Mae demanded, her hood falling backward to show a cap of mussed curls.

"I'm Megan's sister."

"Be careful with that," Rivers said.

"The pistol?" Emma-Mae let out a snort. "It's not loaded. You think I'm nuts enough to come bustin' out here in the snow and ice with a loaded gun?"

"Put it down!"

"I got a license."

"Put the gun down. Now!"

"Well . . . fine." She set the pistol on the coffee table, but held tight to the handle of her umbrella. "It's just you can never be too careful." Her eyes narrowed. "So how'd you get in? I locked up after you all left the last time."

"I have a key," Rebecca said.

Rivers left it at that.

"Well, for the love of all that's holy, I wish someone woulda told me. I hear my cat, Fritz, growling at a squirrel or something and look out the window to see what's got him all riled up, and I see this place—that's supposed to be locked, mind you—wide open! Light on. Thought someone was robbin' it." She sent Rivers a beady-eyed look. "You mighta let me know."

"It was early," he said.

"Hell, yeah, it's early." She let out a frustrated breath. "But it's common decency, y'know, rather than scarin' me half to death. I had half a mind to call the pol—oh, well." She squared her shoulders. "I don't suppose you have any news about Megan?"

"No."

Emma-Mae eyeballed Rebecca. "She's behind in her rent."

"Is she?" Rebecca didn't seem surprised.

"Again." Emma-Mae nodded, her short curls bobbing. "It's due by the fifth, but she told me she'd have the money by the fifteenth, but hell, that's just around the corner, isn't it?" Before Rebecca could answer, she asked, "You heard from her?"

"Not since the other night, no."

"So what am I gonna tell the owner, huh? That I was foolish enough to let her slide on the rent, and now what? I'm gonna evict her?"

"Not yet," Rivers said.

"I figured she was planning on moving in with her boyfriend. They were thick as thieves, at least for a while, and it seemed it was on her mind. She kept hinting she was probably going to move."

"Did she?"

"Well, not in so many words. That's why I didn't bring it up when I talked to that deputy earlier, but I had the feeling she was going to leave, and I just guessed it was probably with him . . . You think he had something to do with her going missing?" Emma-Mae's eyebrows arched. "That's what I read in the paper."

"We're still trying to work out what happened," said Rivers.

"Well, this is a fine pickle. Just a fine damned pickle." Frowning, she crossed her arms over her chest. "So you done here, or what? I know you're the cops and all"—she waved in the air dismissively—"but I got a decent place here to run, other tenants, y'know, so . . ."

"I'm finished," Rivers said.

Emma-Mae cocked an eyebrow at Rebecca.

"Me too." She was already moving to the still-open door.

Emma-Mae swept her pistol from the coffee table and stuck it into the pocket of her puffy jacket. "Good." She snapped off the lights, and Rivers followed after her. The fact that she said her pistol was unloaded didn't ease his mind, nor did the fact that it was tucked in her pocket or that she may or may not have had a license to carry. He'd learned along the way to never let a person with a weapon out of his sight.

He flipped the lock, then closed the door behind them.

Emma-Mae said, "Next time you all think you want in, you talk to me." Then she snapped open her umbrella and hurried across the lot toward the only apartment with a light burning in a window.

"So why did you decide to show up now?" Rivers asked Rebecca as the door to the manager's apartment closed behind her.

"Couldn't sleep." She eyed him as she walked to her vehicle, a small Ford SUV parked in a visitor spot in the snow-covered lot. Snowflakes caught in her hair, glistening a little in the streetlight. "You?"

"Same thing, I guess. Sometimes a case keeps me awake." He glanced at his watch. "You're coming in at eight?"

"Yeah."

"Would you rather come to the station now?" he asked. "I'm on my way."

With a shake of her head, she said, "I'll see you later." She slipped into her SUV, slammed the door shut, and was driving out of the lot within seconds.

As the taillights of her Ford disappeared through the snow, he walked to his Jeep and got inside, where he stared at the closed door of Megan Travers's apartment.

His mission here this morning hadn't accomplished much, certainly not what he'd hoped. No "vibes" telling him what the hell was going on inside Megan Travers's head on the night she'd disappeared. No special insight.

But maybe he'd gotten something much better by catching her sister off guard. Not cool and composed. Not ready. No neatly conspired answers. Over the years, he'd found that sometimes catching a witness or suspect by surprise was an easier path to the truth than a neatly composed, well-thought-out, and often lawyer-crafted statement.

From the corner of his eye, he saw Emma-Mae Frost peering through an opening in the curtains. Next to her, seated on the back of a chair near the window, was a massive silver tabby cat, suspicious gold eyes focused on Rivers, his tail twitching.

Rivers slipped into his SUV and headed for a drive-thru coffee kiosk, where he'd pick up a double-shot espresso, then he'd hit the gym before work and try to unravel some of the ever-tightening knots in this damned case.

CHAPTER 16

Rebecca had nearly done a quick U-turn and gone out the door when she'd found the detective in Megan's apartment. After being caught at James's house, she couldn't believe that she would run into the cops at her sister's home. What were the chances?

"You're just no good at all this cloak-and-dagger stuff," she told herself. She'd driven back to her home away from home in Riggs Crossing, at the Main Street Hotel, a building that had probably been built sometime near the turn of the last century and needed serious updates.

Currently the hotel, like the rest of the town, was decorated for the holidays. A fourteen-foot Christmas tree dominated the lobby, and the massive reception desk was decorated with a lighted garland. Cedar boughs swept up the staircase, and piped in Christmas music wafted through the lobby.

Rebecca beelined up the stairs.

Her nerves were shot.

Too little sleep.

Too many worries.

Too much drama. If she wasn't so concerned about Megan, she would have wrung her younger sister's neck. How many messes was Rebecca supposed to clean up for her sibling?

She didn't want to think about it as she stripped out of her clothes in the closet-sized bathroom and stepped into the shower, where the spray was little more than a mist. Thankfully the water was hot.

James.

His name came floating to her, unwanted.

She frowned, despising the fact that she was forced to deal with him again. She couldn't avoid him, not until Megan was located. "Buck up," she said as she poured shampoo into her palm. She hated the fact that she'd been thrown back into contact with him, and wished to high heaven that she could return to her normal life in Seattle, where she worked in marketing for a high-end bridal boutique, whose owner, Angelica Alfonsi, was hoping to expand from Seattle to San Francisco and L.A. She lathered her hair, rinsed off, and let the hot water drizzle down her back. This wasn't the first time Megan had gotten herself in trouble, not by a long shot, but so far, this was the worst.

Unless Megan, in true drama-queen fashion, was just hiding out somewhere while her older sister worried herself sick and interrupted her life all for the sake of . . . what? Megan's need to be the center of attention? Her desire to hurt anyone whom she perceived was out to get her?

Meaning James?

"For the love of God," she whispered. Certainly, her sister wouldn't be so self-involved that she would want everyone close to her and now the police to be thinking the worst and frantically searching for her. Even Megan couldn't sink that low.

Or could she?

"Don't go there." She turned off the spray, toweled off, and pulled on her bathrobe. As she did, she thought of Detective Rivers.

What the hell was the detective doing lurking in the middle of the living room in the dark like some kind of burglar?

The whole thing was weird.

Rivers had been standing in the darkened room of Megan's apartment when she'd opened the door. His eyes had been closed, his head tilted toward the ceiling, his hands in his pockets; the sight of his shadowed form had given her a shock.

What the hell had he been doing?

Having a religious experience? He'd scared her half to death. Worse yet, the apartment manager had showed up and had been armed and . . . well, maybe not all that dangerous. Still, Rebecca had nearly had a heart attack—make that two—in the span of five minutes.

Everything about this was nuts.

Her mind circled back to James again.

She scrounged a clean pair of jeans and a sweater out of her suitcase and thought that she was lucky James hadn't accused her of breaking and entering.

Yet.

But then maybe squeezing through a dog door didn't really count.

She hadn't stolen anything, but hadn't really learned anything either.

She pulled on fresh underwear and her jeans as she thought about the man she'd once thought she'd loved. James Effing Cahill. Did every damned thing have to circle back to him?

Unfortunately, in this case, the answer was yes.

She snapped on her bra before returning to the bathroom. She started to comb out her damp curls. Did she really believe that he was a kidnapper? A potential murderer? She caught sight of her reflection in the still-foggy mirror and saw that she was actually shaking her head.

"Denial," she accused, pointing the tip of her comb at the image in the mirror. "It's a killer."

This whole situation was just so impossible to comprehend.

But she'd just have to go with it for now.

Detective Rivers was expecting her.

"Find anything?" Mendoza asked as she peered around the edge of Rivers's cubicle. She was carrying a cup of coffee in one hand, and she waved it carefully toward his computer screen, which was open to Megan Travers's Facebook page.

"Nope."

He'd been checking Megan Travers's social media pages and feeds, but her accounts had been stagnant for half a week, no activity. It was as if Megan Travers had fallen off the face of the earth.

Or been pushed by James Cahill.

"What about Cahill's page? You check that?"

"Doesn't have anything personal, just basic information about his businesses—the construction firm, the tree farm, the inn, even the café." Rivers typed in Cahill Industries, and the website came onto the screen with a small picture of James Cahill in jeans and a long-sleeved shirt with the sleeves pushed up that was superimposed over the masthead, which featured pictures of tiny houses, fir trees, and the hotel.

"Busy guy."

"No time for personal stuff on Facebook or Tinder, or Twitter or Instagram or whatever."

Mendoza rounded the edge of his cubicle to look over Rivers's shoulder. "James Cahill is pretty damned hot." She took a sip from her cup as she eyed the image on the screen.

"Save it."

"Even now, with a bandage covering half his head." She nodded, as if agreeing with herself. "I hate to say it, but it's true." Her gaze assessed the obviously posed and pointedly casual image of Cahill on the screen. "I'm telling you, the guy's got something."

Rivers shot her a look as he rolled back his chair to stare up at her.

She lifted her free hand in surrender. "Fine, fine, you don't want to talk about how sexy James Cahill is—"

Rivers snorted.

"I'm just giving you the female point of view, you know. Why he's got all these women fighting for him."

"*All* these women?"

Nodding, she said, "He runs through them. Like water."

"And they fight for him?"

"Well, that's just my take on it. Maybe not fighting literally, but somehow he got pretty damned beat up. And those scratches on his face?" she said, eyebrows elevating. "From a woman. An *angry* woman."

"Or a scared one, defending herself."

"Possibly."

"So tell me about James Cahill's women."

"First off"—she held up a finger—"there was that schoolteacher in Marysville, Jennifer Korpi. I got hold of her on the phone. She'd already given her statement to the Marysville PD, and they forwarded it. I just called to get some facts. She's not only a teacher; she also tutors kids struggling in school and helps out at the local animal shelter. She has a steady boyfriend. Also her brother is her alibi. According to the deputy who interviewed her, she was pretty angry that she would even have to come up with one."

"What happened between her and James Cahill?"

"Short-lived and flared out as soon as he met Rebecca Travers. Korpi said the waning interest was mutual but"—Mendoza shook her head, her black messy bun shining under the overhead lights—"I'm not so sure about that. And they do have a connection, if a weak one. Jennifer's father used to work for the Cahill family in San Francisco, as a groundskeeper."

"But James grew up in Oregon."

"And spent some summers in California visiting Cissy Cahill, even though she's a lot older than he, by fifteen years or so." Mendoza waggled her hand to indicate she wasn't certain of the age difference. "Anyway, according to Jennifer Korpi, that's where he and she first met—at the Cahill estate in San Francisco."

"So how did they reconnect and get together here?"

"It's the whole 'small world' thing. Her brother's a carpenter. Actually, her stepbrother, Gus Jardine. He works for Cahill on the tiny houses or sometimes in the tree lot, as I understand it, so she ran into Cahill again—or something. I don't have all the details yet, but I'm going to schedule a face-to-face."

"Jardine's her alibi."

"Yeah."

"I'll come with you on the interview."

"It's an hour and a half in good weather, probably over two now, and that's if the roads are clear."

"I'm okay with that. So, go on. Somewhere along the way, she and Cahill stopped seeing each other?"

"Cahill doesn't stay with one woman too long. At least, that's his track record. From Jennifer Korpi, he moved on to Rebecca Travers." Another finger joined the first one. "That lasted a few months, until he and the sister, Megan, got together." A third finger stood at attention. "And then, lately, while still involved with Megan, or at least so she thought, he took up with Sophia Russo, a woman who works for him. Pretty fast by most people's standards."

"All within a year?"

She shrugged. "Maybe a year and a half. Still nailing that down."

"Fast work."

"Hmm."

"Anyone else?" His phone buzzed, and he saw that it was, again, the reporter for the *Clarion*, Charity Spritz, so he ignored it.

"Those are the most recent, the ones we know about."

"To start with."

She nodded. "Who knows what might come out of the woodwork when we start digging? Not to mention that we could discover a jealous boyfriend or two."

"Or an old enemy, someone he screwed over or was perceived to have screwed over." He saw her make a face. "But you're focused on the ex-girlfriend angle."

"So far it's the only angle we've got," she reminded him.

"Just the most obvious," he pointed out. "He's rich, or will be. Wealthy heirs attract interest."

"But he's not the victim."

"No . . ."

They both thought about that a moment, then Mendoza said, "He's not the last person to have seen her alive. There's Knowlton, the snowplow driver, and a woman in town, all of whom said they saw her driving after the fight."

Rivers scratched his head and frowned at the image of James Cahill in his battered jeans, work shirt, and well-practiced smile that stared at him from his computer screen. Was it a lovers' quarrel? But with something else at play?

He said, "Megan Travers is missing, not James Cahill. Aside from a few scratches, a lack of memory, and his bruised reputation, he really wasn't harmed. If he was the ultimate target, why take out the girlfriend?"

"Doesn't make sense," agreed Mendoza.

"We know they had a helluva fight." He rubbed the back of his neck, thinking he was missing something. Something important. Maybe he needed coffee. "Come on, let's get a refill," he said, standing up.

As they walked together to the lunchroom, he said, "On the surface it looks like a fight. She and he get into it, it gets physical, he's injured, she leaves in a huff, calls her sister, and takes off." He looked over at his partner as they reached the break room. "And then what?"

"He's found by Knowlton, who calls nine-one-one."

Rivers kept the story going as he worked the Keurig machine, putting in a semi-biodegradable pod of coffee. He hit the button, and the coffee maker started gurgling. "Meanwhile," he said, "Megan Travers and her car disappear into the night. Her cell phone is turned off or dead. All the searches turn up nothing. She's just vanished."

"So she's either dead, her car was run off the road in the mountains and covered in snow, down some precipice, or she's hiding somewhere and is damned good at it, or she was kidnapped, but no one's trying to ransom her."

"So, possibly a prisoner—maybe a sex slave?"

She frowned, lines creasing her smooth brow as the machine steamed and coffee drizzled into his waiting cup. "Or hiding out?"

"Or somehow James Cahill did her in?"

"Even though he was injured—comatose when he was discovered." She tilted her head to stare at him as if he'd gone off his rocker. "You think he had an accomplice? Someone who would kill her? A paid assassin?"

"Lame," another voice from a nearby table said.

Rivers looked over and found Arne Nagley, one of the deputies, seated at a round table and huddled over the newspaper, working the daily sudoku.

Nagley looked up from his puzzle, his eyes a crystal blue, his red hair clipped close to his skull. At six-four, he had to be pushing three hundred pounds, most of it muscle. His nose wasn't straight, had been broken twice in his days as a right tackle for the Washington State Cougars. "This is Riggs Crossing, man," he pointed out. "Not fuckin' Chicago." Then, as if he realized his opinion wasn't called for, added, "Just my two cents, for what it's worth, but you two, *you're* the detectives." He went back to the paper, but Rivers noted the edge to his voice and remembered that Nagley had applied for the position Rivers had landed, a perceived slight, as Nagley had worked for Riggs County for over a dozen years, and Rivers, from San Francisco, had been perceived as an outsider.

Rivers picked up his cup, and Mendoza began refilling hers. She said, "I've been checking on Cahill. Yeah, he's a trust-fund baby, but he hasn't inherited yet. He did borrow from it, though. That's how he bought all the property up here and started his business."

"Make that businesses."

"Right. But he won't be able to get his hands on the bulk of the money until he turns thirty."

"So how does that fit in with a girl gone missing?"

"Dunno. Yet. Just spit-balling," she said as she stirred creamer into her cup.

"We got anything else?"

"The lab came back with the analysis of hair samples found in James Cahill's bedroom."

This was news. Rivers looked up. "And?"

"And aside from James Cahill's and his dog's, they found a couple of others. One blonde, very light."

"Sophia Russo?"

"Seems likely."

"And the other one?"

"Dark. Almost black."

"Not Megan Travers?"

"Nope, hers is light brown and curly. We've got samples from a brush left in her apartment. But this one, dark and straight, was found in his bed. On his pillow."

"*Another* woman."

"Looks like."

That was a new wrinkle, but maybe he shouldn't have been surprised. His eyes narrowed. "DNA?"

"Not yet, and only if there's a root. And it won't help unless it's in the database."

"Or we get a sample."

"Right."

It wasn't much, but something, he thought, as they reached his cubicle. He checked his watch just as the phone rang. He picked up and was told by the receptionist that Rebecca Travers had arrived. Good. Maybe she could shed some light on what had happened to her sister.

Then again, maybe not.

He thought about how she'd walked in on him early this morning at her sister's apartment and felt a rush of heat climb up the back of his neck. Ignoring the sensation, he said to Mendoza, "We're on."

"Rebecca Travers?" When he gave her a nod, she grinned. "Good. Let's go."

Together, they headed to the interview room.

CHAPTER 17

Phoebe Matrix's hip was aching again.

In her bathroom medicine cabinet, she pushed aside her backup EpiPen, antacids, and cough syrup to locate her near-empty bottle of Tylenol and pop two into her mouth before bending over the sink and swallowing from the tap, washing down the caplets and hoping they did the job. Then she hobbled to the living room, where she opened the blinds to another wintry day. Snow covered the parking lot of the Cascadia Apartments, her pride and joy, and she frowned, knowing she'd have to rouse that slacker Dabrowski to salt and shovel the lot again. He always grumbled about it, though she gave him a break on his rent for doing some of the tasks around the grounds. Between her bad hip and other ailments, she just couldn't keep up with the place any longer.

Larry, her fluffy white little sweetheart of a dog, was doing circles at the door, so she found his leash and her jacket hanging in the closet near the front door. As he yapped at her, she slid her arms through the jacket, then snapped the leash to his collar. "I know, I know," she whispered, scratching his ears. "You need to go out." Then she unlocked the front door and let him sniff at the frigid shrubbery in front of her unit. "That's a good boy," she said, shivering as the cold morning air seemed to burrow into her bones. She only hoped Larry would get at his business in a hurry.

At the door, she looked up to spy a woman hurrying out of the far unit and expected to see Sophia Russo heading for her car. Instead it was another woman, not blond, but dark-haired, though most of her head was covered by the hood of her long coat, only a strand or two of dark hair catching in the wind, sunglasses firmly over the bridge of her nose, a scarf covering the lower half of her face. Head down, she made her way to Sophia's little car.

Phoebe had seen the woman before, either coming in or going out of the apartment, a friend of Sophia's, maybe even a relative, not that it was really any of Phoebe's business.

Except if she was staying over more than a day or so, a week, then, by God, Phoebe would have to think about charging her rent.

"Come on," she urged the dog, glancing down at him before looking up again and finding the woman staring at her over the snowy top of Sophia's car. As their gazes locked, Phoebe felt a chill that couldn't be attributed to the cold weather. No, this was something different.

She watched the woman settle into the car and heard the engine start. The driver turned on the wipers to slap away the snow, and Phoebe backed up, calling softly to Larry and nearly tripping as she stepped back into the room. There was something not right about that woman, about the whole situation with Sophia. Phoebe could feel it in her aching bones.

With Larry spinning in circles and yapping for food, Phoebe shut the door and threw the dead bolt.

Something in unit 8 wasn't right.

Rivers and Mendoza reached the interview room.

Seated at the round table within, Rebecca Travers was already waiting. Her back was ramrod stiff, and she was dressed in a black sweater and jeans, having changed since Rivers had last seen her. A thick jacket was folded over the back of the empty chair next to her, a purse placed on the seat. In front of her, an untouched cup of coffee gave off steam, compliments no doubt of Dorrie, the receptionist. The walls of the room were cinder block and painted a pale institutional green; despite two small windows cut high near the ceiling, the room always smelled lightly of Lysol. Today was no exception.

Rivers introduced Mendoza, and as they took seats across from Rebecca, she said, "I already gave my statements to Deputy Mercado." She glanced at Rivers. "Anyway, I don't know what else I can tell you that I haven't said before."

Rivers said, "Bear with us. We might ask a question that will trigger something you haven't thought of before."

She stared at him. Disbelieving.

Mendoza, iPad at the ready, suggested, "Just tell us what you can about the night your sister went missing."

"Okay," she said, exhaling a long breath before launching into her tale. Her story was the same as it had been: On the night she'd gone missing, Megan had called Rebecca. She'd been upset. "Really freaking out, even for her." Megan told her that she'd broken up with James in a nasty fight and had taken off, heading to Rebecca's condo in Seattle. "This wasn't exactly out of nowhere," Rebecca added, nervously twisting a ring on her right hand, further explaining that, during the course of Megan's twenty-two years, there had been plenty of other emotional outbursts, often involving someone she'd been dating. Rebecca had bailed her out time and time again.

"She comes to you rather than your parents?" Rivers asked.

"Always. Our folks are divorced. And Dad is really my stepdad, but he's Megan's 'real' or biological father. My dad left before I was two, and Mom moved to San Francisco, where she met and married Donald Travers a year later and had Megan soon after. That lasted for about eight years. Then they split up. Dad remarried, lives in Chicago, and has two sons who are like . . . maybe just in their teens. Mom stayed in California, found a condo in Sonoma. She's still single, but we don't see her all that much. She's got her own life down there . . ." Rebecca let that trail off, and Rivers thought he saw a hint of sadness in her eyes.

"Your name is Travers," Mendoza said as the furnace rumbled, forcing hot air through the vents.

"Donald adopted me when I was almost four, I think, and my biological dad was all about giving up his rights so he wouldn't have to pay child support any longer—not that he did much anyway, I guess. At least, that's what my mother said."

Mendoza nodded, as if she totally understood. "You've contacted them—your parents?"

Rebecca nodded. "They were . . . are . . . concerned, and I told them I'd keep them informed. I think Mom wanted to come up here, but then thought 'why?' What could she do?"

As far as Rivers knew, neither of Megan's parents had contacted the police. Odd. But then, with families, one never knew. Still, he made a mental note to check with Kate Mercado, the deputy who had taken statements from many of Megan Travers's family and friends.

Mendoza said, "Tell us about her relationship with James Cahill."

Rebecca's eyebrows flicked up, just a fraction, and the corners of her mouth tightened a bit. "I don't know the ins and outs of it. They'd been together for several months, six or seven." Rebecca sighed. "You probably know that I was involved with James first, and so it was kind of dicey between us." Again she twisted the ring. "But lately Megan felt that she could confide in me and . . . and she had admitted that things in the relationship were deteriorating."

"How so?" Mendoza prodded.

"They hadn't been getting along for a little while, maybe a month or so, I'm not really sure, but Megan called me a couple of times, and it sounded as if she'd been crying."

"When was this?" Mendoza asked.

"The first time was a few weeks ago. Maybe around the first week of November. At least, that's when she told me about it. She suspected he was seeing someone else, and she was upset because she'd thought they were . . . exclusive." Rebecca's eyes seemed to darken. "I'm not sure James saw it that way. He . . . he's always been . . ."

". . . interested in other women?" Mendoza asked.

"What Dad used to call 'playing the field.' So yeah. I think Megan thought he was 'the one.' At least that's what she told me."

Mendoza said, "You said you were involved with James Cahill before your sister was, right?"

Rebecca's jaw visibly tightened. "Yes."

"You were in love with him?" Mendoza pressed, and a telltale blush crawled up Rebecca's neck.

"I . . . thought so."

"Until Megan came along?"

She gave a sharp little nod, picked up the coffee cup, then set it down again without taking so much as a taste.

"So would you say she stole him from you?" There was no judgment in Mendoza's voice.

"You can't steal something that doesn't exist," Rebecca said dryly. "James and I dated, yes, but we were never really a couple."

"But he went from you to her, right?" Mendoza said.

"James and I saw each other in Seattle, but he lived here, and once he and Megan . . . once they got together, she moved here to be near him."

"Six months ago?"

"Around that time. Yes."

"But she called you when they weren't getting along?"

"More so lately."

"That must've been awkward," Mendoza observed.

"Well, yes. But I got over it."

Was that a lie? Rivers couldn't be sure. She was twisting her ring again, then, as if realizing it, stopped and put her hands in her lap.

"Is this your sister's handwriting?" Rivers asked and slid the once-crumpled note in a plastic bag across the table. He knew the answer, had seen Megan's loopy scrawl on notes in her apartment.

"Looks like it," she said, nodding, her dark hair showing glints of red under the overhead lights. "Oh, Megan." Sadness came over her then, as if she'd come to the fatal conclusion she might not see her sister again. "I assume you've talked to James." She slid the note back.

"Yes."

"But he can't remember what happened. Right? That's what he says?"

"He's not clear."

She snorted.

"Do you know a woman named Sophia Russo?" Mendoza checked her notes as if getting her information straight, but that was all for show. She'd already started tracking down the woman that Bobby Knowlton had told her James Cahill had been seeing.

She shook her head. "Is she the woman James was involved with?"

Mendoza said, "We don't know."

"Megan didn't give me any names. She was so upset; she just let me know she was coming and was crying. She said she'd tell me all about it when she got to Seattle, but . . ." She let that thought trail off.

"Do you know anyone who would do her harm? Does she have any enemies?" Rivers asked.

"No . . ."

"How about friends she may have called?"

"I tried them," she said.

"Do you have their names and numbers?"

"Some."

"Would you share them?"

"Of course."

Mendoza slid the legal pad across the table, and Rebecca, after checking her phone, used her own pen to write a short list of names and numbers. "I don't really know who her friends are, not anymore, other than the one woman she worked with. The nurse." She thought for a second. "Andie."

"Andrea Jeffries," Mendoza supplied. "We talked to her." She glanced at Rivers, who gave a quick nod, but Jeffries, who had been interviewed by one of the deputies, hadn't indicated she'd been close to Megan, just that they'd worked together for less than a year.

"That might be. I've never met her." Rebecca pointed at the pad with the pen. "Those names are people from, like, high school, people I've met, but I'm not even sure she's in contact with any of them. Don't you have her phone records?"

Mendoza was nodding. "We do."

"And?"

"Not much," Mendoza admitted.

Actually, so far the information was a near bust. The cell phone records had given them nothing, nor had the interviews with her coworkers added new insight. The truth was, they were stymied, and until James Cahill copped to regaining his memory, they were at a dead end, which they didn't tell Megan's sister. But based on the way she was eyeing them and the dismissive way she dropped her pen onto the table, she seemed to sense it.

They asked a few more questions and got no more answers that were of any help. When they were finished and Rebecca Travers stood to leave, her face hardened. "Find my sister, Detectives."

And then she walked out the door.

Forgetting her pen.

Rivers scooped it up. "I'll walk her out," he said to Mendoza, even though Rebecca was in the hallway. Pocketing her pen, he caught up with her and held the door as she walked into the parking lot.

"If you think of anything else—" he began.

"I'll let you know." But she didn't even cast a glance over her shoulder as she walked crisply to her vehicle, a white Subaru parked in the lot. Rivers watched her leave, then returned to the interview room as Mendoza was gathering her iPad and notes.

"She orders us to find her sister?" Mendoza snorted.

"She's upset."

"Yeah." Mendoza was staring at the empty doorway. "But . . ."

"But what?"

"But there's something more going on there. With Cahill. Did you notice? Whenever his name was brought up, she kind of gritted her teeth."

"Like she hates him."

"Maybe." Mendoza's eyes narrowed. "But you know what they say about hate?"

"There's a fine line between hate and love." They walked out of the room and into the hallway, and Rivers added, "You think Rebecca Travers is still in love with her sister's boyfriend."

"It wouldn't be the first time a man came between sisters."

"And you think she had something to do with her sister's disappearance?"

"I don't know. Yet. But I'll find out, and if I'm right, we might just want to talk to Ms. Travers again."

CHAPTER 18

He remembered.

Just like that.

James stepped into the shower on Monday morning, turned on the spray, careful to keep the bandage covering half his head dry, and in that clarifying split second, his memory rushed back—all kinds of images. As he stood under the streaming water in his hotel bathroom, he saw Megan as she had been then. That night. So furious she could barely speak. Tears glistening in her blue eyes, her lips, shiny with lip gloss, pulled back over her teeth.

"You shit!" she'd yelled, shaking and sputtering. "You fucking, two-timing shit!"

He'd just finished a dinner of chili and cornbread—takeout from this very hotel—and had intended to settle down to a night of basketball on TV when she'd burst through the front door.

She held a note in her balled fist, and she tossed it at him. "I was going to leave this," she shrieked. "I—I didn't think you'd be home. I thought you'd be with *her*. Just like you've been for the last week and a half. Right?"

Oh . . . damn . . .

When he didn't say anything, she'd glared at him. "Oh, what? No denials? Come on, James, give it a try," she baited, eyes flashing. "You're not going to try and lie to me and tell me you're not cheating on me with that . . . that . . ."

"With Sophia," he said.

"You admit it!" Before he could answer, she cried, "Oh, I get it! She's here now, isn't she? That damned slut is upstairs in your bed!"

"No." He shook his head. "No one's here."

"But she was. I saw her car . . ."

"Here?" He was trying to keep up with her rant.

"At the inn!" She glared at him as if he were dense.

"She works at the inn."

"But she could walk over here. Leave it there so no one would know and come here and . . . and . . ." Her voice broke, her anger abating at least for the moment. "You made me look like a fool," she said, suddenly sobbing. "Rebecca warned me, but I thought she was just jealous. God, James, couldn't you have at least had the decency to . . . to . . ."

He awkwardly stepped toward her. Reached out. "I was going to tell you."

"When?" she spat, dashing her tears away with the back of her hand.

"I thought . . . after the holidays."

"Oh, yeah, right. Carry on behind my back, so what? I can have a Merry Christmas? So we can ring in the New Year together, and then you were going to lower the boom and come clean? Oh, save me!" She violently shook her head. "You're so clueless. What does Christmas have to do with us? With this?" She threw her hands up. "I loved you, James. I thought you loved me too!"

He didn't take the bait, wasn't about to step into that trap.

She was full-on crying now, sniffing and fighting sobs. "I thought we were going to get married."

"What?" he asked, so loudly that Ralph, curled in his bed near the fire, gave off a startled "woof."

"I thought you would propose to me at Christmas."

"But, Megan, why would you think that? We . . . we've only been dating for . . . for . . ."

"God, you don't even know, do you? It's been nearly six months, James. June. Remember? I do. It was summer in Seattle. You were there for some builders' convention."

And to see Rebecca.

"In your display of the tiny house? Remember?"

He did. All too vividly, despite the fact that he'd drunk far more than usual at the convention. He recalled how she'd come on to him. How she'd told him that Rebecca had been cheating, showing him pictures of Rebecca out to dinner with another man. When she'd wrapped her arms around him and kissed him, sliding her tongue into his mouth, he should have pushed her away, but he hadn't.

"Don't you get it? I love you. God, how can you be so dumb! And then you go behind my back? With *her?* Why? Jesus, James, *why?*"

He wanted to say that it had just happened, that he hadn't intended to get involved with someone else before ending it with her, but it sounded so lame, so cliched, that once again, he kept quiet.

"I thought when you left Rebecca for me, that it was because we had something special, something unique, something like no one else!" She stopped then, her eyes glistening, her misery palpable. "I was wrong. Just another fool. Another girl to fuck and leave."

"No, God, no." But there it was. "I didn't mean . . . Look, Megan, I'm sorry," he said, and that was the truth. He felt like the shit he was. He'd never intended to hurt her, but, of course, he had. "I should have told you."

"You should never have cheated on me in the first place!" she said, and her pain morphed once more into a fierce, bright anger.

"You're right, I should have broken it off before—"

"No! Don't you get it?" she asked, advancing on him. "You should have just been faithful. Is that so damned hard?"

Yeah. It was. But he couldn't say that. He couldn't say anything. He'd already tried to apologize, and she was having none of it.

"You're the worst," she charged, standing in front of him, breathing hard, her face flushed, her gaze scathing. "You know that, don't you?"

He kept his silence.

"A rich boy who grew up coddled, always knowing he was going to inherit a fortune, so you just think you can do whatever you want, don't you? That you can hurt whoever gets in your way."

"Not true," he ground out. Yeah, he'd grown up knowing he'd inherit, and he'd borrowed against his trust, but he'd worked every day of his life, making it on his own, trying not to become a typical trust-fund baby, a label he'd heard one too many times before. But he never intended to hurt anyone, though, of course, he had. Too many times to count.

"What're you worth? Five million? Ten?" she asked, her blue eyes narrowing. "Twenty?"

"It has nothing to do with this."

"You mean 'us,' don't you? It has nothing to do with 'us'?"

"Yes."

"That's where you're wrong! It has everything to do with us and every damned woman you ever took to bed. You think you're so ridiculously charming and good-looking that women can't help falling for you?" Glaring at him, she answered her own question. "It's the *money,* James." She was so close now, he felt the heat radiating from her, saw the bits of darker blue in her light eyes. "It's all about the money. Every damned woman you've dated in your entire miserable life has known you had money. Including Jennifer and Rebecca and that slut Sophia."

He tensed then, wanting to shake her. "Including you?"

She didn't answer.

"Including you?" he repeated.

She angled her chin upward and whispered, "Including me. If you want to know the truth—"

"I do."

"That's what started it all. My interest. But then? Then I was stupid enough to actually fall for you."

For a second, he almost believed her. But the harsh glint in her gaze, the tight, hard corners of her mouth, and the almost crazed expression told him not to trust her. "I already said, I'm sorry, and I am—"

"Bullshit!"

Enough. "Okay. Maybe you should go."

"Now you're throwing me out?" Her rage exploded. "Well, fuck you, James! *Fuck you!*"

"Megan," he started when she lunged at him. He stepped backward.

Too late.

"Bastard!" She swiped at him with her hands, her right fingernails scraping down the side of his face.

"Stop!" He grabbed one wrist.

It wasn't enough. She threw herself against him, and she flailed at him with her free hand.

He stumbled backward, falling, with her atop him.

He remembered his shoulder slamming into the fireplace and his body scraping downward in a single moment. His head bounced against the bricks of the hearth. For a dizzying second, he saw her climbing off him, her horrified expression in his line of vision, the sound of his dog barking from behind the kitchen door ringing in his ears before everything went dark.

"Holy shit," he whispered now as the hot water cascaded over his good shoulder and down his torso. For a second, he was unsteady and propped himself against the tile wall, trying to gain his equilibrium. He ran a hand over his wet face as he steadied himself. Memories assailed him, making him feel weak . . . weaker. He managed to twist off the faucet and reach out of the shower for a towel. Ralph had taken up residence on the bath mat, and he had to nudge the dog aside with a wet foot.

With an effort, he dried himself off. He decided against shaving—the beard would help hide the scratches still visible beneath his stubble—and managed to struggle into his clothes before it hit him that he had no car, no means of transportation. The police were still holding his truck and Explorer, both vehicles being searched for evidence.

"Of what?" he said aloud. But he knew. They were looking for bloodstains or personal items, even DNA. From Megan. No doubt they would find a hair or two, maybe a forgotten tube of lipstick or earring or something personal she'd forgotten, but there would be no evidence of crime. Because there was none.

He hadn't harmed her that night.

Nor ever before.

But there was still something missing, something he couldn't completely recall, a forgotten detail or two of that night that teased at his memory, almost surfacing, but not quite. "What?" he whispered, but whatever was plucking at the strands of his memory was gone, retreating quickly.

He slipped the sling over his shoulder and was about to call Bobby for a ride when he realized he didn't have his phone, either. No wheels, no means of communication other than the hotel phone. "Great," he muttered, about to leave when he spied the bracelet, a single band of glittering clear stones that he assumed weren't real diamonds, left on one of the side tables next to the bed.

Sophia's.

In a flash, he remembered her astride him in the bed, her long legs bent at the knees as she straddled him, the bracelet still catching the half-light washing in from the window. He'd reached up with his good hand to touch her smooth abdomen, stretched taut, the skin silken beneath his fingertips as they skimmed the underside of her full breasts where her hair fell in a sexy tangle, her erect pink nipples peeking through the blond tresses.

Now, his breath caught in the back of his throat as the image faded. He swallowed hard.

What the hell have you gotten yourself into?

Rebecca, Megan, and now Sophia?

That was the problem. He loved beautiful, smart women. In Sophia's case, he couldn't help but notice her. She was everywhere he turned. At the shop, at the café, in town, wherever—it was almost as if she knew instinctively where he'd be, almost as if she were in two places at the same time. Impossible, of course, and maybe it was just his rationalization for not being able to avoid her, to be enchanted by a blonde with an impish spark in her eye, a quick wit and easy smile. She was funny and clever, and he found himself looking forward to being with her. She laughed a lot, a tinkling little giggle that brought a smile to his face. She'd been beyond charming when he'd first met her at the inn, when she'd come looking for a job, and he'd been unable to resist her, couldn't resist her still.

Another memory surfaced, an older one. He and Sophia had been together in another place. Her apartment. She'd found him in the shower, stripped off her clothes, and joined him in the tight space, eagerly running her hands down his body under the hot water. He hadn't been able to resist her then either, and had actually made love to her, pressing her back against the slick tiles as he'd lifted her onto his all-too-ready cock, her legs wound around him, her fingers digging into his shoulders as the spray had steamed the glass. Afterward, he'd watched her dress, enjoyed the show of a reverse strip tease, her winking at him through strands of wet hair, then sliding into her lacy bra and panties as he'd lain upon her bed. She'd licked her lips as she'd pulled on a boot, tugging it over her foot and a once-broken left toe with an effort, then standing proudly in underwear and thigh-high boots, silently daring him to ravish her again.

And he had, pulling her onto the bed and yanking down her panties, pushing himself inside her as she giggled and writhed.

Now the images disturbed him.

Things had changed.

He had changed.

And yet he'd still let her into his bed—this bed at the hotel.

He raked a hand through his still-wet hair and winced as his finger scraped the sensitive area under the bandage. What kind of a mess had he gotten himself into?

He left the bracelet where he'd found it. He'd deal with the glittery bangle, and Sophia, later. Right now, he had other issues, and he still felt a little dizzy. He made a pit stop in the bathroom, eyed the pain pills he'd been prescribed, then thought better of it. He needed a clear, if slightly aching, head today.

After grabbing his jacket, he whistled to Ralph, found his hat, and gently placed the Stetson on his head. Steadier than he had been, he made his way downstairs to a hotel lobby that was beginning to fill with guests checking in or out, suitcases and overnight bags in tow, kids running and playing around a fourteen-foot Christmas tree lit from top to bottom. His stomach rumbled at the scents of maple syrup and bacon wafting from the kitchen area near the bar and dining room, but he didn't stop, didn't want to run into too many people. Instead, he strode down a hallway leading to the rear of the building.

Outside, it was crisp and cold, no snow falling. He crunched across new snow as he crossed the parking lot between the back side of the inn and the front stoop leading to the coffee shop. As he stepped through the doorway, he heard the tinkling of the bell overhead. Skirting a few occupied tables where parents and children were eating, deep into their iPads or phones, or sipping coffee, he walked to the counter, where he ordered a cup of coffee and donut to go, as he had done since he'd established the café.

The quick breakfast would go onto his running tab, so he was free to eat and leave. With the clatter of silverware, the hum of conversation, and notes of "All I Want for Christmas" chasing after him, he walked under an archway leading through the Christmas shop, where one could purchase everything from hazelnuts to tabletop crèches, peppermint-flavored candy corn to Santa hats, glass ornaments to toy soldiers, angel tree-toppers to reindeer night-lights.

Everything Christmas and then some.

Offered for sale by James Cahill.

Why did it suddenly feel so crass? So commercialized?

The selling of Christmas, he thought, stepping around a six-year-old fascinated by the miniature train that encircled the displays.

What had Cissy once told him, on a particularly bleak, rain-soaked San Francisco Christmas Eve?

"You can't sell Christmas, James."

Well, he'd damned well tried. Though he'd known that expensive presents weren't the heart and soul of the holidays, he'd convinced himself in the past few years that he actually was selling joy, that all the shiny toys and ornaments gave people pleasure.

He glanced around. For the first time since creating this holiday bazaar of a store, he felt as if he was commercializing something that should be held sacred, making a profit on the holiday. Since he'd never been particularly religious, the thought surprised him and burrowed deep, bothering him.

With Ralph padding behind, James sidestepped a blond four-year-old boy swatting at a glass rocking-horse ornament displayed on a flocked tree. His mother, a baby strapped to her in one of those front packs, was ignoring him and James did too. Let the kid break the ornament. Who cared?

Walking briskly through the back door of the shop, he stepped into the lot, a wide covered area where pre-cut trees were displayed. Here, customers could pick out their Christmas trees if they preferred not trudging through the surrounding acres of mud and snow with axes and saws, where they could actually cut down their own tree—all part of the Cahill experience brought to them by yours truly, James Cahill.

He made short work of the donut while eyeing a staff of seasonal workers in leather aprons, stocking caps, and gloves, all helping a bevy of customers who milled through the lot, poking through cut fir, pine, and spruce. Most were happy, one couple arguing the merits of a noble fir over a Douglas fir, children laughing, dogs barking, toddlers having their pictures taken on a real sleigh as they waited for Santa.

His stomach soured.

Good Lord, Cahill, get over it!

Just because he'd regained his memory, he didn't need this come-to-Jesus epiphany about the commercialization of Christmas.

He spied Bobby getting out of the cab of a truck, its bed filled with recently cut trees. Tossing the butt of his cigarette into the snowy gravel of the service area, Bobby headed James's way, Ralph bounding to greet him.

"I need a phone," James said when the foreman was in earshot, "and a vehicle."

"You can get one of those prepaid things down at the shopping mart, I think." Bobby bent down and scratched the wiggling, tail-wagging shepherd behind his ears. "And there's a beater of a truck at the shop. The old Dodge?"

"That'll do. Why don't you run me down there? I want to check out the office anyway, catch up on paperwork."

"Okay," Bobby said, fishing his keys from his pocket. "Uh-oh. Trouble. Two o'clock."

"What?" James glanced over his left shoulder and spied Sophia heading in his direction. Wearing a black coat that fell to her knees and a silver stocking cap that shimmered with sequins, she was threading her way through the icy potholes and mud of the loading area.

"James!" she said with a happy smile and the wave of a gloved hand. "Wait up!"

"I'll wait for you in the truck." Bobby took off just as Sophia reached James.

"Hey." He didn't know what to say to her. After finding her in his bed, then remembering his fight with Megan, he decided to tread carefully. Sophia had mentioned that she thought she was the cause of the fight between Megan and him; it turned out she was right on the money.

"How're you feeling?" She was squinting, one hand tucking a strand of blond hair into her sparkling cap.

"Better." He considered telling her that his memory had returned, then decided against it. First, he needed to talk to the police.

"Great." She smiled brightly, her blue eyes warm. She glanced up at the cab of the truck, where Bobby was seated behind the wheel and lighting another cigarette. "So I wanted you to know, the offer's still on the table."

"Thanks, but I don't need to be taken care of."

"I meant about *moving in*."

"Uh . . ." He took a sip of coffee.

"Like a couple, James? Like we talked about?"

He nearly choked on the coffee. "We talked about this?"

"You don't remember."

"No," he said, and it wasn't a lie. Though much of his memory had returned, he had no recollection of a plan to move in with her. Or Megan. Or anyone. "I have a house."

"I know. We talked about renovating it, y'know. Updating it and, while that was happening, living in my apartment. In town. It would be tight, but cozy." Her eyes sparkled. "I'd like that."

He couldn't believe they were having this conversation. He wanted to ask her if she were serious, but he saw that she was innocently sincere. "I don't think that's going to work."

"Why not?"

He glanced at the cab of the truck, where Bobby was trying to look as if he wasn't eavesdropping through the open window as the big rig idled. Another one of the workers was hauling a tree to a vintage station wagon and glanced his way. James was suddenly painfully aware of how visible they were. "Look, Sophia," he said, more softly. "I don't think this is the time or place to discuss this. Right now, I have a lot of things to sort out." He didn't want to go into the fact that Megan Travers was still missing, that Megan had thought James intended to marry her, and for all he knew, he was the primary suspect in her disappearance. Aside from all that, he had a business to run and wasn't exactly a hundred percent.

"We all do," she agreed, and touched the lapel of his coat, a personal, intimate gesture that said to anyone who caught it that they were a couple or, more succinctly, that she considered him hers.

He stepped back, and she let her hand drop. "Later."

She lowered her voice. "Didn't last night mean anything?"

He looked up at the sky, where gray clouds were threatening the sun. "That . . . was great, but it was a surprise . . . I've got to go."

"But—"

"I just need a little space."

He saw a wounded look cross her eyes, and he mentally kicked himself from one side of hell to the other. Why was he always disappointing women? Causing them pain? Was he just that callous and self-serving? Had he been sending out the wrong signals? Or had the women misread him?

"All of the above," he muttered and while Sophia stayed where she was, staring at him, her full lips knotting into a sexy pout, he walked around the front of the truck and opened the passenger door. Ralph was waiting. "Get in," he said to the dog, tossing the dregs from his cup onto the snowy ground. By the time he'd settled into the seat and the shepherd was next to him, head pressed to the window, James saw that Sophia had turned around and was walking toward the hotel.

Had he really planned on moving in with Sophia when he hadn't broken off his relationship with Megan? What had he been thinking? What the hell kind of idiot was he?

"Women trouble?" Bobby asked, ramming the Ford into gear.

He put his empty cup in one of the holders between the seats. "Always, I think."

"Ye-up. Best to settle down with one." He eased on the gas, and the big flatbed started rolling across the pocked parking lot. "Or at the very least settle down with one at a time. That's what I did with Cyn, and it's worked out."

James didn't argue. He winced from a sharp pain in his shoulder when Knowlton turned onto the long, rutted lane that led into the foothills, where his shop and office were located. What was it Rebecca Travers had said her sister accused him of being? A man-whore?

He thought about Rebecca—tall, dark, with red-tinged hair and, he remembered, whip-smart and someone who wasn't that close to her sister. They were half-sisters as it was, but that wasn't the reason. Rebecca and Megan just hadn't gotten along—oil and water. She the calmer, Megan the hothead. He was even surprised that Rebecca was so determined to find her sister. As he recalled, she found her sister irritating.

Guiltily, he remembered other things about the older Travers sister as well, most of which involved laughing and talking and fierce lovemaking. There had been that last night in Seattle, in a hotel room overlooking Elliott Bay. They'd had too much to drink and had been ravenous for each other, as if they'd subconsciously known their time together was doomed.

While the lights of the city reflected on the dark water and they'd kissed wildly, her dark auburn hair spilling around them, they'd become tangled in the bed sheets and slid to the floor still wound in a lovers' embrace.

That had been their last time together, and the thought was disturbing. For the first time in his life, he felt regret over the ending of a relationship and had a sense that he'd missed out.

The one that got away.

Because he couldn't be faithful.

And he wasn't faithful with the worst person possible, the person who could wound Rebecca the most deeply: her self-centered younger sister.

A man-whore, he thought again, deciding that the accusation wasn't too far off the mark.

CHAPTER 19

Charity was getting nowhere fast.

Literally and figuratively.

Driving to the offices of the local paper, she'd found herself caught in a clog of traffic, as a steady stream of vehicles headed south. She could guess where. The Cahill Inn and Christmas tree farm drew visitors from all over the Northwest right before the holidays. This year, with the notoriety and mystery surrounding James Cahill's missing girlfriend, even more people had arrived. Not just searching for Christmas trees at the farm or staying at the inn with its renowned Christmas theme, but because they wanted a glimpse of the place where all the intrigue had started: lookie-loos and gossips.

But they were also readers who would lap up the details of the newspaper's report on the scandal. Details Charity expected to provide. If she could ever get through this knot of traffic, grab a cup of coffee at the shop near the office, and plead her case to her editor, who happened to also be the owner of the *Riggs Crossing Clarion.*

She tapped her fingers restlessly on the steering wheel, then gave a sharp beep with her horn as the older Cadillac in front of her wasn't keeping up with the snail's pace. "Come on, come on," she muttered, wondering just how old the woman behind the wheel was. She was so small she seemed to be peering through the steering wheel rather than over it, and she certainly was in no big hurry.

But Charity was.

The Cahill story was hers! And she couldn't allow some reporter from Seattle or Tacoma or Portland to steal it from under her!

No effin' way. But she was stuck. She'd tried to phone Cahill at his home, on his cell, and through his businesses. And she'd struck out. She gave the horn another impatient tap. He was avoiding her. And it pissed her off.

As the traffic inched toward the main intersection of town, she fiddled with the dial for the radio, hearing snatches of rap, country, hard rock, political talk, and sports before settling on a station that played Christmas carols 24/7. But the notes of "Frosty the Snowman" got on her nerves, and she snapped the damned thing off. Agitated, she reached for her Juul and remembered she'd left it at her apartment. "Shit." She'd given up smoking after college and switched to vaping; now she was trying to wean herself off nicotine altogether as vaping was getting a seriously bad rap. Still, right now she could sure use a hit.

Again the white Caddy lagged, and once more Charity gave a quick, pointed beep of her Hyundai's horn. "Come on, lady! Wake up!" Charity was beginning to understand road rage at a very intimate level. Didn't the old woman see how much space was between her and the truck in front of the Caddy? Of course not. So Charity said, "Screw it," and hit the gas, shooting past the older car and tucking her minivan into the spot in front of the white behemoth, narrowly missing a small SUV speeding in the opposite direction.

For her efforts, she was rewarded with a glare and the finger as the driver, a girl in her teens, whipped by.

Charity resisted the urge to return the favor and gritted her teeth, cranking on the wheel around the next corner and maneuvering her van through a side street. Once she was moving again, she thought about her story on James Cahill and the research she'd already done, searching as best she could for information and backstory on Riggs Crossing's most eligible bachelor. But she had to face the stark fact that there was only so much a girl could do on the Internet.

It wasn't enough.

She didn't feel she had a strong enough hook for the series of articles she intended to write, or for the book that was beginning to form in her brain.

Taking another corner, she sped around the parking lot of a convenience store, then down another side street that ran parallel to the main drag.

Sometimes, damn it, a writer needed something more, something tactile to deal with. It was more than just facts and figures; it was a feeling, an emotional connection to the story that she could convey to readers.

She'd tried dealing directly with James himself, and she'd struck out.

For now.

But, she figured, as she adjusted the defroster, if she could just get some background on him or on his family, she would have something to work with, maybe even something to use against him. She wasn't *really* going to blackmail him or anything, but she needed a bit of leverage to get him to open up, and the place to start was with his family. For some reason, he was estranged from them. Why in the hell would a person intentionally break off with one of the wealthiest families in San Francisco? Well, maybe wealthiest was a bit of an exaggeration, but still, if not billions, the Cahill family was rumored to be worth hundreds of millions. And the whole clan was scandal-ridden. Perfect fodder for her article, her series, and especially her book.

Not exactly chump change.

She veered quickly down a back alley, the minivan sliding around a dumpster, then took a side street and cut across a parking lot before turning a final corner and searching for a parking spot in a lot next to the building housing the *Clarion,* which these days was relegated to the drafty upper floor. The owner of the building had leased the street level to a used-furniture and supposed antiques dealer. Most of the parking slots were marked for Auntie's Antiques, but Charity ignored the signs and took a spot not far from the exterior sign posted near the staircase that read RIGGS CROSSING CLARION, LOCAL, REGIONAL AND NATIONAL NEWS.

A sad day, she thought, when the press was pushed aside for overpriced, worthless junk. *Oh, excuse me—"antiques."* She locked the van, then marched up the stairs and through the heavy door to the office.

Inside, the cavernous second story smelled musty and as old as it truly was, the warehouse space divided by padded cubicle walls that owner/editor Earl Ray Dansen had found in a business liquidation sale. Most of the cubicles were empty as there were only a couple of staff writers who actually worked at the office. The others, "contributing reporters" such as herself, worked primarily from home. The place always seemed wretchedly ancient and, she knew, was the home to nests of mice and probably rats; she'd seen the evidence herself, and Earl was always talking about getting traps or a cat to solve the problem.

"If feral cats are good enough for Disneyland, then they're good enough for me," he'd said on more than one occasion, though no feline mouser had yet shown up.

Today, though, Charity wasn't going to think about cats, rats, or mice as she walked past the empty cubicles.

Along the north-facing wall, beneath a row of high windows, was a long built-in table separated into workstations. This area had been assigned to the online edition of the *Clarion.* Currently, the online department was run by Earl's son, Gerry, a stoner who was forever high; he was clever when it came to high tech, but was way too touchy-feely for Charity.

He was already at his station, she noted, and she skirted his desk as best she could as, always smelling of weed, he'd laid a hand on her shoulder one too many times. With his man bun pulling back his still-thick hair, three days' worth of stubble around his chin, and eyes that seemed to stare straight into hers, he was far too intense for her taste. And when he'd suggested they meet for coffee or drinks, she'd felt her skin crawl.

It wasn't just that he wasn't her type.

There was something about him that genuinely creeped her out.

She managed to get past him without him seeing her come in. Seated at a raised chair at his work area, his head swaying to some inaudible beat from his earbuds, his fingers flying over his keyboard, his back was to her.

Thank God.

Next to Gerry, in her own cubicle, Jeanette Flannery was sipping from a Diet Coke and giggling as she talked into a headset that was buried in her spiky blond hair. She was in her usual uniform of jeans split at the knees, black long-sleeved T-shirt, and tunic-length sweater. Today the sweater was an olive color. Jeanette wasn't a reporter, but a proofreader and techie who helped Gerry and kept her ear to the ground for local gossip.

Charity slipped past her as well and headed to the far corner of the massive room, where the ceilings were so high Charity believed barn owls could roost there.

Earl wasn't in his office, the one glass-walled area, filled by a massive credenza and an expansive L-shaped secretary's desk straight out of the sixties. The desk was a mess of papers, coffee cups, pencils and tablets, two oversized computer screens, and Earl's iPhone. Gathering dust on the credenza behind him sat an ancient Royal manual typewriter, handed down to him by his grandfather.

As far as Charity knew, no one had pressed one of its keys in decades.

Out of the corner of her eye, she caught sight of Earl as he walked along the short hallway that connected to the back exit and restrooms. Tucking in his shirt, he looked up and saw her waiting.

"Something up?" he asked.

No smile.

These days, Earl rarely grinned. What was left of his graying hair was slightly more salt than pepper, his eyes dark, almost black, his face gaunt, his body that of a long-distance runner despite the fact that he was over sixty.

No reason to beat around the bush. As they walked into his office, she said, "I've been doing research on the Cahill story. Background information on James Cahill."

He rounded the massive desk, sat down, waving her into one of the side chairs. "I thought Seamus was on that."

"It's not sports, Earl."

"So."

"You and I both know he's not all that into it. If the story doesn't involve salary caps or yards carried or runs batted in, Seamus doesn't give a rat's ass."

Earl lifted his coffee cup from his desk, then, seeing it was empty, set it down again. "Last I heard he was all over it."

"Depends on what you mean by 'all over.'"

"Watch it, Spritz," he cautioned, putting on a pair of half-glasses and glancing at one of the computer monitors. "Your claws are showing."

"That's a sexist remark, you know."

"Don't know what you mean. Take it up with HR."

The Human Resources Department was nonexistent, but she didn't let it go. "You were intimating that I'm being catty, something *always* ascribed to women."

"What side of the bed did you wake up on?" he asked, but held up a hand. "Wait. Don't answer. That could be described as sexist too."

"Give me a break."

"You give me one," he suggested, squinting as he glanced at his computer screen.

"I just want to dig deeper into the Cahill story."

"You think it's a 'Cahill' story, not a story about a missing woman?"

"They're linked, obviously. You know that. And people, I mean readers, will be interested in his family. The Cahills are rich, high San Francisco society, and have more skeletons hidden away in their closets than all of the bones in Adams Cemetery," she added, mentioning the one graveyard near Riggs Crossing.

"I'm listening," he said, surprising her as he leaned back in his chair and finally focused on what she was actually saying.

Charity pressed on, telling him most of the reasons she wanted to delve into James Cahill's past. He rubbed his chin as she talked, but seemed interested, leaning back in his chair and folding his hands over his rail-thin abdomen, eyebrows knitted together, so she made her pitch to go to San Francisco, and that's when he slammed the door.

"You expect air fare, hotel rooms, and . . . what? A daily allowance for cab rides and meals?"

"Uber rides," she corrected him. "And they've got great public transportation with BART and ferries and cable cars and trolleys and—"

"Hold on. You're getting way ahead of yourself. Way ahead. Look around, would you?" He motioned widely to include the vast space beyond the glass walls of his office. "Does it seem like we've got that kind of money?" He barked out a laugh. "Get real!"

She wasn't about to give up. "This is the kind of story that could sell papers. *Lots* of papers."

Shaking his balding head, he let out a sigh. "Even if I wanted to, if you somehow convinced me to pay for your little trip, I can't." His smile faded as the deepening lines of worry crowded across his forehead.

"This story could breathe life back into the paper."

"We're already on life support as it is. I'm sorry." He spread his hands over the mess on his desk. "No can do."

Charity realized further arguing would prove pointless. "Fine."

As she got to her feet, he gave a warning. "Remember. This is O'Day's story."

She shot Earl a defiant glance. "It will be when, instead of it being about a missing woman, it's the news of a freaking three-point shot right at the buzzer!"

And then she decided to take matters into her own hands and stormed out, yanking open the door and running into Seamus O'Day on the threshold. The older reporter was juggling a half-eaten donut and a cup of coffee. A wave of hot coffee sloshed out of the cup to splash against the front of her jacket and drizzle downward, dripping onto the toes of her boots.

"Oh, sorry," he said, flushing a bit beneath his woolen cap.

"Perfect," she muttered, squeezing past him, which wasn't easy as he was an ex-college football player who, over the past thirty years, had gone to seed and was nearly as wide as he was tall.

She didn't respond when he said under his breath, "You know you should be careful when you're opening doors."

You fucking has-been!

But she didn't say it out loud. Not this time. She'd save those parting words for the time when she could leave the *Clarion*, Riggs Crossing, and the likes of good-old-boy reporters like Seamus O'Day in her dust.

Wouldn't it be perfect if she went down to San Francisco, got the story of her life, and didn't bother reporting it through the rag here in Washington? As Earl had said, there was no HR department, nor did she have any kind of non-compete agreement. She was totally freelance, and therefore she could shop her story around. And she intended to do just that.

Take that, Earl Ray, she thought and smiled as she clicked on the remote to open the door of her van.

James Cahill was her one-way ticket out.

CHAPTER 20

Son of a bitch.

Finally, they were getting somewhere, or so Rivers hoped. At his desk at the station, he checked to make certain he had his keys, shoved back his chair, and, with his blood fired up a little, made his way to Mendoza's desk.

Nose to her computer screen, she was scrolling through reports but glanced up at him. "Yeah?"

"Guess who had an epiphany?"

Her eyebrows shot up, and she must've seen the gleam in his eyes. "Not James Cahill." When he smiled, she said, "Really?"

"So he says."

"Just like that?" She snapped her fingers. "He called to tell you?"

"Yep. He offered to come in later today, but I thought we'd go pay him a visit."

She was already pushing back her chair. "You think he might run?"

"Not so much run as have a change of heart, maybe talk to an attorney."

"What're we waiting for? Let's go." She was already climbing out of her chair and heading for the locker room. After donning jackets and hats, they headed outside, where the sky was the color of steel, heavy clouds threatening, the temperature hovering just under freezing.

Mendoza glanced at the heavens. "Another storm on the way."

Rivers climbed behind the wheel, and she strapped herself into the passenger seat.

"So I've done some research," she said as he backed the Jeep up, then put it into DRIVE and maneuvered around a department cruiser that was just wheeling into the lot.

"On?"

"A couple of things. First, I checked with Deputy Mercado, who had talked to Megan Travers's folks about her going missing, but it was strange. They didn't sound all that worried, not the mother in California nor the divorced father, Donald Travers."

"Sounds like she's pulled this kind of disappearing act before."

"Never quite this bad, but yeah. And I double-checked their alibis."

"Solid?"

"Mom was at a wine tasting in Napa, the dad in Chicago with his family. And then I did a little digging on the Cahill family." She was into her phone again, scrolling down. "They're worth millions, and it's been that way for generations. The family owns a huge mansion on a hill in San Francisco with views of the bay and the Pacific. The matriarch, James's grandmother . . . let's see, her name was—oh, here it is. Eugenia Cahill."

"She's dead?"

"Murdered." Mendoza slid him a glance. "A lot of that in the Cahill family," she added, still reading. "Really thinned them out. James's father and mother are alive, along with his sisters. They live in southern Oregon. Then he has a half-sister, Cissy, who's got a couple of kids and lives with her husband, still in San Francisco."

"That's it?"

She was still reading as Rivers avoided the knot of traffic in the center of town and took side streets as far as the bridge, where he melded in with pickups, cars, and vans heading south. "Well, not exactly. There've been some scandals in the past, scuttlebutt about kids born out of wedlock, which is kind of ironic because one of the big philanthropic organizations in San Francisco that Eugenia was involved with is Cahill House. It was established years ago as a home for unwed mothers when they had such things. Now it looks like . . . let's see. Now it's a resource for victims of family abuse as well as serving pregnant women with no place to turn." Mendoza looked up from her phone as the town fell away behind them and the first snowflakes started to fall. "But the long and the short of it is that James Cahill is going to be hella rich."

He knew that much already, as well as about the scandals in the

Cahill family. You just couldn't be a cop in San Francisco for as many years as he had and not be aware of one of the most socially prominent and notorious families in the City by the Bay.

"Is Cahill at his hotel?" she asked, turning up the heat, adjusting the fan.

"He claimed that he was in his shop where they build the tiny houses."

"A hotel and Christmas tree farm aren't enough for him."

Rivers thought that, if nothing else, Cahill was industrious. He might have been born with a silver spoon firmly lodged between his teeth, but at least he worked for a living.

As the interior warmed, they drove over the bridge. The river below was starting to freeze, ice forming near the banks. A little farther south, past snow-flocked pastures, the Cahill Inn, surrounded by fields of snow-covered evergreens, came into view.

Traffic slowed again, and just before they reached the inn, Rivers turned down the long lane that led deep into Cahill's property, a straight shot of twin ruts of gravel that wound up at the buildings where the high-end tiny homes were constructed. They bounced along the uneven tracks that ran along a fence line bordered by trees that separated this lane from the driveway leading to Cahill's home. As he drove through stands of fir and pine, Rivers couldn't help but think this man-made forest would be a perfect place to hide a body.

Then he reminded himself that Megan Travers wasn't dead.

Or at least not that they knew.

Just over a small hillock, the trees gave way to a wide parking area, trucks and vans parked in no particular order in front of a huge warehouse-like metal building with oversized barn doors. One of the doors was open, lights from inside spilling outside.

Rivers wedged his Jeep between a white van and a pickup from the seventies. "Let's see what our star witness has to say." He cut the engine and threw open his door.

"Possible suspect," Mendoza said as she stepped outside.

"Person of interest."

"How politically correct of you."

"That's me, always PC," he said dryly as they walked into the cavernous building where, high overhead, bright lights lit the beehive of activity within. Framers and electricians, plumbers, finish carpenters, and others worked around three flatbeds on which several homes were in different phases of construction. Electrical wires snaked from under the flatbeds, and a cacophony of sounds assailed them. Nail guns sputtered, hammers banged, saws buzzed, and voices shouted over some hard-rock song Rivers couldn't name.

James Cahill, wearing jeans, work shirt, a jacket, and a black Stetson, stood on one of the trailers, inspecting the steel frame of a house while speaking to a tall, thin man with a red beard whose head was covered by the hood of his sweatshirt. James was shouting to be heard over the din. ". . . so she's insistent. Wants a larger bathroom with a standard tub or at least one big enough to give a medium-sized dog a bath. She's got a couple of schnauzers. Her babies." He winced and rubbed his shoulder under the strap of his sling. In truth, he looked like hell, the scratches in his beard still visible, his complexion ashen.

He must've caught sight of the detectives because he cast a glance their way, then held up a finger to the guy he was talking with and said, "Jake, give me a few minutes, okay?"

"You got it." Jake tossed off his hood and replaced it with a hard hat while Cahill hopped down from the trailer, only to grimace as he landed. His expression wasn't exactly welcoming. "I thought we were going to meet later."

"We were anxious to hear what you had to say," Rivers said. "You mentioned you remembered the night that Megan Travers disappeared?"

James shot a glancc over his shoulder, as if checking to see who might overhear the conversation, which seemed improbable as the shriek of a wet saw chewing through tile screamed through the building. "Let's go into the office, where we can hear ourselves think." He hitched his thumb toward a staircase that climbed to a landing tucked halfway to the ceiling and ended at a large glassed-in room that had a bird's-eye view of the activity below.

"Fine."

Cahill, looking like death warmed over, led the way, only leaning on the railing a little as they scaled the steps.

"This'll be better, or at least quieter," Cahill said as he shut the door behind them and waved them into visitors' chairs. He took a seat at a massive desk. The back wall was lined with cubbies filled with samples of fabric, tile, hardwood, and quartz. And a drafting table sat in one corner, a design partially finished, while a computer screen displayed a 3-D image of the interior of a small house on another desk.

"You said you remembered," Mendoza prodded. She'd slipped out of her jacket and placed her phone on the desk, hitting the record button. "This okay?"

"Sure." Cahill slid into his chair, his arm in its sling resting over his chest. "It all came back this morning."

"Everything?" Rivers asked.

"Some details are kind of blurry, but yeah, it feels right."

"Why don't you just tell us what you recall," Mendoza suggested. "About the last time you saw Megan Travers."

He leaned over the desk and started right in. "I came home to the house as usual, about the same time as I always do. And just like every other day, I'd picked up takeout from the inn—chili and cornbread. Once I got home, I grabbed a beer from the fridge and thought I was in for the night. But I guess I was wrong." He proceeded to explain about Megan arriving and accusing him of cheating on her. How she'd tossed a note at him before things had gotten more violent. According to Cahill, Megan Travers had been the aggressor, working herself into a rage, attacking him, lashing out with sharp fingernails, pushing him. In trying to avoid her blows, he'd stumbled, scraping against the fireplace, his head smacking against the hearth. He didn't wake up until he was in the hospital. Megan was long gone.

"And that's it?" Mendoza asked.

"All I remember." He seemed sincere, though there was a little bit of hesitation.

Rivers asked, "What time was this?"

"Around six-thirty, maybe seven."

The timeline jibed with what Knowlton and the driver of the snowplow had sworn to. It also meshed with the dog walker's story of seeing Megan's car speeding through town.

Still, Rivers wasn't convinced of James Cahill's innocence.

Cahill swore he hadn't had any contact with Megan since that night and had no idea what had happened to her.

Mendoza pushed. "Megan Travers was your girlfriend."

"She had been," he admitted.

"But you'd broken up?"

James's gaze moved from Mendoza to Rivers. "In the process."

"But you were seeing Sophia Russo at the same time."

"Yes."

"Did Megan know?"

"She'd found out. Just like I said."

Mendoza said, "Were you seeing anyone else other than Megan Travers and Sophia Russo?"

"Don't you think two is more than enough?" When Mendoza didn't respond, he clarified, "No, I wasn't seeing anyone else."

"But you'd dated other women in the last year or so." She glanced at her notes. "Jennifer Korpi?"

"Long over."

"And Rebecca Travers. Megan Travers's sister."

Cahill tried not to react; Rivers could almost feel the monumental effort he employed. But it didn't work. A vein pulsed just beneath the shaved area visible beneath the brim of his hat. "We broke up."

"And you ended up with her sister."

"Not my finest hour," he admitted.

"How did Rebecca Travers handle it?"

"She was pissed. At me. Not so much at Megan."

Cahill's return gaze had grown penetrating. Mendoza had hit a tender nerve. "If you're trying to say that Rebecca had something to do with Megan's disappearance, there's not a chance."

Rivers asked, "How do you know?"

"I know Rebecca. She was always there for Megan, always. Megan could be . . . emotional . . ." He pressed his lips together, then continued, "Rebecca was always the calmer one, has a more level head. She would never do anything to hurt her sister."

Mendoza further poked the bear a bit on that subject, but Cahill didn't budge. He was adamant that there was no bad blood between the Travers sisters. Rivers wasn't ready to buy it, however, nor did he think his partner was.

Rivers asked, "How would you describe your relationship with Megan?"

Cahill smiled faintly. "Not exactly rock solid."

"She'd left before," Mendoza said. "Twice, right? You filed missing-person reports."

"That's right." He was wary now.

"Did you fight then, too?" Mendoza asked.

"Argued, yes. Let me be clear—it had never gotten physical before."

Rivers said, "But you were arrested once—"

"A bar fight, a long time ago. Nothing since. Never with a woman."

Rivers let it go. They grilled him more about the confrontation, asking if anyone else had been in the house or had come with Megan, even suggesting that he might have been the aggressor, but Cahill's story was set in concrete.

Finally, James said, "I've told you everything I know. Haven't held back, but there's nothing more to say, and I really have to get back to work." He stood, effectively ending the conversation, and even Rivers had to admit they were getting nowhere.

"If you think of anything else, call us," Mendoza said, picking up her phone. Checking her messages as she scrolled, she stopped and read quickly, then glanced up. "Lab's finished with your vehicles. They're at the garage. You can pick them up whenever you want." She slid the phone into her pocket. "If you need a lift, we're heading into town."

Cahill gave a quick shake of his head. "I'll get a ride on my own." He was obviously anxious to get rid of them. "What about my phone?"

"It's been cleared," Mendoza said. "You can pick it up when you get the truck and SUV. I'll see that it's waiting for you."

"Good."

"Again, if you remember anything else?" Mendoza slid a card onto his desk.

"Got it." Cahill ignored the card and headed for the door, the dog at his heels. Mendoza took the hint and followed, as did Rivers, though as he passed Cahill's desk, he swept a pair of sunglasses off the surface and pocketed them before catching up to Mendoza on the steps. He already had the work gloves, but Cahill was the center of the case, and another one of his personal items couldn't hurt. That was the reason, Rivers told himself. It couldn't possibly be because he experienced a rush at lifting the shades.

He reached the others at the foot of the stairs. Cahill walked them out of the building, where snow was beginning to fall again, big, lazy flakes drifting down from a dove-gray sky. As he left them to return to the warmer building, a smaller car pulled into a spot in the gravel lot, a blonde at the wheel.

"Sophia Russo," Mendoza said as the woman got out of the car and started walking toward the building.

"What do we know about her?" Rivers asked.

"Not enough." Mendoza watched the blonde hurry through the large door, then head straight to the staircase leading to the offices where James Cahill had headed. "Not nearly enough."

CHAPTER 21

"For the love of God, James, at least let me drive you," Sophia said, insistent as she followed James from his office and down the stairs to the shop floor.

"I can handle it." He didn't want her involved in his problems, and truthfully, Sophia was getting pushy.

Bobby, who had delivered some Sheetrock and was heading to his truck, fell into step with them as they headed outside.

"You haven't been out of the hospital that long. I can take care of you," she insisted.

"No." James thought for a second about their lovemaking. Tempting, but no.

Bobby pointed a finger at James. "You do what she says for a few days or you'll find yourself back in the hospital, and we all know how much you liked that."

"Don't think so." James stopped outside the barn door.

"Jesus, man. You look like shit." Bobby woefully shook his head. "What good do you think you're doing here with us?"

"I'm fine."

"It's just for a few days," Sophia said, sending Bobby a "butt-out" glare. "Until you're stronger."

"I'm going home."

"Your place is a friggin' nightmare," Bobby reminded.

"I'll go back to the hotel for tonight, then. If and when you can arrange for a crew to help me get my place back in order, I'll go home."

"And if you fall down the stairs and break your neck?"

"I won't do that." Hiking his collar up around his neck, James started walking toward Bobby's battered Silverado. "If you want to help, drive me to the police garage. Looks like my Explorer's finally been released from custody."

"You're gonna drive?" Bobby questioned.

"Yes, I'm going to drive." James was growing more irritated by the second. He'd never liked being bossed around, and now just about everyone he ran into thought they had a better idea about how he should run his life than he did.

Bobby asked, "What about the company truck?"

"Oh, fu—" He stopped himself before he cursed a blue streak, because Knowlton was right. The cops had both the Explorer and the GMC truck. "We'll make two trips."

"Or she can help out," Bobby said, nodding toward Sophia. "I'll be the lead dog in my truck; you can drive the company rig behind me, and she'll bring up the rear in the SUV."

"I don't need this, Bobby," James said coolly.

Bobby stopped to light a cigarette, bending his head and cupping the end of his filter tip as the snow fell in fits and starts all around him. "If anything goes wrong, we're on the scene to help. That's all." The cigarette bobbled in his lips as he talked, then finally caught. He drew in a big lungful of smoke.

"Fine," James grumbled, not happy, but anxious to get going, to get his life back on track.

With Ralph following at James's heels, the three of them made their way past a delivery truck from a local appliance store that was backing up to the open barn doors. The rear warning signal was beeping insistently as the truck's tires ground over the snow and gravel. Bruce Porter, a jack-of-all-trades, was standing in the open doorway and waving the truck backward.

They crossed the lot to Bobby's pickup, where James found himself once again stuffed inside, squeezed between Knowlton and a beautiful woman, his dog in the passenger well at their feet.

He should just accept Sophia's help, he thought as Bobby put the pickup into gear. Why was he fighting it?

He slid a glance in her direction to find Sophia watching him, a small, almost playful smile on her lips.

That's why, man. You've got no idea what's going on in her head.

"What?" she asked, eyes twinkling.

"Nothing."

She pressed the length of her thigh closer to his, and despite his trepidation, he sensed that he could be easily aroused by her, that he *was* being aroused by her, even though he'd spent too much of the last few days thinking of Rebecca, and even though he wasn't completely convinced he could trust Sophia at all . . . which was a pretty good summation of what his downfall had been ever since he began noticing the opposite sex. His Achilles heel had nothing to do with his heel but everything to do with his goddamned cock.

He ignored his own body's signals as Bobby drove along the lane, wipers scraping off snow and ice, defroster working overtime, every now and then a branch from the thicket between the two lanes brushing the side of the Chevy.

Once they were on the county road leading toward town, Sophia started in again.

"I just think it would be best if you had someone taking care of you for the next week or so," she said.

"We covered this."

"But—"

"No, Sophia."

She rolled her eyes.

"I'm staying at the hotel. Someone's there twenty-four/seven. Just a phone call away."

"The inn's booked," Sophia said.

"I'll figure it out."

"You would kick out a paying customer?" Bobby asked, giving him a look.

"If I had to. I'm capable of making my own decisions," he added with a bit of steel in his voice.

That, at least, ended their pressure campaign for the next forty minutes until they arrived at the garage and James signed the paperwork for both vehicles.

As Detective Mendoza had promised, he was able to pick up his phone as well. Outside the garage, he handed Sophia the keys to his Explorer. "You'll follow me," he reminded her.

She was a tad testy as she said, "I'll drop it off at the inn, where my car is, because I have to head back into town ASAP. I got a call reminding me I'm supposed to be at the police station in an hour. Apparently Detective Rivers wants to talk to me."

CHAPTER 22

The Isolated Cabin
Cascade Mountains
Washington State
December 15

I wait.

Seated on the hand-built couch.

Armed and ready.

Not only do I have two pieces of razor-sharp plastic, but also the metal rack that I managed to unscrew from the back of the bathroom cabinet door. It's heavier. Will be able to do a different, deeper kind of damage.

At that thought, my stomach curdles. I imagine swinging the weapon, feeling the soft thud as it hits flesh, then pulling and ripping open a throat or gouging out an eye with the sharp plastic. How had it come to this?

It's true what they say about isolation and loneliness—they can breed paranoia that, at times, is overwhelming. I'm still sane enough to fall victim to the waves of fear. Then it all grows, becomes stifling and overwhelming. I have to ride it out, to wait, and eventually the terror slowly abates. These attacks usually come at night, dark, disturbing, violent images that leave me quaking and gasping, but come the dawn, I can usually find my center, come back to the bleak reality of my imprisonment. And that's when I plot my revenge.

As I stare through those high, too-small windows, as the snow falls from a leaden sky, my gaze is turned inward.

Will I be able to pull off my brutal plan?

Will I be able to find the strength, the sheer fortitude to slice into the face and neck of a person I once so loved? It seems impossible . . .

Don't forget that person you once cherished put you here. Locked you away. At gunpoint.

Tears build. My stomach sours and knots. Bile rises in my throat and burns my nostrils.

I have to do it. I have to free myself. This cannot go on!

Slowly, squeezing back the betraying tears, I let out my breath, attempt to calm myself by glancing around the small cabin that, though my jail cell, is also now my home—smooth hardwood on the floor, a flickering fire, a convertible couch of faux leather, and even a fluffy blanket. Overhead, the sleeping loft is comfortable, with a thick mattress and downy duvet.

Affordable luxury for the adventurous spirit.

A line from one of the brochures.

And yet it's a damned prison.

My stomach turns queasy at the thought.

Stone walls do not a prison make,
Nor iron bars a cage.

I heard that somewhere—Dad had read it to me, hadn't he?

Yeah, well, Dad, come live in this jail and see if you believe it then. It may not be constructed of stone walls and iron bars, but what about custom moldings, polished granite, gleaming glass tile, and decorative but strong dead bolts that work from the outside? *I know the poem has something to do with the freedom of the spirit or mind, or possibly love, which makes my situation all the more ironic, considering the betrayal of it all.*

Seated on the couch, I stare at the opposing wall, constructed of sturdy, smooth cedar, where a flat-screen television was supposed to be mounted. Of course, that space is bare now. No television or phone or computer allowed. Instead, I've been left with a mountain of books, fiction and nonfiction, but no newspapers, nor magazines, no connection to the outside world.

My life is slipping away. Hour by hour. I tell myself it hasn't been that long, and yet it seems like an eternity.

I walk to the kitchen and glance into the small sink where a half-

eaten sandwich sits, bread stale and dry, pulled pork congealing on a stained paper plate.

My stomach rumbles, then clenches.

I can't be sick. Won't *be sick.*

And then it happens. My stomach lurches.

Frantically, I scramble to the small bathroom, where without any further forewarning, I heave up the contents of my last meal—the sandwich—into the state-of-the-art composting toilet.

Dear God.

Tears bloom in the corners of my eyes, and my mouth tastes sour and foul. This imprisonment has to end!

Shaking, unsure I won't vomit again, I straighten and glance down at my hands. Blood has bloomed on my left palm as I was still holding onto one of the pieces of plastic, gripping it so tightly it cut through my skin. "Shit," I mutter, finally reacting to the pain and grabbing a towel to staunch the flow.

How easily the plastic slit my skin.

And at that moment, I can see in my mind's eye the razor-sharp edge slicing across the smooth skin of a neck, then deeper through soft flesh, and into the hard cartilage of the larynx.

Crunch!

My stomach flips hard, and I throw up the rest of my half-digested sandwich and bile.

As I spit, straighten, and rinse my mouth I wonder: Can I really do it? Draw that knifelike edge across an exposed throat?

For a second, I stare into the oval of the mirror mounted over the small sink and smile weakly at my pale reflection.

Of course, I can.

CHAPTER 23

December 5

Sophia Russo was a looker, Rivers would give her that.

She had agreed to meet them at the station rather than at her apartment, and she now walked into the small conference room with Mendoza. After a quick introduction, she peeled out of a coat trimmed in faux fur and removed her sparkly knit cap. A blond ponytail fell to her shoulders. "Cold out there," she said with a mock shudder as Rivers got to his feet.

"I'll take those," he said and, before she could argue, grabbed her coat and hat to hang them on a rack near the door, his back to the table where the women were getting seated and to the camera mounted high on the wall. As he appeared to smooth the wrinkles from the coat and stuff the cap into a pocket, he deftly slid his hand deeper into the opening to retrieve whatever he could find—in this case, a small lipstick tube that he folded into his hand unnoticed by either Mendoza or Russo or the camera's wide eye.

Once back in his chair, he scooted his seat closer to the table, where, beneath the tabletop, he slipped the lipstick into his pocket.

"Would you like some coffee? Or a water?" Mendoza asked.

She replied, "Maybe a Diet Coke?"

Mendoza made a quick call and nodded as Rivers poured two cups of coffee from the carafe into mugs that had been left on a tray in the middle of the table.

Within minutes, a soft tap on the door announced the arrival of Dorrie Kahn, the receptionist and senior secretary for the department. She swept in and, in her usual efficient if brusque manner, handed Mendoza a can of diet soda. "All we got is Pepsi," she said with her perpetual scowl. In Dorrie's world, there just weren't any good days. "I've been trying to talk them into Coke forever, but the powers that be aren't listening." Lips pursed, she shot Rivers a sharp glance as if he were somehow to blame. "But then, do they ever?"

"Pepsi's fine," Sophia said.

Dorrie smiled tightly, then left the way she'd come, her high heels clicking loudly in the hallway outside the investigator's room.

Mendoza passed the can to Sophia, who quickly cracked it open.

"I don't really get the whole cola-war thing," she said, smiling as she took a sip.

On the surface, Sophia seemed innocent enough. If she was nervous at being questioned by the cops, she hid it well.

"Let's get started," Mendoza said and ran through the preliminaries, typing onto an iPad, and taking notes despite the camera recording the whole interview. After having Sophia state her name, she asked, "What's your address?"

She gave the address, then added, "It's a studio. Cascadia Apartments."

Mendoza asked, "So how long have you been in Riggs Crossing?"

"Six, no, it's almost seven months now."

"What brought you here?"

"Work. I mean it's kinda crazy. I was living in Portland, and—"

"Oregon, right?" Rivers clarified, then took a sip of his coffee, which was tepid and weak. He set his cup aside.

"Yes, they've got that whole 'keep Portland weird' vibe going, and I liked the idea, and there was all the bicycling. It seemed cool, y' know. But the rain. More like a constant drizzle. Y'know, the weird Portland thing got old after a while. So, I saw this job at a Christmas tree farm—well, actually a hostess position at the inn—and I thought it sounded like fun, a change of pace, and I especially love the winter season, y'know? So I applied."

"How'd you find out about the job?" Mendoza asked.

"Online." She said it as a matter of fact, as if that was the way things were done these days, and she was right.

"Is that where you met James Cahill?" Mendoza asked, glancing up from her screen at Sophia. "At work."

"He personally interviewed me," she said, nodding. "Personally." Did her eyes shine a little bit more when she spoke of him? "I started the next week as a hostess, originally, but I ended up tending bar and working the desk at the hotel, as well as waitressing in the café out back during the busy season, just filling in wherever." Then, as an afterthought, she added, "I've also helped out in the office, for the tiny homes."

"As a receptionist?" Mendoza asked.

"Well, yeah, and I took a couple of years of accounting in community college, so I can do more. I kinda do whatever's needed, like bartending or table waiting."

"A jill-of-all-trades?" Mendoza asked and took a sip from her cup.

She lifted a shoulder.

Rivers said, "You moved up pretty fast."

"I'm smart," she said. "I know that sounds like I'm bragging, but it's just the truth. And I'm loyal. There's a lot of turnover at the inn and Christmas tree farm. Some of it's to be expected, as a lot of the work is seasonal, and people move on. And then there are the people who just walk out. No notice. No nothing. I'm always dependable."

There wasn't the tiniest hint of duplicity in her blue eyes, at least none that Rivers could detect, but it still rang somewhat false.

Mendoza asked, "So when did you and James first get together?"

"You mean . . . ?"

"When did you become a couple?"

Sophia had drawn a breath, her eyes sparkling, and it looked as if she were about to launch into the intimacies of her relationship with James Cahill before Mendoza shut that down. Now, the young woman just looked irritated.

"It was a few months ago, I guess . . . It kind of just developed. We were working together more and more closely . . ." Her steady gaze slid to the side. "There was just this attraction. One you couldn't fight. And then we were in bed, just loving each other. I've never felt so . . . womanly."

Mendoza's expression was unreadable. Before Sophia could elaborate, Rivers asked, "What about Megan Travers?"

The girl exhaled and shrugged. "It was over between them."

"Did Megan know that?"

"Of course she knew. Women *know*."

Mendoza prodded, "But James hadn't told her."

"I don't think—I mean no, I'm sure he didn't."

For the first time, Sophia seemed uncomfortable; one hand reached up to fiddle with a tress of blond hair.

"So can you tell us where you were on Thursday?" asked Mendoza, clearly ready to get down to the pertinent facts.

"Sure." Another shrug, this time with a swallow of Diet Pepsi. "I worked until six, in the office, drove into town and went home—no, not straight home." She shook her head, pale hair skimming her shoulders. "First, I went to the gas station and filled up. My tank had been on empty for a day or two. I was practically driving on fumes, so I stopped down at the station on Sixth. After that, I picked up a salad at Charlie's Deli and went home. I thought about hitting my yoga class but didn't go as I was late, so I just showered and binge-watched three episodes of *The Bachelor* that I'd recorded." She met Rivers's gaze before looking at Mendoza again. "Exciting life, I know."

More exciting than you're admitting. At least that's what he suspected. "Did you see James?"

Her eyebrows arched as she took another sip from her soda. "At work."

"What about after work?"

She was already shaking her head. "Not until I went to the hospital. I heard about what happened at work the next day. Bobby Knowlton had told some of the staff, and we all knew. I busted down there to visit him."

"That day?" Mendoza took a sip from her cup but didn't stop typing.

"No. Well, yes. I mean, I went there, but I couldn't see him because he was in a coma. I think the first time I really saw him and we talked was last Sunday. And he wasn't all that great then, either."

Rivers asked, "Did he tell you what happened to him?"

"He couldn't remember, but obviously Megan was behind it."

"Obviously?" Mendoza repeated.

"Well, yeah." She stared at Mendoza as if she were dense. "The scratches on his face? Those were done by a woman."

Rivers agreed.

"I figured he'd finally told her about us, or she'd found out somehow and they'd had a big fight. She attacked him!"

"Rather than the other way around?" Mendoza prodded.

"James would never hit a woman."

"You know that?" Rivers asked.

"Well . . . no . . ." She lifted a hand, as if the truth were obvious.

Rivers leaned back in his chair. "So what happened to Megan?"

"How would I know?"

Rivers said, "If you were to guess."

"I couldn't. And I'm not going to. And don't you guys work in facts? Not what-ifs? All I know is what I heard, that she left James's house after the attack all pissed off, and drove like a maniac, almost hitting a snowplow or something. Supposedly, she was going to drive to see her sister who lives in Seattle or Tacoma, I think, but she never made it."

"Who'd you hear that from?" Mendoza asked as, deep in his pocket, Rivers's phone vibrated. He ignored it.

"Everybody who works for James. Bobby, Leon, Zena . . . you know—work gossip."

Mendoza made a note. "When was the last time you saw her?"

"Megan?" Sophia frowned, her eyebrows drawing into a knot of concentration. "I'm not sure."

"Was it that day?" Mendoza pressed.

"I don't remember . . . I think . . . I think I saw her in town . . ." She was working so hard to recall, her eyebrows knitted. "Megan works in that clinic off Main, right? The McKay Clinic?"

Mendoza nodded. "The McEwen Clinic."

"I saw her there, not inside but out," she said slowly. "She was in the parking lot, getting into her car. It was snowing. Hard. But I saw her. At least I'm pretty sure it was her."

Rivers didn't believe there was any doubt. Sophia seemed like the kind of person who knew exactly what was going on. Especially when it was a woman involved with a man she was interested in.

Mendoza asked, "When was that?"

"A few days ago? Oh, wait. I remember now! Tuesday afternoon. I was on the way to yoga, over in the basement of the Presbyterian church? We meet on Tuesdays and Thursdays, at six, that's why I'm always rushing as most days I don't get off work until five-thirty. Sometimes I'm late and miss the first stretches. I hate that."

"And you didn't see Megan on Wednesday or Thursday?"

"No." Another quick sip from her drink, and it seemed as if her hands were shaking a little. What was it she was hiding?

"She wasn't at the hotel?"

"Not that I saw."

"Or with James?"

"I told you, I didn't see her." She folded her arms over her chest. Defiant. She then told them she'd never actually met Megan, not officially, and that she hadn't been interested in doing so, all things considered. She looked away from the table, to the windows high overhead, and let out a sigh. "I knew *of* her, but that was about it. And before you ask, yeah, I knew she was seeing James and that they were 'a couple.'" She made weak air quotes.

Rivers wasn't buying it.

Sophia must've guessed as much. She licked her lips and fiddled with her hair, adjusting the band around the ponytail.

"Maybe I subconsciously avoided her, or she was avoiding me."

Mendoza asked, "And the fact that they were a couple didn't deter you from . . . getting closer to James?"

"They weren't married or engaged or even living together!"

"So he was fair game?"

She squirmed in her chair a little. "I guess if I'd been hunting, then yeah, but it wasn't like that. I told you. We were attracted to each other, and . . ."

It just happened. In his mind, Rivers finished her thought. Shades of Astrid's weak explanation about her affair.

And so it went. For another fifteen minutes during which they didn't learn anything significant. By the time Sophia slipped on her coat and hat and left the station, Rivers didn't know much more than he had when she'd walked in.

"You believe her?" Mendoza asked, snapping her iPad closed.

"Jury's out."

"She's a little too perfect," Mendoza said. "Too put together. Too beautiful."

Rivers pushed his chair back and stared at the door to the interview room as it hung open, the scent of Sophia's perfume still lingering. "Not her fault."

"Maybe not, but I don't trust her."

Rivers had experienced that same feeling. As they left the room, Mendoza asked, "Do you think she targeted James Cahill?"

"Targeted him before she came to Riggs Crossing?"

They walked toward their respective cubicles. "Think maybe she came to Riggs Crossing specifically because of Cahill? That she knew he was young and single and going to inherit a fortune?"

"There are lots of young, single rich men. You wouldn't have to come all the way to Riggs Crossing to find one." He thought it over. "Where's she from?"

She propped her tablet onto his desk, opened it, and typed quickly. "California," she said.

"Big state."

"Hmm. Right. How about San Mateo?"

"How about it?" he replied, knowing its close proximity to San Francisco. Located about twenty miles south of the heart of the city, San Mateo was on the peninsula. He'd been there dozens of times when he'd lived in the Bay Area.

"Don't you think it's a coincidence that she comes from close to the same place that the Cahill family called home?"

"I come from the area, too. Lots of people do. Including Megan and Rebecca Travers."

"You know what I'm saying."

"I do. But James Cahill is from Oregon. His parents moved there after he was born, I believe."

"But the Cahill family is from San Francisco, originally, and it's where the family fortune was amassed. Maybe we should follow the money."

"Instead of the women?"

"One always leads to the other," she said with an edge of sarcasm.

CHAPTER 24

The dream was so real.

He was with Rebecca. They were lying on the warm shores of a lake, the area deserted, no people, palm trees lining a beach of glittering sand. Far in the distance, on the horizon, was a boat of some kind, a small speck that grew larger as Rebecca started kissing him and nuzzling his ear.

His cock stirred, his erection coming to life as he responded. Her lips were warm and pliant, and he moaned, closing his eyes for a second before opening them and seeing that the boat was nearer, a ship by the size of it, steaming into the bay, moving quickly, black and massive.

Along with arousal, James felt a frisson of fear slide down his spine—there was something wrong here, and just as that thought occurred, the ship hit the shore and the beach started sloughing away to a ravine as dark and cold as a winter's night, and he, clinging to Rebecca, began to fall.

Still she kissed him, oblivious to the danger, to the fact that they were falling into the great, gaping maw of—

She slid her legs around his, beginning to move, and he caught her rhythm while the earth shattered around them.

He moaned.

Spasmed.

His eyes flew open.

Sophia was astride him again.

James grabbed her hips, forced himself not to throw her off him. The room was semi-dark, and her eyes were shut, her head thrown backward, blond hair falling past her shoulders. Her back was arched, her naked breasts shining with perspiration, her nipples protruding. "Oh, God," she whispered hoarsely. "James, oh, oh, ohhh . . ." And then she stiffened and cried out in ecstasy or pain or a little of both.

Dear God, he thought, why did she keep slipping into bed with him? How did this keep happening? Why didn't he wake up? How did she get in and—

She fell forward and lay atop him, breathing hard.

"Sophia, what're you doing here?" He dropped his hands from her hips.

She wrapped her arms around his neck. "Loving you."

"This can't keep happening."

"Sure it can," she said, her warm breath ruffling the hairs on his chest. "I came back for my bracelet, and I saw you and couldn't resist."

"You have a key?"

"From the main desk."

Of course. Because she sometimes worked the front desk and had access to the computer and all the skills needed to make a second key card.

He untangled her arms and slid her off him to one side. "You can't keep coming in here like this."

"Why not?" She looked at him with luminous and slightly wounded eyes.

"A million reasons," he said.

"You worry too much."

"You don't worry enough."

She snuggled close, her head against his shoulder. "Hold me," she whispered breathlessly. "Oh, James, just hold me for a little while . . ."

He lay quietly and stared at the ceiling, remembering the yawning chasm of his dream.

Willow waited in the shadows.

As she always seemed to do.

The hotel was quiet in the predawn hours while most of the guests were sleeping. The few people on staff were at their posts, one receptionist in the office behind the lobby, probably looking at porn on his phone, the lone person on janitorial staff locked in his small room in the basement.

The doors of the rooms were closed, locked for the night, the hallways hushed.

She was alone, and she knew where the cameras were.

On the third floor, she stared at the door of the executive suite, where James Cahill was now recovering and where, she knew, Sophia Russo had made her way inside. Willow thought about creeping closer to the door, even using her passkey to crack it open, but there was the dog, who would put up a ruckus if a stranger entered, and James was probably not sleeping anyway.

She imagined what was going on in that room. Despite his injuries, despite his recent hospital stay, despite the fact that his supposed girlfriend had gone missing, James was fornicating.

With Sophia.

A sin that couldn't be forgotten and certainly not forgiven.

Fourteen hours on the road.

Charity had to give it up for the night.

She'd considered staying with her aunt, but thought better of it.

Too many questions that she didn't want to answer.

Instead, she pulled into the parking lot of a no-tell motel just outside of Oakland and rented a room just as dawn was breaking and the heavyset woman in the small reception area was refilling the coffee pots. The receptionist looked like she could use a shot of caffeine herself, as she kept yawning while she worked, straightening the baskets of fake sugar and fake cream nestled by a row of paper cups, one filled with stir sticks. "Just a sec," she called over her shoulder as Charity, overnight bag in hand, waited at a laminate faux-wood-grained counter.

The receptionist finished her job and said, "What can I do ya for?" in that folksy manner that irked Charity. She wondered if she should have called her aunt after all and suffered through all of the nosy, busybody questions she'd have to have answered as Aunt Maureen grilled her. "Why aren't you married?" "Don't you want children?" "Really, a job as an investigative reporter? In the middle of nowhere? Are you kidding me?"

No, it was better to be here.

"I need a room," she said. "For two nights . . . possibly three."

"A double-double?" the receptionist asked and slipped on half-glasses as she started keying in the request on an aging computer.

"Sure. Whatever." Charity was going to elaborate that it was just her, but held her tongue, signed in, and got the key for a room on the second floor that turned out to be just what she expected: two beds with garish spreads, matching curtains, a desk on which a small flat-screen TV was mounted, and a closet without a door. The bathroom was tiny, but clean enough. And there was Wi-Fi, which she didn't trust, but she didn't have to. She'd brought her own hot spot with her.

Weary as she was, she spent the next half hour unpacking, setting up her laptop, and creating a work area.

Satisfied, she thought about tumbling into bed, but her stomach was rumbling, so she went downstairs, out the front door, and across four lanes of traffic to a diner that advertised "fresh made" pies and an "all you can eat" buffet 24/7. It wasn't much and basically gourmet-negative, but it would have to do. She grabbed a breakfast sandwich to go, brought it back to the hotel room, scarfed it down, then took a quick shower and tumbled into one of the sagging double beds to catch up on a few hours of sleep, after which she would start her investigation. She'd spent most of the trip south thinking about how to tackle the Cahill family and had decided to start by visiting Cahill House, the home for pregnant teens, then drive to the family estate. Once she'd cased the place, she would try to contact friends and acquaintances who knew James. After that, it was Megan's turn. The missing woman's mother still lived in the area.

So far, Lenora Travers hadn't returned her calls.

No worries about that. Thanks to the Internet and Charity's well-honed detective skills, she knew exactly where the woman lived. If Lenora didn't return Charity's phone message, then Charity would make certain they met face-to-face, which would probably be a lot better anyway. Emotions could be hidden in texts and on the phone, but it was much harder to conceal reactions when looking someone directly in the eye. And Charity considered herself a master at reading people.

But why and how would Megan's mother be involved in her daughter's disappearance?

It's true it was not likely.

Still, she might be able to provide answers about the people Megan knew, the places she might hide, about ex-boyfriends and who would want to do Megan harm, a little insight into the missing woman. Maybe something to break the case wide open, courtesy of Charity Spritz. Oh, yes.

CHAPTER 25

December 6

What the hell was she still doing here?

It had been over a day since she'd had the interview with the police, and Rebecca had yet to leave Riggs Crossing. She'd spent a sleepless night staring at the clock, punching the pillow and wishing she could sleep, but memories of her sister kept creeping into her brain: Megan crying on the first day of kindergarten. Megan falling off her bike and scraping a knee. Megan getting caught smoking cigarettes in junior high. Megan's first heartbreak when some kid in eighth grade dumped her, and then the incredible highs and deep lows of her high school years, the high drama that was forever a part of her life.

And then, of course, the betrayal of James Cahill.

Leave.

Everyone knows you're trying to find Megan: The police. James. Even the stupid press. So let it go. Just leave. You've made your point and done all you need to do, all you can do.

So get the hell out.

You can't help Megan.

God knows, you've tried.

Over and over again.

To what end?

So that she could hurt you? Backstab you? Then come running back for you to solve her problems?

Face it, Rebecca: You can't fix her. No one can.

And she doesn't want to be fixed.

No matter where she is; no matter what's happened to her.

Rebecca's heart ached for a second, but she forced that pain backward just as she had all her life.

As she had when her biological father had left.

As she had when her adoptive father, Donald, had divorced Lenora.

As she had when Megan had stolen James.

But she couldn't give up.

Not yet.

She had to make a public statement, begging for Megan's release if she were being held against her will, even though as yet no ransom request had come through. Sometimes women were kidnapped for other reasons, used by their captors. Her skin crawled at the thought of the sex slaves she'd read about, or the people drawn into cults.

Her throat was dry.

She had to do something. Her phone was charging on the small desk in her hotel room, and she snatched it up and scrolled through her recent calls. Reporter after reporter had left messages, the most persistent being Charity Spritz, but she was with the newspaper, and Rebecca thought her plea needed to be televised.

She imagined herself staring into the camera as she begged for whoever held Megan captive, if she were alive, to release her.

That would be effective.

Everyone, including James, would take her impassioned pleas to heart.

But could she go through with it?

Why did she feel like such a phony?

It wasn't that she didn't love Megan; she did. But she was tired of the theatrics, sick to the back teeth of everything revolving around her younger sister. When Donald had left, he hadn't so much as said good-bye to Rebecca. He never called, not once. But he'd kept in contact with Megan.

And hadn't Lenora doted on her younger daughter during that painful period? "She's so sensitive, you know," her mother had said, not thinking that Rebecca too was wounded and in pain.

In the following years, Megan had messed up her life so often, losing jobs and boyfriends and leases on apartments at a head-spinning rate. Yet each and every time, Megan had come running to Rebecca, expecting her calm, level-headed older sister to fix things, to help Megan pick up the pieces of her shattered life, thoughtlessly expecting Rebecca's own life to be secondary.

There was the time Rebecca had come to her rescue when Megan had gotten caught in her own emotional trap and her live-in boyfriend had drained their joint bank accounts, leaving her with an unpaid lease on an expensive apartment and zero money. Rebecca had found someone to take over the lease, a soon-to-be-married couple and clients of A Vision in White, the bridal company where she worked. She'd also allowed Megan to move in with her while she licked her wounds and pulled herself together. Rebecca had helped out with the bills and offered her younger sister as much emotional support as she could. Megan had leaned on her hard and then finally moved on.

That particular incident had been nearly two years ago, before Megan had met James, but it wasn't the only one. Each and every time Megan's shattered life had been thrust upon Rebecca, she'd tried her best to pick up the pieces and glue them back together as best she could.

Until now. Until Megan had stabbed her in the back by taking up with James Cahill. She still remembered the day when Megan had admitted that she'd been seeing James.

They'd been in Rebecca's condo in Seattle. It had been drizzling, raindrops sliding down the kitchen window over the sink. Megan had been nervous, licking her lips, picking at her sleeve, her blue eyes clouded. She'd come over with a message, and she'd refused to sit down. "There's something I have to tell you," she'd said and met the questions in Rebecca's eyes.

"Okay."

"You, um, you said that you thought James was losing interest in you."

Had she? That wasn't quite right. "I think I said, 'James has been distracted lately.'" Rebecca saw the indecision on her sister's face. "Why?"

"Well. I thought you should know that I'm moving to Riggs Crossing."

"To Riggs Crossing?" Rebecca repeated, wondering where this was going. "Because James lives there and . . ." Oh! Her heart dropped like a stone. No! Megan wouldn't . . . she couldn't . . . but Rebecca saw it in her sister's eyes. "Because of James."

"Yeah." Megan was nodding. "Look, I didn't mean for it to happen—honest, I didn't—but—"

"For *what* to happen?" Rebecca demanded. But she knew! She knew, damn it. Megan had somehow, someway wheedled her way into James's heart!

"—but James and I . . . we fell in love," Megan admitted, a little breathlessly, stars in her eyes as if she actually believed her lies. "I'm moving to Riggs Crossing to be close to him."

"You fell in love," Rebecca repeated, feeling the heat crawl up her neck. "With my boyfriend!"

"It wasn't supposed to happen."

"You got that right."

"It has nothing to do with you!"

"It has *everything* to do with me, and you know it." Rebecca was furious and sad at the same time. "This is a mistake, Megan."

"I know you're hurt, and—"

"You don't know the half of it," Rebecca cut in.

"But we love each other."

"I don't want to hear it! Just go. Go to Riggs Crossing. Go be with James. You'll find out, but don't come running back here for me to fix it. Not this time. Because I won't, Megan," she'd said as Megan had started for the door. "This time you're completely on your own!" As Megan had hurried outside into the dark Seattle drizzle, Rebecca had slammed the door after her, locked it, then thrown the dead bolt for good measure. The pain in her heart had been knee-buckling, and she'd slid down the door panels but had sworn to herself that neither Megan nor James would ever know how excruciating their betrayal had been.

That would be her secret, her cross to silently bear.

Yes, that day had been the turning point.

Tears filled her eyes and, furious with herself, Rebecca angrily dashed them away. She stalked to the bathroom, where she turned on the cold water at the sink and splashed it onto her face. "Don't let her do this to you," she told her reflection. "Don't."

She would talk to the media.

She would make her plea for Megan's safe return.

And then she would leave.

And what about James?

She conjured up his face, complete with beard stubble, scratched skin, and bandage over one side of his head. He was thinner than she remembered, the edges of his cheekbones and jawline more defined. Well, that's what dealing with Megan would do to a person.

Rebecca had thought she was well over him, had told herself that James's betrayal was water under the bridge, a good thing. She'd almost convinced herself that she'd been lucky not to get too involved with him before he'd shown his true colors and ended up with Megan.

But she'd been wrong.

So damned wrong.

As soon as she could, she would put Riggs Crossing behind her. Get on with her life.

Her cell phone chirped from the tangled mess of blankets on the bed. Retrieving it, she spied her mother's number and inwardly cringed. She wasn't in the mood for Lenora's questions, which always made her feel as if she were being interrogated, but putting her off was no answer either. Sweeping up the cell, she crossed to the window and looked down on the street below. Streetlights glowed, reflecting on the ice and snow. Traffic moved slowly through the nearby intersection, and pedestrians, bundled in jackets, hats, gloves, and scarves, hurried across the sidewalk. Big, lacy flakes drifted from gray clouds overhead. The phone rang in her hand again.

No time like the present.

Still staring through the glass, she answered just before the call was routed to voice mail. "Hey, Mom."

"For a second, I thought you were busy. Or ignoring me."

And there she was. Lenora Travers. Never one to pass up an opportunity to get in a little dig.

"Just coming out of the bathroom," Rebecca lied.

And there you are, bending the truth to avoid conflict with Mom.

"I won't keep you. I just want to know if you've heard anything from Megan."

Rebecca imagined her mother, tall and willowy, her skin tanned, her hair streaked blond from hours in the California sun, her pale eyes worried. "Don't you think I would have let you know, if she'd called or texted or shown up?"

"Of course, of course, but . . . I'm just so far away."

Your choice, Rebecca thought, which was wrong. She and Megan were the ones who had moved away. "I know." On the street below, a pickup with a tarp over its bed rolled through the intersection, and three preteen girls in matching red caps, giggling, their arms linked, made their way under a wide awning and into the coffee shop sitting catty-corner from the hotel.

"And no ransom call?"

"You think she was kidnapped? Mom, Megan's a grown woman."

"Don't you read the papers or see that information on Facebook? People, women, not just kids, are taken all the time. They—the kidnappers—they pretend to be stranded, and you stop, or they ram you from behind and you get out to do the insurance work and *bam!* They force you back into your car at gunpoint and drive you to some remote place. That's why they haven't found Megan's car!"

"She wasn't kidnapped."

"You don't know that!"

No, Rebecca thought, no, she didn't.

"It's so frustrating," Lenora was saying. "I've left messages with that detective—oh, what's his name? Rivers, that's it. But after an initial conversation, he hasn't called me back."

Rebecca thought about Brett Rivers, how she'd found him in Megan's apartment, where he'd been standing in the dark, all alone, as if he were in some kind of trance or something, his mind light-years away. And the way he'd studied her when she was giving her statement at the sheriff's department. Weird dude. "He's probably just busy."

"He told me he'd keep me posted, but I don't know if he will. He's just as likely to call your father, and you know how that will go." Lenora's voice turned acrid and sharp, as it always did when she mentioned her ex. "Donald and that wife of his would like nothing more than to keep me in the dark—"

"If I hear anything, I'll let you know," Rebecca cut in, hoping to forestall another hate-filled diatribe about Donald Travers. She had her own daddy issues and didn't want to go there. "Promise."

"Well . . ." she said, half-mollified for the moment, "I just want to be kept in the loop, Becky." No one but Mom called her that. And Rebecca hated it. "You're up there, and I can't get away right now, and . . . I'm just so worried about Megan." Her voice cracked. "Ever since she was a child, she was so emotional, so overly dramatic, so . . . well, so . . . 'Megan,' that's what I used to say about her. All her life, she's pulled these incredible stunts."

"You think she's doing this on purpose?" Rebecca asked, astounded that her mother had that much insight into her wayward younger daughter, even more astounded that Lenora would voice it.

"Oh, no . . . I mean, I don't know, but I'm just worried sick, and if I could get away I'd be up there in an instant. You know that. But I've just got so much going on with the holidays and all. I'm one of the hostesses of the holiday ball and bingo championship, and then I'm in charge, I mean, I'm the head coordinator for the Valentine's banquet; it's for charity, a local soup kitchen, and we're already collecting donations, and there's a problem with the caterer and . . ." Lenora choked back a sob. "I'm just so worried."

"I'll let you know anything I learn," she said. "Look, Mom, I've got to get back to work. I'll talk to you later." And she hung up on the lie, tossed her phone back on the bed. She had no interest in her job whatsoever, and as she glanced to where she'd left her laptop and saw that it was open to the website for A Vision in White, she turned her attention back to the street, where she saw, in a flash of blond hair, Sophia Russo pushing her way into the coffee shop across the street.

Her heart lurched.

She hadn't yet met the woman; she'd only seen digital pictures of Sophia that Megan had sent to her phone days before she'd vanished. God, had that only been about a week ago? It seemed a lifetime. Since landing in Riggs Crossing, Rebecca had spied Sophia in the small town twice: once, wrapped in a long coat and fuzzy hat when Sophia had been hurrying out of a strip mall that housed a bakery, a convenience store, a gun shop, and a consignment store that sold "gently used" items; a second time, when Rebecca had been idling at a light and Sophia, in the crosswalk, had walked to her parked car on the next block. That time, Rebecca had watched as Sophia slipped into her gray vehicle and would've lingered longer at the light except that the driver of the pickup idling behind her gave a sharp, angry beep of his horn, forcing her to hit the gas and gun through the intersection. She'd experienced the unlikely urge to follow the blonde that day, because, whether she wanted to admit it or not, Sophia held a fascination for her. She'd quickly circled the block, and upon spying Sophia's Ford disappearing around a corner going the opposite direction, Rebecca had done a quick U-turn and had tailed the gray car down to Aspen Street and the Cascadia Apartments, a nondescript two-storied cinderblock building. Once parked, Sophia had climbed out of her car, keys in one gloved hand, and had walked in knee-high boots to her end unit. As if she'd sensed she was being watched, Sophia had looked over her shoulder before unlocking the door, her gaze fastening on Rebecca for a heart-stopping instant just as Rebecca had driven past.

Sophia hadn't shown any surprise when their gazes collided, and Rebecca would have sworn later that the blonde had actually shown the hint of a smile, almost as if she'd expected Rebecca to follow her.

But that was crazy, wasn't it? At the very least, paranoid.

Rebecca turned away from the window and focused on the open page on her computer, but couldn't find the energy right now to care about weddings or brides or anything to do with romance and happiness and sunny futures. She snapped the laptop closed and returned to the window. Her stomach rumbled, and she eyed the restaurant situated catty-corner at the next block. She should just get going, leave this tiny town and head back to Seattle, but at the thought of her empty condo, she inwardly cringed. And she could work from anywhere as long as she had a decent Internet connection, anywhere in the world.

Maybe she should relocate entirely.

Get farther away from the mess that was her life and out of the drizzle and memories of Seattle.

Since the boutique shop was expanding into markets in California, she could possibly leave Seattle. Maybe a change of scenery was what she needed.

And what about Megan?

Her stomach twisted at the thought of her sister.

And then there's James . . .

Forget him! He betrayed you. Remember?

Staring through the window, past her own pale reflection, she continued to watch pedestrians on the streets as they hurried along the sidewalk or between parked cars, some burdened with packages, all bundled against the cold as the snow fell. A boy on a skateboard slipped through the crowd, an elderly man helped his wife into a parked pickup, and . . . and a lone figure, standing apart from the rest—a woman, she thought, a scarf wound over her neck and lower face. She kept to one side, but her head tilted upward as if she were staring straight at Rebecca.

So what, was Rebecca's first thought, but then, as if the woman realized she had been caught staring, she whirled away, ducking down an alley, the rope of her black braid snaking out behind her. Not blond Sophia, who'd ducked into the coffee shop. Who, then?

"What the devil?" Rebecca asked aloud as she told herself it was nothing and her cell phone jangled, causing her to jump. She nearly ignored it, as she'd already talked to her mother and most every other call had been from anonymous numbers, all of which had turned out to be reporters. They could leave a voice-mail message, she thought, but she plucked the cell from the mess of her bed again, and this time she recognized the number: James Cahill.

Her heart beat a little faster, and she told herself to let the call go to voice mail.

But what if he'd learned something about Megan?

Steeling herself, she picked up. "James," she said without preamble, hoping there was no trace of emotion in her voice.

"Hey, Becca." Her heart twisted as she remembered how he'd always shortened her name. Not Becky . . . Becca . . . and she'd loved it. "I'm downstairs."

"Downstairs? Here?" she asked, then before he could answer: "Why?"

A beat, then, "I remember."

"What?"

"That night. With Megan. I remember."

She swallowed hard. "Oh."

"I thought you should know."

Her heart began to pound. "Tell me."

"Face-to-face."

"No, I don't think—" she started to argue, then looked frantically around her small hotel room: the unmade bed, her computer on the covers, the clothes she'd worn earlier tossed over the back of a chair.

The thought of him in her room—her space—was intimidating. She began cleaning up, straightening the covers. "Not here."

"Where?"

"I don't know, but just not here."

"We'll figure it out." He sounded so sure of himself.

Her heart was hammering. She needed to talk to him. She *wanted* to talk to him. Wasn't that the reason she'd come all the way to Riggs Crossing to begin with? To find out what he knew, what he remembered?

Or was there another reason? Now that Megan was gone—

"I'll come down," she said quickly, breathlessly, cutting off that thought.

"I'll meet you by the front door."

She clicked off and wondered if she was about to make the worst mistake of her life.

CHAPTER 26

"Come on, lady, let's go."

The security guard, a big, burly man in a too-tight uniform, motioned Charity off the front porch as a fine mist, visible in the light from the streetlamps, fell around them. The Northern California night was close, the air as thick as it was cold.

"I wasn't doing anything!" she declared when the guy tried to grab her arm. She yanked it away and glared at Lenora Travers, who was standing in the doorway of her town house. What an A-1 bitch! And she knew it!

Lenora was wearing a long dressing gown cinched tightly around a wasp-thin waist, house slippers, and a pained expression that said it all.

"You're trespassing," the guard rebuked Charity loudly enough for Lenora to hear. She could tell he wanted to prove that he was in control. More softly, into Charity's ear, he singsonged, "Come on. Just get in your car and drive away. Before I have to call the cops."

"You mean the *real* police? You'd actually call them?" Charity demanded.

The security guard made another reach for her arm, this time catching an elbow, his beefy fingers clamping over the sleeve of her raincoat.

"Let me go!" she hissed. "I just wanted to ask her some questions."

"Yeah, well, Ms. Travers, here, she don't want to answer any. You got that?"

Oh, Lenora Travers's attitude was all too clear. Arms crossed imperiously over her chest and backlit by the interior lights, Megan's mother hoisted her chin toward the sky. Eyeing Charity as if she were little more than a cockroach, she announced, "You're not an invited guest."

"I told you I'm with the press."

Lenora's gaze moved to the pseudo-cop. "If you've got this, Hank, I'm going inside." She was already turning away.

"You do that, Ms. Travers. We're cool here." Hank's breath clouded in the air and smelled of his last cigarette mixed with some kind of mint flavoring. *Ugh!*

Charity called after Lenora, "Wait! I just want to ask you some questions about your daughter. Come on, Ms. Travers. Don't you want to find out what happened to her?"

Lenora stiffened, then looked over her shoulder. "I'm sure the police are doing everything they can."

"But maybe I can help. The power of the press and all," Charity insisted, frantic. She'd come all this way and didn't intend to be tossed aside.

"Oh, I seriously doubt that." Lenora walked into her house and pulled the door shut with a soft but definitive *thud* while Hank practically pushed Charity off the porch.

"Damn it," Charity grumbled and only then noticed the other people, curious neighbors who had come out to stand on their small covered porches and watch the show. A seventy-ish woman in a long coat holding a tiny dog under one arm stood on one stoop, and a couple in their sixties, the wife clinging nervously onto the husband's arm, watched from another. The little dog—a miniature dachshund—was growling and yapping its head off, while they all stared at her as if she were some kind of lowlife criminal.

"I'm a reporter, okay?" she yelled at them.

"Come on. You're outta here." The guard pointed her back to her van.

"I'm doing my job!"

"If you know what's good for you, you'll leave. If you don't, it's my duty to call the local PD, as I said before." He glanced at the house, where Lenora was peeking through the blinds. "Or Ms. Travers will do the honors herself. Trust me, she's done it in the past when that little neighbor dog over there"—he hitched a thumb toward the crazed barker—"took to using Ms. Travers's azalea garden as his own personal bathroom. It doesn't take a whole lot to set her off."

"I'm only trying to help."

"Tell that to the officers."

"Shit, shit, shit."

He moved toward her, and she edged closer to her van.

"You've got two minutes to drive outta here," he warned her, and after she reluctantly climbed into the driver's seat, he stepped forward, slammed her door shut, and then all too obviously checked his watch. "Now a minute and fifty-two seconds."

Oh, ha, ha! He was gonna count backward! Very funny.

Asshole.

Charity started the van. She knew it was no use arguing or making more of a stink in this gated community, so she hit the gas and pulled away from the curb just as Hank took a step back. Even so, she nearly clipped him and thought for a vengeful second how good that would feel, then pushed that troublesome thought away. She didn't need to maim anyone or get herself into any kind of trouble or even draw attention to herself. The outburst in front of the neighbors had been a mistake. She still had business here in California, and she obviously would have to use a less-than-direct approach. Not let her emotions get the better of her.

As she drove past the town houses, their identical windows glowing from interior lights, she flipped on the wipers. As the blades swatted away the accumulation of raindrops on the windshield, she plotted her next move. She'd already done as much as she could through the Internet. Next up, she would interview Cissy Cahill Holt, someone who intimately knew all of the skeletons tucked away in the prestigious, if scandalous, Cahill family closets.

Smiling to herself, she passed by the gatehouse where she'd bullied her way past the guard, then turned into a tree-lined street, joining the thin flow of moving traffic, taillights glowing ahead of her, headlights streaming in the opposite direction.

As for Lenora Travers, Charity was certain that bitch would get hers. *What goes around, comes around.*

If not, Charity would make sure of it.

* * *

Rebecca beat back her rising panic.

So she was going to meet James, so what?

She'd forced this issue, had barged into his hospital room, and then sneaked into his house, only to be found out, but she wasn't ready for this, the emotional onslaught of dealing with James and Megan, and the aftermath of their betrayal, and . . .

"Oh, hell," she muttered, giving herself a quick mental slap. She'd started this, and she'd better damned well see it through. The nasty little thought that if she played her cards right and enlisted James's help in locating Megan, he might realize that he'd gotten involved with the wrong sister crept through her mind.

"Stop!" she said aloud. Whatever she'd once thought she'd shared with James, it was over! O.V.E.R.

"Just keep reminding yourself of that," she muttered as she looked in the mirror, snapping her hair into a messy bun. Her reflection looked haunted, as if she hadn't slept in a week. Still, she ignored her makeup kit. "What you see is what you get." Pulling on boots and a jacket, she grabbed her wallet and was out the door.

True to his word, James was waiting for her just inside the hotel's double doors, a Stetson covering most of his hair and bandage, his bad arm hidden beneath his jacket, looking for all the world like some long-legged action-movie hero in battered jeans and beard shadow.

Ignoring the knocking of her wayward heart, she moved toward him with more confidence than she felt.

He looked up and caught her eye. "Hey," he said as some kind of greeting.

"Hi. You ready?" Before he could answer, she pushed into the street.

"You know where you're heading?" he asked, following her out.

"There's a restaurant across the street."

"That's where you want to go? A noisy restaurant?"

Beats the alternative, she thought, imagining being alone with him in her hotel room. And the lobby was out. She'd figured that out as she walked through. It was crowded. There were two people on the circular sofa near the Christmas tree, both heads bent over cell phones, a thirtysomething couple arguing with a desk clerk, their luggage surrounding them, their trio of children playing hide-and-seek around potted plants and chairs and yelling while faintly the strains of "Jingle Bells" added to the general cacophony.

"Doubt we'll get a table," James said.

Rebecca looked across the street through the restaurant's windows and saw a crowd within. The booths were all full, and there was a group gathered in front of the reception area just inside the doors. And hadn't she witnessed Sophia Russo going into it not fifteen minutes earlier? Did she really want to run into the blonde while she was with James? "Where then?"

"Your room?" he suggested.

Hell, no. She thought of the messy bed and lack of seating. And the last time she'd been in a bedroom with James. Shaking her head, she said, "Don't think so. I thought I made that clear."

"Then—?"

"You're the local. You tell me."

"Don't suppose you'd want to go back to the house?"

She remembered hiding in his attic and the disarray. "Isn't it a mess?"

"Being straightened up."

"There must be somewhere closer."

He glanced outside, and his eyebrows slammed together. "There's a bar two blocks down. If we're lucky no one from the press will see us."

"This is a pretty small town. It's not like there are dozens of reporters or the paparazzi waiting outside."

He cocked an eyebrow. "No one from the newspapers has contacted you?"

"Okay, fine." She was anxious, ready to get it over with. "The bar sounds good." It didn't, but they were running out of options. James held the door for two women who were hurrying into the hotel, a woman in a full-length coat holding tightly to the leash of a French bulldog in a tight red sweater. The taller of the two women, a redhead who seemed about fifty, was dragging two roller bags, a scarf covering the lower half of her face as she made her way to the desk, where the couple was still in a heated debate with the hotel clerk while one of their kids was sliding down the banister.

"Come on." James touched Rebecca's elbow with his good arm, guiding her away from the hotel entryway.

The air was crisp and cold enough to fog when they breathed. As they headed down the street, Rebecca glanced to the spot where she'd spied the woman with the long braid on the street, but no one was watching her now. Maybe she'd imagined that whoever it was had been staring at her room; perhaps the woman had just been looking at the hotel.

Then why did she turn away so suddenly when she caught sight of you?

"Something wrong?" James asked as they reached a corner.

Every damned thing. "Nope." She was just unnerved, spying Sophia, then the woman, and now James.

He offered her a smile, but she pulled her gaze from his face. No. Nope. No sexual tension. Nada. Just conversation.

Hands in her pockets, as she'd forgotten her gloves, Rebecca kept in step with James as they crossed the street, turned a corner, and two blocks later, ended up at a redbrick building with a striped awning.

The Brass Bullet Bar looked as if it had been constructed at the turn of the last century and, aside from the addition of several flat-screen TVs, hadn't been updated since the end of the Second World War. High-backed booths lined a wall opposite a walnut bar that stretched the length of the building and was backdropped by a mirrored wall where dozens of bottles glimmered on narrow glass shelves.

Sawdust and peanut shells littered the floor, and the odor of wood dust mingled with the smells of beer and ale.

James led her through the few tables scattered in the middle of the room, and they found a booth near a back exit. She slid onto the bench seat opposite him and saw him wince a bit as he sat down.

"Riggs Crossing's finest," he said with more than a trace of sarcasm. Before she could reply, the bartender arrived, her wild gray curls tied back by a red bandana that matched her western-cut shirt.

"What can I get you?" she asked, sizing up Rebecca.

"Something hot. Irish coffee?"

The barkeep glanced at James. "You?"

"Bud. On tap."

"Anything to eat?" she asked, and though Rebecca felt her stomach rumble, she shook her head. "I'm good."

"Just the drinks," James said. As the bartender/waitress left, he slid a bowl of shelled peanuts toward Rebecca, which she ignored.

"Time to get down to business, so spill," she said, folding her arms across the table. "You said you remembered, so tell me."

He didn't hesitate, which kind of surprised Rebecca, even as she told herself she welcomed it. He just launched in, explaining about the argument with Megan, how she'd come at him when she'd found out about Sophia. How hurt she'd been, how angry. She'd thrown a note she'd written at his face, then lunged at him.

The drinks had come, and he'd stopped to take a sip of his beer, but he'd only paused his tale while the bartender was there. As soon as she left, he picked up again, barely missing a beat. As he spoke, Rebecca searched his face for any trace of a lie. She tasted her drink, the foaming whipped cream sweet and at odds with the warm whiskey.

"I should have told her," James wound up. "She was right. Before I got involved with Sophia, I should have told Megan it was over." He leaned back against the booth. "That's it. That's what I know."

She didn't remind him that this was his MO, moving on to one woman before cutting it off with the previous one, didn't say anything to jog his memory that he'd done the same to her.

Is that jealousy worming its way through your veins, heating your blood, poisoning your heart? God . . . please . . . no . . . not at this late date.

"Go on," she said woodenly.

"That's all. I just said—"

"That's not all."

James regarded her carefully. "Are we . . . talking about something else?"

"Megan."

His gaze narrowed. Moments passed. Rebecca could almost hear the tick-tick-tick of elapsing time. She was pushing. Asking without asking. Angry. Needing to know, but unable to ask him, *Why . . . Why? Why Megan?*

James either read something on her face or picked up the vibe because he said, "I'm sorry."

Jackass. Did he think that would be enough?

She tried to smile, but couldn't force the muscles of her mouth to comply. "Call me crazy. I always thought there would be an explanation. Like . . . love grabbed you by the throat, and you were powerless against it. But then you cheated on her. Like you cheated on me with her."

"She told me you were seeing someone else. A doctor."

"What?" She stared at him. "What are you talking about?"

"Megan said you were seeing someone else," he repeated.

Liar! "That's not true."

He didn't answer.

"Oh, God . . . You mean Michael Dent?" she demanded.

"I don't know his name."

"I never dated him. Megan worked for him. At his clinic. He was going through a divorce or something, was separated from his wife at the time, I think. *Megan* dated him. I never did. I was with you."

His expression was unreadable. He didn't move a muscle. Was he feeling the same distinct shock she was?

"Megan showed me pictures of you with him."

"So?"

"They don't lie, Rebecca. You were with him. Together."

She stared at him in disbelief. "I went to dinner with him and Megan once," she said. "And . . ." And then she got it. "Are you trying to tell me that while Megan went to the bathroom she actually took pictures of Michael and me together? Like we were on a date or something?" she said, staring at him. "And you believed it? Didn't even come to me to ask me about it?"

When he didn't respond immediately, she glared at him. "Are you kidding me?" Her heart hardened. "You believed Megan. Never asked me about it?"

His brows pinched together.

"Really . . . You believed *Megan!* Oh, I see. It was easier. It was the easy way out. You *wanted* to believe it."

He looked about to argue, but thankfully didn't. Because when push came to shove, it didn't matter. Water under the bridge and all that. She reminded herself the only reason that she was here was to find Megan.

"Okay. So I'm a dick," he finally admitted.

She didn't say a word.

"You could at least argue the point," he suggested.

"I could." She waited, all the while aware of his gaze lingering on hers. She didn't back down, just stared back at him. "But I'm not going to."

"Fair enough." He seemed to want to say something else. She could tell he was still processing.

"I don't want to talk about could have beens," she preempted.

"Okay."

"Okay," she snapped back.

His eyes held hers for a second too long. "I . . . should've tried harder."

"Yes. You should've." She wouldn't bend. If she bent, she'd break. "Let's move on."

"You got it." He drained his glass and signaled for another.

"You were telling me what happened," she reminded him, forcing the conversation to the situation at hand, refusing to notice the hard line of his jaw, masked a bit by the beard growth, nor the breadth of his shoulders, nor the way his hair, where it hadn't been shaved, curled behind his ear.

Nor would she admit that her heartbeat was ticking a little faster. "You said she attacked you."

"She did."

"And you couldn't defend yourself? From a woman who doesn't weigh a hundred and fifteen pounds?"

"She surprised me, and I didn't want to hurt her. She was out of her mind. So damned angry, so furious. She came at me teeth bared, nails slashing. I tried to sidestep her as she lunged, but we went down together. I remember that." He rubbed a hand over his chin as the waitress picked up his empty glass and left a full one in front of him.

"And you hit your head."

He nodded.

"And then you blacked out."

"Yes."

"And woke up in the hospital with amnesia." She couldn't keep the sarcasm out of her voice. What the hell was she doing here, listening to this BS? She was sick of it. "So what happened to her—to Megan?" She took a swallow from her drink, barely tasting it, realizing it had grown cold. Her gaze was fastened to him, searching for any kind of reaction.

"I heard she drove away from the house. Bobby thinks he saw her car leaving when he was on his way back to the house and, from what the cops told me, she was on her way to your house, but didn't make it."

Square One all over again.

"Where do you think she is?"

The question surprised her. "I don't know. That's why I'm here."

"But you must have a theory." He looked at her over the rim of his glass as he took another swallow.

"I don't know. She said she was on her way. Called me. Upset. And I waited."

"But she didn't show."

"Right."

"And you have no idea what happened to her."

"Of course not."

One of his dark eyebrows arched.

"You think I know something I'm not saying?"

"It wouldn't be the first time sisters got together."

"Oh, come on. To what? *Frame* you?" she said, her voice rising. "Is that where you're going?"

"You both have your reasons."

"Are you kidding?" she growled. "What part of hell do your thoughts come from? Why would I come all this way and stay here indefinitely if I knew?"

"Good question. One maybe you could answer."

She leapt to her feet, torn between fury and disbelief.

"How would it look if you hadn't shown up, hadn't started demanding answers of the police?" he pointed out.

"You don't really believe that."

She saw, then, that his mood had lightened somewhat, that he was enjoying baiting her a bit. That pissed her off. "Let's get this straight, okay? I did *not* drive over here to 'look' legit . . . to—to throw the police off the scent or whatever it is you're getting at." She felt her eyes narrow as she leaned across the table so that her nose was nearly touching his. "Don't do this, James. Don't try to put this on me. I came here to help find Megan. That is the single reason I'm here."

His eyes held hers as he asked softly, "Is it?"

In a split second, she remembered making love to him, the stretch of his skin over taut, corded muscles, the pressure of his mouth on hers. Her breath caught in her throat. "You are a first-class bastard," she said, the fact that her words were a whisper taking away none of their power. And with that she walked away from the booth and through the sawdust and peanut shells to the door, letting him worry about the tab.

He could damn well afford it.

CHAPTER 27

San Francisco, California
December 7

She'd been stood up.

On the night after she had been unceremoniously hauled away from Lenora Travers's town house, Charity, fuming, had waited at the waterfront, the night closing in on her despite the lights of the city, skyscrapers with their towers of windows glowing against the inky, moist night.

The "contact" she'd made, a person who had called her the night before and suggested they meet near Pier 39, hadn't shown last night, either. She'd been wary, of course, but the caller, whose phone number had been blocked, insisted that he or she—Charity hadn't been able to tell which—had "dirt" on James Cahill, including why he was considered the black sheep of his family, and what stood in his way of inheriting.

Music to Charity's ears. As she'd gone to the meeting spot, she'd had dozens of questions for the informant. Had James Cahill had some previous charge of violence against a woman? Had something happened when he was a teenager, and had the court records been sealed? Had a victim been bought off with some of the Cahill fortune? A dozen questions about Cahill came to mind.

And what had Charity learned tonight?

Nada!

It was so damn frustrating. She'd felt in her gut that something in Cahill's past, along with the ties to old San Francisco money, had contributed to the mystery surrounding Megan Travers. Something deeper, something darker. But was that true? Or had it just been what it appeared? Out-and-out jealousy that another woman had turned his head, forcing Megan to take off? Was it that simple?

As Charity walked through the cold San Francisco night, she toyed with the idea that Megan, known for her mercurial temper and penchant for drama, might have staged her own disappearance. If she had, why hadn't she reappeared? Did James know more than he was saying? If so, what?

And then there were the sisters, Rebecca and Megan Travers, both betrayed. Charity had just scratched the surface about them, but she'd made a mental note to dig a little deeper, discover more about them and their involvement with James. And they too had ties to this city.

So all was not lost.

And there was that information she'd received from Cissy Cahill, related to James and nearly fifteen years his senior. Boy, had that woman had stories to tell!

Enough for one book, and maybe two.

So, really, all was not lost. Even if this jerk-wad had set her up only to bail.

Charity just had to do a little more digging on Marla Cahill's daughter—the other daughter, the real whack job of a totally messed-up family. So perfect for a true crime book, or even a screenplay . . .

So, screw everyone who thought she couldn't make it to the big time.

As she stared out at the dark water of the bay and the thin stream of traffic crossing the San Francisco–Oakland Bay Bridge, Charity imagined her future, how she would show everyone, including those imbeciles she worked with at the *Clarion*, what she was made of. Blustering Earl Ray and his creep of a son would see.

Wrap that around your man bun, Gerry.

She imagined a book contract or a movie deal. Wouldn't that be great? Wouldn't that old has-been Seamus O'Day be surprised? They all would. Everyone at that two-bit rag!

But first things first, she reminded herself.

The story.

She gave the guy five more minutes, then gave up. Though it was late, after midnight, there were still some people about. Not many, but a few, some teetering out of bars, others climbing into parked vehicles or waiting on street corners in the filmy lamplight.

But no informant ready to spill his or her guts about the Cahills.

Luckily, all was not lost, considering the information she'd dug up through Cissy and the nurse, but what they'd told her was just the tip of the iceberg, she could feel it.

She'd never been particularly patient, so the magic that was supposed to be found in San Francisco was lost on her. It was cold and misting, the wind whipping across the bay, rippling the dark water into frothy whitecaps, the haunting cries of sea lions chasing after her.

And there was still Megan's mother to interview, one way or another.

Though she'd been thwarted so far, Charity knew the old bag was scheduled for a fitness session with her trainer and a massage at the club after the workout tomorrow—Lenora Travers's usual midweek routine. Charity planned to be waiting when Lenora stepped out of the door of Club Fit and made her way to her car. Then she would spring. Lenora, surprised, would either make a scene or, Charity was betting, rather than risk an embarrassing spectacle in front of friends she worked out with, would agree to a sit-down. Good. Then maybe she would get somewhere. Maybe Lenora would give up some gem of information about Megan or her sister—the woman James had dumped in favor of Megan—as well as come up with a list of contacts, friends and acquaintances, who would help Charity find out what made the missing woman tick. All under the guise of hoping to locate Megan, of course. Which, really, she would be doing as well, Charity rationalized.

And then there was Cahill House. She hadn't been able to see the records yet, but after she'd visited the place yesterday afternoon and was turned away, she'd received an anonymous tip from a woman who claimed to have been a nurse there years before. She'd refused to give her name, and her phone number had been blocked, but she'd claimed she'd heard from a friend who still worked at Cahill House that Charity had been there nosing around. Then she'd hinted that the Cahills were more involved than just funding the place, that someone in the family might have used the private home for pregnant women to their secret advantage. The nurse hadn't given up much else. Just that tantalizing hint.

"Unwanted babies," Charity had guessed when the woman would say no more.

"I didn't say that. You didn't hear it from me."

"I don't even know who you are. Or if your story is legit."

"It is. Trust me."

"I'd like to, but I need specifics," Charity had said.

"Just know that you're on the right track. Keep digging." And then she'd clicked off, refusing to answer a return phone call or a text.

And what would that "right track" be? Charity wondered, thinking that over, but decided it was worth following. Several hours later, she'd gotten the call from another number, the one that set up this meeting. All of this in less than forty-eight hours. So she'd definitely gotten someone's attention.

Now, wrapping her arms around her middle as a blast of cold air rolled over the bay and seemed to cut through her quilted Kate Spade jacket—well, it was a knockoff, but no one could tell—she started back to her car.

It occurred to her that she might be handling this the wrong way, that she should have stayed in Riggs Crossing, but she'd been stonewalled there. And then she might not have discovered the link with the sisters. No, she was on the right track. She just had to keep going, keep pushing.

The eerie, guttural barks of sea lions rippled across the water, and the cold air slapped her face. She glanced around, nervous, wondering if her contact was watching her, and not for the first time, she wondered if she'd been lured here for a reason, if this was a trap.

Don't be silly. You've just watched one too many horror movies. Besides, you're armed. Pepper spray in your pocket, 9-1-1 only one touch on your phone. Don't let your nerves get to you.

But another low, nearly painful moan from a hidden sea lion caused her skin to prickle. Time to go. Her contact obviously wasn't going to show.

She picked up her pace, gnawing on the different ideas and motives that nagged at her. Her heels seemed to resonate loudly in the moody mist.

But not just her heels, she realized, her heart nearly stopping.

Hadn't she heard a second set, almost echoing her own? As if someone were following her? She glanced over her shoulder just as a car rolled slowly behind her, its headlights temporarily blinding her.

Was there a dark figure there, hidden by the intensity of the car's beams?

Her throat tightened.

A man? Woman?

The driver gunned the engine, and the car, a black sedan, shot past. Charity blinked, but the street behind her was empty. No one visible.

Still, the back of her neck tingled in fear, and adrenaline kicked through her bloodstream. She half-jogged across the street toward the parking garage where she'd left her van. This was crazy. What had she been thinking, agreeing to meet an unknown individual in the middle of the night? Yeah, she had her pepper spray in a front pocket, her phone in her hand, but still . . . She took the stairs, didn't want to wait for the elevator to the third floor and . . . Oh, sweet Jesus, did she hear the hum of the elevator as the car rose?

Heart thumping, trying not to panic, she flew up the staircase and burst onto the third floor, aware how empty the parking structure was. How stupid was she to have been lured here? She, who'd graduated at the top of her class at Fremont High? She broke into a run. She was sweating now despite the cold night, breathing hard.

Her van was parked just as she'd left it, no longer crowded between a Porsche and an SUV. Now her minivan stood alone, one of a handful of vehicles parked on the aging concrete.

She heard the rumble of the elevator as it ascended.

Her throat went dry.

Her heart pounded.

Frantically, she reached into her pocket and hit the remote to unlock her car and heard the beep as her headlights and taillights flashed.

Almost there!

The elevator stopped on her floor just as she reached the van's driver's door.

She slid inside as the doors of the elevator swept open.

Freaked, she jammed her key into the ignition and locked her minivan's doors in one swift motion.

The engine roared to life just as a man in dark jeans, a camo jacket, and a stocking cap pulled down to his ears strode from the elevator car. He took a look at Charity, who was wheeling out of her spot.

Their eyes met.

Her heart jolted.

A gloved hand slid into his jacket pocket.

For a weapon.

Oh. God. No!

Her insides turned to water.

She rammed the minivan into REVERSE.

With a screech of tires, she backed up, swinging around wildly.

Her assailant suddenly in her headlights, she threw the minivan into DRIVE and hit the gas.

He lifted his arm.

Pointed a gloved hand in her direction.

Oh. Jesus. He was going to shoot her! Right here! Right now!

Her heart leapt to her throat.

No way! No effin' way!

She wouldn't let it end this way.

She floored it!

The van shot forward as a nearby Toyota blinked and beeped.

The guy's mouth fell open in shock.

With a shriek, he jumped backward, dropping his weapon.

No. Not a gun, but a fricking car remote, a small keyless entry device.

Not anything like a pistol.

Nothing dangerous.

She cranked the wheel, the van rocking, narrowly missing the man.

"What the fuck?" he screamed, scrambling away, his face drained of color. "You fucking moron!"

Oh, sweet God, she'd nearly run a guy over, just because her jangled nerves got the better of her.

"Dear Lord," she whispered, hitting the brakes for a second.

She thought about stopping completely and apologizing and trying to explain, but to what end? In the side-view mirror, she saw him grab for the remote, which had skittered across the stained concrete floor of the garage. Remote in hand, he was now climbing to his feet and looked as if now he really would kill her. No longer frightened, he was now furious, his face twisted in an ugly, angry grimace, his gaze zeroing in on the back end of the van. The license plate!

"Hey!" he yelled. "Hey, stop!" He found his phone, aimed it to take a picture.

She didn't think so.

She pressed on the accelerator, but kept her eyes on him in the rearview.

"You nearly killed me!" he screamed.

He started running after her, and she felt renewed fear.

"Oh, shit."

In that split second, she decided to get the hell out of there. He obviously wasn't hurt. No harm, no foul, right? And she didn't really want to stop and have him ream her out or even threaten to sue her or worse. Best to keep driving. She hit the gas, then saw the post! So close and directly in her path!

"Shit!" She cranked hard on the wheel to avoid it, but grazed her side-view mirror, ripping it so it hung by wires. The glass was shattered, but she didn't stop. The van spun around the corner, and in the splintered reflection, she spied the guy still chasing her, frantically waving his hands.

"Hey! Stop! Fuck!"

Her heart was already pounding crazily, her breathing shallow, her hands shaking on the wheel. She'd been certain he was going to fire a gun through her windshield, hitting her and causing her van to go out of control, careening through the garage, possibly hitting a pillar or another car or something, but definitely killing her.

But she'd been wrong.

Nope.

Not gonna happen.

With one eye in the rearview, knowing he could catch her, she sped down the two floors to the exit, paid the attendant, and didn't wait for change, just shot out of the building the minute the barricade bar lifted.

Barely glancing to her left, she joined oncoming traffic and suffered the sharp honk of a truck that was forced to brake, then maneuver around her. The driver shook his fist, but she didn't care. "Get over it!" she muttered, but didn't return the hand gesture. Better not to get him pissed off. She wasn't out of the woods yet. No doubt the parking structure had cameras, and if the guy she nearly ran over wanted to cause trouble, he could, she supposed. There was the evidence of her broken mirror, but for now, she'd forget it, deal with the fallout when it came and take her grandmother's age-old advice of not borrowing trouble.

"It'll find you, soon enough," Gramma Jean had said often enough. "It's best not to go lookin' for it."

Amen to that, Charity thought, as she drove toward the Bay Bridge, which stretched across the dark water to the winking lights of Oakland and her small, almost seedy motel room, where the daily rate was still far too steep for the lousy, paper-thin walls, sagging mattress on the bed, and cheesy Internet service. If only she could afford something in the city with a penthouse view, spa service . . . God, even room service would be a luxury over the partially filled vending machine in the hallway of the Good Bay Motel, where there was nothing good about it and the bay was half a mile away.

She eased off the bridge and wound her way through the city streets of Oakland. Her heart rate finally returned to normal, and she loosened her grip on the steering wheel. For now, she pushed the image of the man in the parking garage out of her mind and wouldn't allow herself to dwell on the fact that she'd nearly run him down. It was over. At least for now.

When she saw the neon sign for the Good Bay, she let out her breath. "Home sweet home," she said, almost meaning it, as she wheeled into the lot. The minivan bounced over a pothole in the asphalt.

Clunk!

Something bounced in the cargo area behind her.

Crap!

Probably a piece of equipment that had come loose from its bindings and was shifting. Oh, God, please not one of her expensive cameras.

She pulled into her parking slot and reached for her keys.

Something passed in the rearview mirror, a shadow in the dark, obscuring the back window and her view of the empty lot behind her.

What the hell?

A frisson of fear skittered down her spine.

It's nothing!

She licked her lips and cut the engine, her hands still on the key ring.

And she reached for the door, which was when the cold muzzle of a gun pressed against the back of her neck.

Her insides turned to water.

Oh. God.

Panic flooded through her.

"Don't move," a whispered voice ordered.

Like hell!

Charity yanked the keys from the ignition and swiped blindly backward with her right hand. A yowl of surprise cut through the van.

The gun shifted.

She scrabbled for the door handle.

"No, you don't!" the voice warned.

The door flew open.

She fell out. Tried to get up.

Whoever it was tumbled after her, climbing over the seat and falling atop her, pressing her against the cold, hard pavement.

Charity started to scream, but a gloved hand clamped over her mouth, and in the watery light from a single security lamp, she looked up and saw eyes staring down at her.

Malicious eyes.

Eyes she'd seen before.

A new fear surged through her.

She struggled and saw the butt of a gun being raised with her assailant's free hand.

NO!

Her scream was muffled, resounding only in her head as she twisted and writhed to no avail.

The pistol slammed into her face.

Her nose exploded in a burst of pain.

Blood spurted.

Still she fought, trying to scoot away from this maniac's weight, the rough asphalt tearing at her coat. Her legs were useless, kicking at the air but striking nothing, as the would-be killer straddled her.

Get off me! Get off!

She bit at the hand holding her mouth, the taste of stained leather filling her mouth. The gun was raised again, this time dripping blood.

Wouldn't someone come along? Someone to help her? There was traffic on the street running in front of the motel. Surely someone would see that she was being attacked! *Oh, please!*

The gun came down again.

Hard.

Craaaack!

With a sickening crunch, she heard the bones in her cheek shatter.

Her scream was muffled as agony ripped through her.

Blackness seeped into the corners of her vision.

No!

Charity tried to hit back, flailing wildly with both her arms, fingers raking the air, striking nothing.

Again, the horrid weapon was raised.

Why? Why would this person want her dead?

That, she realized, was the ultimate goal.

Through the haze of blood and pain, she saw the butt of the pistol come down again. With a force born of fury.

Craaaack!

A burst of light flamed behind her eyes. Pain shot through her brain. Blinded, she bit down into the leather glove, clamping her jaws as hard as she could. Her attacker sucked in breath in pain.

"Owww! Jesus!"

Good.

She tasted blood, then tried to bite down hard again, but she was starting to fade, the blackness pulling her under, the world spinning away . . .

Her assailant snarled, "You're *so* dead, bitch."

And it was true.

She let go, and the darkness folded over her.

Then there was nothing.

CHAPTER 28

December 8

The following day, Rivers finished the last bite of his ham-and-cheese sandwich at his desk, wadded the white takeout bag from the local deli in his fist, and lobbed it into his wastebasket. The damned thing bounced off the rim and reminded him of the final shot he'd missed in high school, right at the buzzer, with not only the game but a spot in the state championship playoffs on the line. Yeah, it had been bad.

He'd been the goat that evening, he thought, and for all the wins his team—the Hillside Hornets—had captured, that loss, to the rival Eagles, had given him teenage nightmares for weeks and still stuck in his craw two decades later.

Now, shaking off the memory, he stood and stretched, his spine popping from long hours at his desk. He rolled the kinks from his neck, checked his watch, and realized it was time to go. If they wanted to make Marysville by three, they needed to head out. He strode to the locker area, where he found Mendoza already slipping her arms through her jacket.

"Time to roll," he said as they both checked out from the station, then stepped outside to a day that was crisp and cold, the cloudless sky a brilliant shade of blue. "I'll drive."

Mendoza was already heading to the passenger side of a department SUV as a cruiser with two deputies pulled into an open space. "Got the keys?" she asked.

He shot her a look over the roof of the Jeep. "Yes, Mother."

Her lips twitched as she slid inside, and once he was behind the wheel and driving out of the lot, she asked, "Bad morning?"

"Not so much bad as fruitless," he grumbled. "And cooped up."

"Well, now you're not," she pointed out.

That much was true. They were on their way to meet with Jennifer Korpi, and he'd be away from the phone and computer screen for a good while. He'd spent hours going over reports and statements from witnesses and watched reams of footage taken by street and business cameras in the area, looking for a clue, hoping to spot Megan Travers's black Toyota. There was a tiny bit of hope when a Tacoma couple who had been driving east at the time reported seeing what could have been Megan's car. The timing was right, and it had happened just before the summit, on the eastern slope, where the driver had been forced to ease closer to the side of the road as the Toyota, heading west and uphill, had blown by. But so far nothing had come from the tip.

The snowplow driver who'd been cut off, Bud Frandsen, had come in and talked to Rivers. Frandsen was a big, beefy guy in a baseball cap who was looking at retirement and had been behind the wheel of a plow for nearly thirty years. When asked who was driving the car that had careened out of James Cahill's driveway, he'd adjusted the hat on his head and replied, "I had to hit my GD brakes so hard I nearly slid. Didn't pay attention to who was driving. But the car was a black Toyota, that much I can tell you."

"Was there anyone else in the car, other than the driver?"

"Don't know. Don't think so," he said and, when handed Megan Travers's driver's license picture and asked if she could be the driver, he'd swung his big head side to side and said, "Maybe. Maybe not. I was just trying to keep the rig on the road while cussin' a blue streak." As if to underscore that, he added, "Fuckin' idiot. Coulda got me killed."

Rivers hadn't gotten much more from Olga Marsden, either, a woman near eighty who had been out walking her dog on the night Megan disappeared. Gray-haired and thin, Mrs. Marsden was a widow and sharp as a tack, her dark eyes bright behind big blue-rimmed glasses. She had taken her little Scottie dog for a walk through Riggs Crossing that night, just as, she said, she did every night. "We leave the house just after seven and get home before eight so I can catch up on my shows. I tape *Wheel* and *Jeopardy*, you know, after the news," she'd informed Rivers. "I always walk Bitsy then. He's a Scottie, you know, the fifth one I've owned, and it's been my experience they all like their routines. Bitsy for sure. He doesn't like his routine changed. Puts him in a bad mood."

Though she hadn't been sure, Olga Marsden had thought a woman was behind the wheel of the dark car. "She was driving like a bat out of hell! Just a few blocks from Main Street, if you can believe that. Oh, boy! I signaled for her to slow down, you know, patted the air like this." She mimicked the movement. "But she didn't even notice. Just kept right on going. In fact," the old woman had confided, lifting a "tsking" finger, "I think she actually sped up, if you can believe that."

When Rivers had asked if the driver had been alone in the car, Mrs. Marsden had thought hard, her face screwing up beneath her cap of gray curls. "I think so, but I couldn't swear to it. It happened so fast. I was too concerned about Bitsy, you know. Afraid he might run out into the street. He's a love. Name's short for Bitterroot's Scion; he's registered. Purebred. We just call him Bitsy."

That had been the end of the interview.

Later, Mrs. Marsden's story had been confirmed. Two cameras, one from a service station, another mounted over the parking area of a restaurant, caught glimpses of a dark Corolla hurtling past around the same time as the dog walker said she was out.

Olga's recollection coincided with that of Megan's coworkers as well, both of whom he'd spoken with on the phone and confirmed their previous statements. Ramone Garcia, a physician's assistant, had seen Megan leave at her regular time, right after 5:00 P.M., and his coworker, Andie Jeffries, an RN for the McEwen Clinic, had agreed. The parking-lot camera had filmed Megan leaving work and getting into her Toyota at 5:09. The doctor who owned and ran the clinic, Thomas McEwen, MD, had been at the hospital that afternoon, and there was nothing more that he could add, only to say that everyone who worked at the clinic was trustworthy and that Megan had done a good job as a bookkeeper who worked with the insurance companies. Other than having trouble getting to work on time, Megan Travers had been "an asset to the team."

Rivers wondered about that, but didn't say as much. He directed search teams from both the county and state police to look carefully in the area near or past the summit. It appeared she'd gotten that far, at least, but then what?

He and Mendoza also double-checked Megan's phone records and credit-card receipts. Her checking account had been untouched, no debit activity since the last time anyone had seen her. Unless she had a secret identity or a helluva lot of cash stashed away, or a friend who was hiding her and letting her use his or her funds, there was no way she wouldn't be spending her money for gas, food, and lodging.

His frustration with the case grew. It was over a week since Megan's disappearance, and he had no idea what had happened to her. Was she alive? Hiding? Kidnapped? In a bad accident, trapped somewhere? Or, he worried, dead?

"Any word from the state police?" he asked again, glancing at Mendoza, who was, as usual, looking at her phone.

She shook her head. "Don't you think I would've said?"

"Maybe we can nudge them again."

"Like we did yesterday and the day before."

He looked through the windshield at the vibrant blue sky. "It's clear today. They could send a chopper up."

With a lift of one eyebrow, she sent him a get-real glance. "I think they're on it."

"Just check, would you?"

He reached into a pocket and grabbed his sunglasses as the glare of sunlight off the snow was blinding. The road was clear until they reached the foothills, where the plows hadn't been able to keep up with the snowfall and the road was packed with ice, snow, and, in some spots, gravel.

He wondered about the little Toyota. It too had disappeared. Was it secreted in a garage somewhere? Or already out of the country, as the Canadian border was only a few hours north? Or buried deep in the snow at the bottom of a steep ravine in these craggy mountains?

Traffic cameras had been checked, where they existed, but, of course, there were none in the mountains. As they crested the summit, where snow-shrouded evergreens guarded the road, he wondered if Megan had gotten this far. Had she even made it out of the town?

The crumpled note she'd left came to mind:

J—
I'm leaving you.
This time forever.
You'll never see me again!
M

Was it a suicide note?

Or just a breakup message?

Or a desperate cry for attention from a woman who wanted to shake up her lover? That seemed far-fetched, but he'd seen worse in his years on the force in California. Twice before, Megan had been reported as missing, the reports both filed by James Cahill. This time he'd been in the hospital. Would he have let the authorities know if he hadn't been laid up? The whole case was blurry and undefined, more questions than answers. That would have to change.

Rivers squinted into the lowering winter sun, and Mendoza informed him that yes, the state police were already on it, searching the area from the air.

"And you doubted them," she chided.

"Just double-checking."

"Uh-huh." She glanced out the window and changed the subject. "Pretty up here."

And possibly deadly, he thought, but didn't want to ruin her take on the beauty of nature.

"I'm telling you, that Charity woman, she's driving me nuts!" Lenora said, her words as clipped as they had been when Rebecca was a teenager and had gotten into trouble. It sounded as if she were driving, ambient noise audible over her distressed words. "It's harassment, that's what it is. Harassment!"

"Just avoid her." Rebecca stripped the few things she'd hung from the small closet and tossed them onto the bed of her hotel room. She was finally leaving Riggs Crossing. Something she should've done days ago.

"That's impossible. That little reporter found a way to get past the guard the other night, and I almost had her arrested. She was trespassing and bothering me *and* the neighbors. June? Lives two doors down on my street? She saw that woman in the very same van cruising around the fitness club the day after she showed up here. Following me! Can you imagine?"

Rebecca could. She'd dealt with Charity Spritz herself, knew how determined and nosy she could be. "I don't know what to tell you. She's bothered me too." Though the reporter's calls had definitely waned in the last couple of days. Probably because she was in California bugging Lenora.

"I've called her boss, let me tell you, some vile man, Earl Dean something or other—"

Earl Ray Dansen, Rebecca knew, but didn't correct Lenora.

She glanced at the desk in the hotel room, really just a table, where her laptop was recharging, her notes already stacked, a copy of the local newspaper folded after she'd read every column inch of it.

"—I gave him a piece of my mind. I don't mind if he's got someone trying to find out what happened to Megan; of course, I don't. The more help, the better, but that woman was harassing me, and I'm Megan's mother, have never set foot in that little town, so why in the world . . . Oh, I'm ranting, aren't I?" she said.

"It's okay," she lied. It was easier than arguing.

"I'm on my way to the club, if I can avoid that reporter. After I'm done at the gym, I've got dinner with Mel. I've told you about him, right?"

"Yeah, Mom, you have." *A dozen times. Maybe twenty.* Mel Davis, the sexy, retired stockbroker Lenora had met at bridge club and who was now pressing to move in. "He's a very nice man. Quite possibly 'the one,' if you know what I mean."

The one . . .

How many billion people were in the world? Seven? Or was it eight? What were the odds of finding "the one," who just happened to have joined the same club as you? The "one" who had been married four times already?

Her thoughts ran to James for a second before she shut them down. She couldn't think about him without all the "what-ifs" circling her brain driving her crazy. He could get to her without even hardly trying.

There's no going back.

"Mel has been a big help during all of this," Lenora was saying, and it sounded as if her car had stopped, as the rush of traffic noise had disappeared. "I don't know what I would've done without him." Her voice actually cracked. "He talked me out of coming up there, to Briggs Crossing."

"Riggs, Mom. Riggs Crossing."

"Whatever. Anyway, Mel has been my rock, let me tell you."

"Good."

"And you, dear. Knowing that you're there searching for your sister, putting pressure on the police, I can't tell you what a comfort that is, Becky." Rebecca heard a click, as if Lenora had just opened the door of her Cadillac.

Eyeing her open suitcase, Rebecca said, "I don't know how long I can stay here, Mom."

"Well, you have to. Until Megan's found."

"That might not be happening."

"Oh, Rebecca, don't tell me you're giving up. Not on Megan—"

"It's not that."

"Please . . . just . . . stay. I watch some of those detective shows where the family keeps the pressure on the police and does their own detective work, you know, won't let it lie? It always helps."

"I have a job."

"What's that compared to finding your sister? Didn't you tell me you could do your work anywhere?"

"Most of it," Rebecca admitted grudgingly.

"Then don't give up. You know I'd be there if I could, but I just can't. Not right now. I never dreamed some reporter would come all the way down here. But speaking of that, why don't you go on TV? You know, like they do, and put a plea out for information on her? Maybe you-know-who could cough up a reward. I would, you know I would, but I'm strapped. Oh, dear—I've got another call coming in—Oh! Well, speak of the devil! It's Mel!" Her voice took on a brighter, almost giddy tone that Rebecca had to steel herself against. "Look, honey, I'll call you later, okay? Love you!" And with that she clicked off to take a call from "the one."

Rebecca's lips tightened. There was no way she was going to call Donald Travers and ask for a dime.

But it's for Megan, and she needs it.

That naggy, irritating voice that had been in her head ever since

Megan had gone missing was at it again. Rebecca felt a duty to help her sister, and really, she wanted to, but she'd been played for a fool so many times, duped by Megan so often that she wanted to resist.

This time you don't have much of a choice.

This time she could be in serious trouble.

Rebecca ground her teeth in frustration. Getting more deeply involved was her natural instinct, and she loved her sister, but sometimes it was so damn hard. And James Cahill's involvement made it harder.

Arguing with herself, Rebecca tucked her phone in the side pocket of her purse. She was half packed, ready to return to Seattle and get back to her life. What more could she do here?

Make a public statement. You've thought about it, and Lenora wants you to do it.

Put up a reward—you have a nest egg tucked away.

It's Megan, Rebecca. Megan!

She remembered the little blond four-year-old who had looked at her with such adoring eyes, and a lump filled her throat, even as she called herself seven times a fool. But she had to do it. And she would. She would talk to the police again, put as much pressure on them as she could, even though being around Detective Rivers made her nervous. Not only had he been standing in Megan's darkened living room, like a thief in the night, but there had been the interview, almost an interrogation, at the station. She'd felt as if she were walking on eggshells there, as if he were laying a trap for her, and at any moment she might fall through a hidden door.

Be cool.

You did what you had to.

Everyone thinks you're here to help find Megan.

And you are, aren't you?

"Of course," she said aloud.

So, relax.

But she couldn't. Not yet. Not until—

Her phone chimed again. She picked it up. Saw Angelica's name flash onto the screen. Her boss. Great. Just what she needed. Her stomach, already sour, clenched.

She clicked on. "Hi."

"Rebecca?" Angelica asked, even though she'd known whom she'd called. "Oh, my God, how is it going? Any word on Megan? I've been searching the papers and online, but I see nothing." Angelica had been born near Milan, and though her parents had moved to the States when she was a teenager, there was still a trace of an Italian accent in her speech.

"Nothing yet."

"Oooh. So bad." Angelica let out a long sigh. She was an expressive woman, with wavy black hair and eyes as blue as a summer sky. Her olive skin was flawless and her petite figure perfect for the bridal dresses she created and often modeled. "I'm sorry."

"Me, too."

"Well, I'm calling with some bad news. Two weddings in February have been canceled, and the clients don't want their dresses. Can you believe it? This late. One groom got cold feet and broke it off, and the other clients lost their venue and have to reschedule and now want a summer destination wedding, and this dress just won't do. Never mind that the bride gained forty pounds since the initial fitting and now claims the dress makes her 'look fat' and blames me. I tell you, dealing with bridezillas is not for the faint of heart. *Per l'amor di Dio!*"

For God's sake, spoken rapidly and under her breath, was one of Angelica's favorite phrases. Especially when she was frustrated. Which was often enough.

Angelica wasn't finished ranting. "They both want their deposits back, of course, but the dresses are nearly complete, and what are my chances of selling them—designed specifically for the brides?" She rattled off a further stream of Italian that Rebecca assumed was some form of swearing, but she couldn't be certain. "I'll have to sell them at a discount—that is, if I can. So I'll finish them and send you digital pictures that you can upload to the site and stress the discount?"

"No problem. I was about to head back."

"Here? To Seattle? When your sister is still missing?" Angelica asked, her tone almost accusing. "No, no, no. Family is everything. You should stay."

"I don't think there's any more that I can do."

"No? Surely you need to be there for her when she shows up . . ." Her voice trailed off, and Rebecca understood she meant *if* Megan showed up. "Someone in that town must know something. Someone always knows something they're not telling, but you can find out! And check into her boyfriends. They're always the ones, you know?"

She thought of James and wondered. His attitude did seem off. Should he be more concerned about Megan? He'd told Rebecca about their fight without the right amount of emotion, as if he were talking about someone else or spouting lines from a script. And yet he was found broken and bruised with scars that might never completely heal.

Or was that all in her head? Had James's reaction been spot-on and she, so close to the situation, was simply blind to the truth?

"She might have a secret lover," Angelica suggested.

"I don't know about that," Rebecca said, but, she supposed, anything was possible. For the thousandth time, she wondered about Megan and James's relationship. How had it started? What was it like? She might never know, but it still stung. Probably always would. Her sister and the man Rebecca had once loved. Had they ever discussed her? Laughed at her expense? Had he told her about their lovemaking? Even now, the thought could make her blush.

"You find out," Angelica instructed. "You can work from there. No problem. You know. I'll send you what you need, then I'm flying to L.A., looking at space not far from Rodeo Drive. Wouldn't that be something, to expand down there? Keep in touch, but stay, Rebecca. Your sister deserves it."

CHAPTER 29

Something didn't smell right.

Phoebe Matrix had lived long enough to know when things weren't right. She'd buried one husband and divorced two others, all of them tomcats who couldn't keep their privates in their pants. She'd been foolish to give her heart to any of them, though in truth it had worked out. Didn't she own this apartment building free and clear? Good thing too. You just couldn't count on Social Security to support you in your golden years.

Golden?

Ha!

That was a laugh.

Anyone who'd lived into their seventies knew that the whole idea of those fabulous retirement years was a fool's dream. She'd give anything, including the Cascadia Apartments—lock, stock, and barrel—for a good run at twenty or thirty again. And she wouldn't have married Marvin, Steve, or Charles . . . well, maybe Marvin again. She just would have played her cards differently and would never have let him drive by himself to Yosemite, where somewhere south of Bend, Oregon, his little Chevy Nova had been T-boned by a tractor trailer. No, sirree, she wouldn't have let him take that fateful trip again.

At the thought, she sketched the sign of the cross over her ample breasts and made her way to the living room, where Larry, who had proved far more loyal than any of her husbands, was in position on the back of the couch. His little nose was pressed to the glass, and he was growling, his fuzzy white fur practically standing on end.

Probably at the blonde in the upstairs studio. Sophia Russo. She was always coming and going, never staying put. Or that friend—or was it a relative, maybe a sister or cousin?—the woman about the same age as Sophia who sometimes stayed over, a dark-haired woman who was heavier, with dark eyes and glasses. She was really pushing the "temporary guest" rule. Phoebe had seen her a number of times and had actually run into her once when she'd been hauling out the trash from a unit that had just been vacated. She hadn't caught her name and was pretty certain she wasn't actually living with Sophia; that would definitely be in violation of the lease. Nor was James Cahill living in the building, but he'd been at the apartment a few times and spent the night. Phoebe had caught him leaving in the predawn hours at least twice before his girlfriend, that Megan Travers, had gone missing. Then again, he had his own place, and Phoebe wondered why they didn't just stay out there at the Christmas tree farm? It would be more private. Well, unless the girlfriend showed up when he was with Sophia.

It was all very odd. And interesting. Scandalously so.

Maybe Sophia and James had worked together to get rid of Megan? Could that be possible? Or was it reaching a bit, maybe from watching too many episodes of *Dateline* about missing or murdered women? Her last husband, Charles the Casanova, had thought as much and had even gone so far as to delete the shows she'd recorded. "Why get yourself all worked up over these old crimes?" he'd say in that all-knowing way of his. He'd always tried to tell her what to do. Well, they were long divorced. Good riddance to bad rubbish!

Now Phoebe gazed hard at Sophia's unit, where the living room window blinds were perpetually drawn. That was strange, too, she thought. And all the comings and goings . . . But that was the way of young girls, wasn't it? Hadn't she been forever on the go in her twenties? There had been a day when Phoebe was head of the Tri-City Twirlers in high school, a beauty who could toss a whirling baton twenty feet into the air and catch it in a swooping spin without once scuffing the white boots that were part of the twirling team's uniform. She'd been forever on the go with this friend and that boyfriend. "A whirlwind of a social butterfly," that's what her mother had called her. Who would have thought Phoebe O'Malley would be single and content to knit for hours and actually look forward to outsmarting those idiot contestants on *Jeopardy*?

"The folly of youth," she said, scratching Larry behind his big ears and peering into the snow-covered lot again. "Oh, for the love of St. Peter!" The asphalt was covered with a blanket of white, and that no-account renter in unit 4, Phil Dabrowski, who got a hundred dollars off his rent every month for keeping the parking lot clear of leaves, gravel, ice, snow, and whatever trash floated in, hadn't been out salting and shoveling the parking area.

And here came Sophia again, wheeling into the lot in her little gray car and sliding to a stop in front of her unit. She hadn't been gone but half an hour, and now she was back again. What was she up to?

Larry stiffened and gave a quick round of sharp barks as the girl—well, woman, really—unlocked the door of her unit and slammed the door shut behind her. Even though Sophia worked at Cahill's Christmas tree farm and the hotel attached to it, she didn't seem to have regular hours. But that was the way of it these days, lots of people actually worked from home, on their laptop computers, eating Cheetos and watching *The Bachelorette* or some other television show while they were "working." The world had changed.

She sat down in her favorite Queen Anne chair with her knitting, one eye on the window, and nearly called Dabrowski when she spied him, hunting cap with ear flaps buckled tight over his round head, a heavy camo-patterned jacket seeming to add another twenty pounds to his already rotund girth, crossing the parking lot. In one gloved hand, he held a bag of salt, and he started shaking it onto the icy lot just as the door to Sophia Russo's apartment opened again and she appeared. She'd changed quickly, out of jeans and a long gray jacket to a short skirt, tights, boots, and a tunic-like sweater. A long coat was slung over one arm, a large bag swinging from the other.

On the couch, Larry bristled and growled, his nose making little spots of fog on the window.

"It's all right," Phoebe told him and reached for her knitting basket, where she kept a ziplock bag of his favorite treats.

But Larry was having none of the liver-flavored morsels this morning. Stiff-bodied, he glared out the window as Sophia slid into her car and backed up quickly, missing Dabrowski by less than a foot.

In a hurry.

As ever.

Finally, the dog took the little snack from between her fingers and settled down on the back of the couch again, still watching, but more relaxed. Phoebe allowed herself a little snack as well from the candy dish she kept on the shelf too high for Larry to reach and popped five M&Ms into her mouth.

As the chocolate began to melt on her tongue, Phoebe recounted her stitches, then began knitting again, yet another baby blanket she was donating to the church, which would distribute it, along with her other finished projects—booties, hats, and sweaters—to the needy. Her hands flew, the needles clicked, the fuzzy pink blanket grew, and still she wondered just what it was about Sophia Russo that bothered her so.

Maybe she would have to do some more checking on the pretty blonde herself. After all, she could easily let herself into the apartment and poke around a bit. Honestly, it wouldn't be the first time and probably not the last. And she had the handy excuse of checking for frozen pipes if she was found out.

Phoebe considered it part of her job to make certain everything was on the up-and-up at the Cascadia Apartments.

No funny business. Not on Phoebe's watch.

And something about that Russo girl just wasn't right.

Phoebe felt it in her bones.

And Larry, bless his little heart, did too.

CHAPTER 30

As he sat behind the wheel of his idling SUV, James Cahill stared across the street at the Main Street Hotel, hoping to catch a glimpse of Rebecca. Like a love-sotted fool.

"Moron," he muttered as he noted her car was still in the hotel's lot and contemplated how he could see her again.

It was ridiculous.

Until this moment in time, he'd always known what he wanted.

And he'd gone after it. Usually with single-minded intent. From the time he'd been upright, he hadn't so much as walked but run to get what he was after—and usually, at least according to his parents, straight into trouble, as proven by the number of times he'd broken the law as a teenager. Worse yet, he'd crushed his mother and father by dropping out of college and working construction. Despite their disappointment, he'd been adept with a hammer and saw, could read architectural plans and schematics easily, and was quick to come up with innovative ideas and solutions to problems. He'd scraped and saved, borrowed and used the money he'd already inherited, a small portion of what he would someday come into, to buy forty acres of land here in the foothills of the Cascades and start his own construction company. Within a few years, he was where he was today. Self-made and proud of it.

But now everything he'd struggled for wasn't enough.

Because of Rebecca.

That had been a mistake.

Even if it couldn't have been avoided.

Which really got under his skin.

So now here he was, sitting in his idling Explorer, coffee getting cold in the cup holder, while he drummed his fingers on the steering wheel.

And contemplated what he did or did not want.

"Hell," he muttered, and beside him, on the passenger seat, Ralph snorted as if agreeing.

James had been leaving the doctor's office, driving home, when his mother had called. Again. Figuring he'd put her off long enough, he pulled over in the loading zone of a furniture store, took the call, and talked to her for ten minutes, answering her questions about how he was doing and asking the right ones about his sisters. He hadn't realized until he'd disconnected and let the phone slide into the cup holder that the furniture store was across the street from the back of the hotel, where Rebecca's white Subaru was parked in the lot.

Had that been a subconscious decision?

Picking up his cell again, he was about to punch in her number when the phone rang in his hand, and he saw the number affiliated with a Seattle TV station.

He didn't answer and let voice mail do the honors. Then, before he could talk himself out of it, he punched in Rebecca's number.

She didn't pick up.

He didn't leave a message—make that *another* message. He'd already recorded a voice-mail request that she call him. She hadn't. Nor had she responded to either of his two texts.

It didn't take a rocket scientist to realize she didn't want to see him.

Which stung.

And which, he realized, his lips twisting bitterly, was pretty damned ironic, all things considered. But, damn, the more she rebuffed him, the more interested he became.

Then there was the problem with Megan. Where the hell was she? He was getting more worried about her with each passing day. What he remembered of their last fight was horrid. How angry she'd been. How vicious. How upset.

And it was his own damned fault.

He should never have taken up with her in the first place, never believed her lies.

"You're going to regret this."

Her words haunted him.

And he wondered, if she did happen to show up again, which he hoped for, how he would explain about his rekindled interest in Rebecca. Not that it was a problem currently, considering Rebecca's attitude toward him. Nonetheless, when Megan found out, she'd hit the roof.

If Megan found out, he reminded himself.

There was a chance she would never return.

And as time went on, the thought that she might be dead burned through his brain.

He closed his eyes.

What the hell had happened to her? Less and less he believed her disappearance was an act. More and more he feared something awful had happened to her.

What about Sophia? She still thinks you're a couple. You're not doing much to dissuade her. And Jennifer? Don't forget her. Didn't she call you the week before Megan went missing? Despite your amnesia, you didn't forget that, did you?

"Shit."

Beside him, Ralph pressed his nose to the passenger window and whined.

It was time to go. James slugged back the remainder of the coffee that he'd bought at the drive-thru kiosk a block from the clinic. He hadn't exactly been given a clean bill of health, but Dr. Monroe had told him he could ditch the sling, for the most part, and suggested he might want to get a haircut to even things up; his wound was healing as expected.

James cast a glance at himself in the mirror and decided he looked like crap. A military buzz cut was the only thing that would "even things up." Well, so be it.

He crushed the paper cup, tossed it on the floor, and hazarded another glance at the hotel.

So close, but so far away.

Light-years.

He should just let it go.

Let *her* go.

Like he had before.

All for Megan. Jesus, he'd been an ass. He scraped a hand over his head and wondered what the hell had happened to Rebecca's sister.

And he felt bad. Because he hadn't realized how serious her leaving had been. Even after he'd regained his memory, he'd believed she had just thrown a tantrum, made a scene, hidden out to lick her wounds and make him realize how much he needed her—wanted her.

But he'd been wrong.

And now he was scared, worried about her.

Where could she be?

Dead, Cahill, she could be dead.

Ever since he'd become convinced that her disappearance wasn't an act, she'd been like a ghost, teasing his subconscious, playing tricks on him, coming to mind at the most unlikely of times.

A sharp rap on the side window brought him back to the here and now. A beefy guy in a trucker's cap and jeans jacket had his face to the glass. James rolled down his window as the guy pointed a gloved hand at the loading-zone sign.

"Hey, buddy," he said. "Can't you read?"

Then James noticed the delivery truck double-parked on the street behind him, another burly guy behind the wheel glaring at him.

"Sorry."

"Hey, aren't you—?"

James didn't wait, just rolled the window up, shoved his Explorer into gear, and slipped into the lane in front of the truck. This was getting worse. The publicity behind Megan's going missing was intensifying. And then there was his suspicion that the police thought he was lying, that he'd what? Hurt, maimed, or killed Megan, then faked his own injury, even when witnesses had seen her drive away from his house?

No, they think you staged the whole thing, that you had an accomplice who did the dirty deed while you had a ready-made alibi.

His jaw tightened as he stopped at an intersection. A woman pushing a baby stroller stepped into the crosswalk. He waited, squinting into the sun, and reached for his sunglasses in the console. They were missing, and he was thinking maybe the cops had taken them or misplaced them when they'd searched his vehicle before he remembered he'd left them at the office.

He flipped down his visor, picked up his phone, and after a second's hesitation, punched in a familiar number, then, using his Bluetooth, waited until Rowdy Crocker picked up. Which took a while.

"Yeah? Cahill?" he finally answered as James eased through the intersection.

"Right."

"I figured you'd be calling. Been catching you on the evening news. Wow, brother, you've really got yourself in a mess this time."

"The reason I decided to ring you up."

"What do you want me to do?"

"Find Megan Travers."

There was a laugh on the other end. "Because the police can't?"

"Right." He turned onto the highway leading south, out of town, and hit the gas. "They seem to think I had something to do with it."

There was a pause. "I assume you didn't."

"Jesus, Rowdy, would I be calling you if I had?"

"Rumor has it your memory of that night isn't all it's cracked up to be."

"I didn't do anything other than get into a fight with her and end up on the losing end," James said, irritated. Rowdy was, and always would be, an ass. But a smart, highly skilled ass who had spent time with military intelligence, a decision that helped him get out of trouble when he'd been a teenage computer hacker. Now he was a sometimes PI, sometimes surfer, sometimes completely off the radar.

"I'm not cheap," Rowdy reminded him as James sped past snow-covered fields that glittered under the December sun.

"I don't care."

"Good, cuz you really do get what you pay for."

"Just help me out on this."

"Okay, I'm on the clock. I'll dig up what I can, call you, and tell you if I need any more info."

"Good."

Rowdy asked a series of questions about Megan, and James filled him in as best he could.

"What about anyone else? Info on . . . another girlfriend, maybe?"

James hesitated, then admitted that yes, he had been seeing Sophia, and that there had been other women, including Gus's sister, Jennifer, and, well . . . Rebecca.

He was rewarded with a long whistle. "Have you ever thought of slowing down with the women?" Rowdy asked.

"A time or two," James said dryly.

"Just a thought."

"I'll remember that."

"Good," Rowdy said. "Just one last thing."

"Shoot."

A pause.

"You are innocent, right?"

The muscles in the back of James's neck tensed, and he imagined Rowdy's cynical smile partially hidden by three days' growth of beard shadow. "Again, yes."

"Okay."

"Just do what you can."

"You got it." And then the connection was cut off, and he was left to brood and squint while following a service truck for the local propane distributor. Once he reached the shop, he parked between a van for Riggs Crossing Electric and Bobby's old pickup. A headache was forming behind his eyes, but he ignored it as he cut the engine and stepped outside.

Ralph sprang from the interior to chase a squirrel up a spruce tree, only to whine at the base as the squirrel chattered at him from an upper limb.

"Leave it," James commanded, knowing the squirrel was ever elusive.

Just like Rebecca.

No, Rebecca wasn't elusive. He'd had his chance with her. He'd blown it.

As he walked through the open door, a wall of heat and a cacophony of sounds hit him full in the face. Somewhere beneath the buzz of saws, the rapid-fire tattoo of nail guns, and the hiss of a compressor, he heard the strains of "Roxanne" by The Police.

The crews were in full swing, men and women in hard hats and safety glasses, moving from one site to the other as they worked on three houses in varying stages of construction. The sleek, ultra-modern abode, made primarily from a shipping container, was nearly finished. The second, the ski cabin, was on its platform awaiting tile, and the third, a cottage with a "coastal vibe" requested by the client, was only in the framing stage.

Bobby was in deep conversation with two workers. One was a burly man holding a rolled-up set of plans in his gloved hands, and he stood next to a petite woman wearing jeans, a plaid shirt, and a tool belt. They were locked in a deep discussion, bordering on an argument, that James wanted no part of. But he caught Bobby's eye, and the foreman tilted his chin in greeting as James headed up the stairs to the office. By the time he'd reached the landing, his dog had whipped past him to wait at the door.

"No luck?" James asked the shepherd and took the time to scratch Ralph behind his ears. "Believe me, I know the feeling."

He unlocked the office and glanced down at the houses under construction, as he had a thousand times. He wondered if things were finally getting back to normal.

Yeah, right. Who're you kidding, Cahill? Until Megan turns up, there is no normal.

In his mind's eye, her face, clear as day, came into view, and he remembered her playful smile that could turn a little cruel at times and the freckles that spattered her nose when her makeup had worn thin . . .

That caused him to stop for a moment, and he thought, just for a bit, that it was important. But as close to the surface as the idea was, it quickly submerged again. The muscles in his neck tensed. Though most of his memories were distinct, like Megan advancing upon him during their last fight, some were still unclear, murky recollections hanging in the shadows that had yet to come to the fore. He sensed they were important, yet nothing he could put his finger on, which was the problem. And he was sick to death of trying to figure it out, almost as sick as he was of the reporters constantly calling or accosting him on the street.

The mystery surrounding Megan's disappearance had gone from a local story to statewide and even some national interest, and that "Find Megan" campaign all over social media had gotten all of the conspiracy theorists chatting, commenting, tweeting, or whatever; many of them seemed to think he was not only a person of interest, but the mastermind behind his girlfriend's disappearance. They'd dug into his life, learned about the family fortune and all of the scandals involving the Cahills of San Francisco, so they'd quickly cast him into the same pit as the murderous psychos in his family. He felt as if the press had already tried and convicted him, and that damned Charity Spritz was the worst of the lot.

And then there was Sophia.

He had to end it with her.

Whether he liked it or not, his life was quickly becoming part of a media circus that translated into his own personal nightmare.

But he had to keep moving forward . . . though it would be best to wait until he heard back from Rowdy.

He tossed his keys onto the desk and noted his sunglasses weren't where he'd thought he'd left them. A quick scan of the desktop didn't help, but he couldn't worry about anything so trivial.

He sat at his desk and went through all the old messages that had piled up on his cell phone while it had been with the police. He cringed at the thought of the cops digging through his personal stuff. Nothing was too private for their prying eyes.

Jaw set, he deleted calls from reporters and friends and separated out the business calls before tackling the e-mails just as a scream ripped up the stairs.

"Yeeeeowww! Fuck! Fuck! *Fuck!* Son of a bitch! Son of a fucking bitch!"

What?

James shot to his feet.

Rounded the desk.

Stared out the window with a view of the shop.

Men and women abandoned their stations. Several hopped from the trailer with the ski cottage to rush toward the back of the shop. James focused on the back wall. On the wet saw.

Shit!

A man, doubled over, was at the center of the commotion.

Gus Jardine.

His face ashen and twisted in agony, he was holding his right hand with the other. Blood flowed through his fingers, torn flesh, and exposed bone.

"Jesus." James flew down the stairs, where the saws, hammers, and nail guns had stopped their din. Now it was just sharp conversation and Bon Jovi's "Livin' on a Prayer."

A woman shouted, "Someone call nine-one-one!"

"On it!" Bobby Knowlton already had a phone pressed to his ear.

"Oh, holy shit, look at all that blood," another man yelled. "Gus! You okay?"

James pushed through the crowd that had gathered around the injured man. "What happened?"

"For Christ's sake, Cahill. Are you fuckin' blind? What the fuck does it look like? I cut my fuckin' hand," Jardine said, panicked, black hair falling over his eyes. "Jesus."

Somehow Betsy Idalgo, an electrician who'd been working on one of the houses, came up with a clean towel. "Let's clean it up. See what we've got? Let me see."

"Fuck off! I need an ambulance!" Gus was screaming, snapping the towel from her and wrapping it over his arm, but not letting her look at the wound.

"Hey, man, I was an EMT," she said, her face earnest and firm. "I can help."

James said to Gus, "Let her help."

"Fuck off, Cahill. This is all your fault!"

Tires screeched through the open barn doors.

James looked up and spied an older-model Chevy Tahoe sliding to a stop. The driver, Leon Palleja, leaned across the passenger seat and threw open the door. "Get him in here!" he yelled. "I'll drive."

James said, "Bobby's calling nine-one-one."

"Shit, that'll take forever." Gus, cradling his bleeding arm, barreled through the crowd.

James was on his heels. "I'm coming with," he said to Leon.

"I told you to fuck off!" Gus growled. "Oh, shit, this hurts like a mother!" and he nearly fell into the front seat of the SUV.

"He's bleeding. Bad," Leon said, working with James to strap Gus in.

Gus was sweating. Breathing hard. A wild look in his eyes. "Let's fuckin' go!"

James slammed the passenger door. Got into the back.

Bobby Knowlton ran out of the building. "Ambulance is on its way."

"Call 'em off. Let 'em know we don't need them," James said. "Then you, Bobby, meet us at the hospital. I'll need a ride back. We'll be there in twenty minutes."

"Fifteen." Leon hit the gas as James yanked his door shut. "Hang on!" Leon shoved his truck into drive, cut a tight circle, and sped along the lane, wheels spinning gravel, the vehicle bouncing over potholes, Jardine moaning and cursing in the passenger seat. By the time James had buckled up, Leon had turned onto the county road and was speeding north toward town. Snow-covered fields flew by, fence posts a blur.

"This is your fault," Gus accused, twisting his head around to peer at James with narrowed, pained eyes.

"So you said."

"Your safety standards are for shit!"

"I comply with—"

"You don't comply with crap!" Jardine spat at James, then turned to Palleja. "Jesus, Leon, can we get there already? I'm dying over here." He sent the driver a hard stare even though Leon was ignoring the speed limit, his Chevy Tahoe skating over the road, sliding around corners, passing slower-moving vehicles where he could.

"You fucked me up, Cahill," Jardine repeated. "And I'm going to sue your ass."

Leon whispered something in Spanish under his breath that sounded like *imbécil desagradecido,* which, loosely translated, meant "ungrateful moron," James thought, though either Gus hadn't heard Leon or didn't understand the phrase because he just moaned and leaned against the window, the white towel wrapped over his hand now red.

Jardine was in too much pain to be making any sense, too scared. Let him rant and rave.

Once they'd crossed the bridge, the town came into view, and Leon took a side street, turned two corners, and cut through an alley to avoid the clog of traffic in the middle of town.

The hospital loomed into view.

Gus moaned as Leon slowed to turn into the lane that stretched under the emergency room's canopy. Gus opened the door while the Tahoe was still rolling.

"Hey, man, hold up!" Leon stood on the brakes. The Chevy jerked to a halt. "What the hell? You tryin' to kill yourself? *Dios!*"

"Get me out!" Jardine ordered, seeming not to care about the injuries he could have sustained if his seat belt had failed and he'd tumbled onto the pavement.

"I got him." James was out of the back seat in an instant. He attempted to help Jardine inside.

Gus was having none of it. "Didn't I tell you to leave me the fuck alone?" he snarled, his face pale. Holding his bleeding hand, blood covering the towel and smeared all over his shirt and jeans, he walked unsteadily through the sliding doors of the ER to announce, "I need help. Now."

"You sure do. Let's get it," said a woman behind a wide, curved desk as she picked up a phone.

Within seconds, a male nurse in his late twenties wearing pale blue scrubs hustled to the desk. He was tall, but rangy, his brown hair clipped to stubble, his hawkish eyes intense.

"Let's get you back here," the nurse said to Gus, then to James, "If you can see to the paperwork . . ."

"He doesn't know nothin' about me!" Gus sputtered and sent a hateful look over his shoulder as if James had personally harmed him. "I'm gonna sue you, you fuckin' bastard," he said again, and a smattering of people in the waiting room looked up from what they were doing to watch. "Ya hear me?" Jardine was bellowing. "I'm gonna sue your ass! Count on it." With his good hand, he jabbed a blood-stained finger at James as he was being herded through a wide door by the nurse.

James felt the gazes of the curious land on him. From a short couch, a thirtysomething man was trying to keep an energetic toddler entertained, but he kept glancing up at James, while a woman in her sixties in a nearby chair had her gaze fixed on both him and the information desk. Even the worried-looking elderly couple seated on linked chairs near a ficus tree looked up. They were huddled together while talking in hushed tones, the woman dabbing at her eyes, but their conversation had stopped as Gus began screaming out invectives.

Leon was hovering nearby. "You have a ride coming? Bobby?"

"Yeah. You can go back to work," said James.

"Okay." He gnawed on his lip. "But there's something I think you should know."

"What is it?"

Leon's dark eyes shifted from one side to the other. "It's about Gus. I saw him a little earlier, before he went to the saw and . . ." Leon rubbed a hand over his forehead as if he wasn't certain he should continue.

"And—?" James said.

"And . . . I don't know. I just caught a glimpse of his hand, but I think it was fucked up before he went to the saw."

"What do you mean?"

"Just that it didn't look right. Like maybe it was swollen or bruised, so maybe he shouldn't have been working, you know. Maybe he messed up because his grip was off . . . oh, *qué carajo* . . . what the fuck."

"You think?" James asked.

"I don't know, man, but it seems like now he's trying to blame you."

"Why?"

"You heard him. A lawsuit. Easy money." Then, as if he'd said too much, Leon added, "I'd better go," and took off for the sliding doors. James was tossing over what he'd said when he heard a quiet cough.

"Ooo-kay," the woman behind the desk said, bringing his attention back to her. "Why don't we get started? We can begin with his personal information. As much of it as you know. I'll confirm with him later." The ID tag hanging from a lanyard around her neck indicated she was Sharon Nader, but the picture on the badge was barely recognizable as she'd cut and changed her hair color from a medium brown to flaming red, gained at least thirty pounds, and added cat's-eye glasses. "Have a seat."

"He's right about the fact that I don't know a lot about him," James admitted.

"How are you related?"

"I'm his boss. The accident happened in my shop."

"Well, then, you can tell me whatever information you know. He'll fill in the blanks." She glanced up and added, "He seems pretty verbal."

James nodded. "As I said, he works for me. At Cahill Industries. In the tiny house division."

And that's when it clicked. She finally looked up from her computer monitor enough to connect the dots. Her eyebrows quirked up over the rims of her glasses as she took in his lopsided haircut, the head stitches, and the claw marks still visible beneath his beard.

He wasn't surprised. Everyone in town knew he was the last person to have seen Megan Travers in Riggs Crossing before she went missing, and he assumed all of the employees at Valley General had known he'd been a patient there recently as well.

"Okay, Mr. Cahill," she said a little more coolly, her smile tighter. "Let's start with his name."

CHAPTER 31

The old nun who introduced herself as Sister Rosemarie was as much a sentry as a principal, Rivers thought when she introduced herself at St. Ignatius Elementary School in Marysville. Her expression was as severe as the coming storm. In a long navy skirt, matching cardigan over a white blouse, and sensible boots, she studied their IDs and badges with suspicious, icy eyes, then peered at each of them over the tops of half-glasses perched on a hawkish nose and held in place by a beaded chain that looped around her neck.

"Ms. Korpi is expecting you?" she asked.

"Yes."

"All right then. I'll take you to her room. This way." The end of a rosary dangled from one of the pockets in her voluminous skirt as she led them briskly past a statue of the saint for whom the school was named and then headed up a short staircase and down a corridor, where their footsteps echoed on the worn floor.

She paused by the open door to room 8. "In here," she said and led them inside a cluttered room filled with tiny desks, science projects, and artwork. "Ms. Korpi?"

A woman of about thirty was standing between a cluttered desk and the whiteboard stretching across the front wall. Bible verses were scripted on all the walls, jingle bells were hanging in strips from the ceiling and artwork was everywhere. In gray slacks and a pink sweater, she was holding a cell phone to one ear and looked up quickly as they entered, holding up a finger. "Oh, geez," she said into the phone. "What is it with him? . . . But he's okay? . . . When will he get there?" She glanced up at the clock as Rivers surveyed the room.

Windows ran along one side, each decorated with a cut-out angel and fake snow. A terrarium was positioned on the back wall near a sink, and a small Christmas tree decorated with paper ornaments listed near a row of hooks near the door.

Jennifer was ending her call. "Sure. I've got a few things to take care of and then, yeah, I'll be there . . . okay. Sure . . . I'll call . . . Thanks, Tabby, I'll talk to you later." Then she disconnected and stuffed the phone into the pocket of her slacks. "I'm sorry."

Sister Rosemarie said, "Everything okay?"

"I think so. Or maybe not. No one knows." She was obviously upset. "My sister . . . That was Tabitha on the phone, and she was calling about our brother, Gus. According to Tabby, he was in an accident at work. A bad one, got his hand caught in a saw." She visibly cringed at the words. "I guess his hand is pretty messed up, possible nerve damage, and he could lose a finger or two. The local hospital is sending him to a specialist in Seattle. A hand guy." She glanced at the clock mounted over the door again. "I said I'd go over and be with him."

"I'll put him in my prayers," the nun said, her fingertips flicking to the beads of the rosary draped from her pocket, then, as if remembering her mission, said, "This is Detective Rivers and Detective Mendoza. They said you were expecting them."

"Yes." Korpi glanced at the clock over the door. "I am."

"Do you want me to stay?" the principal asked.

"Oh, no . . . no, it's fine," Korpi said, though she looked like a doe caught in the headlights of a fast-approaching semi.

"Then I'll be in my office."

"Thanks."

With a final disparaging glance at the detectives, Sister Rosemarie swept out of the room, her boots clipping down the hallway, the rosary rattling.

"Sorry . . ." Korpi said to the detectives. "She doesn't like any sort of trouble."

"No trouble," Mendoza assured her.

"Well, you are the police, and to Sister Rosemarie that means trouble. One of the parents might see. Oh, the scandal." Then she heard herself and added, "Forget I said that," as she walked to the door and pulled it shut. "Sorry, I'm a little . . ."

Nervous, Rivers thought, and remembered that one of the hairs found in James Cahill's bedroom belonged to a dark-haired woman. Korpi's own hair was a shade about the color of coffee, her eyes big and brown.

". . . distracted, because of Gus. Would you like to sit down?" Then she looked at Rivers's over-six-foot frame and glanced at the small desks. "We could go to the library if you'd like to sit down."

"This is fine," Rivers assured her. He wanted her to be as comfortable as possible and thought the classroom would provide more privacy.

"Okay, good. It's weird, you know, that you're here to talk about James, and Gus works for James and got hurt and . . . small world, I guess. Sometimes I think the universe is trying to tell me something. Or maybe God," she added, as if realizing she was in a parochial school.

"How so?" Mendoza asked.

"Well, it's kind of odd, y'know? You all coming here from Riggs Crossing to ask about James Cahill and Gus getting hurt at his shop right before you get here. His shop in Riggs Crossing. I mean, what a ko-ink-ee-dink!"

Maybe. Rivers considered it, but really didn't put much faith in coincidence.

"So what is it you want to know?" Korpi asked as she made her way back to her desk and leaned a hip on the edge. "Oh, right. About my 'relationship' with James." She made air quotes, her fingertips the same shade as her sweater. "Well, if you want to know the truth, it was the biggest mistake of my life."

"How so?" Mendoza asked, and Rivers guessed that she was recording as her phone was in her hand.

Korpi arched an eyebrow at Mendoza. "You've met him. He's what Gus calls a 'chick magnet,' which I think really means big trouble. We didn't date that long, but it certainly wasn't exclusive, at least not on his part. There were always women coming out of the woodwork." Her lips twisted wryly. "Not only is he too handsome for his own good, but he's got money, and that . . . oh, it's stupid I know, but he has that bad boy attitude that some women find so attractive."

"Is that what attracted you?" Rivers said.

"No." Then, "Maybe." With a sigh she shook her head. "I really don't know. He was different from the other men I'd dated, and yeah, his don't-give-a-sh—damn attitude was refreshing. He seemed more real, you know, but looking back, maybe I was being played. Anyway, it didn't last all that long."

"Because of Rebecca Travers?"

She lifted a shoulder. "Maybe she was a symptom and not the cause, y'know. James doesn't seem to be a one-woman kind of guy."

Rivers asked, "How did you meet?"

"I already told this to the Marysville cops."

"I know," Mendoza said, "but humor us."

She picked up a purple tension ball from her desk, then realized what she was doing and dropped it quickly. It landed between one of three coffee cups and a stack of papers. "We knew each other as kids when my father worked for his family and he'd come to visit, and then we reconnected when Gus took the job at his shop last year. At the time, I thought it was 'fate,'" she admitted ruefully, "but now I realize it was all just a big, fat mistake." She sounded bitter, heard herself, and said, "I just wish this was over. I just hate being involved."

"So, how did you reconnect?"

"Oh. I thought that was pretty obvious. Gus introduced us. Well, technically reintroduced us. We all got together for drinks, and James and I clicked and . . . well, you know . . . one thing led to another. Before I could think twice about it, we were dating and yeah, I was fantasizing about being in love. Then along came Rebecca Travers, and"—she slapped her hands together—"poof. That was that. What do they say? 'Over before it really began'? Well, that's how it felt."

Rivers thought she felt a little worse than she was admitting and decided to push it. "So where were you on the night Megan Travers went missing?"

Jennifer Korpi blinked, surprised. "You think I had something to do with that? Really? It wasn't Megan who broke us up. It was that sister of hers—Rebecca. I thought I made that clear a second ago." Jennifer's voice held more than a smidgeon of irritation, and she let out a huff of disgusted air. "As to your question. I was with Gus the night Megan went missing. We grabbed a pizza at Mario's. Ate it back at his place and watched the game. The Hawks were on."

Rivers knew the Seahawks had been playing the Forty-Niners. He'd watched the Seattle team lose the lead and go down in the fourth quarter.

Jennifer wasn't finished. "As I said, I already told the Marysville police about it. Wait." She stopped as if a sudden thought struck her. "Didn't Gus back me up?"

"He did." Mendoza was nodding.

"Well . . . ?" Holding up a hand as if that explained everything, she looked at Rivers, silently accusing him of being dumb as a stone not to come up with what she considered an obvious conclusion. Her phone buzzed, and she said, "Excuse me, I really have to take this," then answered quickly and walked to a corner of the room, turning her back on them. Mendoza watched her, while Rivers moved around a bit. He walked to her desk and saw a still-wet tea bag in one of the coffee cups as he heard her part of the conversation. "Hey, I'm with the police now . . . yeah, the missing woman thing . . . soon, I think . . ."

He noticed the tension ball and, shifting his body so that his back was a shield and neither woman could see his actions, plucked the purple sphere nimbly from her desk and slipped it into his pocket before continuing through the room. A glance up confirmed what he'd thought—no cameras surveying the room. Walking along the windows, where the rain peppered the glass and the tape on a paper angel was failing, one of its wings sagging, he eavesdropped on the private conversation.

"Yeah, I know . . . won't be long. Then I need to run to the hospital. Gus was in an accident . . . I think he'll be okay. But I really have to go now," Jennifer was saying. "Yeah. Love you too." She clicked off as Rivers reached the leaning Christmas tree and terrarium. The lizard inside blinked his eyes slowly.

"Sorry," Jennifer was saying as Mendoza scanned her phone and Rivers wended his way back through the desks to take up his place near her desk. "He's expecting a ride. Car in the shop." Then before anyone could ask, she added, "Harry Sinclaire. My boyfriend. I met him last year." She inched her chin up a bit, a little proud—the spurned woman getting a little of her own back. "Kind of ironic, as I met him when I was still with James. Harry was buying one of those tiny houses James builds for a mountain cabin. He's a great guy, by the way. Harry, that is. And yes, if you want to know the truth, he helped me get over James."

Was she? Really over James Cahill? Something about her attitude seemed off for a woman who'd moved on. When they'd first walked into the room, she'd seemed scared, but sometimes that happened with cops. Now she was almost smug. Her phone rang again. "Oh, geez. It's Tabitha again. Probably calling with an update on Gus." She bit her lip. "I didn't know this would take this long."

Mendoza said, "I think we got everything we needed." She checked with Rivers, who gave a swift nod. "Thanks for your time, and if you think of anything else that might help with the investigation, give us a call." She slid a card into the teacher's hand.

"Like I said, I don't even know her."

Mendoza smiled. "Just in case."

"Okay." Jennifer nodded and answered the phone as they walked out of the room, down the hallway to slip past the somber statue of St. Ignatius and the even more dour visage of Sister Rosemarie standing behind the counter in the school office. Upon spying their approach, she flew out of the office to unlock the doors and escort them outside to stand under the portico. Winter dusk was settling in early, the security lights in the parking area beginning to glow, a persistent rain falling from low-hanging clouds, their Jeep one of only a few vehicles in the lot.

"I trust you got everything you need," the nun said, frowning as she glanced at the county-issued SUV with its light bar and police markings.

"We're good," Mendoza said.

Rivers nodded and added, "Thanks," as the wind whipped Sister Rosemarie's skirts and rain gurgled in the gutters.

"Let me know if you need to return."

"Will do." Mendoza flipped up the hood of her jacket while skirting puddles on the way to the Jeep. Rivers thought he heard her mutter, "Fat chance," under her breath, but he couldn't be certain.

As he slid behind the wheel and Mendoza strapped herself into the seat belt, he asked, "So, what did you think?"

"Not sure," she admitted as the buckle snapped into place just as Rivers started the engine. "Everything checks out." She chewed on her lower lip. "I don't know . . ."

"Too much of a coincidence that her brother works for James?"

"She seemed to think so."

"But—?" He drove onto the side street and flipped on the wipers.

"But Riggs Crossing is a small town. James Cahill is a major employer in the area. It's not that odd."

He squinted against the headlights from oncoming traffic. There was something about the conversation that nagged at him, scratched at his brain, but he didn't know what. Maybe it wasn't so much what was said as how it was said.

As he turned onto a main road leading east out of the city, he wished he could've had a few minutes alone in Jennifer Korpi's classroom, to stand amid the jingle bells, paper angels, and Bible verses, to delve deep and pick up any dark images submerged beneath all the Christmas cheer. Something didn't feel right in there, but he doubted if the gatekeeper of St. Ignatius Elementary, Sister Rosemarie, would allow him inside or give him free rein in the classroom, and he wasn't about to break in.

He didn't have to.

He had her tension ball in his pocket.

CHAPTER 32

Willow summoned her strength.

Then quietly, holding her breath, slipped through the back door of James's house.

Her heart pounded, and her pulse was jumping as she stood in the kitchen, straining to hear even the smallest of noises, any sign of life within the darkened interior. Not from James; she knew he was at the hospital because of Gus's accident—the news of him nearly cutting off his hand had spread like wildfire through the shop, inn, and Christmas tree farm. But what about the dog?

Biting her lip, she stepped noiselessly across the hardwood. She half-expected the shepherd to come barking and snarling from some hidden corner of the house, but she heard no sound of toenails clicking rapidly on the floor, no low menacing growl, just the hum of the refrigerator and the soft rumble of an old furnace pushing air through the ancient vents.

She eased into the kitchen and through the dining area.

Slowly, her eyes adjusted to the half-light, a bit of illumination from a front porch light seeping through the windows to give the interior a ghostly glow.

She had a right to be here.

Earlier, she and that obnoxious Sophia had been here, cleaning the place—washing, scrubbing, vacuuming, even changing the bedding. Sophia had been in charge. Bossing her around. God, that woman could be a bitch when she wanted to be. Some of the time, she was actually easy to get along with, but cross her and you awakened a monster. And she was secretive. Willow had seen her with her sister when the sister had dropped her off at work one day, but Sophia never wanted to talk about her. Usually chatty, she just clammed up. A real Dr. Jekyll and Mr. Hyde. She was beautiful, of course, but other than that, Willow couldn't fathom what James saw in her. Willow had said as much to Zena, which had probably been a mistake, because Zena was always running off her mouth and Zena knew that Willow was in love with James. Oh, well, soon the world would know.

It turned Willow's stomach to be so subservient to Sophia, to allow Sophia to boss her around, but she told herself it was temporary. Willow just had to bide her time. Besides, she had a secret. She'd been in this house before. A few times. But always by herself. Always when James and the dog were away.

He'd never known.

She just wanted to spend a little time alone in James's home, to fantasize what it would be like if she were his lover—no, more than that, if she were his wife. Even though he barely knew her, that would change, she would make certain of it.

And it wasn't as if she hadn't played out this fantasy before.

That will change, my love.

Except now there was another problem. She had to deal with not only Sophia, but Rebecca Travers as well. Willow had hoped that since Megan wasn't around, James might finally notice her, but of course that had backfired. Sophia was all over him, and James had this odd fascination with Rebecca.

Willow frowned at that, felt bile rise up in her throat. Sophia had let it slip that James had once, fleetingly, dated Rebecca. Had he fucked her? Probably. Just like he was still doing with Sophia. It made Willow sick, but she reminded herself that Rebecca and Sophia were just passing fancies. Just like Megan. Once they too were out of the picture . . .

Scraaape.

Her heart leapt to her throat.

What the hell was that?

So close!

So damned close!

She froze.

Maybe she should leave . . .

Scraape!

Again, the horrid sound.

Her heart knocking wildly, she looked over her shoulder and—

Scraape!

Startled, she jumped, then noticed a branch moving against the panes, grating across the glass.

Oh. God.

She tried to calm herself, then kept going, easing up the stairs, which seemed to creak loudly with each of her footsteps. What if she were wrong about being alone here? What if James had returned and parked in the garage—she hadn't double-checked there—and even now was resting in his bedroom?

But the dog—the dog would have heard her, she reminded herself, every one of her nerves strung tight. No, she was the sole person here. The weird vibe she was feeling, that someone was watching her, that someone was actually in the house, was all in her head, her own paranoia at sneaking around uninvited.

On the upper story, she slipped into his room, where the light was even dimmer. Tiny bits of illumination filtered from the lamp on the front porch and reflected on the snow-covered yard.

She ran her fingers over the comforter on his freshly made bed, a task Sophia had insisted upon doing by herself.

Fine.

She hesitated at the head of the bed.

Do it. Do it now!

Almost angrily, she threw back the covers, exposing the sheets. From the front pocket of her sweatshirt, she retrieved the gun, James's pistol, which she'd taken on an earlier visit to his dining room—not stolen, just borrowed—and loaded with a clip she'd located in a separate drawer.

A bullet was definitely in the chamber.

Carefully, she laid the Glock on a side table before stripping out of her hoodie, sweater, and ski pants and allowing the cold air in the bedroom to caress her skin. She toed off her boots and socks, then, her hair uncoiling in a rope down her back, she fell onto the bed, lying upon the cool sheets, *his* sheets, staring up at the ceiling, *his* ceiling in this, *his* room.

Slowly, Willow let out her breath.

This was so right. Where she was supposed to be.

She imagined him with her, his hands on her skin, skimming over her abdomen and breasts. Her nipples tightened, and to enhance her pleasure, she reached for the pistol, curled her fingers around it, and with her finger on the trigger, slid the Glock over her body. Cool polymer, so like steel it felt the same, slid up her legs and over her waist. Fear and lust, excitement and desire coursed through her blood, pounding in her brain.

Perspiration dotted her forehead and dampened her spine.

Stretching, she licked her lips, considering the feel of James's mouth, hard and demanding, upon hers. Her breathing became shallow as she undulated, and she moved the muzzle of the gun downward again, past her navel.

Imagining she was with James . . . She could almost taste him, feel him . . . ooh.

As she touched herself, she felt the first spasm of pleasure rip through her body.

Then the next . . .

She dropped the gun, her fingers digging into the sheets.

"James!" she cried out, bursting with desire. She writhed and shivered. And then . . . and then . . . and then . . . and then the frustration as she remembered she was alone.

Tears stung her eyes.

How pathetic.

She sniffed. Refused to cry.

No more.

She wouldn't allow herself to be the victim, not again. Not ever.

Rolling over, she buried face deep into his pillow and breathed deeply. But she couldn't smell his scent. No remnant of aftershave or male musk. Nope. Just the irritating fragrance of a clean pillowcase.

Nothing was working today!

Her fantasy just wasn't complete.

Annoyed, she sat up and noticed that a hair had escaped from her braid and lay against the stark white of his pillowcase. She almost swept it away, but thinking twice, decided to leave it.

For James to find.

Or Sophia?

Or Rebecca?

The vengeful cockles of her heart warmed.

Surely, James's interest in Megan's sister was fleeting, maybe just the result of some weird need to comfort her, possibly even because he felt guilty about Megan going missing.

Eventually, though, he would come to his senses.

Eventually, he would understand that he and Willow were destined to be together.

Eventually, Willow thought, he would be hers.

But she would have to be patient. As she'd been all of her twenty-two years. Always overlooked, always outshone, never in the spotlight. Especially when her sister was around. From her birth, she'd never measured up, had never been as smart, or as cute or as charming as . . .

Don't go there.

Pushing onto her elbows, Willow reminded herself it was time to leave. If she didn't want to get caught, she needed to make tracks. James could return at any moment, and she would have trouble explaining why she was here, naked in his bedroom.

That would ruin everything.

She leaned over the side of the bed to pick up her clothes, and as she did, her phone fell out of the pocket of her hoodie. She scooped it up automatically, intent on tucking it away again when inspiration struck.

Why not a memento?

A selfie?

Yes!

Without thinking twice, she leaned back on the bed, and adjusted her braid to fall over one of her bare breasts, coyly exposing the nipple, just a bit. Then, angling her chin just right, she stared at the camera and snapped several pictures of herself in different poses. One on her back; another on her stomach looking over her shoulder; then, just her boobs, no face, just the tip of her braid visible; another of her naked buttocks again with her braid; and finally her bare breasts, the Glock, barrel pointed up at her chin, placed between them, her braid wound around its handle. Oh, Lord. How phallic was that?

Her own private gallery.

She giggled.

Someday—please God—she would share them all with him.

And they would make their own. Together. Maybe even a sex tape. She tingled at the thought of filming him with his muscular back covered in sweat, his eyes fixated on hers as he pried open her willing legs and . . .

Her heart swelled as she pictured it, and the pulsing in her private parts . . . mmmm.

Oh, love, soon!

For now, though, she'd keep these to herself. The only person she dared confide in was Zena, who was her best friend and coworker, but no. Not yet. Zena had changed with her pregnancy, and Willow wasn't sure she could be trusted, not with something like this.

She could possibly tell her sister, but if she spilled the beans about James tonight, Willow was sure to get a lecture, and God knew she didn't need that. She'd had enough over the years from her older and—ugh!—wiser sibling. No need to suffer through that kind of torture, not again.

For a brief second, Willow considered staying here, in his room, in his bed, and surprising him, but, again, the timing wasn't right. Reluctantly, she rolled off the mattress and straightened the bed, making sure the long hair was visible on his pillow. If anyone ever suggested it might be hers, she'd deny it, then, if it were proven to have come from her scalp, finally just admit that she had been in his room cleaning. That would explain it.

But Sophia would know.

"Good," she said aloud.

Smiling, feeling like she finally was getting the upper hand, she reached for her sweatshirt and—

Crreeeak!

The noise came from outside the bedroom, as if someone or some *thing* were outside the doorway, maybe on the staircase.

Fear sluicing through her, Willow froze, strained to listen, hardly daring to breathe over the wild knocking of her heart. Maybe she was wrong about the noise; maybe it was the echo of that damned branch scratching against the kitchen windowpane.

She heard nothing.

Still, her insides clenched.

Had the noise all been a figment of her imagination?

No! It had been from *inside* the house.

Throat dry, she dressed quickly, noiselessly, and, with her ears straining for any other unlikely sound, carefully tugged on her boots.

Suddenly, bright illumination washed across the window, throwing the bedroom into relief.

Headlights!

No—oh, no!

Inching to the side of the window, Willow watched in horror as twin swaths of moving illumination played upon the trunks of the trees guarding the lane and sparkled against the blanket of snow covering the yard.

James was returning, his Explorer roaring toward the house!

Oh, crap!

"No, no, no," she said under her breath and hastily zipped up her boots. She scrambled out of the room, more concerned about being caught by James than by whatever imagined threat she thought she'd heard inside the house.

She didn't have much time, probably not enough. Her heart in her throat, she thundered down the stairs as fast as she could. On the final step, she turned, slipped, and twisted her ankle as she fell. "Shit!" she hissed. She got to her feet. Pain shot up her leg. She sucked in her breath. No matter what, she couldn't be caught. Not here!

Scraaape!

The damned tree branch.

Had to be.

Willow shoved back the horrid feeling that still lingered. The sensation that someone was watching her. Following her.

Get over it! It's just your nerves. For God's sake! Move! James is coming. And he'll have his stupid dog.

Oh. Jesus, oh, Jesus, oh, Jesus!

Frantic, she hobbled through the kitchen and out the back door, turning the lock swiftly. Pain burned through her leg as she worked her way down the long, dark porch and down a step into the woodshed. No windows. Just a dirt floor, dry, dusty air, and cobwebs in total darkness.

Hurry, hurry!

Lurching forward, her ankle throbbing, she ran a hand along the rough wood siding, her gaze fixed on the door at the far end of the shed. She'd left it ajar and caught a glimpse of white snow through the crack.

Good.

If she could just get outside—

Bam!

Her shin crashed into something right in the middle of her path.

Pain shimmied up her leg.

She cried out, then bit back the scream.

What the fu—?

The chopping block! A stump James used to split wood. An axe imbedded in the top.

She caught her breath. Heard the ever-nearing roar of a big engine as James's Explorer got closer.

Tears sprang to her eyes.

She couldn't be found out.

Not now. It would ruin everything!

Limping and flailing her hands in front of her in the darkness to prevent another injury, she half ran to the door and threw it open.

Cold air slapped her in the face.

She ignored it and ran, slipping and sliding, aching and mentally cursing as she followed the path through the orchard, where bare branches swatted her face, the same path she'd broken earlier.

Bright beams bore down on the buildings.

Willow flattened herself against the far side of an equipment shed. Heart thudding, she silently prayed she wouldn't get caught.

The shed was less than fifty feet from the garage!

Panicked, she searched for another escape route, her eyes scouring the surroundings.

Oh, God, was there movement in the hedge of fir trees?

A shadow out of place beyond the pump house?

Her heart skidded.

It's nothing. Just your imagination.

But the snow-laden branches appeared to shift a bit, as if someone were passing by in the night.

All the spit dried in her mouth.

Stop it! If you have to worry, worry about James.

All the while the Explorer, tires crunching over the snow, reached the end of the lane, wheels turning, the headlights intense as they splashed over the face of the farmhouse and garage.

Freaked out of her mind, Willow silently screamed. Her leg ached, and she realized she'd probably left a trail of blood in the snow . . . well, too bad. She just had to get out of here.

Before James—

The door of the detached garage rumbled open, light spilling from inside.

She didn't dare breathe.

He drove his SUV inside, then cut the engine.

She inched to the corner of the shed and carefully sneaked a peek.

She heard the Explorer's door open, then close with a thud.

Her heart was clamoring, and she bit her lip just as he stepped out of the garage. Her heart clutched at the sight of him. So tall, so handsome. He strode across the yard to the front steps.

His dog too was out of the Ford and streaking to the front yard, where he cut wild circles in the snow while the garage door rolled downward, destroying the light as it settled with a clunk.

Willow let out her breath. In a few minutes, she would be able to slink away from here in the darkness and—

Snap!

What?

The sharp noise came from behind the shed.

Scared spitless, she searched the darkness surrounding the back of the shed, then the rows of firs lining the far side of the yard.

Nothing.

Then what the hell was that noise?

An animal? Coyote? Wolf? Puma?

Or had the sound been human? Someone stepping on a twig?

From the front yard, the dog let out a soft whine.

No!

She turned her attention back to the house.

Ten yards away, the shepherd was staring straight at her, eyes focused on the corner of the shed where she was cowering.

His dark ears were pricked forward, his nose in the air, his eyes seeming to lock with hers.

Oh. God.

Go away! Just go away!

Jesus Christ, she was surrounded!

Willow's heart leapt to her throat.

The shepherd began to whine louder, advancing slowly, tail low.

Her insides turned to water.

She couldn't outrun him, even if her ankle wasn't throbbing, her bruised shin on fire. And where would she flee to? Backward to whatever danger was lurking beyond the trees?

Please, dog, just let me be!

She tried to pull back, duck away.

Too late!

The dog bolted.

Growling and snarling, he came, running straight at her.

No! No! No!

Willow braced herself.

A piercing whistle cut through the night.

Then the sharp command, "Ralph! Come!"

She waited, shivering, rooted to the spot.

"Leave the damned squirrels, would ya?" James ordered.

The dog whined but didn't round the shed.

"Come!" This time louder. More authoritative.

Oh, please . . .

She waited.

Nothing.

Swallowing hard, she took a quick glance around the edge of the shed.

James was on the porch, his long frame silhouetted in the faint light from a single bulb. "That's it. You come on, now. It's freezing out here."

Willow pulled back.

The dog whined plaintively.

"Leave it!" James ordered, his voice firm.

Willow's heart was beating so fast she thought it might fly out of her chest. A nervous sweat chilled her face. What would she do if James decided to investigate why his dog was behaving oddly? What if, at this moment, he was walking this way and she'd have to explain herself? Could she say that she'd just come by to check on things after she and Sophia had put the house together? Would he buy that she left rather than bother him? She squeezed her eyes shut for a second and heard the sound of keys jangling, then the creak of a door opening.

Then, more softly, over the frustrated whine of the shepherd, James said, "That's a good boy. Come on in, now. What's the matter with you?"

With a soft thud, the door was closed.

Oh, thank God.

Willow sank against the rough boards of the shed.

Her pulse pounded in her temple, and she let her breath out slowly, but she couldn't stay here another second. It was too damned dangerous. She sent a nervous glance back to the row of trees, saw nothing, and dared to look at the house again. James was turning on the lights, settling in. Patches of warm illumination from the windows reflected on the snow.

Go!

Screwing up her courage, she took off, running brokenly across the parking area to the lane. She ducked through the hedgerow of firs, then scrambled over a fence, her leg throbbing. On the far side, she took off, hobbling along the icy lane that paralleled James's driveway, the twin ruts that led from the county road to the shop where the tiny houses were built. She'd parked her car on the far side of the inn. If she could just get there . . . She cast a glance over her shoulder, just to be certain she wasn't being followed.

The snowy landscape was empty, almost eerily so.

Willow was alone—as she had been most of her life.

She limped along the lane, and finally the hotel and café came into view, Christmas lights sparkling, customers still searching for that perfect tree even in mid-December. Man, oh, man, she thought, crossing the parking area in front of the hotel, if she had a husband and family, she would clean up the last dish from Thanksgiving, then drive to the nearest lot, buy a tree, and decorate it immediately, to stretch out the holiday season.

Not if, *Willow.* When. *Remember that. When you and James are married and have children . . .*

She spied her car where she'd left it and felt a rush of relief.

She'd gotten away with it!

Despite the phantom voyeur and the nervous dog.

No one would ever know.

She almost smiled.

She'd go home, have a hot bath, maybe a glass of wine, and pretend she had never been inside all by herself, never lain on his sheets in his bed in his room, had never taken his gun and . . .

The gun!

Why didn't she feel its weight in her hoodie?

Oh, no, no, no . . . She reached into her pocket, found the key to James's house and her phone, but the pistol . . . ?

Her anxiety cranked up three notches.

Forcing herself, she double-checked every pocket.

Nothing.

The Glock was definitely missing.

She went cold inside.

Hadn't she picked it up? Or had she dropped it when she missed the last step on the stairs?

Let it go. Just get out of here. It's his gun anyway.

Hurrying to her car, she told herself that James might just think he'd misplaced it and she and Sophia had found it and left it. She'd explain to Sophia that she'd run back in and put it . . .

Are you nuts? That nasty, nagging voice in her head cut into her thoughts. *The police searched for the gun, too. And now it has your prints all over it. How're you going to explain that one?*

She couldn't.

She slid behind the wheel and glanced in her rearview mirror.

Round haunted eyes stared back at her.

As she started the car, the voice in her head wouldn't shut up.

"*Face it, Willow*," it taunted. "*You're screwed.*"

CHAPTER 33

Sophia snapped her hair into a quick bun and glowered at her reflection in the bathroom mirror.

James was slipping away.

She didn't understand it.

But she sensed it. Like sand sifting beneath her feet in an outgoing tide, James Cahill was leaving her.

Angrily, she turned on the shower. She'd thought, stupidly, that his interest in her had begun to wane when Megan went missing, that some sense of guilt was drawing him away, but that wasn't quite right. Nope. That wasn't it. The real shift in his feelings had come when Rebecca had come sailing back into his life.

To find her sister.

Oh, right.

Like she even cared about Megan.

What a joke!

Wasn't it bad enough that she had to deal with one sister turning James's head, but a second? That just wasn't fair!

The room had started to steam. She flipped the switch for the fan and heard nothing. Not the slightest whirr. No big surprise there. The place was falling apart, and that old bat Phoebe Matrix was too lazy and greedy to get anything fixed. You'd think since she owned the place, wasn't just the manager, Phoebe would take better care of things. But she didn't. Instead the old woman spent her hours and days peering out the window, spying on her tenants, when she wasn't doting on that yappy little dog of hers or complaining about her ailments: a bad knee, arthritis in her back, diabetes, and her deathly aversion to peanuts. As if anyone cared.

Sophia pulled off her sweater and bra, then wiggled out of her skinny jeans and undies.

The shower pipes groaned as Sophia stepped into the phone-booth-sized shower with its stained panels. In the thin spray, she scrubbed off her makeup, careful to wash around her hairline, under her chin, and around her neck.

She thought of James again and was instantly pissed that she'd let him slip through her fingers. He was the one—the only one. It wasn't that he was smart and sexy, it was that he was rich. Even though he hadn't yet inherited the fortune he was due to receive, he still had money from all of his business ventures. Sophia knew. She had checked.

And once he inherited . . .

She lathered, then rinsed, turned off the shower, and stepped into the foggy bathroom to swipe at the mirror and crack the door. She let down her hair, letting it fall over her shoulders, covering the freckles on her neck, then found fresh clothes.

She set her jaw as the moisture in the room dissipated and goose bumps rose on her skin in the cold air. She'd made love to him, tried her best to be sexy and sweet, and . . . oh, it wasn't working!

But she had a plan . . .

She snagged her bathrobe from the hook on the back of the old door and slipped it on, the thick white terry cloth drying the remaining droplets from her skin. Then she hurried downstairs and decided to call Julia.

Her sister would know what to do.

She always did.

But all Julia would do would be to caution Sophia not to lose her heart.

Well, too late for that!

Julia would remind Sophia how high the emotional stakes were and to play it cool.

As if she could!

Cinching the belt tight around her waist, she speed-dialed her sister. Noticing the date on her phone, she smiled to herself. Only a couple of weeks until Christmas . . .

She felt a warm rush of anticipation, her fingers skimming the terry cloth over her abdomen.

Things were bound to change.

Willow made it home. Her ankle and shin throbbing, she climbed the creaking exterior stairs to her little apartment. The lower floor was empty, the once-upon-a-time bakery no longer there. Sweet Scents had closed over a year ago; the ovens, tables, chairs, and counter were all gathering dust, and a FOR LEASE sign was fading in the grimy window.

She should move.

Though the bakery had been noisy—the baker arriving hours before dawn and pans clattering, a radio playing some classical music, the sounds drifting upward through the vents—she'd liked it. With the aromas of freshly baked breads and sweet cakes, yeast, cinnamon, and coffee wafting into her sparsely furnished unit, she'd felt a part of something. At almost any hour, Willow had been able to walk through the back door of the bakery, where the baker, Mrs. Nottingham, greeted her. A chubby, round-faced widow, Elsa Nottingham had been forever wearing an apron dusted with flour and had never forgotten to save Willow a day-old muffin or scone, which she'd handed out happily, along with a bit of grandmotherly advice that Willow had always ignored.

But those days were long gone, and this winter, Willow's studio was drab and cold, her blankets thin, the space heater inconsistent, the entire building feeling forsaken and empty.

Currently, she was the only occupant of the building as the only other apartment, most recently occupied by an elderly man, was now vacant and had been for over six months, which left Willow as the single tenant in over five thousand square feet of neglected building.

All in all, it was depressing.

But that was bound to change.

Once James realized . . .

Oh, God—what about the gun? If he found the Glock in the bedroom—

Angrily she pushed that thought aside and unlocked the apartment.

Inside, she turned on the space heater. As it clicked to life, she peeled off her clothes and dropped them into a bathroom hamper.

Her ankle was already swollen and discoloring rapidly, and the scrape on her shin was crusted with blood. She cleaned the scrape, decided it wasn't all that bad, and applied antiseptic lotion and a row of Band-Aids. In the medicine cabinet, she found a near-empty bottle of Tylenol and tossed back the last two capsules, taking them dry. Gingerly, she stepped into flannel pajamas she'd bought years before, the print of pink French poodles and gray Eiffel Towers nearly indistinguishable.

Paris.

The City of Light.

Would she ever really get there?

Of course! James would take her.

Maybe for their honeymoon!

Feeling slightly better, Willow turned on the lights on her tiny artificial tree, made a cup of herbal tea, and sipped it while surfing through the channels on her old TV. She settled on a movie channel playing some inane romantic comedy. Then she crawled into her bed, a twin she'd had since she was eight, and propped herself up on the pillows. When the movie ended, she switched to the channel that played heart-and-hearth-style Christmas movies, filled with glitter and hope, the bad guys always found out, the hero and heroine destined to find happiness and Christmas forever . . .

She let herself be drawn into one movie and then another, and finally clicked off the TV sometime after one. But sleep was elusive. Listening to the wind, she stared at the ceiling, twisted the ring she wore—her mother's engagement ring, with its tiny winking diamond—and fantasized about being married to James, to sharing Christmas with him in the farmhouse that she would decorate from top to bottom.

Smiling at that thought, she started to drift off, to finally feel sleep embrace her. She would dream about James tonight and think about his big hands on her body. "Someday, my love," she whispered and dozed, slumber taking her to a happy place, a safe place, so secure that she didn't hear the footfall on the exterior steps, nor even rouse when her lock was gently pried open and the intruder slipped inside. So deep into her dream was she that she barely stirred as the barrel of the pistol was placed near her right temple.

Blam!

It was over in an instant.

One quick pull on the trigger.

Willow's body jerked like a marionette.

And then there was nothing.

James didn't like it.

His house—all clean and spit-polished.

He tossed his keys and wallet onto a side table near the front door and eyed the front entryway, then peered into the living room, where every magazine was in a rack, not a speck of dust to be found, his slippers lined neatly on the hearth, where the slightest bloodstain was still visible.

With his dog tagging along, James walked to the kitchen, where he shrugged out of his jacket with less difficulty than he'd had four days earlier, then hooked it, along with his hat, on a peg near the door to the back porch.

Though he'd agreed that Sophia could straighten up, she hadn't waited for him to help out as he'd suggested. She'd done it behind his back while he'd been working, though she might have expected him home sooner.

Who could have predicted the accident at the shop?

Leon, who thought maybe Gus had staged the accident.

And Bobby, who held his own suspicions.

Knowlton had driven to the hospital and given James a lift back to the shop. A cigarette dangling from his lip as he drove, Bobby had said, "I'd tell you to fire Jardine's ass, but that wouldn't look good right now, him being in the hospital and all, with him yellin' that he was gonna sue ya? But he's been slackin' for a while now. Came in late today, did ya know that? Looked tired as hell and kind of beat up, as if he'd been out all night boozin' or whatever." Bobby had sent James a knowing look as he'd turned into the lane to the shop. "And it's not the first time. But . . ." He'd shrugged, smoke swirling around him in the old Silverado's cab. "All things considered, you can't can him. Not now. Jesus, what an idiot. Most people are more careful around whirling blades than Jardine. It's like the guy has a death wish or wants to be able to sue you and collect disability or whatever." He squashed the butt of his Marlboro in the ashtray. "Like I said, if I were you, and I ain't, I know, but I'd take the next opportunity to shit-can his ass."

Too late for that now, James thought. Gus Jardine had run the tile saw through his hand, ripping through muscles and tendons and nearly slicing off two fingers, which might have to be amputated, and there was talk of nerve damage.

A nightmare.

And an accident that could have been avoided if Jardine had followed the safety practices that were not only written in the handbook, but posted on the job site and that were simply commonsense.

Surely, he wouldn't have injured himself on purpose, as Leon had suggested. What kind of nutjob would take his chances with an electric saw?

James swore under his breath as he refilled Ralph's water dish, then opened a fresh can of dog food, added some kibbles from a container on the counter, and set the bowl on the back porch.

Before Jardine had been carted into the ER, he'd been screaming that he would sue James. Instead of worrying about healing, Gus had been focused on a lawsuit, and he seemed hell-bent on making James pay.

James couldn't help thinking that there was more at play than the accident, that Gus was pissed about James's breakup with Jennifer, which had happened a while ago. Still, there was something there.

He walked back to the front of the house, where, in the living room, pillows had been placed strategically on his couch. On the other side of the staircase, fresh flowers had been arranged on his dining room table, new bottles of his favorite scotch gleamed on the sideboard, and the glass in the windows was clearer than it had been in months.

James told himself he should be grateful, but Sophia was pushing too hard, all under the guise of helping.

It was suffocating.

And it had to end.

Despite the sex.

Which, he had to admit, was good.

Just . . . a little empty. At least for him.

Or was he rationalizing? Because of Rebecca?

His head was beginning to ache as he headed up the stairs, where the rails were smooth, the carpet runner recently vacuumed. His jaw tightened as he noted that the second floor had undergone the same transformation as downstairs. His bed was made, the room had been dusted, even the old fixtures in the bath were shining like they hadn't since long before he'd moved in.

He ran a finger along the top of his TV, and it came away without a speck of dust.

It all felt like a new pair of too-tight, polished dress shoes when all he wanted was a beat-up pair of comfortable slippers. Opening the closet, he found his shirts sorted by color, slacks the same, shoes in neat rows and polished.

This—the closet organization—was something Rebecca would never do.

And there she was again. Invading his thoughts. Causing him to draw comparisons. Rebecca was the source of his irritation with Sophia. It wasn't just that Sophia was pushing hard; it was that Rebecca wasn't pushing at all. In fact, she seemed to think he was the lowest of all lowlifes.

Maybe he was.

Angrily, he pushed a pillow off the chair near his closet, then yanked off his boots. His shoulder twinged a bit, but he ignored it and headed back downstairs. In the dining room, he opened one of the bottles of scotch and poured himself a stiff drink.

Ralph had already settled into his bed as James grabbed the remote and clicked on the television. Sipping slowly, he started channel surfing, searching for a sports update. Instead, he caught a glimpse of Megan's face. He paused, his gut tightening, the whole world crashing back on him as he stared at the smiling image: blue eyes twinkling, her lips parted, sparkles of sunlight in her light brown hair.

He'd seen that very photo in her apartment.

". . . if anyone has seen Megan Travers or has information about her whereabouts, please contact the Riggs County Sheriff's Department," a woman's voice said as a number for the department was posted on the screen beneath Megan's photo.

James's heart twisted a little as he looked at the woman who had turned his head; he had once thought he could fall in love with her.

In the picture, her hair was straighter than he remembered, her freckles hidden by makeup, her eyes as pale as ever.

Where the hell was she? What had happened after she'd left this very room? She'd turned his head because he thought she was more lighthearted and fun-loving than Rebecca, a woman with a glint in her eye that hinted at darker pleasures. And he, damn it, had been moved. Stupidly. Whereas Rebecca had been rock-steady, Megan had been constantly shifting, a puzzle he'd found intriguing. But he'd soon found out how free-spirited and ever-changing could easily devolve into mercurial and nasty.

Absently, he touched the scars nestled in his beard. Constant reminders of Megan's temper. As Megan's picture was dropped from the screen and the reporter, a narrow-faced woman in her twenties, started talking about the weather, James tuned out. He stared at the blackened fireplace, the hearth, where still a hint of bloodstain was visible in the mortar, a discoloration that Sophia hadn't been able to bleach away.

He'd originally thought Megan's disappearance had been a stunt, a way to get back at him. He could hear her voice now, as if she were in the room.

See what it's like if I left. Not so great, huh? And how about if I were dead? How would you feel then?

Dead.

The word he hadn't wanted to face seemed to hang in the air.

It had been so long since she'd disappeared, though, he had to face it.

He finished the rest of his scotch in one swallow, clicked off the TV, and refused to dwell on Megan's fate. No one knew what had happened to her. With another drink at his side, he spent a few hours on the computer the cops had deigned to return to him and tried to bury himself in his work.

He had designs for future tiny homes to look over and even a proposal from a contractor who wanted him to partner on larger buildings in the area—or at least the contractor had showed interest *before* Megan had gone missing and James had become persona non grata. His notoriety was spreading. He'd noticed it in the hospital when he'd been in the emergency room, and later when he'd picked up a pizza. He'd called the order in, but when he'd walked up to the counter, he'd caught the sideways glances of patrons at the smattering of tables in the pizza parlor, people who had recognized him and quickly turned away, afraid to catch his eye. Where once he'd been the darling of Riggs Crossing, a major employer in the area, a man who was known to donate to any number of charitable causes, he was now considered toxic or, at the very least, dangerous.

This was a small town. He needed good relationships and the trust of the townspeople.

He wondered if the best way to combat the negative publicity and speculation was to hit it head on. Speak to one of the reporters who had been dogging him, tell his side of it.

He sipped his second scotch. Decided he'd wait until Rowdy had gotten back to him—Rowdy, whom James was counting on to prove his innocence.

Or not. Remember: You're not completely clear on what happened that night.

Drumming his fingers on the table, he attempted to dismiss the nagging notion that he might somehow be at fault—if not directly, at least indirectly. "Oh, hell." Scraping his chair back, he walked to the kitchen, where he finished his drink and set his glass into the gleaming sink.

He had nothing to hide. He'd phone a reporter and tell his side of the story—consequences be damned. Sliding his phone from the back pocket of his jeans, he quickly scrolled through his missed calls. The last member of the press who'd left a message was Charity Spritz, the reporter he'd nearly thrown off his front porch. She was local. She would do.

It was after ten, but she'd practically been salivating to hear his side of the story. "Today's your lucky day," he said, hitting the CALL BACK button on his phone.

His call went straight to voice mail.

Rather than leave a message, he clicked off. Thought about it. He could try again in the morning. If he didn't have a change of heart. Maybe by then Megan would have returned. Maybe by then Rebecca too would call him back.

And maybe by then pigs really would fly.

His cell rang in his hand. He checked the number. Not Charity Spritz, as he'd expected. The caller was Sophia.

His jaw tightened involuntarily. He didn't want to talk to her. Wasn't certain he ever wanted to see her again. It was time to end this. Long past time, really.

He clicked on, but before he could say a word, Sophia said, "You're home, right? I'm coming over."

"Yeah, I am, but I don't think that's—"

"I'm on my way."

"No, Sophia, don't come."

But it was too late. She'd already disconnected.

CHAPTER 34

"I just think it might help," Rebecca Travers was saying from the other end of the connection.

Rivers, holding the phone between his ear and shoulder while clutching a bag of groceries, unlocked his door and stepped into his condo.

Rebecca had phoned to tell him she wanted to make an appeal for Megan's safe return via a televised press conference. And, she'd said, her family was willing to set up a reward for information leading to Megan's safe return. Since the investigation had stalled, Rivers had agreed, knowing full well the headache that would ensue when all of the fake tips started coming in, each one having to be checked out. It was remarkable how often a few hundred dollars could loosen someone's tongue, and Rebecca was offering five thousand. That amount might spur someone to come forward. Rivers, however, wasn't betting on it. "Okay, I'll set it up with the PIO," he said. "She'll get in touch with you."

"Thanks."

He clicked off as he dropped the paper sack onto the counter near the refrigerator, beer bottles clinking as the bag nearly toppled. "Steady," he ordered the bag and retrieved one bottle before stuffing the remainder of the six-pack and a jug of orange juice into the refrigerator. After shrugging out of his jacket, he cracked open one of the beers and retrieved a wrapped deli sandwich from the bag. As he added extra mustard to the ham-on-rye, he called Roxy O'Grady's number and left a message that included Rebecca Travers's request and cell number.

Only then did he take a bite, washing it down with a long swallow from his bottle of Heineken. As he consumed the sandwich, he thought about the missing woman and wondered how she'd disappeared without a trace.

"You'll figure it out," he said without a lot of optimism as he eyed the small personal items he'd "borrowed," all laid out on the counter separating the kitchen from the living area of his condo:

James Cahill's work gloves and sunglasses.

The necklace from Megan Travers's apartment.

A tube of lipstick from Sophia Russo's coat pocket.

Jennifer Korpi's tension ball.

Rebecca Travers's pen.

Yeah, of course, it was a little crazy—well, maybe *a lot* crazy, but he felt compelled to touch the personal items from a case, to feel a physical connection to those involved, be they suspects, victims, or perpetrators.

But, at the very least, it kept him focused.

Once, when he was still married to Astrid, she'd come across him with the items he'd lifted for a particularly grisly case in San Francisco, where a serial killer had actually run a stake through each of his victims' hearts, as if he thought they were vampires. The killer had been insane, of course, but Astrid, upon finding her husband's tokens from the victims, had seemed genuinely alarmed before collecting herself.

"You're crossing a dangerous line here, darling," she'd said in a tone of amusement tinged with worry as she'd entered his den, a glass of wine in one hand. "You've got your little 'treasures,' just like the killer with his souvenirs, yes?" She'd eyed him curiously as she'd slung a leg over the corner of his desk, then picked up an earring from one of the killer's victims. Rubbing it between her manicured fingers, she added, "This isn't just unusual, you know. It's freaky. And vastly illegal."

He hadn't said anything, just watched her from his chair.

"You could lose your job." She eyed him over the rim of her glass, her short, sun-streaked hair catching in the light from his desk lamp.

Not if I don't get caught. Not if you don't rat me out.

"Or they could . . . send you away, to a psych unit. When you add this to that trance thing you do—how did you describe it? getting into the victim's or the killer's head?—I'm telling you, you're one step away from the loony bin." He'd felt his jaw grow so tight it had ached, but he hadn't said a word. "Oh, well, it's your funeral, I suppose. Just, please, don't take me with you."

Wouldn't dream of it, "darling."

"Face it, Brett, you're disturbed. Deeply disturbed." She'd dropped the earring back onto his desk and made a sour face. "Some secrets are better kept locked away." Tapping a fingernail on the desk's surface near the bow from a patent-leather shoe of another victim, her green eyes glinting, she'd said, "This isn't a game, you know. It's your life. *My* life. Our life."

And she'd been right, he thought now.

He'd wondered over the intervening years if, indeed, it was a game with him, getting away with something.

Or was it a deeper psychological anomaly?

Whatever the reason, tonight he was undeterred. He swiped a paper towel across his face and hands, then tossed it and the wrapper into the trash.

In the dining area, he took a seat at one of the bar stools and started the ritual.

First, he picked up Megan Travers's necklace, fingering the delicate links and looping it between his fingers, touching the small, glinting cross dangling from the chain. Closing his eyes, he waited for an image to come. To feel her. To sense her emotions.

He thought the images would come slowly, but he'd been wrong.

In a sudden burst, a kaleidoscope of pictures of Megan flashed behind his eyes: Seated at her desk in the clinic, fingering the cross nervously. Talking on the phone, rapidly, heart pounding. Worrying about . . . an unborn baby? Hopeful? Or not?

Was she pregnant?

Rivers felt a bit of her joy, her anticipation. And something else. Worry? Or disappointment?

Concentrating, he forced his thoughts to the night she disappeared, to her confrontation with James Cahill.

Closing his eyes, he slowed his breathing.

And there she was—Megan panicked and furious, running through her apartment.

I'll kill him. I will. I'll kill his cheating ass!

She kicked off her shoes, banged a toe on the corner of her bed, swore, and then stopped short. *I'll make him suffer. All of them. I'll just leave and not tell him where I'm going. Make him miss me. Make them all miss me! What about Rebecca? And Mom?*

"Like they ever cared." She said the words aloud, her toe throbbing. *Mom has her own life. Dad doesn't give a shit, and Rebecca . . . well, she'll get by. Besides, she's never forgiven me for stealing James away. She'll be glad if she thinks I'm dead . . . that's it. They'll all think I'm dead. I'd love to be a fly on the wall when they realize I'm gone. But I can't give myself away—they have to expect to see me.*

She ran to the living room to scrounge in a drawer for a pen and notepad, then jotted out a quick note on the coffee table, stripped off the page, and tossed it into a bag. Still angry, she changed out of her scrubs, taking off her necklace and dropping it onto the edge of her dresser, where she'd left a drawer open. And then . . . and then . . . nothing.

Of course. She hadn't been wearing it when she'd driven to James's place.

Letting out his breath, he dropped the necklace onto the counter, where it pooled. Another swallow from the green bottle of beer. So Megan had planned to disappear, at least in those moments when he'd caught a glimpse into her head. Not exactly reliable information, though—gained from a vision while holding a discarded bit of jewelry.

One step away from the loony bin.

Astrid's little dig seemed more like a prophecy at this point.

"In for a penny, in for a pound," he told himself and picked up Sophia's lipstick.

He fingered the tube, opened it, and noted that the pale gloss was nearly gone, as if this were a favorite shade. In his mind's eye, Rivers saw Sophia at a darkened bar where the bartender was rattling a shaker of ice. With a sidelong glance her way, he poured a martini and set the frosty glass in front of her. She passed the lipstick to her friend, and the other woman applied a sheen to her lips.

Rivers slashed a little of the pink gloss across his palm. It felt slick and warm, and when he closed his eyes, he saw Sophia's lips, close up, as if in a magnifying mirror.

It has to be perfect.

He blinked. It was as if he'd heard a woman's voice in his head.

Don't overdo. Just a shimmer. Thin lipstick, thick makeup. Apply the coverup everywhere. You can't let any flaw show through. No sign of pimples, no hint of freckles.

He twirled the tube in his fingers and stared at it. Clicked the cap on and off. There was something odd about it and the voice he heard. What was all that about?

What's any of it about?

Good question.

He set the tube aside to pick up Jennifer Korpi's squishy tension ball. It molded to his fingers as he kneaded it in one hand and again closed his eyes. For a second, he got nothing and then . . . then he felt the anxiety, the fear. The more he massaged, the stronger the vibe he got. Jennifer was worried, yes. And there was something about her sibling . . . her sister? No, no. Her brother. She was worried sick about him, didn't want to get involved . . . but she was. Rivers felt it in the fear pulsing through her blood, the guilt sliding through her heart.

Guilt?

His face grew taut as he concentrated, his grip squeezing and releasing, squeezing and releasing the malleable ball, but no firm image came to mind . . . and yet . . . there was something.

"What?" he said aloud, startling himself. Jennifer had found out about her brother being hurt while he and Mendoza were at the school, but she hadn't picked up or touched the tension ball after learning the news, so that couldn't be it. She'd been worried about Gus Jardine *before* she heard of his accident. He was still holding the ball, and James Cahill's face came into view. He felt the sting of her tears, the overwhelming sadness that he'd left her, the shame that she'd been fooled, the deep-seated pain.

Rivers rolled the ball between both palms, as if he were working clay.

He sensed a spark of anger.

At a woman.

Rebecca?

Megan?

Someone else?

Jaw tight, he squeezed for a few more minutes but got nothing more, nothing solid. Only wisps of feelings.

This wasn't getting him very much. Setting the ball on the counter, he eyed it as he finished his Heineken. Jennifer Korpi, despite her protestations, hadn't completely gotten over James Cahill. So why lie about it?

Pride?

Embarrassment?

Or something more?

With no answer, he stretched his fingers, then reached for the ballpoint pen that he'd swiped from Rebecca Travers.

He felt nothing.

He closed his eyes.

Concentrated.

Felt a little sizzle.

A tingle of emotion.

What was it?

Anger?

Sadness?

Disgust?

He rolled the pen between his index finger and thumb.

The images were faint.

An argument?

Pain.

He saw Rebecca's face and then another . . . Megan's visage, pale and watery, came into view. She'd held this pen, if only once, because he saw her only faintly. His throat closed for a second. Could this have been the utensil she'd used to write her hastily scratched note to James? He felt his heart thud in anticipation. Had Rebecca been there? In her apartment? Did Rebecca Travers know a lot more about the night her sister had disappeared than she'd admitted?

He sensed the presence of a man—James Cahill?—but couldn't call up his face.

"Come on. Come on," he whispered, his teeth sinking into his lower lip. "What were you doing?"

But the image faded, just the hint of deep emotion lingering a second. The rift between the two sisters ran deeper than Rebecca was saying. Was she here searching for Megan out of genuine concern, or were her demands that her sibling be found just an act? His eyes narrowed as he eyed the pen. Her feelings for her sister were mixed.

And those for James Cahill?

Hate?

Love?

Time would tell.

Rivers set the pen down and stared at James Cahill's work gloves and sunglasses. Had he worn them recently, when the bright rays were blinding against the snow, or had they been sitting on his desk since last summer, taken off and becoming part of the landscape that he never noticed?

No time like the present to find out.

First, Rivers picked up the polarized shades, feeling the plastic between his fingers, trying to find images. He saw himself, as James, behind the wheel of his SUV, the dog usually on the seat next to him. James was worried. About the business, about finances, and about women. He had to break up with one because of the other . . . but neither one was right for him. He knew that; he'd probably known that for a long while. Through Cahill's eyes, Rivers saw images of the women, but the one that came into the clearest focus was Rebecca Travers, and the phrase *the one that got away* seared through his brain.

The images of Megan were filled with anger and guilt.

There was no memory of Jennifer Korpi, but Sophia was ever present.

Sophia excited James, and sexual images flashed before his eyes—her wet blond hair as she stepped from a shower; her long legs as she bent over and worked them into a boot that was too tight due to her broken toe; her smooth, perfectly round rump; the freckles that bridged her nose and were visible on the back of her neck. And then, again, the image swung to Rebecca.

With Rebecca's face came a deep searing regret as other sexual images came to mind, her auburn hair curling from the mist of a rainstorm, her perfect breasts and the curve of her spine, the little mole beneath one shoulder blade that he always kissed when he was making love to her and she was face down on a pillow, the way her lips parted when he touched the underside of her breast.

Rivers tore off the sunglasses. Dropped them onto the counter.

Felt like a voyeur.

Make that a thief and a voyeur.

And dirty—invading others' most intimate of thoughts while his own pulse was racing.

"Careful, darling," Astrid seemed to whisper in his ear. "You're going to get caught and when you do—oh, my. The you-know-what is really going to hit the fan. Face it, Brett, you're sick." She laughed then, that trilling, nasty little Astrid laugh. "Do you get off on this? Does it feel good? As I said, 'Sick, sick, sick!'"

"Go away," he said aloud and realized he was sweating, his heart pounding. That happened sometimes.

He hadn't been born with this gift—or, more accurately, this curse. He'd never had this kind of insight until late in high school after a bout with pneumonia and a fever that had spiked and fallen only to spike again. He'd spent nearly a week in the hospital, when the prospects for his recovery had been touch and go. He'd been in a semi-conscious state for seventy-two hours, and when he'd finally come to, he'd realized that he'd missed two important basketball games and that his girlfriend, Belinda Sommers, had started seeing Juan Martinez, the fastest tight end the Eagles football team had ever seen and one of Rivers's best friends.

Belinda hadn't mentioned that she'd started seeing Juan when she'd broken up with Brett once he was home. She'd thought she'd given him back a simple class ring that she'd kept on a chain around her neck. What neither of them had known at the time was that the ring had been so much more. When Rivers had returned it to his finger, he'd been stunned by images of Belinda making out with Martinez in the back seat of his classic Dodge Charger. Rivers had felt her passion, her fear of getting caught, her excitement at being with Martinez, but she'd never experienced one ounce of guilt about cheating on her hospitalized boyfriend.

Rivers had figured he was better off without her and had tossed the damned ring out of his bedroom window.

The class ring had been his entry into this new world. His first, but far from the last, and now Rivers couldn't help but use whatever this insight was to his advantage.

Now he was a little calmer, the perspiration on his forehead receding.

Letting out a sharp breath, Rivers picked up the work gloves, once tan leather, now stained on the palms, the stitching stretched, a small hole near the index finger of the right hand. He slipped the gloves over his hands and closed his eyes, seeing images of James driving a tractor in the spring, lifting baled trees onto a trailer while snow was falling, riding a horse through the woods, another horse beside him, a woman rider laughing as they splashed through the icy banks and slow-moving current of a stream. But he couldn't make out the woman's face, nor the color of her hair, nothing about her.

The image shifted, and he felt anger, dark and seething, saw the axe lifted high, then come crashing down, splintering wood, sending kindling spinning. Another chunk was placed on the chopping stump. Another ferocious swing. *Crrraaack!* Pieces of wood splitting and flying away from the blade. And again. And again. He felt the sweat, the strain of muscles as the axe was swung hard and fast, sensed the anger burning through the axe-wielder's blood.

Anger at a woman.

Hate. Rage. Blind fury.

Megan's face floated into view, no longer a smiling girl with honey-colored hair and a quick, sexy smile. Now . . . red-faced, teeth bared, she screamed, "You don't love me. You never loved me!" They were outside, near a stable where horses peered from their stalls. She picked up something—a grooming brush?—and hurled it at him. It bounced against the wall, near a stable door, and the chestnut in the stall shied and reared, neighing in fright.

"Are you nuts?" James demanded, and as he calmed the horse, Megan ran out of the stable through an open door into the night. It was winter. Snow lay on the ground. But it was not the night she disappeared.

Squeezing his eyes shut, Rivers switched his thoughts to the night of the altercation, the night Megan had vanished. He saw nothing, felt nothing. Whatever secrets the gloves held about the evening Megan disappeared, they were keeping.

Rivers stripped them off, pulling them inside out. *This is certifiable, you know it is.*

He noticed the stain then, a dark red blotch on the inside of the left palm. Blood. Cahill's? Or someone else's?

"Fuck." He couldn't take them to the lab without admitting he'd picked up the pair out of protocol, not collecting them as evidence. And they were tainted with his own damned DNA. Even if they could be tied to the crime, if the blood was maybe Megan's, which seemed highly unlikely, a defense attorney would turn him inside out on how he'd procured the gloves. There was no explaining it away. Furious with himself, he tossed the gloves onto the counter, walked around a post to the kitchen, opened the fridge, and pulled out another bottle of beer. He was sweating and breathing hard, as if he'd picked up that damned axe in his first vision and swung it, over and over again.

"Dumb ass," he muttered before opening the bottle and taking a long, cold swallow. Closing his eyes, he counted to fifty. Then a hundred. His heart rate slowed, but he still felt beads of sweat around his hairline.

Shaking off the images, he carried his beer to the living room window and past the small yard to the street beyond. Snow was falling, thick and heavy, dancing in the blue glow from the streetlamp. One of his neighbors on the far side of the cul-de-sac was backing out, garage door rolling down, crimson brake lights flashing as the back tires of the old Cadillac reached the sidewalk. He snapped his blinds shut and rubbed the back of his neck, then finished his beer.

Rivers knew he was missing something, something he couldn't *feel* in the personal items. Something just out of reach.

Oh, hell.

Maybe Astrid had been right.

Maybe he was sick. Or perverted. Or bat-shit crazy.

Stealing personal things, trying to get a sense of the owners from them, nosing around in their most private thoughts, attempting to learn more about an ongoing case, risking his reputation and his job . . . that wasn't the definition of sanity.

Not by anyone's standards.

Astrid's warning floated back to him.

Some secrets are better kept locked away.

CHAPTER 35

What had James said?

"No, Sophia, don't come."

The horrid words rang in her ears as she started her car and backed out of her parking slot at the apartment building.

Don't come? He was rejecting her?

"Ridiculous," she muttered, her breath fogging in the frigid interior. As she turned the heat on full blast, she caught a movement in the unit that sat catty-corner from her own, the larger apartment that jutted out to form an L around the edge of the parking lot: the owner's unit. The curtains were open, lights on, yapping, piece-of-shit dog standing at attention, flashing his teeth on the back of Phoebe Matrix's couch.

As ever.

The landlady was a busybody and a pain in the ass. Watching. Always watching. And even showing up at James's inn. Once when Sophia was tending the counter in the Christmas shop attached to the café, Phoebe had the nerve to come in and purchase little snow booties for the dog. All the while she'd been in the shop, she'd lingered, the cur in his hand-knit sweater under her arm as she'd fingered several tree ornaments, perused the Christmas cards, and touched a festive display of a miniature town complete with a tiny train that actually circled the small houses on a perfect little track. Of course, she'd kept an eye on Sophia, even asking a coworker about her.

As if the old bat knew what Sophia was up to.

She'd even tried to chat with Sophia at the register, her purse flopping open as she'd counted out the exact change. Sophia had gained a glimpse inside: tissues, lipstick, notepad, rain bonnet, and EpiPen; a glasses case was visible for just a second.

Driving away from the apartment building, Sophia shoved the nosy old woman out of her mind, at least for the moment. The old busybody could be dealt with later. Right now, Sophia had more important things to think about: specifically, James. What the hell was he thinking?

Her gloved hands tightened over the wheel.

She knew James wanted her.

Had always known.

From the first time they'd met.

But other people always seemed to get in the way, she thought sourly as she drove out of town, her windshield still showing spots of ice, her wipers scraping as they batted at the ever-falling snow, her once-broken toe starting to throb from the too-tight boots. She should have worn the suede ones, but these were sexier, and James would appreciate the effort—he always did.

A song was playing on the radio, some Christmas oldie that reminded her of growing up as a lonely child in Fresno, but she refused to think about that now.

"No, Sophia, don't come."

"Like hell," she ground out as she buzzed through town, gunning the vehicle as a light turned amber. Her phone jangled, and she saw that it was Donna, her boss at the inn, probably calling her to come to the bar and fill in. Well, forget that. She ignored the call. Didn't pick up.

She had to keep her thoughts straight, make sure she didn't trip up. James was wavering. She could feel it, and that just couldn't happen. She blew out a breath. Right now, it seemed as if everyone was against her, creating roadblocks. At work, she caught the sidelong glances. Both Zena and Donna were watching her as she mixed drinks. She caught them staring, and that miserable foreman, Knowlton, wasn't her friend, either. She'd seen the way his eyes tracked her, and it wasn't in the usual appraising way of so many men. Nope, he was suspicious.

And then there was Rebecca Travers.

She punched the gas, and her car slid a bit at the nearest corner, just at the edge of town. The trouble was that James was definitely intrigued with Megan's sister, and that was a problem. A serious problem. Worse yet, it seemed as if Rebecca was interested in James as well. Really? Even though he'd dumped her for Megan and was probably the prime suspect in Megan's disappearance. Still, she wanted him? What was wrong with her? Was she too playing a secret game? Well, if so, it had to end, and fast. Her eyes narrowed as the interior of the Escape finally started to warm.

She caught a glimpse of her reflection in the rearview mirror, strands of blond hair wisping from beneath her cap. It was then she realized she hadn't been as careful with her makeup as usual, had used less mascara than usual, and no blush, and she'd lost her favorite tube of lipstick. She'd even forgotten to make certain her foundation covered the slightest of her flaws, including the freckles that bridged her nose and the back of her neck. Well, too bad. She still looked good. Beyond good. Sophia knew she was gorgeous. She was just having a confidence problem. In the driver's seat, she straightened her back, sat up taller. "You can do this. He loves you. You *know* he loves you. How many times has he said, 'Sophia, I love you with all my heart'?"

Well, not that many.

Maybe never.

But she knew he did, damn it. A woman can sense these things!

Fingers wrapped around the steering wheel in a death grip, she was still thinking dark thoughts about Rebecca when she saw lights from the inn glowing through the snowfall. Good, she was almost there. She set her jaw. It was time to use every one of the feminine wiles she had tucked away in her arsenal.

After watching the local news, Rivers switched off the television. He was considering a shower or another beer and leaning toward the beer when his phone rang. The display registered an unfamiliar number with a San Francisco area code. He answered, "Detective Rivers, Riggs County Sheriff's Department."

"Glad I caught you. Jasmine Tanaka, detective, San Francisco PD." Her voice was serious.

"What can I do for you?"

"We've got a body down here. Female, early thirties. She didn't have a purse or cell phone or any ID. The vehicle she was found in is registered in Washington to Charity Spritz, address in Riggs Crossing."

He went cold inside. "You sure?"

"We pulled up Ms. Spritz's driver's license, and it's obvious that she's the victim. Her address is Riggs Crossing, and after a little digging, we found out she's a reporter. She had your name and number written on the inside of some papers I found in the van, so I thought I'd call you."

"We've met. Most recently, she was all over a missing woman case we've got going." Briefly, he filled in Tanaka about Megan Travers's disappearance.

"Why do you think she was in San Francisco?"

"No idea," he said, then corrected himself. "There's a loose connection. James Cahill, the boyfriend I told you about, his family hails from down there."

Tanaka knew all about the Cahills; her ex-partner, a retired cop by the name of Anthony Paterno, had dealt with a couple of bizarre cases involving members of James's family.

"So what happened?" Rivers asked, but he already knew, the hairs on the back of his neck rising.

"Not sure. She was registered in a motel in Oakland and had been there as recently as two days ago, according to a clerk at the motel who had seen her going into her room. Her body was found at the airport in the 2006 Hyundai minivan that was registered to her. It's a little odd; she had surveillance equipment in the vehicle, and we're checking that out too. Anyway, her body could have been left for days or weeks before she was found, but whoever drove the van there used her credit card to prepay for the space, then did a lousy parking job, boxed someone in, and that someone complained. Airport security checked it out, saw the body, and called nine-one-one.

"Looks like she was killed somewhere else—not enough blood in the van, and we're working all that out, piecing it together. This much is certain: Ms. Spritz didn't drive herself to the airport, and she damned well didn't die of natural causes. Definitely homicide. She was attacked, has all kinds of defensive wounds. We've bagged her hands, hoping to get some scrapings, hopefully DNA from beneath her nails, trace or fingerprints or DNA in the van, but it's still early on.

We'll know a lot more in a day or two. The only thing we're sure of is that, for whatever reason, random or targeted, she was murdered."

It was now or never.

Phoebe Matrix had watched Sophia Russo climb into her little gray car and wheel out of the parking lot. The only problem was that Phoebe had no idea how long her tenant would be gone. Didn't matter, she told herself. She'd be quick. She slipped on her rubber boots and heavy jacket, then, telling Larry to guard the place, hurried out the front door, closing it before her little dog could escape.

With more dexterity than most people would believe, she hurried along the overhang of the L-shaped building and made her way to the Russo girl's unit, then, using her key, let herself in.

The place was fairly tidy, more so than Phoebe had expected, the living room free of a lot of clutter, just a jacket and a sweater left over the back of a small sofa. In the kitchen area, the countertops were clear, only a few glasses in the sink. Phoebe was surprised, as the unit was small, a studio with a loft. So often tenants with little space had clutter, but not so with Sophia Russo.

She didn't know what she expected to find, maybe nothing; it was just that Sophia was a bit of a mystery.

And then there was Sophia's involvement with James Cahill. That was the root of it. With that other girl—Megan—missing and Sophia taking up with James *before* Megan had so conveniently disappeared, it all seemed more than a little suspicious.

Phoebe peered into the bathroom, which was slightly messier. So much makeup, which was ridiculous. The girl was a knockout, a blond bombshell, as Phoebe's father—God rest his soul—would have said back in the day, but the shelves and counter were littered with liquid makeup, concealers and blush, lipsticks in a variety of colors, and eye shadows and liners and pencils, and oh . . . it seemed ridiculous for a girl with so much natural beauty. But then, hadn't Phoebe seen as much in her lifetime? The pretty ones were the most vain, the most concerned with appearances, spent the most time in front of the mirror trying to cover flaws.

Still, there was nothing out of the ordinary . . . now, wait just a second. What was that? The door to the tall cabinet in the bathroom was ajar, as if it couldn't close, as if the little cabinet was overstuffed.

Phoebe opened the door and, at first, saw only stacked towels, but wait!

What the devil?

On the shelf above the towels, tucked behind some linens, was a Styrofoam human head, molded with female features and topped with a dark wig, coffee-brown hair cut shoulder-length with bangs. Phoebe touched it carefully and decided it was made from human hair. She knew a little about wigs as she had two friends who had gone through chemo; each had purchased a wig, one with synthetic hair, the other with human. This was the real deal. "Well, I'll be . . ." Phoebe whispered. Next to the wig was a glasses case and inside a pair of owlish glasses, very much like the glasses she'd seen Sophia's visitor wearing. The coffee-colored wig was the exact shade and length of that friend's hair.

She explored a little further, moving the towels a bit, and discovered something else—some kind of padding that could be strapped around one's body. To add pounds to an otherwise slim figure. Who would do that? Only someone who wanted to conceal her identity.

Phoebe's heart began to quiver, and she was suddenly perspiring. What in heaven's name was Sophia involved in? She touched the fine strands of the hair again and eyed the glasses. Clear glass, she discovered. These items were obviously part of a disguise. Was Sophia living a double life? But why? She couldn't help but wonder if this had something to do with that other girl's disappearance. Quietly, she replaced the items and decided she had to leave.

For now.

She couldn't go to the police—so what if her tenant had glasses and a wig? Big deal . . .

But it was. Phoebe knew it in her heart.

She hurried into the living area again and felt as if she were being watched, then panicked as she thought Sophia might have installed cameras in her home. These days there were all kinds of sophisticated home security equipment available. She swept her gaze over the few pieces of artwork on the walls and the tabletops, but saw nothing that looked suspicious. And even if there were cameras, that was just too bad. She had her rights as a landlord, even if she did stretch them once in a while.

Outside, she closed the door firmly behind her before locking it.

She hastened to her unit, slipping a little on a patch of ice, and decided to give Dabrowski a piece of her mind. How difficult was it to keep the walkway clear?

Inside her own unit, she took off her coat and slipped off her boots, then looked around. Where was the dog? "Larry?" she called, instant anxiety sizzling through her blood. Had he gotten out? Had someone been in her unit? She pulled her old high-school twirling baton from the umbrella stand, a handy weapon she'd kept for all these years, then, panicking, searched her apartment. "Larry?"

Her heart was beating a frantic tattoo when she couldn't find him.

"Larry? Here, boy. Come on now."

Nothing.

Heart in her throat, she kept searching, peering under her bed and behind her favorite recliner.

"Larry!"

She was having trouble breathing, fear shooting through her, when she heard a muffled yip. Her heart leapt. "Where are you—?"

Another sharp bark.

From the kitchen! She opened the pantry door, and he burst out, yapping wildly.

Relief flooded through her as she crouched, and he sprang into her arms. "Silly boy, how did you get in there?" She scooped him up as she straightened. He rewarded her with sloppy kisses that made her giggle. "You know you've been naughty, don't you, hiding from me?"

But it was her fault. She must've left the pantry door ajar, and Larry, always curious, had somehow gotten caught inside, the door swinging closed behind him.

Still, it was odd, she thought, as she carried him into the living room.

"All's well that ends well," she said, but she was left with an uncomfortable feeling, her nerves slightly jangled. As she took up her spot on the couch and stared out at the parking lot, her gaze moved to unit 8. All locked up.

So, what about the disguise?

It was odd.

She decided to keep the baton at her side.

Larry gave off a sharp bark, and before she picked up her knitting, she reached for his treats. "Sit," she commanded, and he obeyed, his eyes focused on the treat in her hand. "Good boy." She rewarded him, and he ate hungrily, then spun in tight circles, hoping for more. "Okay, fine." She gave him a few more of the liver-flavored treats, then brushed her fingertips on her sweatshirt. "My turn." Though she knew she shouldn't, she reached into the candy dish and counted out five M&Ms, then plopped them all into her mouth. The chocolate was delicious, definitely melting in her mouth and sliding down her throat and . . .

No!

Her eyes widened at the taste of peanuts—peanut butter.

What??!!

It couldn't be.

Frantic, her throat closing, she stumbled into the kitchen, found her purse, and opened it. The EpiPen. Where was it? Fingers scrabbling inside, she gave up and emptied the bag on the counter. Coins rolled and fell to the floor, tissues and lipstick and her glasses and wallet tumbled onto the Formica. No EpiPen!

It was always there. It had to be! But no. And her phone . . . where the hell was her phone?

Oh. Dear. God.

Her lungs were so tight she could barely breathe, couldn't think.

Gasping for breath, she opened the cupboard where she kept her medications, but her spare EpiPen also was missing.

Panic tore through her, and she slipped on her way to the front of the unit. She threw open the door to the parking lot and tried to scream, but her throat was too constricted . . . Stumbling, she was vaguely aware of Larry streaking across the parking lot as she fell against the door of Dabrowski's unit. She managed to hit the doorbell and hear it peal inside as she slid to the ground, her head landing with a thud on the cold, cracked concrete.

"Sophia, what're you doing here?" James demanded.

She couldn't believe it. He was actually denying her!

He stood steadfastly planted in the door frame of his house, blocking her entrance. And he wasn't happy. Even though his face was in shadow, his silhouette backlit by the interior lights, she sensed his annoyance.

"I wanted to see you," she said, shivering on the porch despite her coat, gloves, and boots. It was freezing, the slap of the wind racing around the corner of the porch sharp against her cheeks.

"I thought I told you not to come."

"I know. But I had to," she said, offering him a smile as snow fell from the inky sky. She tried to hide her own irritation because he was lying. Lying *to her,* acting as if he didn't care, as if it were over as he filled the doorway, looking sexy as hell, his battered jeans hanging low on his hips, his long-sleeved shirt half unbuttoned. But of course she saw his eyes. Even shadowed, they were cold, as cold as this winter night. And just as unyielding.

"I just can't do this anymore," he said. "We can't do this anymore."

"Can't do what?" She knew what he was talking about, of course, but she wasn't going to make this easy for him; she was going to make him say the words, actually spit them out.

"You know," he said, his gaze finding hers.

"I don't," she said stubbornly.

"We can't see each other anymore, Sophia."

"Are you kidding me?" After everything she'd given up to be with him? He was really, seriously ending it? "Why?" she asked, inching up her chin. "After all I've done for you. I even spent all day cleaning, Willow and I, but it was my idea to make this house perfect for you. We've shared so much, you and I. I can't believe . . . why, James?"

"We both know it's just not right. Megan's still missing—"

"That—she—her being gone—has nothing to do with us," Sophia argued, starting to feel the first bit of desperation.

"The police seem to think I might have had something to do with it."

"Did you?"

He stared at her as if she'd gone mad. "Of course not."

"Then what's to worry about?" she asked, trying to tamp down the anger that was starting to pulse through her. "We'll get through it," she said calmly, though her hands fisted and rage that he would even consider breaking up with her pulsed through her brain. But she couldn't let it get the better of her. She reached forward to touch his arm. "Couples have their ups and downs."

She let her hand fall away under his stony glare and barely noticed as a lock of hair escaped the braided plait beneath her cap. "We can get through this, James. Trust me."

Did he falter a bit? Was she getting to him? God, she hoped so. After all, she'd staked her entire future on James Cahill. He was the one. The only one.

"It's not just that," he said.

"Then what?"

"I think it's time we both moved on, Sophia."

"Oh my God," she whispered. "You're really breaking up with me?"

He didn't answer.

But she got it. Finally. And fury seared through her. "It's because of Rebecca Travers!" she said, spitting out the name. "She got to you, didn't she? All of her concern over her sister. I should have seen that coming. What a bitch! You know it's not real, don't you? She doesn't care about Megan. She never did!"

"How do you know that?"

"Come on, James. You and Megan were seeing each other on the sly, weren't you? While you were still 'going with' Rebecca?" She glared at him as a cold wind cut across the porch and rattled the branches of a nearby tree, blowing snow over the railing. That stupid strand of hair blew over her eyes again. Angrily, she took off her cap and tucked that irritating lock under her braid.

Damn it all to hell! Didn't he see? Didn't he know they were supposed to be together? She wanted to scream at him, but she forced her anger back.

"Don't do this now," she advised, returning her hat to her head, her hair now secure. "You've been through a lot." She reached up and touched the still visible claw marks in his beard. "Everything is . . . strange right now. Weird. But it'll be better." She forced a tremulous smile. "I can make it better."

He pushed her gloved hand away, and when she stepped a little closer, intent on passing into the hallway behind him, he shifted, making it impossible for her to enter. Frantic, she spied the dog behind him, staring at her through the small space between James's waist and the door frame, appearing no more welcoming than his owner.

"James," she whispered, heartbroken.

"It's over," he said firmly.

"No." Her throat clogged as she shook her head. "I don't believe it." That was a lie. She saw by the set of his jaw that he meant business, and she knew from dealing with him how stubborn he could be.

"I think we've said enough."

Oh, God, he wasn't budging. She bit her lip and felt tears start in her eyes. "Don't do this. Not now."

He didn't respond. Didn't back down. "Good night, Sophia." He started to close the door. "Go home."

The door shut in her face, and she heard the click of the dead bolt.

She sagged a bit.

Never before had he been able to resist her.

But then her spine stiffened, and she reached up to start pounding on the door, her fist tight. She would make him see!

You still have the upper hand. He just doesn't know it yet.

She held her fist back, poised, taking a moment. She had to be careful. She couldn't ruin this, and she did have an ace up her sleeve. She hadn't been sure when to play it, but now was definitely not the time.

Stepping off the porch, she flung a dark look over her shoulder, half-expecting James to have changed his mind, but the door stayed firmly shut.

You son of a bitch.

You miserable, two-timing prick!

Her jaw clenched, and she wanted to pound on the door or, better yet, use her own key and sneak in, find him in bed again, and change his mind with sensual ministrations of her lips and tongue on his body. But not now. She needed to back off. To make him want her. Becoming a hysterical female at this point would only drive him further away.

But the rage that was always simmering in her blood threatened to overtake her. Who was he—so privileged, so entitled—to break it off? He had no idea of her struggles, how she'd had to scrape and climb, how hard her life had been, how loneliness had been her only friend, while he'd grown up knowing in the back of his mind that no matter what, he had a legacy, a fortune waiting for him.

She felt that little telltale tic start near her eye, and she was determined he would never see it, never have a glimpse of the other side of her.

Gritting her teeth, she strode back to her car, breaking new tracks in the snow while telling herself this wasn't the end, was *not* the last time she'd see him. They were meant to be together, and he'd realize it soon enough.

She'd make him see.

But she would have to bide her time.

Once inside her SUV, she cast a glance at the house—a pitiful old building, really, considering James's wealth or soon-to-be wealth—then backed up and put her Escape into gear. As she nosed toward the lane, she saw the porch light snap off.

"Bastard," she muttered under her breath, that oath stinging a bit. Hands clenched over the wheel, she silently vowed James would regret this night forever. Before you knew it, he'd be begging for her to get together with him again, and not just for the sex he liked so well. He'd be down on one knee, ring in hand, professing his love and pleading with her to marry him.

There was more than one way to handle this situation, to ensure that he would never let her go.

That thought warmed her from the inside out.

Just you wait, James Cahill, just you wait.

You're going to want me again, and it's going to hurt so bad, so damned bad you won't be able to think.

CHAPTER 36

December 9

It was barely seven in the morning, and already Earl Ray Dansen was having a bad day.

Well, hell, weren't they all bad?

The heyday of print newspapers was long gone, and it was a miracle he was able to publish a paper edition of the *Clarion* at all. As he stood in his office, the ancient furnace unable to keep up with the cold that drifted through the thin walls of the big, open space, he surveyed what seemed like acres of empty desks in the old warehouse, and he felt that he, like the newspaper he'd worked on for over fifty years, was a relic from a bygone era. Journalism had been swallowed whole by technology, the Internet, and everybody not giving a good goddamn about real, hard news. Everything now was opinions and spin, and slick anchors on cable news.

Not like the old days, the good old days.

His cell phone buzzed, moving like a huge flattened cockroach as it vibrated across his desk.

Ignoring the call, he eyed the counter along the far wall, where the digital edition was being formed, and noted that Gerry wasn't at his station. Again. Probably out smoking dope or getting another fucking tattoo. When the hell would he grow up? Thirty was already in his damned rearview.

At least Jeanette was at her area, ostensibly proofing tomorrow's edition. Seated on a stool at the raised desk in her split-kneed jeans and sloppy camo jacket, her spiky blond hair showing dark roots, wide gold hoops dangling from her ears, she was bent over her computer.

He glanced at the huge, near-empty space that housed the *Clarion*. Charity was in San Francisco, and, of course, Seamus O'Day wasn't at his desk at this hour. Seamus might not show up at all, preferring to work "at home" or "in the field," which usually meant the stool next to the video poker machines at the Brass Bullet.

Earl should really fire him and give Charity his stories.

The phone was still vibrating as Earl wondered about Charity. She'd been practically rabid to work on the Megan Travers story, all amped up about James Cahill being behind the girl's disappearance, but when Earl had refused to cover an all-expenses-paid vacation in San Francisco, she'd gotten really pissy and said she'd go on her own dime. He hadn't believed her, but she'd been MIA ever since, and he figured if she came back with something worthwhile, a sensational story, then maybe he'd comp her for her gas or motel room or meals. Then again, maybe not. He'd wait and see, but in the back of his mind, he wondered if she ever would return. She had big plans, Charity Spritz did, and he didn't think it included writing human-interest stories for the *Clarion* for the rest of her life. She'd said as much.

Again the phone caught his attention.

Well, speak of the devil. Charity's number popped onto the screen.

Earl Ray scooped up the phone just as it disconnected.

"Shit."

He returned the call.

No answer.

What was that all about? He left a message. "It's Earl. Call me back."

He clicked off and immediately heard the sound of chimes indicating she'd texted him.

Good.

He hated to admit it, but he kind of missed having her around here.

She was a spunky thing. Full of fire. Even if she did rub O'Day the wrong way. But at least she had life. His gaze wandered to the door, where his son, in sloppy jeans and a T-shirt, his hair wound up in that stupid man bun, slowly sauntered to his workstation. Probably stoned out of what was left of his mind.

Irritated, Earl Ray glanced down at his phone as the text message came onto the screen. "What in fuck's name is this?" The picture was of a naked woman lying in a bed, her eyes staring upward, her mouth rounded as if in surprise, a pistol pointed at her head. Her hair was black and braided, the plait falling over one pale shoulder to curl at her breast.

He'd seen her, he thought, but couldn't place her. What was Charity doing? The message accompanying the photo was simple:

ANOTHER VICTIM.

"Another one? Who's the first?" Earl said aloud. What the fuck kind of game was this? And then he noticed the small hole at the woman's temple where a barely discernible splotch of blood matted her hair. "Holy fuckin' shit," he whispered, adrenaline pumping through his bloodstream. "What the hell?" A story! Quickly he punched out Charity's number, wanting an explanation. Who was this girl? Where had he seen her? Had she killed herself? Or had someone else done it? How the hell had Charity gotten the picture?

The phone rang several times.

"Pick up!" he growled. What was wrong with her? She'd just called him, damn it.

More rings as Earl paced in front of his desk.

Finally, Charity's recorded voice asking the caller to leave a brief message and number. Really? For the love of—! "It's Earl," he said sharply, as voice mail began to record. "Got your message. Call me."

Then he clicked off and stared at the photo again, and with a creeping sensation born of being in the business for so long, he felt a little frisson of excitement. Charity was teasing him with this picture, but he knew in his heart she was onto something big. Something earth-shattering.

"Hey!" he called over to the online department, where Gerry was talking to Jeanette.

His son glanced up as Earl, half-jogging, made his way past the empty desks and cubicles to the Internet department.

"Take a look at this." As he reached Gerry, he held out his phone so that both his son and Jeanette could see the small screen. "You know this girl?"

"Maybe?" Gerry said in his usual fog.

"Sure. That's Willow." Jeanette had been sipping from a super-sized soda cup. "Uh, Willow . . . what's her last name?" she asked Gerry.

"Valente?" Gerry offered, his eyebrows slamming together over bloodshot eyes as he studied the image on the phone. "Oh, shit, yeah, that's her. Yeah. Pretty sure. But how . . . I mean . . . she's naked?" He stared at his father as if Earl Ray had been looking at porn. "What is this?"

"Don't know. It's from Charity."

"In San Francisco?" Jeanette pulled a face. "What would Willow Valente be doing down there?"

Gerry let out a strangled sound. "It looks like she was being dead, that's what she was doing." He paled and took a step back. "Maybe I can find something on the Internet." He kicked out his stool and began typing on his keyboard.

"Dead?" Jeanette repeated. "I thought she was just naked." She leaned in closer, her eyes popping. "Oh, God, you're right." She too turned ashen, her hand flying to her pale lips as her soda cup slipped to the floor, ice and cola slopping onto the carpet. "What the fu—what is this?" She was already reaching for a tissue on her desk, then bending down to sop up the mess.

"I have no idea," Earl Ray said, but it was something.

Something damned important.

Something that might just breathe some much-needed life into the *Clarion*. As Jeanette was picking ice cubes from the floor, Earl started for his desk when Charity texted him again. "About damned time." But he wanted to talk to her in person and was about to punch in her number when he saw that the message was actually another picture. "What the fuck?" he said as the image filled his screen.

"Oh, shit! God." Gerry was practically hyperventilating. "Dad! You gotta see this. It's about Charity. Jesus, can this be right?" Jeanette had straightened and was staring at Gerry's screen. She let out a scream.

"No, oh, no!" she cried.

But Earl hardly noticed. On his phone, he saw a picture of Charity herself. Not a selfie. This one showed her face beaten and bruised and . . . for the love of Christ . . . it appeared as if she, like Willow Valente, was dead as the proverbial doornail.

At his desk in the station, Rivers swilled black coffee, eyed his computer screen, and studied the information sent over from Detective Tanaka in San Francisco. Graphic pictures of the dead woman confirmed what they already knew: Charity Spritz had been murdered. The theory was that she'd been caught off guard at her motel in Oakland, where the attack had taken place, possibly in the parking lot—though there were no cameras or witnesses at the scene. Then her body had been taken to the airport and left. The SFPD was working with the airport security cameras and the airlines, hoping to find out if the killer had flown out on a late-night or early-morning flight, but that could take a while.

Tanaka, though, had assured him that they were working around the clock on Charity's murder. Rivers knew firsthand how the SFPD handled homicide cases. They were efficient, but it would take time.

He wondered how Charity Spritz's homicide connected to Megan Travers's disappearance. There had to be a link.

He heard Mendoza's footsteps before she appeared at his desk. With one glance at the computer screen, she stopped dead in her tracks. "Oh, jeez. Brutal."

He agreed. No matter how many violent attacks and murders he'd witnessed, he'd never become inured to the savagery or the viciousness of what one human could do to another.

"What was Charity Spritz doing in San Francisco?"

"I'm hoping someone at the *Clarion* might have some insight. I've got a call in to Earl Ray Dansen, but he hasn't gotten back to me yet."

"Don't newspaper people get in early, like hours before dawn?"

"Apparently not Earl Ray."

"Maybe he's just busy."

They locked eyes, and he said, "Hey, we're talking about the *Clarion.* Remember? You and I are working on the biggest story to come their way since Barton Scruggs stole Hugh Lambert's prize bull a couple of years ago."

She smiled faintly. "Okay. You're right. He'll be calling. But in the meantime, take a look at this." She handed him her cell phone, where a text message read I NEED TO TALK TO YOU. IT'S IMPORTANT.

"Who's this from? What's it about?"

"I don't know what she wants, but it's from Andie Jeffries."

"The LPN who worked with Megan Travers at the clinic?"

"One and the same. I called the number back immediately. Set up an appointment, and if we don't get going, we'll be late. Thought you might want to tag along."

He was already pushing his chair back. "You thought right." He grabbed the jacket he'd slung over the back of his chair and slipped into it as they walked outside.

"And by the way," Mendoza said as they reached his SUV, "don't make the mistake of calling her Andrea. It's Andie. She let me know that."

"Got it. But what's it about?"

"Don't know. Wouldn't say on the phone, and I have no idea why. Probably didn't want someone to overhear her or something. Maybe we'll find out. Whatever the reason, she wants a face-to-face, so we're obliging. And it won't take long. She's due at work at nine, and she didn't want to meet at the clinic for some reason, so we agreed on Lucy's Diner."

"Andie didn't want to be seen talking to the cops?"

"My guess is she doesn't want anyone at her work to know or have the press find out. That's probably the same reason she didn't want to come into the station." She slid into the car and buckled up as Rivers settled behind the wheel.

"Lots of people are skittish or scared or weird around cops," Mendoza said, stating the obvious. "They seem to think we're the bad guys."

"And yet they call us when they're in a jam."

"Um-hmm."

"Let's see what she has to say."

Snow was falling again, lazy flakes drifting from a steel-gray sky as they drove the mile out of town to Lucy's Diner. He cut the engine, and they headed inside, where they were met with a wall of heat. The scents of frying bacon and brewing coffee filled the air, while clicking glasses and buzzing conversation muffled the piped-in music, which seemed to be in the form of oldies from the sixties.

Mendoza led the way to where Andie Jeffries had tucked herself into a corner booth. Her long fingers were busy shredding the paper from the straw that was stuck into a tall glass of what appeared to be cola. Her gaze was fixed on the glass, as if she were studying the bubbles rising between small ice cubes. So lost in thought was she that she nearly jumped out of her skin when they approached.

"I shouldn't be doing this," she said as they slid into the booth opposite her.

"Doing what?"

"Risking everything . . . I mean . . . it's . . . it's probably nothing anyway." Dressed in faded blue scrubs beneath a navy jacket, she was a pale, impossibly thin woman, not yet thirty, her eyes a light brown, her dishwater-blond hair secured at her nape by a leather thong. And she was nervous as hell, still tearing the tiny strips of white paper.

A waitress swung by with a pot of coffee and filled two of the four cups waiting on the table. She asked brightly if they wanted to see a menu, but they declined.

"Okay. Sure. Sugar and cream are on the table," the waitress said, nodding, red curls bouncing. "Let me know if you need anything else." And she was off, coffee pot in hand, swinging toward a booth closer to the door, where three men in heavy jackets had settled.

"So what's so important?" Mendoza asked, her iPad and phone already on the table, ready to record.

Andie blinked as if she were going to cry, then looked through the plate glass of the window. "It's Megan. I mean, I should have called you earlier, but I was so scared, and I didn't believe anything had happened to her, and—" She hiccupped, placed the back of her hand to her mouth, and tried to steady herself. "Bruce would kill me if he knew I was here, talking to the cops."

"You know where she is?" Rivers asked, thinking this might finally be their break.

"No." She was shaking her head and sniffing, looking scared.

Rivers felt his pulse tick up.

"Who's Bruce?" Mendoza asked.

"My boyfriend . . . Bruce Porter . . . he . . . um, he had a little trouble. Drugs. But it's all over now. He's been through rehab, and he's clean. Has been for six, no, almost seven months . . . well, anyway, he works for James Cahill, out at the shop. He . . . um . . ." Her voice squeaked. "James gave him a chance once he proved he wasn't using. Just janitorial stuff at first, y'know, sweeping up and keeping track of the tools and . . . well, anyway now he does more, helps out now putting up Sheetrock or laying subflooring or whatever." She sniffed, on the verge of tears. "And he needs the job, y'know. We both do."

She looked absolutely miserable.

"Did something happen?" Mendoza prodded.

She squeaked, and the hand came up to her lips again as she blinked to stave off tears. "I'm just explaining that this is a very small town, and we're all connected. Like my sister. She works here at Lucy's. She's a cook and . . . and . . ." Andie let out a small sigh, and Rivers noticed impatience tightening Mendoza's lips. She looked like she wanted to rip the words out of Andie's hesitant throat.

"Go on," Rivers encouraged, taking a swig from his cup.

Andie sniffed again. "It's . . . it's what Megan said to me." She finally lifted her eyes to meet Rivers's. Her voice a bare whisper, she finally confided, "She said that if anything happened to her, you know, like she went missing or . . . worse . . ."

Almost imperceptibly Mendoza leaned forward.

". . . she, um, said that it would be James Cahill's fault." Andie closed her eyes, and tears were visible in her lashes. "I want to say this off the record, okay?"

A little late for that.

"I mean, like, I don't want to testify." Swallowing and sniffing, turning the glass in her hands, she added, "Bruce and I . . . we've got a baby coming. Just found out this week."

"What exactly were her words?" Mendoza asked.

"I told you." Andie closed her eyes for a moment. "She said, 'If anything happens to me, it's James, his fault.' "

"When did she tell you this?" Rivers asked as his cell phone vibrated in his pocket.

"I don't know the date, but a couple of weeks or so ago. Like maybe a week before she disappeared."

"She was angry."

"Oh, man, really mad at him. Again. He'd blown her off or something, and she suspected he was with another woman."

"Did she say who?"

"I think . . . I mean, he'd been seen with Sophia Russo. Again. Like it had happened before, and I really didn't think much of it. Sophia works for him and, you know . . . sometimes Megan jumps to conclusions and gets all kinds of upset. That day she was really, really pissed, jabbing her arms through her sleeves, grabbing her things out of her locker in a rush. She threw her phone into her bag and was swearing. She was really mad. Like really, and she said, 'If anything happens to me, it's James. Okay? It's James. He's such an effin' prick!' Only she used the 'f' word, you know?"

"What happened then?" Mendoza asked.

"I don't know. She was out the door and let it slam behind her. I saw her peel out of the parking lot. She nearly hit a kid on a skateboard, but luckily she missed him."

"You don't remember exactly when this was?"

She shook her head.

"Did you see her afterward?"

"The next day at work, and she acted like nothing had happened, y'know?" She rotated the glass once more, and Rivers noted her fingernails were chewed, polish gone at the tips. "Anyway, I told Bruce, and he said to forget it, that it was nothing, that she was upset. You know like when someone gets mad and says, 'I could *kill* him,' but it's just because they're upset; they're not going to kill anyone."

Mendoza eyed her.

Andie added, "So I didn't say anything, just kept it to myself, like Bruce said." She looked miserable. "But now . . . But now she's been gone over a week, and I saw on the news that the police were asking for help, there's even a 'Find Megan' group on Facebook and Instagram and whatever. So I thought maybe I should tell you." Her face crumpled.

"You were right," Mendoza said.

"But it's off the record, right?"

Rivers asked, "Did she and James fight often?"

"I don't know."

"Was it ever physical?" he pushed. "Did she come in with bruises or—"

"No! Nothing like that. *She's* the one with the temper."

Rivers wondered about that.

"Was there anything else she said or did that was odd in the days leading up to her disappearance?"

Andie shook her head. "Not really. She was maybe a little tenser than usual, but with Megan, it's kinda hard to tell. Like I said, she's pretty emotional." She checked the clock over the revolving pie case in the corner and sucked in her breath. "Oh, darn. I gotta go." She started gathering her coat. "I'm gonna be late, and Doctor McEwen has himself a little fit if you're, like, more than thirty seconds late."

"If you think of anything else, call me," Mendoza said, but Andie was already sliding out of the booth and race-walking to the glass doors.

"Don't count on it." Rivers reached for his wallet and paid for the three drinks, noting that Andie hadn't taken so much as a sip of hers. He wondered about her, and about her boyfriend who wanted her to avoid the law. That was the trouble with this case, he thought as they walked outside to the blast of raw wind blowing across the parking lot. The more answers he found, the more questions that arose. It was beyond being idled or stalled. It felt like actual backpedaling.

He slid behind the wheel and flicked the starter, his Jeep's engine roaring to life. He needed to get back to the essence of it all, he figured, as Mendoza buckled up, and that was:

Who would benefit most if Megan Travers were out of the picture? That person was the key to it all.

Sophia Russo was the first person who came to mind. With Megan out of the picture, she could be the center of James Cahill's attention.

What about Rebecca Travers? Sure, she seemed interested in what had happened to her sister, but was it just an act? She and her sister had been at odds often enough, and Megan had stolen Mr. Wonderful—James Cahill—away from her.

He pulled out of the lot and headed back to the station.

Jennifer Korpi was another ex who was connected with Cahill and, despite her protestations, didn't seem over him.

Or was this whole scorned-woman thing overrated?

According to Andie, Megan thought James Cahill was capable of doing her bodily harm. *If anything happens to me, it's James, his fault.*

Was he a murderer? One with an accomplice? So that he could suffer an attack, but survive, and whoever was involved with him would take care of Megan—follow her? Chase her down? Did that hang together?

Charity Spritz had been in San Francisco when she'd been murdered. What had she dug up? Maybe something about the Cahill family? Something someone didn't want anyone to find out?

Or had it been about Megan? She and Rebecca had grown up in the area. He wondered again what Charity Spritz had known, what she'd been doing in San Francisco, and what, if anything, her death had to do with the mystery surrounding Megan Travers.

If Rivers was a betting man—and he was—he'd put his badge on the line, wagering that the two cases were linked. But then, that was an easy bet. Charity Spritz had been onto something in San Francisco, something that had gotten her killed.

CHAPTER 37

At noon, Rivers counted three news vans in the parking lot and twice that many reporters gathering around the steps to the Sheriff's Department. Rebecca Travers, pale-faced but determined, stood next to the public information officer, Roxy O'Grady. Travers was speaking into the microphone, making a plea for her sister's safe return, and all eyes were on her as a cold wind blew, rattling the chains of the flagpole and rushing through the branches of the bare shrubbery surrounding the brick building.

". . . and to anyone who has information that leads to locating Megan, we are offering a five-thousand-dollar reward. My family just wants Megan back. Thank you."

Rivers thought her speech had seemed heartfelt, despite her lack of tears, but Mendoza wasn't convinced.

"That woman has ice water in her veins," she said. "I don't trust her."

Rivers was on the fence about Rebecca Travers, not convinced she was innocent, not completely trusting her, but then he was suspicious of most people. He watched as she concluded her plea, then took a step back as the PIO took over. Roxy O'Grady asked anyone who had information to call the department and offered up the Sheriff's Department's phone number.

Thankfully, neither Rivers nor Mendoza was asked to speak or update the public on the case. O'Grady, all five feet, two inches of her, handled the questions the press called out to her, and she was up to the challenge. Fiftysomething, petite O'Grady was as fit as most women half her age. With short, near-white hair and a few premature wrinkles, she was attractive and absolutely no-nonsense, firing back answers quickly until the briefing took a sudden turn and a reporter, a lanky man with curly brown hair sticking out of a green cap, looked up from his cell phone and called out, "Is your department investigating the murder of Charity Spritz?"

"Here we go," Mendoza said under her breath. "The news is out." Until now, there had been no reports of Charity Spritz's homicide in Riggs Crossing. But that was changing.

There was a murmur through the small crowd collected at the base of the steps as other members of the press consulted each other or their mobile devices. Rebecca Travers visibly started, and she turned her questioning eyes toward Rivers.

O'Grady said, "We've just recently heard about the suspected homicide of Ms. Spritz."

Rebecca blanched, took an involuntary step back.

The newsman in the green cap pressed on. "It's being reported that she was killed in San Francisco. Can you confirm that?"

"We're still getting details from the San Francisco Police Department as the investigation is ongoing."

"She was rumored to be working on a story about Megan Travers," another reporter, a woman in a yellow coat, said. "Is Charity Spritz's homicide connected to Megan Travers's disappearance?"

"As I said, the investigation is ongoing."

More questions were thrown out: Why was Spritz in San Francisco? Who was a suspect in her death? How did she die? Was there any person of interest? Would the Sheriff's Department here work with the force in California?

All the while, Rebecca seemed to shrink back from the barrage of questions, outstretched microphones, and clicks of photographs. O'Grady handled it all, responding over and over again that the investigation was ongoing, there was nothing to report, and when there was, the public would be informed. She thanked them all and stepped away from the podium, a signal that the conference was over. As the reporters dispersed, Rebecca, her dark eyes grave, her jaw set, headed toward Rivers and Mendoza.

"This is true? Charity Spritz is dead? Murdered?" she demanded, obviously stunned.

Rivers nodded.

"But . . . but . . . She was just at my mother's house the other night.

Mom called and complained, said she was being harassed by her! She—Mom—she had the security guard come and escort Charity out of the gated community. She was really upset."

That was news. From the corner of his eye, he noted that Mendoza was already taking notes on her phone, and the green-capped reporter was drawing near.

"Let's go inside," Rivers suggested, shepherding them up the remaining steps and holding open the door.

As they walked inside, the warmth of the building enfolding them, Mendoza said, "We need to talk to your mother."

"You need to talk to *me*!" Rebecca charged and stopped in the main lobby, where glass windows separated them from officers who were working at the front desk. "You knew about it, and you didn't tell me," she charged, her shock having given way to anger.

Rivers said, "There's nothing to tell."

"Like hell! You can't expect me to believe it's just coincidence that the reporter who has been calling me day and night and showed up at my mom's house because she was investigating Megan's disappearance is *dead. Murdered.* Is that what you want me to think?"

"I don't believe in coincidence."

"Neither do I. Charity was all over Megan's disappearance. Now she's dead? Murdered? There has to be a link."

"We're working on it, but haven't discovered a connection yet," Rivers said.

"Well, find out." Her eyes sparked, and she sent Mendoza a scathing glance. "Can't you do something?"

"We're working—"

"Yeah, yeah, I know. You're 'working on it, the investigation is ongoing.' I heard. Well, do something more, will you?" Lips tight, she spun back to face Rivers. "This smells, Detective, and let me tell you, it smells rotten."

With that, she turned on her heel and was out the door.

From his chair at his desk, James asked, "You heard anything about Gus?"

Bobby stood and stretched, his back popping loudly. "A little."

They'd had a short meeting about delivery of the houses under construction. The consensus had been that not one of the three could be delivered before Christmas due to (a) delays in the delivery of everything from cabinets to special-ordered plumbing fixtures and lights and (b) the changing work schedules as the holiday approached.

"Bruce called him this morning. Surgery went okay, I guess," Bobby said as he squared his Mariners cap on his head. "They were able to stitch him up, and the nerve damage seemed minimal, at least that's what Porter got out of it, but it's hard to tell. Gus was probably still doped up on painkillers when they talked, and it'll take time to see what kind of range of motion Gus has with his fingers."

"How long will he be in the hospital?"

Bobby shrugged. "Bruce didn't say. Don't know if Gus knows for sure." He eyed James. "You know he's a loose cannon."

"Jardine?" He rolled the plans for the container house and snapped a rubber band around them. "Yeah."

Bobby looked about to say more, then held his tongue as he reached for the door.

"What?"

"Well . . . this is just hearsay, y'know, but one of the guys in the shop—Lloyd—he was workin' near Gus, and he thinks . . . God, this is crazy . . . but he thinks it looked like Gus shoved his hand right into the saw."

"What?"

"I know, I told you it was crazy. Who would do such a thing?" He scrabbled in a breast pocket of his work shirt for a crumpled pack of cigarettes.

"Why would he want to injure himself?" James asked, thinking of Leon Palleja's earlier comments along the same lines.

"Who knows? It's just what I heard."

"From who?"

"Oscar Aaronsen," Bobby admitted with a scowl. "He, Oscar, I mean, was working the skill saw, not far from where Gus was cuttin' tile, and out of the corner of his eye, he sees Gus adjust a tile, obviously at the wrong angle, and then what does he do? Close his eyes and ram the tile at the wrong angle so that the blade goes right between his fingers and he starts screamin' and cussin' and . . . oh, well, like I said, it's freakin' nuts. Just a rumor."

Was it?

"Forget I said anything. It's gossip. That's all," Bobby said, and he took off, but James wondered. He felt as if he were at the vortex of some strange whirlpool where nothing was as it seemed and reality was blurred.

He stared through the windows to the shop, where work went on as usual: Carpenters, electricians, and plumbers milled around the houses being constructed; saws screamed; and rock music thudded. It all appeared the same, but it was different. Vastly so. Now beneath the calm exterior of a normal workday lurked the presence of something darker, something where people went missing or worse, or men risked life and limb to intentionally mutilate themselves.

Why?

Of course, no answer came to him. He switched on the small television mounted over a file cabinet, the volume just loud enough to mute some of the noise from the shop, and turned to the stack of invoices on his desk.

The invoices swam in front of his eyes, however, and he found concentration impossible. He rubbed his jaw, felt the tracks of the claw marks on his cheek beneath his beard, and wondered about Megan. Guilt tore at him. His actions, taking up with Sophia, had been the spark for her anger, the reason she'd attacked him, the impetus for her driving out of Riggs Crossing to who-knew-where. He hadn't physically assaulted her, but his actions had propelled her out of his door and into the night. He closed his eyes and tried to remember what had happened. Was there something more?

And now Rebecca was in his life again.

No—that was wrong. She'd made that pretty clear. The damned thing of it was, he wanted to see her again—despite all the mess of their lives, of . . . and that's when he heard her voice.

For a second, he thought he was imagining it. He glanced up sharply and focused on the small television screen, and there she was, standing on the steps of the sheriff's office and asking for help in finding Megan, even offering up a reward. Snatching up the remote, he increased the volume, then kicked back his chair and rounded his desk to plant himself in front of the small screen. His chest constricted at the sight of her in a long coat and boots, wind pulling at her hair as she spoke, flanked by cops.

For a second, he lost his concentration—the boots, the hair at her nape, the . . . and then whatever wayward thought had pulled his attention away disappeared, and he was caught up in watching Rebecca, chin angled, eyes direct, pleading for the safety of Megan. His heart twisted painfully.

Megan had betrayed her.

He had betrayed her.

But there she was, standing strong, fighting tears. As she quit speaking, a short woman cop took over, asking the public's assistance in locating Megan, whose picture suddenly filled the screen: straight, near-blond hair that fell to her shoulders, blue eyes twinkling, an easy smile, and a smattering of freckles visible over her short, straight nose.

Again, his thoughts were broken, and there was something in the picture that tugged at him, teased at his memory, and gave him pause. Something important that was too elusive to catch, when the screen split, and half the image was of a black 2010 Toyota Corolla and the license plate number for Megan's car.

He ignored the invoices that he'd been working on. Leaning his hips against the edge of his desk, James tried to conjure up the thought that had been teasing him—something that had caught his attention while staring at Rebecca on the stairs of the Sheriff's Department, then again when Megan's picture had flashed onto the screen. What was it? He squinted as he thought. It hadn't been that they resembled each other, because they didn't, not in looks nor temperament, so what?

Before an answer came, another bit of streaming news flashed onto the screen: LOCAL REPORTER FOUND MURDERED IN SAN FRANCISCO.

"What?" he said aloud. A picture of Charity Spritz came into view, and his stomach sank. Murdered? *San Francisco?* He stared at her image as the reporter explained that her body had been found in the city, but police thought she'd been killed elsewhere.

His head was pounding with the news, and the questions she'd asked him while standing on his doorstep flitted through his head.

"You're from San Francisco," she'd said, and when he'd denied it, she'd pointed out that his family had been. Which was true.

He'd refused to talk to her, and now . . . now she was dead? Killed in the very city she'd mentioned? His blood ran cold. *What was this?* He knew in his gut that Charity's death was linked to Megan's disappearance.

Had to be.

His cell phone vibrated on the desk.

Rowdy Crocker's name came onto the screen.

James answered in a heartbeat. "Yeah?"

"And 'hello' to you too."

James wasn't in the mood for games. "Did you hear about Charity Spritz?"

"Christ, yeah. I'm all over it."

"Jesus." James stared through the glass to the shop below, but he didn't see his employees working on trusses or planing rough wood or mudding Sheetrock; instead, he saw Charity Spritz, her gray eyes assessing him beneath a fringe of dark bangs. She'd stood on his porch as if she'd owned it a week earlier.

"Hey, man, you okay?" Rowdy asked.

"No," James said, then focused on the conversation. "What've you got?"

"Too much to discuss on the phone. I'm already in my car. I'll meet you at your place in fifteen. That work?"

"Yeah." James reached for his jacket, searching for his keys. "I'll be there."

"We got a hit," Mendoza announced as Rivers strode into the station. He'd gone outside, walked around the block, and returned with a coffee for himself and a "skinny vanilla latte with light whip," which he'd heard Mendoza order several times when they'd stopped in for coffee at the local shop.

"A hit?"

"Response to the press conference."

"Legit?"

"Maybe. A couple from Tacoma called in—on speaker phone so they both could talk, very confusing—but they think they spied Megan's car that night, but not on the main road to Seattle. They were staying at a friend's cabin and met a car coming the other direction, and the husband swears it was a black Toyota Corolla, but he couldn't be certain of the year."

"Where have they been?" Rivers asked, handing her the cup as they made their way to her desk. "I mean, how could they be in this state and not know we were looking for her?" Megan Travers's disappearance had been all over the news.

"That's just it. They've been out of town. They flew out the next morning and have been on a family vacation in Mexico, and after that they spent a week with their son and his family in Salt Lake. They just got home last night and caught up on the news, saw the press conference, and put two and two together."

Rivers asked, "So where did they see the car?"

"That's the interesting part—on a little mountain road, not more than a lane, where people have second homes. It's sparse. Hardly anyone lives up there year-round. Just summer homes. Cabins on a creek and in the woods, that sort of thing." She took a sip from her cup as she settled into her chair, and he stood next to her to view the monitor on her desk.

Rivers's mind churned. "Does one of the cabins belong to James Cahill?" he asked, focused on her computer screen. An aerial shot, where a small spur of a county road was visible, came into view. Maybe this really was something.

"Nope. Not Cahill."

"Then who?"

She zeroed in on one plot of land. "I checked the county records for all of the lots in the area, and most meant nothing, but the registered owner of this place," she tapped the screen with a fingernail where the roof of a cabin was visible through the tree branches, "just happens to be one Harold Sinclaire, aka Mr. 'Good Guy' Harry."

"Harry Sinclaire?" The name rang a bell. "Jennifer Korpi's boyfriend?" he asked, surprised. Though he hadn't discounted her as a suspect, Rivers hadn't really thought the nervous schoolteacher James Cahill had once dated was involved in Megan's disappearance. She hadn't seemed the type, despite what he'd felt while holding her tension ball: the sadness, the anger, maybe even a hint of jealousy. Nonetheless, this was something, and that familiar tingle in his blood that came with the thought that they finally had something to go on, a lead, singed through his veins.

"Yep. Jennifer's current main squeeze, as my grandma used to say.

One and the same." Mendoza seemed pleased with herself. "How do you think Sister Rosemarie would like them apples?"

He allowed himself a laugh.

Mendoza said, "I think we should go and check the place out."

He was already reaching for his keys, and within minutes, they were driving west out of the city. With Mendoza navigating the GPS, Rivers kept to the main road, then, near the summit, turned onto a county road that was packed with ice and snow. They met few other vehicles as the road twisted upward through dense old growth laden with snow, fir trees and pines that spired high into the sky.

"Here!" Mendoza said as they rounded a sharp curve and she spied a narrow one-lane bridge that spanned a frozen creek. The lane was unplowed, with only a few visible ruts. They decided to walk in and trudged through knee-deep snow in places to the third house in, a rustic, two-storied cabin with a steeply pitched roof, the walls built of rough-wood siding that had grayed over the years. The doors were locked, but a few of the windows didn't have the shades drawn. They peered inside, their breath fogging the panes, the interior dark.

"No one's in here," Mendoza said, frowning. "The place looks almost abandoned."

He agreed. "Probably only used in the summer." They walked along a snow-covered path to the detached garage, which was little more than a shed. Its door too was locked tight, but there was a window in the side door, and the shade was broken, falling at an angle that left a long, uneven sliver of the pane unobscured. Using his flashlight and ignoring the blinding reflection from the beam reflecting on the glass, Rivers peered inside. The beam swept over a stack of wood and a few garden tools to land squarely on the hood of a small black sedan.

"Son of a bitch," he whispered as he stared at what he firmly believed to be Megan Travers's 2010 Toyota.

CHAPTER 38

The Isolated Cabin
December 15

It's now or never!

I hear the vehicle approach, engine whining as the car climbs the hill, tires crunching through ice and snow.

With difficulty, I swallow back my fear. My nerves are jangled, my emotions strung raw. I have to do this. And I have to do it now!

This is my one shot. If I fail now, I'll never have another chance. If I fail, I could be signing my death warrant.

You can do this, you can.

But my confidence wavers. Even though I've got the plastic bits in one pocket and the metal hook rack in the other, I feel my determination start to crumble as I envision the scene, sense the imminent attack.

But. Oh. God.

My stomach clenches.

I've played and replayed the scenario in my mind for hours on end. While struggling to get to sleep in the loft, I've imagined it often:

A sharp rap on the door.

A familiar voice.

The jangle of keys.

The door being flung open.

"Hello?" will be called out.

One step inside.

And then strike!

Swift as a cougar leaping from a mountain ledge, I spring from the loft, weapons extended like claws.

My adversary looks up.

Too late!

With deadly aim, I gouge eyes, ripping flesh and ocular matter as I blind my jailor.

Then I go for the throat.

Slashing.

Blood spurting.

Gurgling air rasping through a severed trachea.

I feel sick at the thought.

Bile rises in my throat.

The whining engine is nearing. I climb the ladder, as I've done dozens of times, peek through the row of impossibly small windows near the ceiling. Headlights flash through the trees, illumination splaying on the frozen trunks.

"Give me strength," I pray, then feel disgust at my weakness, my supplication to a deity who has abandoned me. I don't need God's help in crippling and killing my captor.

Nor do I need Satan's.

I only need to remember who did this to me and why.

And then I'm ready.

I can do this.

But I'm thwarted.

This time, my captor doesn't step inside, just shoves a bag of groceries through the partially open door before locking it again.

What?

NO!

I scream in frustration.

But it's too late!

I hear the car leave and take my dreams of escape with it.

CHAPTER 39

Rowdy Crocker had lied.

He hadn't been twenty minutes away.

Probably not even ten, because when James got home, he found Crocker's ancient Ford pickup in the driveway and Rowdy himself seated in James's recliner, an opened bottle of beer on the table beside him, reading glasses propped on the end of his nose while his fingers flew over the keyboard of James's laptop. His brown hair was long and shaggy, falling over his forehead, his jaw covered in half a week's growth of beard, and he wore camouflage pants and jacket over a black Megadeth T-shirt that had seen better days.

Ralph gave a quick bark at the sight of him.

"You're okay," Rowdy said to the dog without glancing up from the screen. He grabbed his bottle, took a long swallow of beer, and said, "Don't you have anything to eat around here?"

"What the hell are you doing?" James asked.

"What's it look like?" Rowdy peered over the tops of his reading glasses and gave an exaggerated shrug. "Uh . . . helping?"

"By breaking into my house and—"

"—and grabbing a brewskie while cleaning up your damned computer? Well, yeah, if you'd call what I did 'breaking in.'" He frowned up at James and gave an exaggerated sigh. "A key on the sill over the back door? Really? Why not just post a neon sign with an arrow that says, 'Look Here for Key'?"

That burned James; an intruder would have to walk through the woodshed or around to the very back to another door just to get to the locked door.

"You said you had information."

"I do. And a helluva lot of it," Crocker said, leaning forward and snapping the footrest of the recliner down as he sat upright. He set the computer on a side table. "Let's go get you a beer, and we'll discuss." Grabbing his own bottle, he headed for the kitchen, his heavy work boots clomping down the hallway.

Just like he owned the place.

James followed. "Have you found Megan?"

"No."

"What, then?" James tried and failed to keep the irritation out of his voice. He'd known Rowdy since junior high, expected some of his high jinks. It was all part of the Rowdy Crocker package. But it was still irritating as hell.

"You know that Charity Spritz was murdered?"

James nodded, still bothered. "Heard it on the news, just in the last hour."

"You have any idea why she was in the Bay Area?" Rowdy was already at the fridge and pulling out two more bottles.

"I can guess."

Rowdy glanced over his shoulder. "I can do better than that." He found the opener he'd left on the counter and opened both new bottles, then finished his first bottle and left the empty in the sink.

"I've set up in the dining room. That's where I saw your computer and thought I'd clean it up; you know, you should get a better security system for it. Any hack could get into your files."

"Just like any hack could get into my house?"

Rowdy barked out a laugh. "If the shoe fits . . ."

They settled at the table, where Rowdy's open laptop sat next to his iPad and two cell phones. "Rudimentary, I know. But it's what we have to deal with."

James could only imagine what Rowdy had in his own home, a cabin in the woods that was supposedly "off the grid" but was actually equipped with the latest in technological equipment, everything from cameras to recording equipment, computers with layers of security, and the kind of spying equipment a CIA operative would drool over—or at least that's what Rowdy claimed.

Taking a chair next to him, James drank from his bottle as Crocker settled in, working the keyboard, and Ralph curled at his feet under the table.

"Okay, as I said, I haven't located Megan. Not yet. But I will tell you this, the police have just found her car."

"They have? How do you—?"

"Remember my 'don't ask' policy."

Crocker demanded ultimate secrecy.

"Just trust me. They got it. I haven't pinpointed the location, but in the mountains."

James's heart was pounding. "But what about Megan?"

"She's not with it. From what I understand, they found her belongings—her phone, her laptop, and purse. They're checking into it as we speak." He slid a sideways glance at James. "But you might prepare yourself. They haven't started looking for a body yet."

James sucked in a swift breath. "You're saying she's dead."

"I'm saying it's a very distinct possibility." No joking. Rowdy was serious. "The kicker is that the property is owned by Harold Sinclaire."

"Sinclaire?" James repeated. "He bought a tiny home from me."

"This cabin isn't a tiny home; it's been there for half a century, probably longer, but the connection is that Sinclaire is involved with Jennifer Korpi."

"What?"

"Small world, I guess."

"But Jennifer . . . I mean, she would never be involved in anything like this," James said. "Doesn't make any sense. You're sure about this."

Crocker gave him a long look. "You know who you're talking to?"

"Okay. Right."

"And didn't you say that her brother, Gus Jardine, he's going to sue you for an industrial accident?"

"Right." James snorted. "The thing is, several people who worked near him think he did it on purpose. How crazy is that?"

"Maybe not so crazy."

"So he's after money? Going to sue me?"

Crocker cracked his neck. "Maybe it's more than that. Take a look at this." Again his fingers flew over his keyboard, and within seconds, a picture of a mangled hand came into view, torn tissue, exposed bone, and ligaments visible in the flesh.

"Holy crap, is this Gus's hand? How the hell did you get that?"

Crocker didn't answer, just shot him a reminding glare, then pointed to the screen. "See here, on the palm, on the inside of the first knuckles. It's been cleaned up, so you can see the tear in the flesh, but if you look closely, here under the ring and middle fingers, there is another set of bruises."

"From the saw."

Crocker shook his head slowly. "Look at the marks, several deep but small impressions, almost semicircular."

James just stared, his mind racing, his muscles tensing. "You're saying this is a bite mark."

"A human bite mark," Crocker corrected.

James was following Crocker's theory. "You think Jardine *intentionally* screwed up his hand to cover up the fact that his hand was bitten?"

Suddenly, Crocker scraped back his chair, rounded on James, and grabbed him from behind, his right hand covering James's mouth.

James reacted, every muscle tensed as he was about to throw Rowdy off of him. "Hey!" he cried, but his voice was muffled, nearly silenced. Ralph jumped up, growling, hackles raised, ready to leap at Crocker as he released James.

"Get it?" he asked, breathing hard.

James did. The "attack" was just a demonstration. And he was following Crocker's train of thought. "You think Gus Jardine killed Charity Spritz?"

"I think it's a strong possibility." He slid into his chair again. "I already did some checking, and he could have done it on the night she was killed and gotten back here in time to look good." He changed the image on the screen, and this time it was a person leaving a van in a parking lot. "At the San Francisco airport. Does that dude"—he indicated the man in black hurrying from the van—"does he look like Jardine?"

"Maybe," James allowed. "Maybe not."

"I'm working on that."

"Good." James stared at the screen as Rowdy replayed the short film over and over. The guy had the same build as Gus Jardine, but his face was obscured, his clothes dark and without anything distinguishing. "But why would Gus Jardine kill Charity Spritz?"

"Because she knew something, or was going to find out something."

"About him. Or his sister?"

"That's the million-dollar question. Or one of them. Why do you think Charity Spritz was in Northern California?"

"Probably checking into my family. She said as much."

"To you?"

"Well, she came over here, wanting an interview, and brought up the fact that my family was based there, so I would assume that's a reason she went there."

Crocker took a big swallow from his bottle, but kept looking at his computer screen. "You're right. And I think she hit pay dirt. You probably know that your family has more than its share of nutcases."

James tensed but couldn't deny it.

"The Cahill and Amhurst family tree has a lot of branches and roots and is a real clusterfuck when it comes to the gene pool."

He knew that much. His full name was James Amhurst Cahill; his mother was an Amhurst, a child born to one of his grandfather's mistresses. She ended up marrying his stepfather, Nick, a Cahill.

"And you, my friend," Rowdy said in awe, "you're one of the few heirs to the Amhurst fortune. It's not the Cahills who will make you rich, though they'll do their part, but the Amhursts . . ." He let out a long, low whistle, and Ralph, from beneath the table, lifted his head, ears pricked.

"I have sisters. And a relative in San Francisco with a couple of kids. They'll inherit."

"Will they?"

James tensed.

"Your grandfather's will. He left the lion's share of a huge estate to you. Almost all of it. In trust. Your sisters? Not so much. And that half-sister, Cissy, she gets a nice chunk of change, but you, my friend, are the big winner in the Family Fortune Sweepstakes!"

James asked, "What does the inheritance have to do with Charity Spritz and her murder?"

"Well, that's just the thing, isn't it? Remember I said there was this pretty messed-up and comingled gene pool where all sorts of Cahills and Amhursts were involved with each other, with kids conceived out of marriage, those who were once called 'illegitimate,' though that's not PC today. You had a whacked-out half-cousin or something, a woman who did some major damage a few years back, right? Like your mother's half-sister's secret daughter or something."

"Something like that."

"Created a lot of scandal."

"At the least." The woman had terrorized Cissy, nearly driven her insane. Cissy had barely survived.

"Right." Crocker nodded, agreeing with himself. "A real nutjob. Well, guess what?"

James's stomach knotted. He didn't know what was coming, but he sensed it was bad. Real bad. "I couldn't."

"I haven't got all of the details yet," Rowdy admitted, "but it looks like she had a kid before she started all of the mayhem for your family. A daughter, I think, though I don't have all the details. And she gave the kid up for adoption through—drum roll, please"—he waited expectantly and looked a little deflated when James didn't respond—"through Cahill House, of course, that place in San Francisco your own family started for pregnant teens."

James's bad feeling was getting worse by the second. "So what exactly are you getting at?"

"It's pretty damned clear, isn't it? I think Charity Spritz found out about that baby and knows where he or she is. She talked with a nurse who had worked at Cahill House during those years, but so far, I haven't found out what was divulged."

"Do you know the nurse's name?"

"Not yet, but I'm working on it."

"Shouldn't we tell the cops?"

"What?" His head whipped around. "No. I don't trust 'em, and you shouldn't either. Remember why you called me in the first place: You're still their number-one suspect. They don't need any help. They have the technology and manpower to figure this out. If you want me on your side, then the cops are out. You decide." He checked his watch, then finished his beer. "Gotta run. I just wanted to talk to you face-to-face."

"You think my phone's being bugged?" James asked.

"Just being careful. By the way, I swept this place since the cops searched it. Looks clean."

"Not every cop is dirty."

"Yeah, I know, but you just don't know which ones are clean. So . . . let's just keep all this on the down low." Rowdy snapped his laptop closed and pushed back his chair. "I'll let you know what else I find. Shouldn't take too long. And then we'll settle up." He stuffed his equipment into the battered case and headed for the front door. "And, James," he said, as he stepped onto the porch, "be careful, okay? The reporter's dead. Probably because of you. And a woman's missing, again, probably because she was close to you, so watch your ass, okay? And while you're at it? Why don't you try hiding your spare key someplace where a three-year-old can't find it?"

CHAPTER 40

Darkness had fallen by the time the search crew was finished going over Sinclaire's cabin, and the cold was getting to them. Rivers rubbed his gloved hands together to conjure up warmth, while Mendoza stomped her feet in the snow.

Upon spying Megan Travers's car in the garage, Mendoza had called for backup and gotten a search warrant. Rivers had phoned Harold Sinclaire, and Sinclaire, shocked, had agreed to meet them at the property and had given them the code to a lockbox near the front door with a hidden key. With the owner's permission on top of the search warrant, Rivers and Mendoza had searched through the house and grounds. The car in the garage had turned out to be Megan Travers's, and her phone, laptop, and purse were inside.

But the woman hadn't been in the car, nor the trunk, nor the house. No body of Megan Travers. Or anyone else. Yet someone had driven the car to the cabin, and the keys to the car, and presumably her apartment, had been left in the Toyota's ignition. They were still puzzling it all out when, along with another couple of deputies, the tow truck had arrived, the driver managing to back the huge rig with its flashing amber lights over the narrow bridge and between the trees to park in front of the garage where the Corolla had been stashed.

"No clothes," Mendoza remarked. "Nor any kind of overnight bag—no makeup kit or bag for prescriptions." She frowned as she shone the beam of her flashlight over the car's interior. "I get that she was angry and left in a huff, but she had the presence of mind to bring her laptop and iPad and phone with her."

"Maybe they were already there, in the car."

"But she knew she was leaving. She wrote the note at her apartment and didn't return, right?"

"Yeah. She got off work, went home, changed, and then drove out to Cahill's house, got into it with him; things got physical and she took off, nearly hitting the snowplow and driving like a bat through town, calling her sister and . . . then what? She didn't just drive here."

"Not unless it was some kind of disappearing act on her part, which I doubt."

"Agreed."

"So she either planned to meet someone here, or got a call and came here because of that call, or was forced to drive here."

"And then what?" Rivers said just as he caught a glimpse of a new set of headlights, beams reflecting on the snow as a white Range Rover came into view, growling across the bridge spanning the creek. As Rivers watched, the SUV stopped to onc side of the series of ruts created by the other vehicles. The driver's door swung open, and a beefy man no more than five feet, eight inches tall swung out, slamming his door shut.

"Harold Sinclaire," Rivers told Mendoza.

"What the hell is this all about?" Sinclaire demanded, his eyes wide, his face flushed. He was dressed from head to toe in red and black snow gear, a matching knit cap pulled down over his ears, all adding to the image of a spark plug. "Are you kidding me?" he said. "Megan Travers's car is *here?*"

Rivers nodded. "In the garage. We're going to tow it back to the department's garage."

"But why?" Harold asked, astounded, his eyes round. "I mean why would she end up here . . . or her car end up here? What the eff is this all about?"

"That's what we were hoping you could help us with."

"I have absolutely no idea." He turned his gloved hands palm up to show his state of confusion.

The passenger door of his Range Rover opened, and Jennifer Korpi, bundled in a long coat, stepped out, picking her way through the snow in high-heeled boots that were more fashionable than functional.

"What's this all about?" she asked, glancing at the tow truck, its lights flashing as it winched the Toyota onto its bed.

"You know what it is, honey," Sinclaire said. "I told you I want to get rid of this place. It's just a headache. All the upkeep with snow in the winter—I'm always afraid the roof might collapse, or the pipes freeze, or raccoons make nests in the attic—that's happened before, and what about someone siphoning off the propane?" He turned to Rivers. "Who would do that? Clear up here? Who the hell would drive all this way to steal damned propane? I was just lucky some snowshoers saw it happening, or when I came up here after the new year, I wouldn't have had any heat!"

"When was that?" Rivers asked.

"Dunno. A month ago maybe . . ." He glanced at Jennifer for confirmation.

She nodded. "Maybe four, maybe five weeks ago. After that big storm. Which was . . . just before Thanksgiving, I think." She bit her lip. "I just don't get why this is happening. Why Megan's car is here. It doesn't make any sense."

"Yeah," Sinclaire agreed. "Her car is here, but she isn't?"

"And the garage was locked. Does anyone else know the combination to your lockbox?" Rivers asked.

"No." Sinclaire shook his head. "Well, aside from the two of us and the neighbor." He pointed down the snow-covered lane. "Frank Miller. He comes up here more often than we do, and so he can get in if he sees something wrong. But that's it, right, honey?" He glanced at Jennifer, who didn't meet his eyes. "Honey?"

She let out a sigh. "Well, remember? We gave the code to Gus once. He was delivering firewood."

"But he never showed. The wood deal fell through." Sinclaire shrugged. "Doesn't matter. Gus isn't involved in all of this."

Rivers wondered.

Gus Jardine's name kept coming up. Just here and there, always on the fringes.

"I'm telling you I'm gonna sell this place," Harold said, draping an arm around Jennifer's shoulders. "We just don't need the headache."

Sinclaire and Korpi watched as the Toyota was secured onto the flatbed and the tow truck lumbered off, almost too big for the little bridge spanning the creek.

Rivers hoped they would get lucky, that fingerprints or some other bit of evidence would be located in the car, that there would be a clue to what had happened to Megan Travers, but he wasn't betting on it.

By the time they left the cabin in the woods, it was after seven, and they stopped at Lucy's, ending up in a booth near the one where they'd met Andie Jeffries, Mendoza sliding onto one high-backed bench, he opposite her. The place was crowded, conversation drowning out the oldies music, several waitresses hurrying from one table to the next, the sizzle of a deep fryer adding to the cacophony. Mendoza ordered a meatless burger and sparkling water. Rivers decided on chicken-fried steak and french fries with a Coke, as he was still on duty. A beer would have to wait.

"You're killing yourself," Mendoza observed when the orders came and thick gravy oozed over the side of his plate.

"In more ways than one, I'm sure." He grabbed the bottle of catsup and squeezed out a huge puddle onto his plate, right next to a pile of steaming fries. "And the jury's still out on fake meat. You know, it can be made with some kind of three-D printer. How nutritious can that be?"

"But oooh, so yummy." She cut the damned thing in half, exposing layers of pickles, tomatoes, onions and lettuce, before she took a big bite. "You're missing out."

"I'll take your word for it."

"You notice how Gus Jardine's name keeps coming up?" Rivers asked, once he'd taken two bites of the steak. "Always on the periphery, but there."

"Uh-huh. Which links Jennifer."

"Maybe." Rivers thought about it. Took a swallow of soda. "Maybe there's another connection."

"Other than that his sister was dumped by James Cahill?"

"For Rebecca Travers, not Megan."

Mendoza raised one hand and tilted it back and forth to indicate she wasn't convinced. "Maybe it's the samey-same. You know, get back at whatever woman he's currently dating."

"Thin." He cut off another bite of steak, plopped it into his mouth.

"I can see your arteries clogging from here." She grinned, teasing, her dark eyes flashing.

"You're just jealous."

She snorted and stared at his plate. "Hardly." Then she looked up at him again. "Okay, if you don't buy my theory, then what?"

"Not sure yet. Maybe Gus Jardine has another connection to Megan."

"So what is it? Why would Jardine—what? Kidnap her? Force her to drive to Sinclaire's cabin? Then . . . snowshoe out? Have another vehicle waiting? What would he do with her?"

"Maybe they were in it together," Rivers said, thinking aloud. "She fights with Cahill, meets up with Jardine; they stash the car, and she hides out."

"Why? Makes no sense. What would be the point? Revenge for Megan, but what's in it for Jardine?" Her eyebrows raised inquisitively, and then she made a bleeping sound, like the buzzer on a game show when the contestant fails. "Not buying it."

"Yeah, me neither," he admitted and grew quiet as he finished his meal. Nothing was making sense, but he felt as if they were getting closer to piecing it all together. Jardine was involved. They just had to figure out how.

Once they were on the road again, Rivers drove toward the station, and Mendoza, as ever, was on her phone, scrolling through messages and e-mail. He'd just pulled into the lot when she said, "Uh-oh . . . what's this?"

"What?" he asked as he nosed his Jeep into a parking slot near a department cruiser.

Her eyebrows knitted as she stared at the screen. "It's weird." But there was an edge of excitement to her voice. "Let's go inside. I want to bring it up on my computer. Bigger image." She was already unbuckling her seat belt and opening the passenger door.

Rivers followed her to her cubicle, where she peeled off her coat and slung it haphazardly onto a filing cabinet; then she slid into her roller chair and pulled it close to her computer monitor. "It's from the lab," she explained. "DNA on the hairs found in James Cahill's bed." Her fingers were flying over the keyboard and working the roller ball of her mouse. "Here . . . look." The report came onto the screen. "Three specimens," she pointed out, "all different. One male. James Cahill and two others. One is from Megan Travers—it matches the samples we took from a brush in her apartment, and the other one . . . look here. Female as well, undetermined, but get this—related to Cahill."

"What?"

"A cousin, probably, not a first cousin, but someone related to him on his mother's side."

"His mother?"

"Right, Kylie Cahill, who was Kylie Paris, but who, it seems, is really an Amhurst." She glanced up at Rivers, who was standing behind her, bending over to see the screen. "I've done some research. The Amhursts are even richer than the Cahills, or were, and the two families intermarried or got sexually involved with each other over the years, and there were several children who were born to mistresses."

"Including Kylie Paris."

"Right."

"So James Cahill was sleeping with someone related to him?"

"Distantly related, but yeah," Mendoza said, disgust pulling at the edges of her lips. "The way he goes through women, this shouldn't be a surprise."

"To us," Rivers thought aloud, "but I wonder if it will be to him." He stared at the report and the label: UNKNOWN FEMALE.

Mendoza rolled her chair back to stare up at him. "The Unknown Female is a blonde," she pointed out.

"So Sophia Russo is his cousin," he said, the wheels in his mind whirling.

"Imagine that." She shook her head. "Some kind of cousin. As I said, 'distant.'"

"I wonder if he knows?"

Mendoza shook her head. "Maybe not yet, but he will soon enough."

Rivers's cell phone went off, and he glanced at the screen. "At last."

"At last?" Mendoza was still looking at the DNA results on the computer monitor.

"At last—Earl Ray Dansen," he said and answered. Dansen and he had been playing phone tag for most of the day. "Rivers," he said into the phone.

"It's Earl Ray, down at the *Clarion.* Glad I finally caught you."

"Me too. You know about Charity Spritz."

"Jesus, yeah, I know. Can't believe it." He sounded stunned. "Horrible."

"Can you tell me what she was working on?"

"The Cahill story. But, uh . . . look, I think it would be better if we talk face-to-face. I've got something I need to show you."

Rivers checked his watch. After seven. "How about now?"

"I'm stuck here with tomorrow's edition. I was hoping you could come to the office."

"That works. We're on our way."

Heart pounding, Sophia waited for the results of the pregnancy test. Her hand was shaking, her stomach in knots as she stood in the bathroom of her apartment.

What if she was pregnant?

What if she wasn't?

She didn't know what to wish for.

Heart beating like a jackhammer, she was totally alone, waiting for her sister to return.

Julia had been acting strange lately, had been jumpy, and Sophia really couldn't blame her. Everything was weird. Sophia had seen on the news that that reporter woman, the one she didn't like, Charity Spritz, had been murdered in San Francisco.

The thought of it gave Sophia a really bad feeling when she'd seen it on television.

And that wasn't all of it.

First off, Gus had been involved in a freaky accident with a saw at the shop. He'd torn up his hand so badly that he might never have full use of it again. But then, Gus was an idiot. He might have done it on purpose and blamed James, looking for a lawsuit and a huge settlement.

Then Phoebe Matrix—that old busybody of an apartment owner/manager—had suffered some kind of allergic reaction or diabetic seizure or something and had been rushed to the hospital. Sophia had seen the EMTs arrive and had talked to her neighbor, the older guy who was always cleaning up around here, in unit 5, Phil Something-or-Other. He'd said the old bat had made it to his door, and he'd called 9-1-1. According to him, Phoebe might not make it, was in a diabetic coma. He was pretty upset about it as he'd ended up with Phoebe's miserable little dog.

Sophia couldn't help but feel bad for the older woman, even if she was a pain in the ass.

But she couldn't be distracted.

Bad shit happened.

Occupational accidents and comas occurred all the time.

But a murder? Of someone she knew? That was different.

She closed her mind to all those things and stared at the pregnancy test stick. Even if the world around her was spinning out of control, this—a baby—could change everything.

She felt her teeth sink into her lower lip.

Sitting down on the lid of the toilet, she knew she'd made a mistake. She'd lost her heart. To James. That hadn't been part of the plan.

And now . . . God, and now, she was losing him, feeling him slip between her fingers. Because of Rebecca Travers. Her heart ached at the thought. How could it have happened? Why would he take up with Rebecca again? It just wasn't fair.

Sophia had thought—no, prayed—that he would fall in love with her, really fall in love, and that no other woman could turn his head.

And then Rebecca had shown up.

Sophia's blood began to boil at the thought of it. Because it was her own damned fault. But she wasn't alone in that screwup; Julia had been involved too. In fact, the whole Megan going missing thing had been her idea.

Life was so damned unfair!

She squeezed the stick in her hand so hard that she caught herself, noticed the impression on her palm, and reminded herself that she had to stay calm and keep her temper under control.

It wasn't as if the unfairness of the universe were a new thing.

It always had been unfair.

She thought of her years growing up, alone and isolated, an only child of cold-hearted parents who eventually divorced and shuffled her back and forth like some piece of unwanted furniture.

And then . . . and then, miracle of miracles, through a genealogy search company, she'd connected with Julia and learned a whole lot about who she really was. The first time she'd seen her twin, Sophia had been stunned. It had been like looking into a mirror. After connecting on the Internet and, yes, seeing pictures of each other, they'd finally met face-to-face at a little bistro in San Mateo. Sophia had watched as Julia had locked her car and walked into the outdoor area of the restaurant, which faced the street. Sophia couldn't believe it. They were so much alike! From the blue of their eyes to the white-blond of their hair to the same dimple. Julia's hair had been a couple of inches shorter, and she'd dressed with a little more flash, but they were definitely identical. They'd eaten Italian food and talked and laughed, and the hole that had been in Sophia's heart began to slowly close. Finally, after years of loneliness, Sophia felt connected to someone who was truly like her—so much like her that it was a little eerie. At first, they became friends, learning all about each other, each explaining how they'd felt incomplete. It was as if Julia had insight into Sophia's mind, and they started hanging out, talking about the future, and within a week or two, Julia had explained that she'd done more research on their family, their biological family, and had discovered that they were related to one of the richest families in the Bay Area. They were, by rights, heirs to the Amhurst fortune, and as they spent more time together, Julia hatched a plan to reclaim what was rightfully theirs. However, it involved a "little bit" of deception, Julia explained. Well, it had turned out to be more than a little bit, and Sophia had resisted, didn't like lying or "playing" a guy the way Julia had suggested in order to get to James Cahill, but then Julia had said it was fine, she would go it alone. She really didn't need Sophia to be a part of the plot.

"I just thought you'd want to," she'd said as they were driving into the city one day, the traffic stalled as they were trapped on the Bay Bridge. Rain had been steadily falling, the water on either side of the bridge choppy, cars all around them. "I'm going to do it! I'm going to make James Cahill fall in love with me. It would have just been easier if you helped me out, you know. He's got a wandering eye, but we'll see to it that he is kind of like blinded by us—can't get away from us, you know, sees us everywhere he goes so that he can't get us—or you—or me—out of his mind. We'll be everywhere—looking hot, hot, hot—always ready to be with him, you know, sexually or romantically or whatever, so that he never gets a chance to find someone else; then we could really get him to marry us. Other guys will look at us, but we'll only have eyes for James!"

"Marry?" Sophia repeated.

Julia's eyes twinkled mischievously. "Of course, silly." She laughed in delight, her enthusiasm contagious. "How else are we going to get what was really ours in the first place?"

Julia had explained how their mother, Deidre, had given the twins up for adoption even though she herself had been estranged at one time from her mother, their grandmother, Marla Amhurst, who had married a Cahill—James's father!

"So he's not related to us?" Sophia had asked, intrigued, and really, James was handsome. She'd seen pictures Julia had on her phone.

"Not really. His mother is half-sister to our grandmother or something like that. It's no biggie. But the point is, he's rich, rich, rich. Going to inherit mega millions, and I'd like to be a part of it. I thought you might want to also."

Sophia had stared down at a picture of James.

"I don't know . . ."

"Well, that's fine." Traffic had begun to move again, and as they inched across the dark water, Sophia had thought of her life, how lonely and empty it had been, and now she and Julia could be together.

So Julia had dropped it for a while, but as the weeks had bled into months and they'd become closer, Sophia had slowly decided her sister was right. Julia had sworn no one would get hurt, not really. They were just reclaiming what they should have gotten in the first place.

Eventually, Sophia had agreed to go along with the plan. After all, it was all about family, wasn't it? Finally, she had a sister and not just a sister but an identical twin! Everything would work out. Julia's enthusiasm had been contagious. Also, the more time they spent together, the more like Julia Sophia became. They could finish each other's sentences and thought so much alike it was weird—but in a good way. And Sophia eventually came around to her sister's way of thinking. Hell, yes, they were entitled to a piece of the family fortune!

Then she'd met James.

At the heart of the scheme.

At the heart of everything.

How the hell had that happened?

And then there was something else . . .

As much as she hated the idea, she had a sneaking suspicion that Julia had something to do with what had happened to Phoebe, but she wouldn't go there—at least not yet. Certainly, her sister couldn't have tried to kill the old bat. Sure, the old lady was a snoop and irritating, but . . . seriously, her twin wouldn't go that far.

Or would she?

The uneasy feeling persisted, because though she'd tried to convince herself differently, Sophia had noticed a darker side to her twin. She hated to think of it as evil; that wasn't it really, but Julia was quick to get mad, her temper explosive, and little things irritated her. Worse yet, she was always suspicious, and she'd taken to the idea that Phoebe Matrix was onto them, like she was a master spy or something. Julia had mentioned that living here would be a lot easier if Phoebe wasn't around . . . well, that was true, but so what?

Sophia chewed her lower lip, refused to think of the time that Julia, in California, had berated a coffee barista for sloshing coffee on her, yelling at the girl, calling her an "idiot," and threatening to sue the shop, causing such a scene that the girl, all of sixteen, maybe, crumpled into tears and ran away from her station with all the patrons and workers in the coffee shop looking on. Only when the girl was completely humiliated had Julia been satisfied. Another time, a feral cat had made the mistake of crawling into the open window of her car and sunbathing. Julia had discovered it and threw open the door, finding an umbrella to shoo the skinny thing out. She'd landed a blow, and the cat had turned and hissed, ears back, needle-like teeth showing before jetting across the street and nearly being run over by a passing pickup. "Too bad the truck missed," Julia had remarked, eyeing the feline as it skittered down an alley. For the next two hours, she'd been in a dark mood. And how about all the times Julia had claimed that life wasn't fair, that she'd gotten a bad deal, that she would "get back" at anyone who crossed her. She'd gotten a look in her eyes that had actually caused goose pimples to rise on Sophia's skin. No matter how many times Sophia had warned her to "calm down" or "chill out," Julia hadn't. In fact, once, when discussing how unfair the situation was, Julia, who had been chopping onions with a vengeance in the kitchen, had nicked herself, blood dripping, onion juice getting into the cut. She'd whirled, holding the knife up between their noses. "Back off," she'd warned, and in that second, Sophia had felt her heart clutch, and she'd wondered fleetingly how far her twin could go, just how dangerous Julia could be. Julia's eyes had narrowed behind the bloody blade and, ignoring the drips from her fingers falling to the floor, she'd glared at her twin and warned, "I thought you of all people would understand! Either we're in this together, Sophia, or we're not!"

"Wow," Sophia had responded, and that had sent Julia spiraling into an even darker, more desperate mood.

Julia had tensed, her teeth bared, and for the briefest of seconds, Sophia had worried for her life. Then her sister had muttered, "Oh, fuck it!" and tossed the knife into the sink before hurrying to the bathroom for a Band-Aid.

So now, was it possible that Julia had done something to Phoebe Matrix? That seemed unlikely. Still, she felt a chill in her blood and had to tell herself she was letting her imagination run wild.

How had this all turned out so awful? When Julia had contacted her last year, Sophia had been ecstatic. Through one of those genetic-testing companies, they'd found each other, met at the bistro, and were both taken aback. Not only a sister, but a twin!

It had been a little spooky, but so exciting.

And then, eventually, Julia had told her about her plan to get their hands on the fortune that was rightfully theirs. Though reluctant at first, Sophia had eventually embraced the scheme, even the part about pretending to be one person. Twins might scare James off, but one girl who was always around would keep him interested, or so they'd hoped. And it would be fun, Julia had insisted. They could make a game of it, fool everyone in Riggs Crossing. That sounded a little lame to Sophia, but she hadn't said so—Julia had been so excited. Sophia hadn't wanted to burst her bubble. Julia had also insisted that they deserved their piece of the "San Francisco old money pie." After all, hadn't they both suffered enough? Sophia was an only child whose parents were wrapped up in their own lives, their marriage brittle, their interest in their only child waning as she'd become a teenager. And Julia had ended up with younger siblings whom her parents had doted upon. She'd been little more than a slave helping take care of them.

Neither Sophia nor Julia had been given a fair shake in life!

So Sophia had put her reservations aside and gone along with the plan:

Get close to James Cahill. Real close. Be always around, so that he can't imagine life without Sophia. Eventually marry him. Get what was due to both of the twins! The goal was to walk down the aisle before he inherited his millions.

She'd found it an exciting challenge to try and catch his eye and flirt with him, to steal him away from that awful Megan. That part hadn't been hard. The difficult part had been to try and avoid falling in love with him.

And she'd failed.

Worse yet, his wandering eye had moved on.

To Rebecca Travers, of all people! A woman he'd already tossed aside!

Neither she nor Julia had seen that coming.

But now . . . now . . .

Sophia glanced down at the stick in her hand, to the tiny results window, and sure enough, just as she'd expected, it indicated that yes, indeed, she was pregnant.

With James Cahill's child.

Her heart soared, and a slow, satisfied smile spread across her lips. All her doubts about having a baby fled, and tears starred her eyelashes, tears of a newfound joy.

Take that, Rebecca Travers!

Game over!

CHAPTER 41

Rivers wasn't sure what he expected from Earl Ray Dansen, but it certainly wasn't two digital pictures, one each of two dead women. The first was of Charity Spritz, her face battered and bruised, similar to the photographs Detective Tanaka had sent to him. The second picture, according to Earl, was Willow Valente, lying on a bed, a bullet hole visible in her temple.

"Jesus," Mendoza whispered.

"Where did you get these?" Rivers demanded, stunned, his jaw tight as they stood in what had once been the reception area of the newspaper's offices. One of the fluorescent lights overhead was buzzing, hinting that it was about to go out, and the entire suite of offices beyond seemed empty.

"Came from Charity Spritz's phone." Earl scrolled down and showed Rivers and Mendoza the text message: ANOTHER VICTIM.

"What the hell?" Rivers said under his breath. The killer was obviously taunting them—or, at least, taunting Earl.

"I'm going to have to take the phone. Evidence," Rivers said, his mind racing. Pictures of two dead women, obviously from the killer. Somehow the murderer had killed Charity Spritz in the Bay Area, then come to Riggs Crossing to take Willow Valente's life. Or possibly the other way around; he didn't have a timeline on Valente yet. His insides turned cold.

"Yeah, I figured you'd want this." Earl frowned, but he handed over his cell. "But just so you know, I'm running with the story. Both homicides. They're the *Clarion*'s. Exclusive."

"Whoa. Wait. Not until we investigate. Check and find out if this really is Willow Valente. This could be staged," Mendoza said. "We just don't know yet. She may be still alive."

"She's not," Earl said with confidence. "Look at that picture."

Mendoza reminded him, "If she is deceased, you can't run her name until we notify next of kin."

"Yeah, yeah, I know the drill. But the minute you do, we're going to put it out in the digital edition, and then as the lead for the next printing."

Rivers couldn't do anything about that. "Is Willow Valente a friend of Charity Spritz?"

Earl lifted a shoulder, puffed out his lips, thinking. "Not that I know of. Never heard her speak of her."

"Had she talked to her recently?" Rivers asked.

"Hey." Earl Ray scowled. "Didn't I just say, 'I don't know'?" Then he swiped at the air dismissively, as if he were swatting at a bothersome fly. "I guess it's not all that odd. I don't keep track of my employees' personal lives. Unless Charity had been working on a story on Valente, I have no reason to connect them."

"So she hadn't?" Rivers pressed.

"That's what I'm saying, not that I know of."

"What do you know about Valente?" Rivers figured Earl Ray had already started doing some research.

"Not much. We did do some checking, for the story. All I know is she's twenty-three, grew up around here, has an older sister who lives outside of Olympia. Can't think of her name right off the top of my head . . . no, wait!" He snapped his fingers. "It's um . . . Fern. Another woodsy name. Last name of Smithe, with an 'e'."

"You talked to her?" Mendoza asked as she typed in the information on her phone.

"No."

Rivers asked, "What else?"

"She—Valente—holds down, well, held down two jobs. Basically maid service at the Cahill Inn and then janitorial work at the McEwen Clinic."

Where Megan Travers had been employed.

"Does she have any friends?" Mendoza asked.

"Haven't gotten that far. Don't know."

"Okay." Rivers needed to get moving and took a step toward the door. Mendoza was ahead of him, already calling for deputies to check out Valente's place.

"Hey, man, I want my phone back ASAP!" Earl jabbed a long finger at Rivers. "Tomorrow."

"ASAP," Rivers assured him.

As they clambered down the staircase from the newspaper offices, Mendoza said, "She lives out on Taylor's Creek Road, an old building just on the other side of the train tracks. I've got the map on my phone." They sidestepped an old Volkswagen van emblazoned with AUNTIE'S ANTIQUES. "Deputies should be there by the time we arrive. Wait—Deputy Brown is calling."

"Let's go."

Rivers drove east toward the outskirts of Riggs Crossing, past the center of town, where people were still on the streets and bright Christmas decorations were visible on the storefronts. The town was bustling, a happy holiday fever in the air.

It was all directly at odds with his grim mission. Squinting against oncoming headlights, he thought about the person who had been photographed at the San Francisco airport. Had the killer left Charity Spritz to hop a plane, then land somewhere—Seattle? Spokane? Then what? Find Willow Valente and kill her within twenty-four hours? If so, it seemed that it might be easy enough to track down airline information. But on whom? Who would want both women killed? And why? He couldn't believe these killings were random. There had to be a link between them. His first thought was James Cahill. But he couldn't see Cahill flying to and from San Francisco. Driving would take . . . fifteen or sixteen hours, maybe longer, each way. Nonetheless, Cahill and the missing Megan Travers had to be part of this. And what about Harold Sinclaire's cabin, where they'd found the black Toyota Corolla? How did it all hang together?

"Okay," Mendoza said into the phone as he drove past an abandoned gas station. "Just hold her there; we'll want to talk to her . . . yeah, I'm sure . . . anyone would be, but still, we need to talk to her . . . okay, we'll be there in ten, maybe less." She clicked off. "Apparently we weren't the first to call in Willow Valente's death. A coworker was already checking on her when Brown and his partner got there. They're holding her so that we can talk to her."

"Good." Rivers flipped on his lights, blew through the next intersection, and half a mile farther, turned onto Taylor's Creek Road.

"She—the coworker—is more than a little freaked out."

"Who wouldn't be?" Rivers asked, his stomach knotting. The once sleepy little town of Riggs Crossing now was on the map. In December alone, two women had been murdered and one was missing.

And it wasn't yet Christmas.

Restless, Rebecca unpacked her bag, folded her few sweaters, jeans, and leggings and placed them once again in the drawers of the small dresser in her hotel room. She had intended to leave.

After doing her duty with the press conference, she'd planned to go home to Seattle, to restart her life, to leave finding Megan to the police and to get as far away from James Cahill as possible. The man messed with her mind, and she didn't need any of that, thank you very much.

But then her mother had called.

"What?" Lenora had cried when Rebecca had explained that she was returning to Seattle. "You can't! Not until Megan's found. You have to find her, Becky!"

"That could take a while."

"And it will just take longer if you're not there to rattle the police's cages!"

"I've done enough 'rattling,'" Rebecca had thrown back.

Lenora had driven her point home. "You let the police know that you won't take 'no' for an answer. Be the squeaky wheel, Becky," Lenora had insisted. When Rebecca had mentioned she thought Detectives Rivers and Mendoza were all over the case, her mother had scoffed. "I doubt it, but you make sure they're not slacking off."

Rebecca had thought about the detectives. She wasn't sure she liked either one—Rivers seemed odd, and Mendoza had a chip on her shoulder the size of Mount Rainier, but she felt they both were on their game, that they would leave no stone unturned in locating her sister. And being here, stuck in the hotel room, spinning her wheels and sick with worry about Megan, letting her fears assail her, wasn't healthy.

"Mom—I have responsibilities in Seattle. You know, like a job."

"Oh, phooey! How many times have you told me you could work from anywhere as long as you have a laptop?"

Rebecca silently cursed herself for being so forthright with her mother as Lenora went on, "I'm sure Angelica will understand."

Before she could argue, Lenora had claimed another call was coming in and disconnected.

Yeah, right.

So bogus, Mom.

But Lenora had been right about one thing. Rebecca could work from Riggs Crossing. As long as she had her laptop, an Internet connection, and electricity. Well, and inspiration. There was always that. And it was in short supply lately.

Worse yet, Angelica had given her blessing for Rebecca to stay in Riggs Crossing when Rebecca had phoned her.

"It's where you belong. Until you find your sister. There is nothing more important than family," Angelica had said breathlessly as she was nearly out the door to catch a flight to L.A., where she was certain the next Vision in White shop would be established. There was no arguing with her when she was in a rush. "Look, you stay there, do what you can do, and keep in touch. E-mail or text or call. This will all work out. I only pray you locate Megan, and soon. If you find out anything, call me!"

"I will."

"Good. Gotta run if I want to catch my flight! Hopefully by this time next week, we'll have a Southern California location! Wish me luck. *Ciao!*"

"*Buona fortuna a te!*" Rebecca had said, but Angelica was already gone, leaving Rebecca with a phone pressed to her ear as she stared out the hotel room window at the familiar street below. Suddenly, she felt very, very alone in this small, out-of-the-way town, where everyone appeared to know everyone—except her.

Megan was still missing.

Charity Spritz had been murdered.

And James Cahill was involved with Sophia Russo. That didn't sit well. There was something about the woman that bothered her, even though they hadn't really met. Her feelings were jaded by her sister's opinion, but there was something about Sophia that seemed fake or suspicious or—

"Stop!" she said aloud, as she didn't know the woman. The truth was that James Cahill's interest in other women, including Megan, still bugged her. Which was ludicrous, all things considered. "Get over it," she said through clenched teeth. Her time with James was over, and it was for the best. She just had to focus on Megan.

Where the hell was she?

When Rebecca had first driven to Riggs Crossing, she had been certain that this was just another one of Megan's overly dramatic diva stunts. Now, though, she wasn't as convinced. Never before had one of her sister's disappearing acts been so lengthy. Or so worrisome.

This time, the situation felt different.

She remembered the frantic phone call she'd received from Megan, how freaked-out the younger woman had been. Now, Rebecca felt foolish to have thought she was being played. She should have realized Megan's panic was real. But how could she when Megan was such a drama queen, such a great actress . . .

But Megan hadn't been acting or playing a part when she flipped out after her fight with James. She'd been furious, and for the first time, Rebecca wondered if Megan had been distraught enough to do something rash, hurt herself or worse. That didn't feel right. The idea of suicide was hard to imagine, as Megan had always displayed a zest for life. Yes, she was emotional, her temper legendary, but she wouldn't harm herself. And certainly not just to prove a point.

The last person who had seen Megan had been James Cahill and she, Rebecca, had walked out on him the other night. Before getting any answers.

Maybe it was time to fix that.

He wouldn't exactly be rolling out the red carpet for her, but she'd track him down. He had to know something more.

Before she could talk herself out of it, she snagged her keys from the dresser, slipped on a jacket and scarf, and headed out the door. Her near-frozen Subaru was waiting for her in the parking lot, and after giving the windshield a quick swipe with the ice scraper, she climbed behind the wheel and headed out of town.

She stopped at James's house, found he wasn't home, and drove to the inn, where she spied his Explorer parked and collecting a layer of snow.

First, she checked the hotel, its lobby festooned in ribbons, lights, poinsettias, and, of course, a Christmas tree that climbed nearly two stories. One man sat reading near a fire burning in a river-rock fireplace; another couple emerged from an elevator. Music and laughter filtered in from the bar, where people had gathered on bar stools and café tables.

But the front desk stood unmanned, no receptionist at the computer.

Rebecca waited anxiously, searching for a bell to ring, but could find none. Irritated, she looked for anyone who might be able to help her and spied two women huddled deep in conversation beneath a glowing EXIT sign that marked a hallway leading toward the rear of the building. The older of the two, a wasp-slender woman with a dour expression and over-permed brown hair, was agitated, a muscle near her forehead ticking. A name tag was pinned to her jacket. It read DONNA BUNN, MANAGER, and she was speaking rapidly, almost out of breath. "—never happened before. It's just not like her not to call in if she wasn't going to show up for her shift."

"I know," the shorter, younger, apple-cheeked woman agreed. Her name tag read MARIBELLE EDWARDS, KITCHEN STAFF. Thick-waisted, with horn-rimmed glasses and hair tinged purple, she looked like she'd been crying and kept swiping at her nose with a tissue and then lifting her glasses to dab at red-rimmed eyes. "I've texted her. Nothing. I even called. Three times. No answer. I'm just zipped to voice mail."

"Maybe she lost her phone."

"Maybe, but I can't help but worry after what happened to Charity Spritz," Maribelle said, sniffing loudly. "She's my neighbor, you know. Or was. Geez, that's weird to say. She lives in the same apartment building as I do, and now they're saying on the news that Charity's dead. Murdered! I just can't believe it. I saw her just the other day and waved to her when she was getting into her van. Ooh, this is horrible."

"We shouldn't borrow trouble. Maybe it's nothing. Just a stomach bug. Or something. She's always calling in sick anyway." Donna's mouth pursed. "And if it is . . . well, I'll deal with that later. Anyway, Zena's shift ended an hour ago, and I asked her to stop by and check in on her. They're friends, you know." She pulled a cell phone from the pocket of her jacket and scowled at the screen. "Of course, Zena hasn't texted. Those two are a pair. So unreliable! She might not have even gone over to Willow's!" Donna must've seen Rebecca because she said hastily, "I gotta go," and forced a smile.

"Just keep me in the loop!" The shorter woman hurried to the women's restroom, and Donna pasted a smile on her wan face. "Sorry," she said as she stepped to the reception area and stood behind the desk. "What can I do for you?"

"I'm looking for James Cahill."

"The owner. Oh." Her neatly plucked eyebrows drew together. "He's . . . well, I'm not sure where he is. Let me check." She made a quick call on her cell phone, talked softly, then clicked off and pasted on her smile again. "He's supposed to be in the lot," she told Rebecca. "At least that's what Bobby, our foreman here, thinks."

"The lot?"

"Yeah. The Christmas tree lot. Out back." Donna motioned toward the rear of the building. "Next to the café. You can get there through that hallway," she said, motioning to the short corridor where she and the other woman had so recently been deep in conversation.

"Thanks." Rebecca was outside in a shot, crossing the parking area and ducking under an archway to the lot where cut trees were displayed beneath strands of lights. Gravel paths led through the clusters of spruces, pines, and firs, while Christmas music played softly from speakers attached to the exterior of the café. Rebecca barely noticed. She cut past a few customers and scanned the area just to spy James, dog at his heels, striding through a back gate to the surrounding forest of uncut trees.

"Great," she muttered, hurrying after him.

While this part of his property was well-lit, music lilting, the smells from the café tantalizing, the adjoining hilly acres were shrouded in darkness, thin moonlight casting foreboding shadows over the snowy ground. Rebecca took off after James, ignoring the nagging thought that he might not be all that happy to see her. She had ditched him the other night.

Well, too bad. It was time they worked things out.

To find Megan.

And, truthfully, to put her feelings for James Cahill to rest forever.

"Closure," she said aloud—such a popular term these days—and probably impossible with James.

Well, so be it.

CHAPTER 42

As he left the lighted lot, James's mobile phone began to buzz. He answered without looking at the caller and regretted it the minute he heard Sophia's breathless voice.

"We need to talk," she said without preamble.

"I thought we were on the same page," he said, irritated as he searched the ground while walking through the rows of trees that had been planted seven or eight years prior. He was on a mission, trying to find Bruce Porter's phone, which must have dropped out of his pocket as he helped a customer cut and carry one of the fresh Douglas firs.

But Sophia was having none of it. "I need to see you."

"We've been through this." He wasn't going to be budged. And he needed to get off this call so he could punch in Porter's number to find the guy's cell.

"I'm serious." And she sounded it. "It won't take long."

"Then tell me now." He stepped through a row of spruces.

"You need to hear this, from me. Face-to-face. It's not the kind of thing you discuss on the phone."

Jesus-God, did Sophia know something about what happened to Megan? What else could be so damned important?

"Just tell me."

"I'm serious: I need to see you."

Shit! His hand clenched over the phone. "Fine." He didn't have time for this.

From somewhere in the distance, he heard someone calling his name. "James?" A woman.

"I'll come over," Sophia was saying a little more brightly.

"No!" He didn't want to be completely alone with her, not at his house. Not a good idea. "Meet me at the inn. In the bar."

"No, no. I work there. It could . . . it could get awkward."

"Why?"

"James?"

On the phone, Sophia insisted, "This is important," and the edge to her voice finally compelled him. "Listen," he said into his phone as he scanned the darkened woods. "I gotta go! Meet me in an hour. At the inn. That's the best I can do."

"But—" He clicked off the phone and dialed Bruce's cell number, listening for the ringtone and the woman who was . . . where? Out here in the uncut trees looking for him? Really?

"James!" the woman—Rebecca?—yelled again.

What was she doing out here?

Bruce's phone started going off, some Latin-beat ringtone warbling through the night. James headed toward the sound and saw the very dim light of the phone's face, partially buried in the snow in the midst of a stand of noble firs. As he snagged the cell from the ground and dropped it into his jacket pocket, he wished to high heaven he hadn't agreed to meet Sophia for whatever "urgent" reason she'd concocted.

He had to convince her it was over.

Intent on catching up to James, Rebecca half-jogged to the spot where she'd last caught a glimpse of him, pushing forward into this man-made forest, avoiding stumps and saplings, the cold air brittle against her cheeks, branches catching on her hair, clouds beginning to gather overhead.

"James?" Squinting, she tried to make out movement between the firs and pines, but the woods were quiet, the lights from the tree lot becoming more distant. "James?" she yelled, hoping to catch his attention, then louder, "James!"

Nothing.

Damn the man.

She stubbed her toe on a stump and nearly fell. Smothering a curse, she slid her phone from her pocket and turned on the flashlight app to illuminate her path.

"James?"

Still no response, but she felt as if unseen eyes were watching her, zeroing in on the bright light from her phone.

Just your imagination.

Get over it.

Still, she paused, straining to hear.

Was that the sound of footsteps behind her?

The hairs on the back of her neck stood on end.

Whipping around, she shone her light into the darkness.

Nothing.

No one.

Just eerie blue illumination and the sough of a breeze rushing through the branches of the evergreens, a battalion of dark sentinels surrounding her.

"Pull yourself together." Slowly, she swung the flashlight's beam over the snow-packed earth, where the light glinted and pierced the shadows.

She decided she'd never find him in over forty night-dark acres of man-made forest. What had she been thinking? The smarter move would be to go back to the café, buy a hot cup of coffee, and sip while watching for him to return to his Explorer. An even smarter move would have been to phone or text him.

She started to punch in his number as a gloved hand reached out from the darkness and snagged her forearm. "Rebecca? What the hell are you doing here?"

She whipped around, face-to-face with him. "God, you nearly gave me a heart attack!" She yanked her arm from his grasp. "I came looking for you. You weren't at the inn, and they said you were out here."

"They were right."

"I've been thinking," she rushed on. "We, um, we didn't leave on the best of terms the other night."

"You walked out on me." And as he said it, his words still hanging on the night air, Rebecca's heart clutched. She thought about another time, when the situation had been reversed, when he'd left her for good. For another woman—her own damned sister.

As if he too had realized what he'd said, he let out a huff of disgusted air. "Damn." He grabbed her arm again, more gently, and muttered something under his breath about being an idiot. "Look," he admitted, "I don't know how to say, 'I'm sorry,' you know, about everything that happened between us." He paused as if waiting for her to interject something. She didn't. Wasn't going to let him off the hook, not about this.

"And even if I could, it doesn't seem enough."

"It isn't."

"What would be?"

"Nothing."

"I was an ass."

Again, she kept her silence, noticed the first flakes of snow drifting from the sky.

"Probably still am, all things considered."

"No 'probably' about it." Then she brushed the air with her hand, dismissing it. "Maybe we shouldn't go there right now."

"When, then?"

"Never," she said quickly, nodding sharply in agreement when she heard her own words. "Yeah, never would be a good time."

Even in the half-light from the snow's reflection, she saw him wince. "Okay," he finally said. "Listen: I'm trying to apologize here. And it's not easy."

"Good."

"The appropriate thing would be for you to say, 'It's okay.'"

"But it's not. And it never will be. But we still have to find Megan. So either you work with me or you don't. That's what I came to tell you, to clear the air—the recent air. I'm just letting you know that I'll be around here in Riggs Crossing, and I'm not leaving until I know what happened to my sister. I just need to find her. I didn't want to believe that something bad had happened, wouldn't even admit it to myself. It was just easier to think that this was one of her stupid stunts. But this feels different. Even if it started out that way, if she intended to fall off the face of the earth for a while to get everyone worried about her—you know, a big act to get attention—somehow something went terribly wrong." She met his gaze. "I would think you would want that too."

"I do," he admitted, his breath smoky in the night air. "Right now, the police seem to think I had something to do with it."

"Did you?"

"What? Jesus. No! You can't still think—"

His phone chirped loudly. He checked his cell. "It's my foreman." He didn't answer, but before he could say anything, it rang again. "Bobby again."

"Take it."

Frowning, he asked, "What's up?" then stood stock still. The conversation was one-sided. "Shit. What? . . . Whoa, whoa, whoa . . . slow down." His eyes found Rebecca's, and in the half-light she saw the strain on his face, the worry. "Holy Christ," he finally said, then, "Stay put. I'm on my way." He ended the call, jammed the phone in his pocket, and grabbed her hand. "Come on." He'd started jogging, dragging her with him toward the glowing lights of the Christmas tree lot, hurrying along a row of spruce trees laden with snow.

"What?"

"One of my employees. She didn't show up for work today."

"And," she prodded, hurrying to keep up with him.

"I don't have all the details. Don't know if it's true, but . . . what they're saying is, is that she's dead."

"Dead?" She stopped in her tracks, jerking on his arm so that he turned to face her. "Who?"

"Willow Valente. Maid service. Christ, she can't be twenty-five." He tugged on her arm again, pulling her behind him, the dog loping beside them.

"What happened?"

"Don't know." His jaw was set as they cut through the evergreens. "But we're damned sure going to find out."

CHAPTER 43

Rivers and Mendoza were far from the first cops on the scene. By the time they'd arrived at Willow Valente's out-of-the way apartment, two other department-issued vehicles were parked in the lot, their lights strobing the night. A crowd had started to gather, and one deputy was putting up a barrier of yellow tape, another keeping track of who came and went. Rivers and Mendoza signed in to the crime scene, donned boots to cover their shoes, and hurried up the exterior stairs.

In the sparsely furnished unit, the victim lay in her bed, just as the first cop on the scene had found her, in exactly the same position as Rivers had seen her on Earl Ray Dansen's phone.

Her television was flickering in the corner, a cup of what looked and smelled like some kind of flowery tea was cold on a nearby table, the gun pointed at her head where a bullet hole was visible just above her temple. Blood had matted her black hair, then trailed onto her pink pillowcase, where it had congealed in a dark pool. "James Cahill's Glock?" Rivers asked, pointing to the gun in the victim's hand.

Deputy LaShawn Brown scowled. "Don't know. But looks like it." A tall, beefy man who would still regale anyone who would listen about his glory days as a college football star nearly twenty years earlier, Brown was a dedicated cop. He'd settled down with a wife and two teenage daughters, his ball-playing days far behind him. Nearly six and a half feet of muscle, he probably weighed nearly three hundred pounds and was as intimidating as anyone on the force. "Just gotta check the serial number."

"Who discovered her?"

"A friend who's also a coworker," the deputy said, pulling out the notepad from his back pocket. "Zena Wallace. When our girl here"—the deputy nodded at the corpse in the bed—"when she didn't show up for work and didn't answer any texts or calls, her boss got worried and sent Ms. Wallace over here."

From first glance, it appeared as if the victim had committed suicide. But that was a BS theory since Earl Ray Dansen and the *Clarion* had been sent pictures of the scene, *after* she'd pulled the trigger.

"Was the door locked?"

"Nah. And according to the friend, that was odd."

"Forced?"

"Nope."

Mendoza asked, "What time was that?"

"Not quite an hour ago—you can check with nine-one-one for the exact time. Wallace found the body, freaked the hell out, and called nine-one-one. No, wait, I think she called someone else first." Another quick scan of his notes. "She couldn't get through to her boss, so she called Robert Knowlton, who is an overseer where they work."

"At Cahill Industries," Rivers said.

Brown was nodding. "Right. Soon as we got the report, Taggert and I, we drove over here, found her—Ms. Wallace—outside. Then we came upstairs and discovered this one"—he hitched his chin toward the bed to Willow Valente's body—"right here."

Rivers asked, "Where is Ms. Wallace now?"

"Down in the car. With Taggert."

"Did Knowlton show up?" Mendoza asked the question as she checked out the small apartment.

"Yeah, he's down in the parking lot. Or was. His story checked out. He only came because he was called."

Mendoza asked, "The ME on her way?"

Brown gave a quick nod. "Should be here within the half hour."

"And the crime-scene guys?" Mendoza pressed.

Brown rubbed his chin. "S'posed to arrive any minute."

"Good." Rivers had seen enough. He and Mendoza walked carefully down the exterior stairs, where the night was cold, new snow falling softly, the darkness abated by the single security lamp casting a gray-blue pool of light over the parking area of what had once been a bakery and the blue-and-red flashers from the light bars of the deputies' vehicles.

Mendoza tapped on the driver's-side window of the occupied, idling cruiser. "We'd like to talk to Ms. Wallace," she said as the window was rolled down, Deputy Taggert behind the wheel.

Taggert nodded. "Here?" she asked, short brown hair visible beneath her hat.

"Unless she'd rather go into the station," Rivers said.

"No. Oh, God, no!" the woman in the passenger seat said around sobs. "I can't. I just can't. I . . . I'm pregnant."

Looking up at them, Taggert rolled a world-weary eye. Even though she was barely fifty, Taggert was jaded, thought she, personally, had seen and heard it all.

From the passenger seat, Zena said, "I have to get home. My boyfriend. He'll be missing me."

"Fine, we can talk here." Mendoza leaned down to look past Taggert to the passenger seat, where the woman was shredding a much-used tissue.

They climbed into the back seat, which was warmer than outside, and conducted a quick interview in which Zena explained her concerns about her friend.

"She . . . Willow would call in sick, y'know, all the time, and it's not like she was pregnant like me or had a good excuse and Donna—uh, Donna Bunn, she's our supervisor—had said before that she was on her last nerve with Willow or something like that."

Rivers adjusted himself so that he could face Zena as Taggert adjusted the heater and defroster. "Was Willow depressed?"

"What?" Zena Wallace seemed shocked at the idea. "No—I mean, maybe. It would be hard to tell." She blew her nose. "She was so quiet. Could have always been depressed, for all I know."

"Any change in her attitude lately?" Mendoza asked.

"No. She didn't seem any different than usual."

"Had she ever talked about suicide?"

"Geez, no!" Zena reacted by dropping a hand and covering her abdomen protectively as if she didn't want her unborn child to hear.

"It wasn't suicide," Rivers reminded Mendoza.

"Just covering all the bases," Mendoza said, but kept her gaze on Zena Wallace. "She have a boyfriend?" Mendoza asked.

"No. Well. Uh. Not that I know of."

Rivers suggested, "Enemies?"

"Oh, Geez, no! Willow? Uh-uh. There isn't—wasn't—anything to not like about Willow. She just kind of blends into the woodwork, if you know what I mean. Kind of always around, but not loud or pushy or . . ." Zena started crying again and fanned herself with her hand. "Sorry, it's my pregnancy hormones, you know, I'm like, I mean, my emotions are all over the place."

"She has something she wants to show you," Taggert said, interrupting another of Zena Wallace's crying jags.

"What's that?"

"Oh." Zena sniffed loudly as the windows in the cruiser started to fog. "It's just so weird. I finally got a text from Willow, right before I came over here and . . ." She shuddered, scrolled, then handed her phone, through the open partition, to Rivers in the back seat. On the small screen was a photograph of the dead woman, but in these images she looked very much alive, still nude, but posing suggestively with what appeared to be the same gun that took her life.

Rivers's eyes narrowed. "When did you receive this?"

"Like an hour ago . . . maybe. Hour and a half? I don't know." Her voice cracked.

Only ninety minutes ago, but the woman in the bed appeared to have been dead for much longer. "Did we find Willow Valente's phone?" he asked Deputy Taggert.

"Not that I know of."

"I'll call upstairs to Brown," Mendoza said and punched in a phone number. Rivers knew she didn't want to take the steps up to the apartment again, was trying to minimize any alteration to the snow pattern on the stairs in case the killer had left a footprint or some trace evidence.

Rivers asked Zena Wallace, "Did she ever send you something like this before? Any other suggestive pictures or—?"

"No!" Zena squeaked. "Are you kidding? It's not like I'm a perv—or she is, for that matter. I mean, I never thought Willow would do anything like that. She's kind of weird, like I said, a little quiet and shy. So . . . I don't get this. I don't get it at all. It's just not like her."

". . . okay, thanks," Mendoza said and disconnected. "No phone found yet," and her gaze collided with Rivers's as they both understood that the pictures of Willow with the gun were sent to Zena Wallace's phone *after* Willow Valente was dead. So, no, she hadn't offed herself, not without an accomplice. She had been murdered.

Mendoza glanced at Zena's phone, where the picture of the nude girl gazing seductively into the camera was still in the frame. "That's not Willow's bed," Mendoza pointed out. "Not the twin bed upstairs. Willow's has different sheets too and a white headboard. This bed"—she pointed to the screen—"doesn't have one at all. And is much larger. Check out how she's sprawled across it."

But the bed in the small image on Zena's phone looked familiar. And then Rivers got it, and he felt a frisson of excitement surge through his blood.

Mendoza was asking, "You're certain Willow doesn't have a boyfriend?"

"I already told you: no!" Zena was shaking her head violently.

"One she might have recently broken up with?"

"I never heard of one." She glanced out the passenger door window and ran the tip of her index finger over the condensation that had collected, despite the efforts of the cruiser's heater.

"What about James Cahill?" Rivers asked.

"What? Are you nuts? No! Geez, I don't know how to say it any clearer!"

But Rivers recognized the bed in the picture, where a nude Willow was staring provocatively into the camera's eye, as belonging to Cahill. He'd seen it when going through Cahill's house.

"Oh, Lordy," Zena sighed. She fought a new spate of tears.

"What?" Mendoza asked.

"I wasn't lying when I said she didn't have a boyfriend, but she did have this major crush on James. She was half in love with him." Zena started shredding the tissue again. "Well, maybe more like totally in love with him. But it was a complete fantasy."

"How so?" Mendoza prodded.

Zena rolled her expressive eyes. "He, like, doesn't even know she exists. Or . . . existed. It was like she was invisible to him."

"But you know she had a crush on him?"

Nodding, Zena blinked back tears. "Oh, yeah."

"So why would she be in his bed?" Rivers asked. "With a gun?"

Zena looked absolutely miserable and dabbed at her eyes with the shredded Kleenex. "I don't know," she said, "but as I said, she's a little weird."

"Does she have any friends or family in the area?"

"I don't know." She thought for a second, her forehead wrinkling. "Wait. She never talked much about her folks, but she has a sister."

"Do you know her name?"

"No. Just that she lived in Tacoma, I think . . . or maybe it was Everett, somewhere on the other side of the mountains. She never called her by anything other than 'Sister.' Not 'my sister,' just 'Sister.' I joked once that I thought maybe her sister was a nun, but she didn't seem to think it was very funny." She rubbed her slightly protruding belly and started to cry softly again. "This is so awful."

"Maybe Fern," Mendoza supplied. "Could that be her sister's name? Fern Smithe?"

Zena thought. "Maybe . . . yeah. I heard her say that name once in passing—that it was Fern's birthday or something."

They asked a few more questions, but got nothing more. The ME arrived, and a couple of minutes later, the crime-scene team in their van pulled into the lot, waved through a growing crowd of onlookers by one of the deputies.

Rivers eyed the crowd, wondering if the murderer could be hiding in plain sight in its midst.

It wouldn't be the first time a killer had come back to get his rocks off by watching all the hoopla he'd created. In the short while since Rivers and Mendoza had arrived at the apartment, the bevy of the curious on the far side of the barricade had grown. Onlookers had stopped, some in their idling vehicles, others braving the cold night in ski jackets or wool coats, boots and caps, their breath fogging as they chatted with each other. The press, in the form of Seamus O'Day from the *Clarion*, was in attendance, but so far no news vans. That was bound to change quickly. Once the word got out not only about Willow Valente, but also that Charity Spritz had been murdered, more would arrive.

But as he climbed from the back of the cruiser and stretched his back, he eyed the throng of lookie-loos on the other side of the yellow tape, but no one caught his eye; no one seemed the least bit suspicious or out of place.

Yet he sensed that he was getting closer, that soon the killer would show his hand. Sending the pictures was a sign and a stupid one.

He was going to nail the bastard and soon; he could feel it as surely as the cold breath of the night that made him turn up his collar.

What had Andie Jeffries said?

If anything happens to me, it's James. His fault.

Rivers was just tossing that around in his mind when—speak of the devil—James Cahill's Jeep roared into the lot. He was at the wheel, but he wasn't alone.

Rebecca Travers was right at his side.

How damned convenient.

"She lives here?" Rebecca asked as James parked his SUV in the lot of a two-storied building.

"I guess so." James wasn't certain, but he'd gotten the address from his employee records at the hotel when he'd dropped off the phone and left Ralph with the staff.

Judging by the activity in the parking area—an array of police cars, vans, and an ambulance—this had to be the right spot.

A small crowd of onlookers was being held at bay by a couple of deputies, and Bobby Knowlton stood outside his truck while smoking a cigarette, the blue-and-red flashing lights of a couple of police vehicles playing weirdly on the snowy pavement and reflecting in the large windows where baked goods had once been displayed.

As James climbed out of his Explorer, he noticed the cops, Rivers and Mendoza, walking away from a cruiser and heading in his direction. His jaw tensed, and his stomach clenched into a tight knot.

"James Cahill," Rivers called out, as they approached. "We need to talk."

Great. "Okay." From the corner of his eye, he saw Rebecca round the front of his SUV so that she stood next to him. "Just let me ask one question. I got a call from Bobby." James hitched his chin toward the foreman. "He said that Willow Valente committed suicide. Is that right?"

"She's deceased," Rivers said, "but we haven't figured out the cause of death yet." Mendoza glanced from James to Rebecca and back again.

"Was she in an accident?"

"We can't say at this time," Rivers said. "But we'd like to ask you a few questions."

"You mean 'more' questions. I've already given a statement." James's voice had an unwanted edge to it, and he gazed up to the second floor of the big building as more passers-by pulled over, engines of cars, trucks, and vans rumbling through the night.

"Not about this," Rivers said.

"This? Listen, I don't know anything about Willow! My foreman called me, and I drove over here. That's it. End of story."

Unmoved, Rivers said, "It's just a few questions. We can do it here. Or at the station."

"I told you—"

Rebecca's gloved hand grabbed hold of his forearm, steadying him.

"Okay, okay. I don't care. We can do it here." James didn't bother to hide his irritation.

"Maybe the station would be better," Rebecca suggested as she cast her gaze over the onlookers being held back by a hastily made barricade of yellow crime-scene tape and sawhorses.

"Fine," he finally agreed. "The station."

CHAPTER 44

Sophia was furious.

She'd been stood up! After agreeing to meet James here, in the very bar in which she worked.

Her blood was really boiling now.

She'd been in the bar for nearly an hour, sipping a damned soda while waiting for James and practicing how she was going to tell him he was going to be a father. He'd be shocked, maybe even deny the possibility, but he would come around. And then he'd realize they were meant to be together.

Except that he hadn't shown.

Her back teeth ground together as the strains of "I Saw Mommy Kissing Santa Claus" lilted through the room and groups of friends or couples laughed and talked, oblivious to the drama that was Sophia's life.

A couple of men at the bar eyed her. She knew them. She'd served them, for God's sake. She jabbed her straw into her drink, causing the ice cubes to swirl. James couldn't keep treating her this way. Not now. Not when she was about to become the mother of his child! At that thought, she actually smiled.

But she couldn't wait any longer. She'd taken the car the second Julia had arrived at the apartment, and now her sister would want it back. After all, the hatchback really did belong to Julia.

Sophia finished her drink and stood, left a few bills on the table, and tried to call James again, but this time her call went straight to voice mail. She texted him for the third time:

Where r u? We need to talk. Now!

He was avoiding her. That was it. She walked into the lobby, where she spied Donna at the front desk.

Oh, God, she didn't want to talk to her boss. She didn't want to talk to anyone. Just James!

She was headed for the front door when Donna looked up from her keyboard and held up a hand. "Sophia!"

She probably wanted Sophia to work someone's shift. Well, no way.

"Sophia!" Donna said, more loudly, and to Sophia's surprise, her boss actually left her post at the reception desk to walk briskly across the lobby, past the Christmas tree, not even bothering to kick back one of the "presents" that had escaped from underneath the glittering boughs. "Sophia, have you heard?" Donna's face was a little whiter than usual, her eyes worried beneath her curlicued bangs. "About Willow?"

Oh, dear God. She was going to ask Sophia to fill in for that near-mute maid with the snaky black braid and the ever-watchful eyes, the girl who helped her clean up the mess that had been James's house. "What about her?" Sophia wasn't all that interested. Willow was weird, and the way she gazed at James sometimes was really unnerving. Beyond creepy. If ever there was a stalker in the world, Sophia thought, it could well be Willow Valente.

"She's dead."

Sophia froze. She thought she'd heard wrong. "What?" Was this Donna's sick idea of a joke?

"I finally heard from Zena. Willow's dead."

"Jesus," Sophia squeaked out. "What happened?" Had the girl been in some horrific accident?

"Zena's there now, at Willow's apartment. The cops have been interrogating her and Bobby; she'd already called him. Now they're talking to James and a woman he was with, the one who came here and asked about him."

"What woman?" Sophia demanded.

"The one who was on TV, Megan Travers's sister."

Rebecca! Sophia's stomach dropped, and she thought she might be sick. "They all went there? To her apartment?"

"They went when they heard the news. First Bobby, then James and the woman. I know because James left Bruce's phone here at the front desk for him to pick up. Apparently he'd lost it."

Sophia didn't care about Bruce's damned cell. "So, wait. Back up a sec. What happened to Willow?" This was getting crazy.

Donna lowered her voice, looked from side to side as if she expected someone from the FBI to be listening. "Zena went to check on her, because, you know, she didn't show up for her shift, and she found her in her bed. Zena said it looked like she'd shot herself."

"*Shot* herself?" Sophia recoiled, took a step back. This was horrible. "Suicide?"

"That's what Zena thought, but the police don't seem to think so because they have a picture of her, someone had it on their phone and sent it to the newspaper."

"What?" Sophia couldn't believe what she was hearing. A couple, clinging to each other, walked out of the bar to the front door and out into the night.

"I know, I know," Donna was saying. "Zena overheard a couple of the cops talking or something. She's not supposed to know." Donna looked over her shoulder, checked the desk area. "Anyway, the picture was supposedly taken *after* she died, so they think the whole suicide thing was staged."

"Oh . . . wow." Sophia didn't realize it, but she was slowly shaking her head, denying everything Donna was saying. "I can't believe it."

"I know. And it gets worse." Donna's voice softened to the barest of whispers. Sophia could barely hear her over the conversation spilling out of the bar.

"How can it get worse, if she's dead?" Sophia asked, horrified.

"Zena said there was a digital photo of her . . . naked." Donna pulled a tube of lip gloss from her pocket and ran it over her lips. "A very sexual shot with a gun, and it looked like the pistol that killed her!"

"So maybe her boyfriend took the picture?" Sophia said.

"Did she have a boyfriend?" Donna asked. "Someone who would get off on her in sexy poses?"

"Don't know." Sophia had to step out of the way when a couple in matching peacoats swept in through the doors and headed into the bar. "I never heard that she did, but I didn't pay attention."

But Donna was shaking her head and recapping the lip gloss. "Me, neither. I was always just concerned that she show up on time . . . Oh, I have to run." Donna scurried back to the desk, where an elderly man was approaching from the elevator.

"Wow," Sophia said, her thoughts on Willow. Dead? Suicide? It didn't make sense. She cinched the belt of her coat around her, then pulled her knit cap from her pocket and tucked her hair into it before heading outside, where the night was sharp and cold, a bit of snow falling. It was odd to think Willow had offed herself, but Sophia couldn't let herself get too wrapped up in it. After all, she'd barely known the weirdo.

What did bother her was that James had stood her up to check on Willow. And he'd been with Rebecca.

That would have to end, she thought, as she slid into the frigid interior of Julia's car and crammed her key into the ignition. And end now.

Sliding the Glock, encased in a plastic bag, across the table in the interview room, Rivers asked James, "Is this your gun?" He and Mendoza were seated on one side, Cahill on the other, a manila folder unopened between them. Every second of the conversation was being recorded by cameras and microphones. Rebecca Travers had angled to be in the room as well, but Rivers hadn't allowed it, of course. Protocol. Also, he wanted to interview Cahill alone to study the man's expressions, to observe the slightest of his reactions.

Currently, Rebecca was in the waiting area with a deputy.

Rivers wanted to talk to her, too, but first things first. Right now, James Cahill was up to bat.

A tic had developed near Cahill's right eye as he eyed the weapon. "Can I pick it up?"

Rivers nodded. "Just leave it in the bag." The pistol had been tested for prints already and had been fired into a water tank to see if the bullet fired in the lab had matching striations to the one that would be extracted from Willow Valente's skull. Just to be certain the gun wasn't a plant.

Cahill studied the pistol. "Yeah. I think so. I mean, it looks like mine. And mine's registered, so you should already have that figured out. I gave you all that information when I told you it had been stolen."

Mendoza nodded. "We checked the registration."

"Then why are you asking me?" he asked.

"Confirmation." Mendoza's gaze held his.

"Where did you find it?"

"Next to Willow Valente's head. In the bed with her."

"Jesus. Are you fuc—kidding me?" Cahill couldn't take his gaze off of the gun. "What was it doing there?"

Rivers leaned back in his chair. "I was hoping you could tell us," he said as Cahill slowly shook his head from side to side.

"I have no idea. The last time I saw it—I told you—the Glock was in the dining room, which is really my office, in a drawer on the sideboard. That's where I keep it, and it's never loaded. You know this already. I filed a damned report. It wasn't in the house when you guys searched it. Obviously, it was stolen. By the killer or his accomplice! For God's sake, I had nothing to do with it!"

"And you put the gun in the drawer in your dining room when?" Mendoza asked.

"God, I don't know," he snapped, then took control of his temper again. "Look, I don't remember. Hell, I still don't remember some of the things that happened a couple of weeks ago. But . . . maybe when I moved in. I never use the thing and don't recall taking it out of the drawer. I've had it for years, bought it from a dealer in Seattle, but . . . I just don't need it." He slid the plastic-encased Glock back to Rivers as if he never wanted to see the pistol again.

He seemed sincere, but Rivers didn't trust him.

"So what was your relationship to Willow Valente?"

"Nothing. I mean, she was an employee, obviously. On the payroll."

"And that was it?"

"Yeah." He shrugged. "Uh, she helped Sophia clean my house after you guys trashed it doing your thing, but I didn't ask her to. I knew her well enough to say 'hi,' but that was about it."

"When was that?"

Cahill glanced at the calendar on his watch and gave the date, then said, "Sophia insisted, and Willow helped her. I'd been camping out at the inn after I got out of the hospital . . . so . . ." His voice faded.

Rivers took out the pictures of Willow in James's bed from the manila folder on the table. He'd copied the images from the digital images that had been sent to Zena Wallace and printed them out once he'd arrived at the office. "How do you explain these?" He slid the pictures out of a folder and sent them James's way.

"What are these?" James took a quick glance at the nude shots and scooted his chair back, distancing himself from the photos. "Why the hell are you showing me these?" He gestured quickly at the pictures. "Because she has the gun?"

"Look a little closer," Mendoza suggested.

"Why?" Swallowing hard, Cahill inched his chair closer again. "I mean, she's naked, and she's got the gun and . . ." His already pale face lost all color, and his mouth fell open a bit. "Holy shit." He looked up at Rivers. "She was in my bed?" he said, and he seemed dumbfounded. "In my bed with the gun and . . ." He held up both hands, palms out. "I don't know what this means, but wow . . . oh, wow. I don't get this. The only time, *only* time she'd been in that room was to clean it."

"You're sure?"

"Hell, yes . . . To my knowledge, she has never been in my bedroom or my house except that one time . . . wait a minute." He stared at Rivers. "What you're saying is that you think because you have pictures of her in my bed with the gun that she and I . . ." To his credit, he seemed disbelieving, his mouth falling open. "No . . . just no! This—whatever it is, is nuts!" And then it appeared to have dawned on him. "You've been in my house again," he charged.

Rivers gave a curt nod. "We checked." And then Rivers laid it out, explaining that they'd checked his house again, found a long black hair in his bed, presumably from the dead woman. To be certain, they'd stripped his bedding and taken it, probably looking for semen or blood . . . or whatever.

"Jesus H. Christ!" Cahill came out of his chair. "I had nothing to do with any of this! Nothing!"

"And yet your name keeps coming up, and you are at the center of it all."

"No way, I—"

Mendoza cut him off. "What was your relationship with Charity Spritz?"

Cahill's head snapped around to stare at her. "The reporter. Nothing . . . holy crap, what the fuck are you suggesting?"

"She called you."

"Well, yeah! Constantly. Ever since Megan went missing. She wanted to interview me, but I wasn't into it. I mean she was a real pain in the butt." He explained that Charity Spritz's calls were insistent, nearly to the point of harassment, that she'd shown up on his porch, and that he'd finally decided to call her, only to have her not respond. ". . . I guess now that I know what happened to her, that explains it. Wait a minute. Don't tell me—was she killed with . . ." He glanced at the Glock again.

"No," Rivers said. "Strangled."

"Jesus . . . and you think . . . ?" Cahill looked sick. "As I said, this is freakin' nuts!"

Rivers had just seen the official autopsy report, where he'd noted that Spritz's larynx had been crushed, the hyoid bone broken, along with injuries sustained in a severe beating. Hopefully, though, the scrapings under her fingernails would help ID her killer.

The interview lasted over an hour, but in the end, Rivers and Mendoza didn't learn anything more. When Mendoza asked why he was with Rebecca Travers, James reacted a little, bristling.

"I don't see it's any of your business, but she and I want to find out what happened to Megan."

"So you're not involved with her romantically?" Mendoza persisted.

"No." But his eyes had flashed a little.

"You were."

"Yes."

"And you dumped her for her sister."

He hesitated, then nodded. "I made a mistake. I broke up with her based on a lie."

"That Megan Travers perpetrated."

A muscle worked in his jaw. "As I said, it was a mistake."

"So you aren't taking up with her again?"

Just the tiniest bit of hesitation. "No."

Rivers didn't believe him. "What about Sophia Russo? You've been seen with her."

"Are you two involved? Romantically?" Mendoza added, putting a finer point on it.

"We were," he admitted. "That's over."

Rivers asked, "Does she know it?"

"Yes." A muscle twitched in James's jaw, visible just over the scars in his beard. "I made that crystal clear."

"You're certain about that?" Mendoza said, her eyebrow crooking, but James Cahill didn't rise to the bait. Then he dropped the bomb. "Is she related to you?"

"Is she what? Are you kidding?" he said, in visible distress. "Related to me? Hell, no! She's a woman I met here. You people are sick." He scraped back his chair and held up his hands, palms toward the cops. "I think we're done here."

And they probably were for now. "Just one more thing," Rivers said, and texted the officer staying with Rebecca Travers.

"What?"

When Rebecca stepped into the interrogation room and sat down next to James, they told her they'd located her sister's car.

"Where?" Rebecca asked, her hand at her throat, her eyes round. "What about my sister? Is she—?" She couldn't get the rest out, and James took her hand, gave it a squeeze and pinpointed Rivers in his glare.

"We haven't found her," Mendoza admitted. "Just the car and some personal belongings. The car was parked in a garage near a mountain cabin, a garage owned by Harold Sinclaire. Does she know him?"

Rebecca, ashen, shook her head. "Not that I know of."

"I know him." James scowled, ran fingers down his beard. "I sold a tiny house to him." His eyebrows drew together, creating more havoc with his uneven haircut.

Mendoza's head snapped up. "When did he buy the tiny home?"

"Last year sometime . . . end of summer maybe," James said. "Was that it? Was she in one of my homes?"

"No. The cabin is at least fifty years old, maybe more, built solidly on a foundation and with a garage," Rivers said.

Mendoza eyed Cahill. "Do you remember where Sinclaire's tiny home was delivered to?"

"It wasn't. Sinclaire hauled it away himself on a trailer."

"To take it where?"

James leaned back in his chair, rubbed his chin. "I don't know. It was built to code, was small enough to be considered an RV."

"Then I guess we need to know where it landed," Rivers said aloud, and Mendoza made a note. "It's registered, right? To Sinclaire?"

"Yeah."

"We'll need copies of that paperwork," Mendoza said. "You know that Harold Sinclaire is dating Jennifer Korpi. You were involved with her, too, right? A while back?"

"That's right," James clipped out, and beside him, Rebecca tensed, shifted in her chair. "What does that have to do with anything?"

"Just something we're trying to figure out," Rivers said.

"Then do it. This has nothing to do with me."

"Then why would a friend of Megan's say that Megan told her not long before she went missing that if anything happened to her, you were the guy responsible?"

Rebecca gasped, her eyes rounding.

"That's a lie!" James said, and he was on his feet. "I don't know where you're getting your information, but that's all fucked up." He leaned across the table, his features tight, a vein popping in his forehead, his lips barely moving, as he said, "I never, ever lifted a finger to her. We're done here." And with that, he and Rebecca Travers walked out of the building.

Rivers and Mendoza followed them, and Rivers noted that when Cahill attempted to guide her by the elbow past the front desk, she shook him off. And she made certain she pushed the door open herself.

"You set him up."

"Maybe."

"So what do you make of that?" Mendoza said as the glass doors swung shut behind them.

"What's the old quotation? 'Hell hath no fury like a woman scorned'?"

Mendoza's eyes narrowed as she stared through a front window, watching James Cahill drive away, Rebecca Travers in the passenger seat. "And what does it say if she was scorned for her own sister?"

"Nothing good," he said, watching the taillights fade into the slim stream of traffic. "Nothing good at all."

It took James hours to fall asleep at his room at the inn. No way could he have faced his house, where the cops had torn the place up again. After a frosty drive back to the inn, during which Rebecca had barely spoken a word, he'd dropped her off. He'd waited until she'd driven off, then surreptitiously followed her back into town from a distance. From a side street with a view of the Main Street Hotel's parking lot, he'd watched as she found her usual spot, locked the car, then walked inside the brightly lit hotel.

All the while, as condensation had collected on the inside of the windows of his Explorer, the questions the cops had fired at him in that airless room during the interview had ricocheted through his brain—his gun being found at the murder scene, pictures of Willow in his bed, the insinuations that he was involved in her death and Charity Spritz's in San Francisco. And how was Jennifer involved—why had Megan's car been found on her boyfriend's property? And Sophia—they thought she was related to him?

No—that was just wrong! All of it was wrong!

He'd known he couldn't sleep in his bed at the house, at least not tonight.

The thought of Willow Valente lying on his sheets, posing naked with the gun while taking selfies, made his skin crawl. So he'd checked himself into the suite at his own inn, the very set of rooms he'd occupied upon getting out of the hospital; they were fast becoming his home away from home.

And there he lay, staring up at the ceiling, a million thoughts running through his mind: Megan missing; the two women dead—murdered; Sophia refusing to believe their affair was over; Gus Jardine threatening to sue him; Rowdy reminding him that the cops weren't on his side; Megan's car found at Harold Sinclaire's mountain cabin, yet no sign of her; and Rebecca . . . God, why couldn't he just forget her? She'd made it clear that she wasn't interested in him.

Nonetheless, the cops were focusing on him, and even now, in his suite at the inn, he couldn't breathe, felt that there was a noose surrounding his neck and the rough rope was slowly, inch by inch, being tightened.

He threw off the covers and swore.

Nothing was making sense, but it was obvious the police had trained their sights on him.

Rivers considered him a suspect, possibly suspect *numero uno*.

Mentally exhausted but still jangled, he finally went into the bathroom, looked through his overnight case, and found some over-the-counter sleeping pills and tossed back two, washing them down with a mouthful of water.

He glanced at the clock just before two and, with Ralph snoring on his bed, had finally fallen into a fitful sleep, deep enough that he didn't hear the door open, nor the shepherd's soft "woof," but not so encompassing that he didn't feel the weight of another body settle against the mattress.

His eyes flew open, and he physically started at the sight of Sophia, her blond hair shimmering in the thin light, her eyes luminous, her body naked.

"What the hell?" He scooted up in the bed. He flung himself out of the bed so quickly that he felt a jab of pain in his shoulder. "What do you think you're doing?" he asked, still so groggy he thought he might be dreaming.

But she lay back on the bed, and instead of seeming petulant, she was actually smiling. "I told you I needed to talk to you, and you stood me up."

"I know . . . I'm sorry about that. But, hell, you have to leave. Now." He blinked, wiped a hand over his face—this was no dream.

"I don't think so."

"Seriously? Do you want me to call security? Do you know what's happened around here?" The events of the night before came crashing back, and he was incredulous that she was so brazen as to show up in his room. Again. He mentally kicked himself up one side and down the other for not double-locking the door.

"I heard about Willow, if that's what you're talking about."

"Yeah. That's one thing. Look, I don't have to explain. You just need to leave and stay away from me. It's over. You can . . . you can get another job. I'll give you a decent severance package, good references, and—"

"No!" she cut in sharply. Her smile fell away. "I'm not leaving, and for God's sake, you're not firing me." Her eyes narrowed almost evilly. "Not tonight, Daddy."

"What?" What was she talking about, *Daddy?* She never called him that, thank God.

"I've been trying to tell you! I told you it was important." The smile, harder-edged now, returned. "You're going to be a father."

"A what?" Had he heard her wrong? "A—?"

"Father," she repeated smugly.

"No. Wait. Are you kidding?" What was she saying? This had to be wrong. But the expression on her face convinced him, and his heart dropped to the floor. The room seemed to shrink, and he put a hand out to steady himself against the wall. Her words echoed through his head. *A father. You're going to be a father* . . . For a second he couldn't breathe, couldn't think.

"Not kidding. Uh-uh. I'm pregnant, James." The hard edges of her face cracked, and tears came to her eyes, her voice softening, her smile now tremulous. "I know it's a shock," she said, her voice sounding as if it came from a long distance away, "but it's true." As if she had anticipated his reaction, she reached into the purse she'd slung onto the floor and extracted a stick, an implement he recognized as being a part of a pregnancy kit.

Holy shit, she wasn't kidding. His heart thudded, resounding in his ears. This couldn't be happening! Couldn't!

"Go ahead," she encouraged and reached over to snap on a light.

His eyes adjusting, he focused on the little bit of plastic. Every moment of his life had ended up here.

He swallowed hard.

Picked up the stick.

Read the indicator.

True to Sophia's words, it read POSITIVE.

The floor seemed to buckle.

"I know this is hard to take in, but trust me," Sophia said, a tremulous smile on her lips. "This is a good thing. Trust me. The best! You, James Cahill, are going to be a daddy."

CHAPTER 45

December 10

Rebecca tossed and turned, sleep eluding her.

Hours passed, the digital clock mocking her as her thoughts swirled with images of her sister.

1:18—Megan at seven, riding her bike and crashing, her pigtails askew, her knees and palms scraped and bleeding.

2:33—Megan, twelve, sobbing and clinging to Rebecca when she'd found out she'd been cut from the junior high play.

3:07—Megan, her hair freshly streaked at sixteen, returning home and upset, as she'd been fired from her first job at the Burger Hut because she'd been found smoking weed in the parking lot with an older boy. "It's just not fair," she'd complained over and over.

3:42—Megan, an adult, crying wretchedly and begging Rebecca to take her in as her boyfriend had taken all their money and the rent was due on their expensive town house.

4:11—Megan, just this year, a gleam in her eye, admitting she was "in love" with James Cahill and was moving to Riggs Crossing to be with him. She hadn't meant to hurt Rebecca, not really, it had "just happened."

Rebecca had hated her sister then.

Had sworn she'd never help her again.

And now—Megan might be dead. Rebecca had to face that damning fact. Ever since learning about Megan's car being found abandoned in a mountain cabin, the deep-seated fear that Megan was no longer alive had been gnawing at her, chasing away any chance of sleep.

"Enough!" Rebecca said aloud, sitting upright and flinging off the covers. She threw herself out of bed and felt a lump the size of Montana in her throat, her eyes stinging as tears threatened.

She hadn't realized how much she'd believed that Megan would be found alive, possibly injured, but alive! Now, though, with the discovery of Megan's abandoned car, it seemed as if Megan was truly gone, as if she were dead.

Don't give up hope. You don't know that!

Until they find her body.

Oh. God.

She had to do something.

She couldn't just sit in this hotel room and wait for news, cling onto a little thread of hope and pray that the police would locate her sister.

What if Megan were still alive? There was still a chance, right? If so, Rebecca had to find her.

She stalked to the small bathroom, used the toilet, and twisted on the shower. She thought of the two women who lived here and had been found murdered. Had the same fate happened to Megan?

Don't go there!

Angrily, she threw off her oversized T-shirt and kicked off her underpants. Then she stepped under the shower's hot spray and closed her eyes, the water stinging against her skin before washing over her. The pressure from her mother was unrelenting. She'd have to do some detecting on her own because she was the one who understood her sister better than anyone else. She thought about the last time she'd tried to snoop and how James had caught her in his house. She'd have to be more careful, just find out something—anything—to point the police in the right direction.

As she lathered her body, she wondered, who had the most to gain with Megan out of the way?

The simple answer was: Sophia Russo.

Because she wanted James, who hadn't been able to break up with Megan.

So maybe Sophia had taken matters into her own hands.

That seemed pretty rash, but Rebecca had seen enough true-crime mysteries on late-night TV to know that truth was stranger than fiction. She would just have to be careful.

Sweat pouring down his face, Rivers ran on the treadmill located in the second, or spare, bedroom of his condo. He never had overnight company, so he'd converted the room into an office/gym. He'd pushed a desk into one corner, while a set of weights, the treadmill, and a stationary bike were all aimed at a television mounted high on the wall opposite his filing cabinets, the equipment dominating the room. Currently it was 4:00 A.M., and the news of the day was breaking on the East Coast. Not that he was paying attention.

He hadn't been able to sleep, his thoughts chasing one after the other about the ongoing investigations that had stalled over the last week. The loose ends kept running through his mind: Why had Charity Spritz been killed? What had she learned? Did it have anything to do with Megan Travers, who had grown up in San Francisco? Who was the mystery woman related to James? Why was Megan Travers's car located at that out-of-the-way mountain cabin? Where was she? How was Jennifer Korpi involved? Did it have to do with her brother, Gus Jardine? And what about Sophia Russo, the woman who had caught James Cahill's attention while he was still involved with Megan Travers?

He kept running and swiped at the sweat on his forehead with the towel that hung from his neck.

His calves started to ache, and he was breathing hard.

What about Rebecca Travers? Was she as innocent as she tried to be? And how was Willow Valente involved? Why was she murdered? And by whom? Why stage her death to appear a suicide, then take a picture of her dead body and send it to a newspaper, the same newspaper Charity Spritz worked for, the same newspaper that received pictures of Charity in death?

What the hell kind of nutcase were they dealing with?

Or was it more than one case? Were the murders and disappearance linked or separate crimes?

The latter seemed unlikely. On a side note, he'd learned that the owner/manager of the Cascadia Apartments, Phoebe Matrix, was in the hospital, in a coma, one of her tenants having called 9-1-1. The only reason he noted her condition was that Matrix was the landlady for the building where Sophia Russo, a suspect in the case, resided. It might just be coincidence, but James Cahill too, the man who had been dating Sophia for a while, had been in a coma recently.

And Rivers had never put any stock in coincidence.

He hit the INCLINE button, and the treadmill responded, its nose inching upward so that he was running uphill, the sweat rolling off his muscles and dripping off his nose, his calves and thighs protesting.

The answer to the case was right in front of him, he was sure of it, he just couldn't see it.

Why?

Because he was wearing blinders?

Was he too focused on James Cahill, who was at the center of the investigation, linked to the victims, suspects, and crime scenes? Could Cahill really be completely innocent?

"No way," he said aloud.

Today, he promised himself, things were going to break.

He would make them.

First, by leaning on Bruce Porter.

He'd viewed the footage from the airport parking-lot security tape that Detective Tanaka in San Francisco had sent, and all they could determine from the grainy black-and-white image was that the individual appeared male, though there was no certainty in that hypothesis. Just because the driver leaving Charity Spritz's parked van was nearly six feet, that was no guarantee. In an oversized sweatshirt, face obscured by a hood, and loose jeans, the figure could be a woman in disguise.

But he was betting on Gus Jardine. The reason? Teeth marks on Jardine's hand. Rivers had learned about Gus's injury from a surgical nurse who hadn't been able to keep her mouth shut despite the current HIPAA rights of patients. She'd called, spoken anonymously, but swore there had been a human bite mark on Jardine's palm that had been visible, despite the damage done by the tile saw. Also, she'd insisted there had been other marks on him, bruises on his arms and torso that he claimed were all due to the accident, but the nurse didn't buy it—she'd seen her share of injuries from a struggle. She'd found a way to send over the pictures of Jardine's wounds, including the bite marks, and Rivers had forwarded the info to Tanaka, who had promised to have a lab take an impression of Charity Spritz's teeth for comparison.

Rivers had discovered it was possible to fly back and forth to the San Francisco area with enough time to kill Spritz in between. Unfortunately, Gus Jardine's name hadn't shown on any flight manifests.

Of course, he could have driven—but that would have pushed it time-wise. Why would Jardine go to all the trouble to follow Charity to San Francisco to kill her?

Rivers only hoped the scrapings beneath Charity's fingernails would ID the person who attacked her.

Bruce Porter, Jardine's friend, might have the answers.

He shut off the treadmill and television and faced the day.

Forty minutes later, he was walking into the sheriff's office.

At this hour, it was quiet, the furnace rumbling a soft but constant background noise. The arrests for drunk driving, bar fights, and domestic violence usually having tapered off, and few cars on the road, so not so many accidents—this was usually Rivers's favorite time of day, far before dawn, when his mind was fresh and the rest of the world slept.

The day shift wasn't due to arrive for a couple of hours, only a few cops on the graveyard shift hanging out at their desks or rummaging around in the lunch area. The phones too were quiet, the fax machine stilled, no personal cells playing ringtones.

Rivers ditched his coat in his locker, then headed directly to the basement, where it seemed five degrees cooler and was much more silent. The air here wasn't fresh, dust evident despite the overriding odor of a cleaning agent used on the floors. He made his way through the labyrinth of corridors until he came to the evidence room, where Neville Dash was singing under his breath, his smooth baritone a reminder of his claim to fame: appearing on *American Idol* and "making it to Hollywood" years before. Of course, he'd been cut from the show, made a stab at a career that didn't get off the ground, and eventually joined the force here, but he kept right on singing.

"Oh, the weather outside is frightful—" He looked up as Rivers approached. "Well, hey, Detective," he said, flashing a mouth full of straight white teeth. "How's it hanging?"

"It's—going," Rivers said as Dash chuckled.

"Whatever you say." In uniform, he was seated at a desk, glasses perched on the end of his nose, his naturally curly hair receding so that it was little more than a black fringe around a shiny mocha-colored pate. "What's up?"

"Need to get into the evidence locker. Double-checking the victim's things."

"You got it. Which one?"

"Victim is Willow Valente. I think all of her items have been processed." Rivers knew they had been, but had double-checked.

"Oh, yeah."

So he wouldn't be messing with any evidence.

Dash asked, "You taking anything out?"

"No. It'll just be a sec."

Dash eyed Rivers above the tops of his half-glasses. "Good. Less paperwork that way. Just sign in." He waved to the board sitting on the counter separating the evidence lockup from the hallway, even though Rivers already had the pen in hand. He'd been through the same drill hundreds of times.

"Did we get the items from Megan Travers's car?" he asked.

"Coming in later, once they get everything off the phone and computer. The lab and tech guys are still processing."

"Let me know. I'd like to take a look."

"Whatever you say."

Once he was alone with Willow's things, Rivers went over each item: the girlish pajamas with the French poodle and Eiffel Tower print; the underwear, white and plain; a band that had tied off the end of her braid; bandages that had been recently applied to cover wounds with fresh blood; and the ring, an engagement ring with a tiny diamond that winked under the sizzling fluorescent tubing, which gave off a weird bluish light.

There were cameras here, of course, so he was careful as he studied each bit of Willow Valente's life. He started with the bandages, picking them up and examining each. At first nothing, and then a sharp pain, in his shin, and he saw a darkened room with cobwebs and an axe imbedded on a stump. James Cahill's woodshed. Fear pounded through Willow's brain, and she ran, as if she were being chased.

Had her attacker been pursuing her? At James Cahill's farmhouse? Willow had been in his bed with a gun, taking selfies, so . . . Rivers tried to imagine what had happened, the order of the events that had led to her panic. And her ankle was already throbbing.

When nothing more came, he picked up the ring and studied it, just in case anyone was manning the cameras. But what he was really doing was holding the tiny circle of gold between his fingertips, feeling its energy.

Images flashed before his eyes. Lying in James Cahill's bed. Fantasizing about him. Playing with his gun, then running, frightened out of her mind, afraid of being caught. Twisting her ankle as she panicked and ran into the woodshed and pell-mell into the stump he used for cutting wood. She kept moving, fear and adrenaline propelling her to the outside, where the world was bright with snow and cold as ice.

Was someone following her?

She wasn't sure.

Headlights!

James's SUV!

And the dog! The damn dog was staring her down. More frantic running, falling over a fence, into a car, finally home. *The gun! Where's the damned gun?* Freaked out of her mind, she tended her wounds, told herself not to worry. The image changed. She was in bed with tea and a stupid movie, and then . . . He squeezed his eyes in concentration, hoping that Willow had seen her assailant in those dark hours. She was dozing and dreaming about James as something cold and hard touched her temple, and then her eyes were fluttering open . . . nothing.

Shit.

She'd seen nothing, just feared she'd been chased. But not by Cahill.

Frustrated and disappointed, Rivers called Dash, who, humming loudly, made certain the meager items found on Willow's body were returned to their plastic bags, and Rivers headed back upstairs, where he ran into the ever-insufferable Arne Nagley at the landing. Brow furrowed, short red hair recently gelled, Nagley scowled at the sight of him.

"Mornin'," Rivers said and got only a grunt for a response. If nothing else, Nagley held a grudge, Rivers thought, as he kept going and found Mendoza sitting at his desk, staring at his computer. Hearing his footsteps, she spun his chair around to face him. "Let me guess," she said, her expression stony, her eyes flashing. "You were down in evidence. And you were going through Willow Valente's things."

"Just checking."

"Did you take anything?" she demanded.

"Of course not."

As if she hadn't heard his denial, she said, "Because if you did, that would be reason for you to lose your job. It could throw off the whole case."

"I said, 'I didn't.'"

Her gaze narrowed just a fraction. "Then I don't have to turn you in." When he was about to protest, she held up a hand. "I know," she said solemnly. "I know."

He felt suddenly hot inside and saw his entire career disintegrating before his eyes. Worse yet, he saw the case over which he'd felt so much angst being destroyed. Thrown out of court, a murderer walking free. Because of his actions.

He looked his partner squarely in her suspicious near-black eyes and said, "I took nothing." And for once he wasn't lying.

CHAPTER 46

Sophia stared across the street at the park, where mothers in scarves and hats and boots were playing with children bundled against the cold. One woman was helping her three kids build a snowman; another, holding a cup of coffee, waited at the bottom of a slide for her toddler to come screaming and giggling down the corkscrew curves to land at her feet, where a puddle had frozen over, the ice broken by so many tiny, booted feet.

Heartsick, she knew she had to stop the madness.

She couldn't go through with her part of the scheme. She just couldn't. It was all getting out of hand—way out of hand. People were dying! Being murdered! That wasn't supposed to be part of the plan.

But how could she tell Julia? How could she back out?

She walked back from the taco stand, where the woman behind the counter had said "Merry Christmas" as she'd bagged up three tacos for Sophia—three! From the second she'd found out she was pregnant, she'd been ravenous. She trudged the three blocks to the apartment and, as she was unlocking the door, caught a glimpse of that Dabrowski dude walking Phoebe's little dog along the bushes at the side of the parking lot. Sophia wondered about the landlady, how she'd had a seizure or something and ended up in a coma—Phoebe, who'd kept her EpiPen with her always. How the hell had that happened?

Sophia's stomach turned a little as she stepped into the warm studio. She had a sneaking suspicion that Julia had something to do with it, but she wouldn't go there—at least not yet. Certainly, her sister couldn't have tried to kill the old bat. Sure, the old lady was a snoop and irritating, but . . .

Maybe she was imagining it all. Her hormones were so out of whack, and everything was falling apart. Including her relationship with James, despite her pregnancy.

It seemed everything was falling apart. But she couldn't allow herself to go down that path. She had to stay positive.

If she could.

She tried to concentrate on the good news that Julia had shared with her. Julia had proven to Sophia that they were distant relatives to the Amhursts—big San Francisco money, and instead of the fortune being divided between a kabillion heirs, most of the estate was funneling down to James Cahill, since he had Amhurst blood. Yes, the twins and James were related, but not close enough to be weird or anything.

Over the course of several months, Julia suggested that the girls get a piece of the pie. After all, hadn't they both suffered? Sophia was an only child whose parents were wrapped up in their own lives, their marriage brittle, their interest in their only child waning as she'd become a teenager. And Julia had ended up with younger siblings whom her parents had doted upon.

Hadn't Sophia always felt that something was missing in her life? That missing something was Julia, and they'd hit it off famously, so when Julia started hatching her plan, Sophia had gone along with it: Get close to James Cahill. Real close. Marry him. Get what was due both of them. The goal was to walk down the aisle before he inherited his millions.

But Sophia had screwed up the plan.

She'd fallen in love with James and then gotten pregnant.

While he was falling for Rebecca Travers.

Everything was so messed up!

She unwrapped her now-cold tacos at the little table in the kitchen and considered telling James everything—to come clean with him.

How would he react? Would he throw his arms around her and embrace her, tell her that she and a baby were all he ever wanted in the world and nothing else mattered? "Oh, come on." Even she couldn't believe that fantasy. So, then, would he reject her and be horrified that she was a part of anything so horrid and underhanded and . . . oh, Lord.

And what about Julia? If Sophia dared tell James everything? Oh. God. Her insides turned to ice, and her heart nearly stopped. Julia would be upset. Angry, of course. But she wouldn't completely lose it, would she? Yes, Julia was tunnel-visioned when it came to James and his fortune, but she wasn't truly dangerous, surely not deadly.

Right?

Surely, Julia wouldn't hurt anyone.

Or would she?

Things had been icy between Rivers and Mendoza ever since she'd let him know that she was on to his little bit of kleptomania. Or was there such a thing as a *little* kleptomania? Like being a little alcoholic? Rivers didn't believe it. But he rationalized that his need to take things wasn't to see if he could get away with it, or because he had a need all the time to filch things; it was because he thought those items could help him with the investigation.

As such, he needed to touch the gun. The murder weapon. To feel it in his hands. It had been fired into the water bath and tested, examined for prints and DNA, so, he figured, he was safe. So he was back at evidence, bullshitting with Neville Dash, wishing him a "Merry Christmas," and finally holding the Glock that had been used to murder Willow Valente. He had to be careful, because of the cameras. As it was, there were going to be questions, but he didn't worry about the consequences of what he was doing; he'd deal with all that afterward.

He held the pistol.

Tested its weight.

Closed his fingers over the butt and placed his index finger on the trigger.

With a jolt, the gun nearly flew from his hand, the recoil unexpected. The images in his brain scurried like cockroaches skittering away from light. But he caught sight of a hunter tracking Willow down, seeing her as wounded prey because of her limp, following her to her room, and waiting outside, anticipating, having difficulty tamping down the excitement of the kill.

I'm going to get you, and I'm going to do it with the gun you took from him, you little bitch. Just see how you like it.

Rivers felt the tingle of the killer's excitement.

Using the pre-made key, one that had been stolen from Willow's purse weeks earlier, the killer entered, spying the flickering television and the pathetic little bed, the pink, girlish pajamas with all the French symbols—as if she would ever go to Paris—and that stupid long black braid. Ugh.

You'll never have him, and you won't be able to talk even though I know you're suspicious. You saw us exchanging the car, even though I was in the wig and the fat suit. You watched, and you suspect there is more than one Sophia, so, Willow, you little freak, "a-fucking-dieu."

Again the recoil, and this time, he caught sight of a gloved hand wrapping Willow's fingers around the gun as blood oozed from the little hole at her temple. Then the single thought that there was still someone standing in the killer's way, someone who had to be dealt with.

The sister . . .

"You're backing out?" Julia said, shocked, her eyes narrowing on her twin. She'd just gotten home from their yoga class, and Sophia had dropped the bomb that she wanted out of the plan.

No way. No effing way was Julia about to let that happen. Not after having worked on this intricate scheme for years, an idea she'd started sculpting the minute she'd found out that she was related to the Amhursts and, as such, the Cahills—a fortune whose size she couldn't even imagine. And she could imagine a pretty damned big one. "Is that what you said?" And before Sophia could answer, Julia added, "You can't back out now. You're in too deep—*we're* in too deep." Julia felt anger and fear. What the hell did Sophia think she was doing? Taking control? Making decisions? No way. Sophia didn't have the brains to take charge. All she would do would be to mess things up! No, no, no! Tamping down a rising sense of panic, Julia tried her best to stay calm, to reason with her sister.

"What exactly does that mean, 'in too deep'?" Sophia asked, and Julia didn't like the glint in her eye or the way she hoisted her chin upward, almost as if she were superior to her twin.

Yeah, right. Sophia could only hope.

"Tell me you didn't have anything to do with those people dying," Sophia demanded.

"People?"

"Like, you know, that reporter in San Francisco?"

Oh, God, she was blowing this, ruining everything they'd worked for! Julia put on her most innocent face and dropped her bag and yoga mat by the door—the bag and mat Sophia had picked out when they'd worked out how they could pretend to be one person, to ensure that James would notice them, to provide alibis for each other. "You can't be serious, Sophia. I was right here. You know that." They'd been together; Sophia couldn't argue the fact.

But there were others . . . Julia began to worry. What if Sophia started putting two and two together and figured out that Julia really was a part of Charity Spritz's murder and Willow Valente's murder and Phoebe Matrix's near murder? That one still bothered her, but she had to keep her cool, not let on. Not yet. Sophia was already about to blow it. This was no time for her sister to go rogue.

"Then what about Willow?" Sophia charged. "You never liked her."

"*You* never liked her," Julia reminded her twin. "*You* thought she might be a problem."

Sophia rolled her eyes—big and blue, so like Julia's. "James would never go for someone like her," Sophia said. "She was just too weird." Sophia walked into the kitchen. Julia followed and saw there was half of a beef taco, cheese congealing on a plate near a takeout bag. No wonder the place smelled gross. Following her sister, Julia wadded the thin paper around the remaining taco shell and meat—geez, Sophia could be such a slob sometimes—and tossed it into the trash while Sophia ran the tap and filled a glass of water.

"Well, if you're asking. I didn't kill her, okay?" She leaned a hip against the counter. "Do I look like a murderer?"

"Do I?" Sophia turned her head to peer over her shoulder. "What you look like is me."

"Funny, I thought *you* looked like me."

"Not so funny, not really." She drank half the glass of water down. "But it's perfect."

"Is it?"

"Oh, come on, Sophia. Do you think I really killed Willow? I can't believe it!" Julia said. "Geez, get a clue."

"She was shot with James's gun. You were in his house. You could have stolen it."

"*You* were in his house too. *You* could have stolen it."

"You weren't here the night Willow was killed," Sophia accused.

Julia shook her head and opened the refrigerator, pulled out a can of Diet Coke. "Yes, I was."

"Not all of the night. I heard you go out."

That was the problem with this damned apartment. Too small. And though Julia slept in the loft, while Sophia had the bedroom, it was tricky coming and going without being seen or heard. When Sophia was at work—no problem, Julia would don her disguise and do whatever she wanted, as long as she had the car. That, of course, was an issue in this Podunk town with zero cabs and no Uber or Lyft drivers who wouldn't recognize you.

Julia probably should have rented a house, as there were too many prying eyes in this building. Though it didn't have cameras, there was always the nosy landlady to deal with. Or there had been. Julia had managed to take care of Phoebe. Julia was a master at opening locks, and finding the EpiPens hadn't been hard; the old lady was always talking about herself.

Too bad she hadn't died.

Yet.

But Julia would take care of her. The switched-out candy had been brilliant, or so she'd thought. And come on, why was the old lady eating candy at all—what with her constant complaints about diabetes? Julia concentrated. Maybe she should put the peanut powder in the old woman's Metamucil . . . or come up with some other kind of accident. Slipping on the ice would be good. Maybe if Julia let that stupid little Larry dog out, and he ran into the street, and Phoebe, running after him, slipped and fell on the ice and hit her head . . . at night. That would be best. She'd have to work on that, but Phoebe, the old snoop, had to go!

Julia cracked open the soda. "I bought groceries after the shift I worked."

"I know what time you got off," Sophia reminded her. "It was *my* shift."

"So I got groceries and had a couple of drinks, down at the Brass Bullet." She went back to the living room and carefully peered through the blinds to spy on Dabrowski shoveling snow, Larry—that stupid little yappy dog he'd inherited from Phoebe Matrix—sniffing the bushes lining the parking lot.

"Ask Bruce, if you don't believe me," she said, snapping the blinds shut, then returning to the kitchen. "He was there—at the Bullet."

Sophia looked as if she were about to say something, but didn't.

"So what? Now I can't even have a drink?" Julia demanded and, to make a point, took a swallow from her can.

"You just need to be careful. And I think this is wrong. I mean, what we're doing. The whole scam. It's just not right."

"When did you come up with a change of heart? Is this because you and James had a fight?" Sophia had confided that she was giving James a little space, that they'd had a disagreement, so Julia assumed all of her doubts arose from the fight—whatever it had been about. Sophia had been a little closemouthed about it. Now she touched her twin on the shoulder. "You knew this could get messy. So don't think you can back out now. You're in this, Sophia. It's too late now to grow a conscience."

Sophia appeared absolutely miserable, almost near tears, her throat catching. She shrugged off Julia's hand. "Is it—is it really worth it?"

Hell, yeah, it is. What was wrong with her? They had a deal. A pact. Made between two women of the same blood! And stupid Sophia intended to blow it? After all the years of planning to get back at the Cahills for turning their backs on them, now . . . *now* Sophia was going to throw in the towel?

"We're talking millions," Julia reminded her, trying to remain calm. "Tens of millions, maybe hundreds of millions. Who knows? But more money than we would ever see in our lifetimes." Julia softened her voice a little, tried to be placating. "Listen. We're just getting back what's rightfully ours. Remember? We were cut out when that whack job of a mother gave us up for adoption. Didn't even let our father know we existed."

"And now he's dead," Sophia supplied, as if she were sad at the thought.

Well, who knew if their old man had really kicked off, but Julia had spun that story well enough that Sophia had bought it. And really, as far as Julia was concerned, whoever had been the sperm donor who had impregnated Deidre, he didn't exist, not to her. She never wanted to know who he was, so she planned to just keep him where he should be: dead in the ground.

Sophia set her near-empty glass in the sink, where a couple of other dirtied plastic dollar-store plates sat. What the fuck? Couldn't she find the dishwasher? That was the difference between them. Sophia had grown up somewhat pampered, if ignored by her parents, and Julia had been forced to work hard, to take care of her younger siblings. It was like she'd been an unpaid maid—a slave! So still, after all these years, after finally finding her sister, she was the damned workhorse, had made the plans, secured this apartment, bought the car with money she'd saved working as a barista in a mom-and-pop coffee joint, scrabbling for every damned dime she'd saved.

"What about Megan Travers?" Sophia asked, finally getting to what, Julia suspected, was really bothering her. "Is she dead too?"

Julia let out a disgusted sigh. "Of course not."

"Prove it."

"What?"

"You said you kidnapped her. The cops found her car at that cabin, but she wasn't there. I read where they're going to take cadaver dogs up there. Are they going to find her? Buried on the property? Stuffed in a basement?"

"This is crazy!" Julia snapped, her anger surfacing. What the hell was wrong with Sophia? "You've been watching too many made-for-TV 'true crime' shows."

"Prove it," her sister said again stubbornly.

"What? You want a picture of her?"

"Not unless it's date-stamped." Sophia was thinking now, and that was dangerous. "The plan was to kidnap her, right? Not harm her. So, what happens after we get James to marry me—us—huh? We can't just let her free after keeping her prisoner. She'll rat us out!"

"Not if we cut her in. And trust me, Megan Travers wants a share."

"She's in love with James!"

"She's in love with his money. Like us."

Sophia bit her lip. "It's more to me," she admitted, and Julia rolled her eyes.

She couldn't let her twin mess this up. Not after all the work. "Just pull yourself together, and go through with the plan. You think he'll marry you—us, right? Now that the competition's out of the picture."

"But it isn't," Sophia whined. "He's been with Rebecca Travers."

"I know!" Julia spat out, then tried to tamp down her rising frustration. Why was her sister being such a pain? "I'm dealing with that. Rebecca's a lot smarter than Megan was, and James dumped her. For Megan. She won't be fooled, won't trust him again." Julia would make sure of it. Because Sophia was right—Rebecca was a problem, a serious problem. But Julia knew how to deal with problems. "We'll just keep plying him with sex." She arched an eyebrow. She and Sophia had both been in James's bed, and it hadn't been a problem . . . yet . . . But that might change. She sensed the difference in James. Was he just suspicious because of the recent murders, or was it because of that damned Rebecca Travers attempting to turn his head? The problem was that the more Sophia and Julia took turns sleeping with James, the more he could notice that they were different. Though physically they were nearly identical, their personalities were not perfect mirror images. That's where the problem might lie, Julia suspected. It would be their mannerisms or their temperament or their sense of humor that were different and might tip him off. She'd reasoned, originally, that if he was with each of them equally, he might just think "Sophia" was moody and ever-changing, but she'd miscalculated. James was sharper than she'd first imagined, and fooling him was getting more difficult as time wore on. And now Sophia was balking.

Not good. Not good at all.

Something had clearly changed. Sophia wasn't playing along. Instead, she stared at her twin with round, accusing eyes. "You said, 'was,'" she said, in a voice so low Julia had trouble hearing it.

"What?" What was she talking about? Julia's muscles tightened.

"You said, "'Rebecca's a lot smarter than Megan *was.*' Like Megan doesn't exist anymore," Sophia said, obviously getting upset. "Like she's dead."

"Oh, God, Sophia, get over it. A slip of the tongue. A mistake, damn it!"

"Was it?"

"Yes!" Julia let out a long sigh, but inside she was panicking.

Sophia's new attitude was more than worrisome; it was dangerous! "Of course it was. Oh, for the love of—you said you wanted proof, right? That Megan's still alive? Well, let's go." She was already reaching for her gloves and hat, her mind spinning.

"Now?"

"Yes. Just let me get the damned wig. I wouldn't want that goon in room five to get smart about us."

"Phil?" Sophia pulled a face.

"Yeah, that's the one. Dabrowski."

Sophia actually grinned, a glimmer of her old self shining through. "Smart? Not a chance."

"You call him 'Phil' now?"

"He told me to."

"Yeah, but you never told me." Shit! That was the problem. Sophia was getting sloppy, and people were getting suspicious. Several people at the inn had looked at her strangely, and Willow had certainly begun to figure out that something was up with Sophia. It wouldn't be too long until someone—possibly the damned cops or even James—realized what was going on. And what would happen when Sophia actually married James? Was there a chance she would betray Julia, turn on her? Convince James that Julia was the true, the only bad seed? What would happen when the "we" became "I"? That would never work. "We have to keep our stories straight," Julia reminded Sophia. "To make sure that when we talk to someone, we let the other one know. Otherwise, this will never work."

"I do! With James, at least." But there was something in her voice that gave the lie away. Sadly, Sophia was becoming a liability.

"Good. Remember. I need to know. Everything." Julia was already walking to the bathroom to grab her wig, glasses, and fat suit. She only had one outfit that worked with the larger size, but it didn't matter, because she had the coat that she always wore and that seemed normal with the winter weather. "I'll drive," she said once she'd slipped the glasses over her face and the disguise was in place.

"Of course." Sophia slipped on her own coat. "Aren't you always in charge?"

"Always."

From habit, Sophia tucked her hair into her silver knit cap, exposing the freckles on the back of her neck. Those damned freckles!

Though Julia and Sophia were born identical twins, their twenty-odd years of life experiences had made them different. Sophia had freckles from sun exposure, Julia did not. Sophia had broken a toe, and it hadn't healed properly, Julia had not. Sophia had never had female problems, Julia had. But the freckles—how many times had Julia warned her sister to wear makeup over them and cover them with her hair. Right now, they were exposed and visible. Jesus! What a *huge* mistake. Was Sophia a moron?

Julia scooped up the keys she'd left on the kitchen table; then they were out the door. While Sophia was slipping into the passenger side and adjusting her seat belt, Julia double-checked her pocket, her fingers brushing something hard and cold and ready.

Perfect, she thought. It was finally time to deal with her suddenly holier-than-thou sister. This day had been bound to come, she thought, backing out of the parking spot and spying Dabrowski and that miserable, growling Larry in her rearview mirror. She just hadn't thought that it would come this soon.

CHAPTER 47

"Megan's been up here all this time?" Sophia asked as Julia drove along a rutted lane that wound, snakelike, through the forest. The sun had set, darkness slipping through the firs that towered overhead, wind rushing noisily through the boughs. They'd been in the car nearly an hour and now drove through a locked gate to a clearing high on a hill, where a tiny house sat, unique and out of place.

"Uh-huh."

Sophia knew that this had been the plan all along: set up Megan's mercurial temper, make her so jealous she'd go off on James, have a massive blowup and run, as the sisters had learned was Megan's MO. Then they'd planned to kidnap her and take her to a remote spot, where they would, Julia had said over and over, keep her until James had gotten her out of his mind. Julia had been insistent that Megan would eventually go along with them in ripping off the Cahill fortune, but, as Sophia saw it, that was the weak link in the plan.

One of them.

"You worry too much," Julia had told her. "Trust me, we've got this," and Sophia, so longing to be close to her sister and, in truth, to get her hands on a little of the Cahill estate, had gone along with the scheme.

Now, though, she wasn't convinced that they could pull it off.

Or that she wanted to.

Her feelings for James had changed all of that. Even though she was more than a little morose, as after him telling her he needed "a little space to process what was going on," she'd actually seen him with Rebecca—twice since Sophia had told him about the baby.

What kind of father would do that?

It pissed her off and made her sad and messed with her already volatile hormones. And here it was, almost Christmas. All of her dreams about them sharing the holiday together seemed to be crumbling. This wasn't the way it was supposed to be. Not with a baby on the way.

She hadn't told Julia about the baby, didn't know how her sister would take the news. She would confide in her, of course, but later, when Julia wasn't so damned uptight.

Julia parked a few yards from the front door, and as Sophia climbed out, the wind slapped her in the face, stinging her eyes. She noted the small windows running along the front of the home.

"No electricity," she thought aloud.

"It runs on propane from a propane generator."

But she didn't hear it running.

"Plumbing?"

"Water tanks collect the rain and snow. The house has all been retrofitted," Julia said. "It's mobile and compact, kind of an all-in-one home."

"Where'd you get it again?"

"A friend of a friend's estate when the owner died suddenly." Sophia understood; the paperwork was tangled up in red tape that was yet to be untangled. "And this land?"

Julia actually smiled, her eyes twinkling mischievously. "Well, that's kind of cool, really. This is all part of James Cahill's property. He bought it years ago, for expansion. But no one ever comes up here. I had the house brought up here on the sly, with a little help from Gus way back in September before the snows, and . . . I thought it was ironic that it was a tiny house James's company had constructed and he didn't even know I bought it and had it hauled onto his own damned land, property he never visits and won't use for years, I figure. It all seemed fitting somehow." She appeared pleased with herself, as if she thought she was oh, so clever.

"So Megan's inside?" Sophia asked, eyeing the place skeptically and walking toward the door, Julia just a step behind.

"That's what I've been telling you."

"*Locked* inside?"

"Well, of course. Until she comes around . . . I can't let her out. It would spoil everything."

"*If* she comes around." Sophia was shaking her head. This wasn't right. And the women who had died, been murdered? "We can't do this. Julia, really, we can't lock someone up. I don't know what I was thinking . . ."

"The same thing I was: about the money."

The tone of her voice stopped Sophia short. It sounded as cold as this blustery December day.

"Yes, but I was wrong. We both were. We have to find a way to get out of this. We have to work with Megan, explain that we made a mistake, convince her to understand and—"

She felt it then. Something hard against the back of her neck. In an instant she knew. Julia had a gun, the barrel pressed against her nape. Oh, God, no—She swung and started to spin, but it was too late.

The next second, her life swam before her eyes.

Once they caught up with him, Bruce Porter rolled over like a dead fish. He'd been out of town, visiting his sick brother, he claimed, but was back for the holidays, and the thought of going to prison again was enough to get him talking.

"Look, I don't want no trouble," he said as Mendoza and Rivers stood on the front porch of the little bungalow he shared with Andie Jeffries. In stocking feet, he stood on the other side of the screen door, wearing jeans, a T-shirt, and a baseball cap. A television was rumbling in the background. "For God's sake, we're supposed to go to Andie's folks' house in an hour."

"Just tell us what you know about Gus."

"Oh, fuck. Give me a sec." He reached to the side, and Rivers had his own hand on his service weapon, but Bruce was only grabbing his jacket. He slid it on, stepped into a pair of nearby slippers, then pulled the door shut behind him. Huddled under the porch lamp, they stood on the front porch on a street where a few houses were decorated, blow-up Santas and snowmen swaying in the breeze that rattled down the street lined with parked cars, trucks, and SUVs. "Look, I don't have much time. Andie's in the shower. We're goin' to her folks for dinner in an hour. And anyway, I don't know much, just that Gus was in some trouble, and he stuck his hand in that tile saw to hide some kind of evidence—a wound, I think."

"A wound from what?" Mendoza asked.

"A fight, I guess. I dunno. I asked him about it, and all he said was that it was 'big trouble.' Well, really he said 'big effin' trouble,' but he used the 'f' word, y'know." He seemed a little embarrassed and looked down a lot, the bill of his cap shading his eyes. "I don't want no trouble, like I said. I've got a good thing goin' here with Andie, and we've got a kid comin', and I don't want to blow it. This—whatever Gus is involved in—has nothin' to do with me."

"Was he out of town?" Rivers asked and gave him the date of Charity Spritz's murder.

"I don't know." He looked to the side, rubbed a hand around the back of his neck, obviously weighing his options. "Oh, Christ . . . maybe so," he finally admitted. "Gus had me pick him up at a motel by the airport in Spokane and told me not to say anything to anybody, and so I didn't."

"Do you know if he has fake ID? A passport in another name?"

"No . . ." But as he thought about it, he paled. "Oh, shit, I don't know nothin' about that." Rivers could see the wheels turning in his head. "I thought—I mean he said he'd gone to Las Vegas and didn't want anyone to know cuz he's got this gambling habit. You think . . . oh, shit!" He let out his breath and adjusted his hat. "You think he killed that reporter woman?" Porter turned in a small, tight circle under the light fixture. "I can't believe it. I mean . . . holy shit!" And then the true seriousness of the situation hit. "Look, I swear I knew nothin' about any of that, I just gave the guy a ride, okay?" He looked over his shoulder. "Jesus, I just heard the water go off. She's gettin' out of the shower. She can't know nothin' about this . . . she'd be so pissed!"

He started to turn toward the door. "Wait a second," Rivers said. "Does Gus know Sophia Russo?"

"What? Hell yes, we all do. She works at the hotel as a bartender and sometimes does a shift or two at the café and the Christmas shop."

Mendoza asked, "Do they hang out?"

"I dunno. Not that I know of. Look, I gotta go. Andie can't find out about this!" With that, he was inside, the door pulled shut behind him.

"A relationship made in heaven," Mendoza remarked as they trudged through the snow and across the street to the spot where

Rivers had wedged his Jeep between a jacked-up Ram pickup and a Dodge minivan that showed spots of rust. "She doesn't want him to know that she's talked to us, and he's afraid she'll find out that we were asking him questions. I give it six months—baby or no baby."

"So much for the whole 'love conquers all' theory." Rivers unlocked the Jeep and slid inside as Mendoza got into the passenger seat and shot him a look. "You're divorced, right? Go ahead, tell me about love being the ultimate victor." He didn't respond as he pulled away from the curb because he heard Astrid's voice again, her deep-throated chuckle, as she said, "I guess she's got you there now, darling, doesn't she?"

"You know you're an idiot, right?" Julia said, dragging her sister's twitching body up the two steps and into the interior of the tiny house. Sophia was spasming and flailing, trying to gain purchase, hoping to strike her twin, but she had no control, couldn't use her hands or legs after being jolted with the stun gun. Julia really hated to do this, but she had no choice. Sophia was going to ruin everything.

She turned on the heat, saw the propane fire spark to life, and watched Sophia struggle and flounder.

"Mmmmeeee . . . ggggggaaaa . . ."

"Megan? You want to know what happened to her?" Julia asked. "Oh, she's here. Right out there." She pointed to the front of the small building, toward the trees surrounding the clearing. "In the yard."

Sophia's eyes widened even farther, and drool started to slide from her mouth.

"Oh, come on!" Julia said. "You really believed she was alive? That I was stupid enough to think I could convince her to be a part of our plan and just pay her off and she'd go away and never bother us again? Get real!" She stepped over her sister's twitching body, avoiding a weak kick Sophia attempted. "How lame are you?"

Of course, Sophia couldn't answer.

"Pathetic!" Julia said.

Sophia started to cry.

Like a damned baby.

Tears running from her eyes, ruining her mascara, causing her nose to redden.

"Oh, stop!" Julia was having none of it. "Come on. You know we had to get rid of her. So that James could focus on you. On us." She crouched down so that her face was close to her twin's. It was like looking in a bloody mirror, she thought—well, aside from Sophia's now mottled complexion and the waterworks making her eyes red and puffy. "You think I'm a monster, don't you?" she taunted. "You wonder just how far I'll go. I can see it in your eyes."

Sophia reacted, coiling, trying and failing to hurl spit right in her twin's face and failing miserably, the spittle running down the corner of her mouth.

"Oh, now you've just made a mess of your face." Straightening, Julia scowled. "You're just lucky I really wanted a sister and right now I can't find it in my heart to get rid of you too. So you stay here, okay? And you think about everything we've done, how involved you are, how you tricked James, how you were a part of the scheme to fleece him and get rid of the other women in his life!"

"Nnnnnnnnnoooooo . . ."

"Oh, shut up!" She stared down at the wretched being that was her identical twin. So alike they were, and yet so very, very different. "Rebecca's got to go," she said and felt her heart warm a bit. Now that she had free rein, that she didn't have to worry about Sophia messing things up, that she didn't have to rely on her twin for every little, inconvenient alibi, she could deal with Rebecca Travers on her own.

In fact, if push really came to shove, she might find a way to use her sister as the sacrificial lamb, though she probably couldn't go through with it.

Just like she didn't have the heart to kill her.

A flaw. One she'd try to correct.

She remembered to slide Sophia's phone out of her pocket, then started for the door again.

Sophia, damn her, lunged upward.

Nearly got her feet under her, but stumbled and twirled, her arm flailing outward in a wild arc.

Thwack!

Her fist connected, banging against Julia's shoulder before Julia could spin away.

"You bitch!" Julia cried, scrambling to the door before her twitching, gurgling, wild-eyed thing of a sister launched herself again. Fingers fumbling, she locked the door and swore loudly, the wind tearing at her jacket and slapping her in the face. Never had her sister attacked her. Never!

It was time to get away before Sophia was able to control her body again.

She just needed time to cool off and put things in perspective.

Of course, Sophia would try to escape.

Who wouldn't?

But soon enough, Julia thought, alone up here in the middle of no-damned-where, Sophia would realize that she had to acquiesce, that Julia knew what was best. For both of them.

They were twins, after all.

That should count for a lot—maybe everything.

Julia climbed behind the wheel.

As she drove through the surrounding forest, she plotted her next move and felt her anger returning. She'd have to do this alone.

"You stupid, stupid bitch," she ground out, fury coursing through her veins. Her shoulder was really throbbing now, and she rubbed it. She'd probably have a major bruise. At the gate, she got out and locked it, worried a little about the tracks going into the woods, but couldn't let it bother her. More snow was predicted, though, so the bad weather should take care of any impressions in the snow.

She should just let Sophia rot up there and die. Alone. Not knowing when anyone would come for her. If ever. Serve her right.

No way, no effin' way was Julia going to lose out now. She got back into her car and headed back to town, the wheels of her hatchback slipping a little with the ice that had built up on this rarely used Forest Service road, the damned heater not throwing out enough warmth. God, it was hell to have to scrimp and save and sacrifice!

She was so close to the Cahill money, she could almost taste it. That fortune was going to be hers. While her mother, Deidre, and her grandmother, Marla, only wanted revenge, Julia wanted more. And she'd thought Sophia was on board.

Until the idiot had fallen in love with James.

Julia hadn't spent the last three months wearing ugly wigs, brown contacts, and thick glasses, forcing prosthetics into her cheeks, and strapping on that degrading fat suit to alter her appearance for nothing. No way.

She rounded a corner, taking it a little too fast, and she fought the steering wheel for a second, still wound up in her thoughts.

She probably should have reversed the roles, let Sophia wear the disguise while Julia had seduced James, but really, Sophia just didn't have the brains to pull it off, and Julia had had a few brushes with the law that would have been a liability had she been found out.

Some of her anger gave way as she turned onto the main road; she was altering her plans and seeing the next few weeks in a different light.

Now it was just a matter of becoming Sophia, slipping into her skin. She'd been playing with the idea for a while now. If anyone asked about the sister they may have glimpsed her with, she'd explain that Julia had to return home. Family emergency or something.

It would all work out. Julia just had to become Sophia permanently. She'd already filled in at the inn and the Christmas shop a few times—the rest would be a snap. As for James, she'd already been his girlfriend for a couple of nights as Sophia, and he hadn't noticed any difference.

Yeah, yeah, yeah . . . she'd make this work.

For now.

But then there was Sophia. Could she really get rid of her twin? Permanently. At the thought of it, her stomach soured, and she felt tears fill her eyes. Julia had felt so alone for so long. All those years, she'd sensed that she was missing something . . . someone . . . and then the miracle of that connection through modern science. Miracle of miracles, she'd actually found a sibling, and a twin sister at that! What were the chances?

Could she really destroy the miracle that fate had cast her way?

Would she be able to end Sophia's life—one now so entwined with her own?

Her throat closed, and she told herself not to think about it.

She took in a deep breath and saw the town of Riggs Crossing appear in the distance.

First things first. She would channel her sister, become Sophia, hook up permanently with James, and get rid of Rebecca Travers forever.

How perfect would that be?

CHAPTER 48

Sophia slowly regained control of her body, and as she did so, she paced the perimeter of the tiny house for the hundredth, maybe five hundredth time. It was small, compact, and locked tight. The windows were screwed shut, the door locked tight.

Fury consumed her.

Fear chased after her.

How could her own sister have done this to her? She rubbed the marks on her neck left by the stun gun.

Had it been Julia's plan all along?

She kicked at the door in frustration.

This was supposed to be Megan's prison, not hers!

But that had been a lie; Sophia knew it now. Of course, Megan would never have gone along with their plot; she'd been a fool to believe it, and maybe she hadn't, really. She thought about Megan's body, frozen and . . . somewhere nearby.

Would Julia release her?

Would she ever be found?

Flopping onto the built-in couch, she eyed her surroundings for the thousandth time. Simple layout: living area on one end with a desk cove, kitchen in the middle of the structure with a small bath at the far end. Two lofts, one on either side of the living space: a large sleeping loft complete with bed on one end, and a much smaller storage loft on the other.

Julia had left food in a small freezer and books to read, a gas fireplace for heat, as if she'd been planning Sophia's imprisonment all along. Bile rose up in her throat, and her stomach squeezed painfully.

She grabbed a pillow from the back of the couch, hugged it tight, and started plotting her revenge.

If and when Julia ever dared show up again, Sophia would be waiting.

But what if she doesn't? What if she leaves you up here to die? Alone? Waiting? Never knowing.

It's not as if she hasn't killed before.

Sophia set her jaw. If Julia had wanted her dead, she would have killed her already.

No. She was coming back.

And then, Sophia vowed, the tables would be turned.

Rain was pouring from the heavens as James took the exit off the freeway and drove into the heart of Seattle.

He'd spent two restless days trying to pull his life together and think straight after Sophia's announcement that she was pregnant.

He was going to be a father.

He'd been shell-shocked at first.

And still couldn't believe it.

She had every reason to lie, and he knew it, but would she really be that devious? He intended to find out.

He'd told her he needed some space, that he had to process the news and get his mind straight. She'd been wounded, but couldn't do much more than agree. That wouldn't last long. So he had to work fast.

Hence his quick trip over the mountains to this city set steep on a hillside, views of the gray waters of Elliott Bay visible through skyscrapers that knifed into the clouds.

He mentally berated himself for trusting in her birth control. He'd been an idiot. But what was done was done. And he could handle being a father. But first, he insisted on going with her to a doctor's appointment to confirm the pregnancy.

He pulled into a parking structure in the heart of the city and parked on the fifth floor, taking the stairs down to the street, where rain was falling steadily. Turning up his collar, he walked to the waterfront and watched seagulls swoop over the churning water of the bay, where a ferry was just leaving the dock.

The thought of marriage had flitted in and out of James's head, and he told himself it was the right thing to do, the *only* thing to do.

If she was pregnant.

Time would tell, he thought, heading uphill. As he passed by the window of an Italian restaurant, he noticed his reflection in a storefront window. He'd finally gotten a haircut and trimmed his beard. He didn't look so much like a freak any longer, but he still felt uneven and disjointed inside. The pain in his arm and shoulder had finally ceased, and the scars on his chin beneath his beard had almost disappeared, but he was profoundly changed forever.

Not only was he going to be a father, but Megan still hadn't been found, despite the location of her car coming to light. In Jennifer Korpi's boyfriend's garage. What the hell was that all about?

Was Megan even still alive?

Or was she, like two other women in town—Willow Valente and Charity Spritz—dead, murdered?

Would he ever know?

Would he ever stop parking across from the Main Street Hotel to make certain that Rebecca was safe for the night?

It was all so very wrong.

He sidestepped a skateboarder zipping between pedestrians and spotted the sign of the store he was looking for half a block uphill, just past a little café where he and Rebecca had met for coffee. His jaw tightened with the memory, then, with a crowd that had waited at the corner, he crossed the street before heading into a small store where all kinds of electronic devices were on display, the shop that Rowdy had recommended. Once inside, he zeroed in on the surveillance section and found a pimply-faced kid behind the counter who couldn't have been eighteen but enthusiastically showed him devices he claimed were "state-of-the art, nearly military-grade" equipment.

James didn't believe that line of bull, but found a tracking device that would do the trick and bought it.

Once on the wet sidewalk again, he hiked three more blocks through the rain to a jewelry store he'd found in a city search on his phone. The window display of necklaces, earrings, bracelets, and rings glittered brightly against the backdrop of the gloomy day. James stared at the diamond rings sparkling beneath the subtly hidden lights of the display.

Could he really do this?

Be such a hypocrite as to buy a tracking device so he could find out where Sophia went—on the same day as he purchased an engagement ring?

Ten days later, Julia was barely holding it together.

Frantic inside.

She tried to keep her mind on business.

With a smile pinned to her face, she was about to close the little Christmas shop attached to the café, but she was dealing with one last customer, a pudgy woman stuffed into a bright red jacket at least two sizes too small, a Santa hat partially covering her short brown curls. Her chapped lips were pursed as if she'd sucked on a lemon, and she was showing Julia an ornament she'd plucked from the display tree and complaining that it wasn't available in off-white or ivory. Apparently snow-white "just couldn't possibly" go on her tree.

"I'm sorry; it's all we have left," Julia said, trying to keep her voice light, but she was irritated. For Pete's sake, it was two days before Christmas, and the woman was decorating her tree *now?* Just so she could get the fifty percent off the sales price?

"Isn't there anything you can do?" Pudgy pouted.

"I'm sorry." Julia wasn't. "Maybe you can find something else?"

"I've looked! Everything's picked over."

Well, duh. Again, two days before Christmas!

"Don't you have some in the back? I swear I saw a bone-colored one just last week. Maybe there are others."

"Everything we have is out," Julia assured the old bag.

"Well, this just won't do." Pudgy scowled and puffed herself up even more, straining the zipper running down the front of her jacket. "I guess I'll just have to look somewhere else."

Good luck with that!

"I'm sorry." But there wasn't the least trace of sincerity in Julia's tone; in fact, she was being sarcastic

And Pudgy knew it. She slapped the delicate ornament into Julia's hand.

"*And Merry Christmas to you too!*" But Julia didn't utter the overused phrase.

Pudgy adjusted her Santa's hat and walked out in a huff, the door with its little tinkling bell over the threshold slamming behind her.

Good riddance, Julia thought, and wondered how long she would have this job—such as it was. Sophia had indicated that, during their fight, James had suggested Sophia find employment somewhere else but had acquiesced as it was the busy season. However, the holidays would soon be over. She hadn't dared approach James, as Sophia had also told her that James needed a little time to sort things out.

Whatever their fight had been about, it had been a doozy, nearly ruining everything they'd worked for. Sophia had only confided that it had been about Rebecca, which was a pisser.

So Julia would be patient. She hadn't come this far, spent all the years plotting and hatching her plan, only to rush things and blow it at the end. If James needed a little breathing room, she'd go along with that. For now, he seemed to be thawing a little, waving to her if they met in the bar. She'd give him some breathing room, even though she hated it.

She'd seen him, of course, usually from a distance, and she had caught his eye, smiling and waving. He'd returned the favor, though his smile hadn't touched his eyes.

It was all she could do to get through the days.

Everything was falling apart. That damned Phoebe Matrix hadn't died, had come out of her coma. No telling what she would tell the cops, and beyond that, there was Gus, out of the hospital and supposedly recovering, but he was a powder keg, ready to go off. She'd bought his silence by promising him a hundred grand, but she was willing to up it, and besides, he was the one who had killed Charity, so it was to his advantage to keep his mouth shut!

Julia had known from the moment Sophia had mentioned that Charity was at the bar, sniffing around, that the reporter would be trouble. She'd been looking for James that night, had been on the trail of a story, and, of course, had made the Cahill–San Francisco connections while snooping around. Julia and Sophia both knew Gus from working for James. With a little alcohol poured into his friend Bruce, Sophia had learned that Gus would do anything for a buck—Bruce had repeated, "anything"—and he had let it slip that

Gus knew a guy who could make fake IDs, great ones, within a matter of days. With that knowledge, Julia had gone to work. And Bruce Porter—bless his little ex-con hide—had been right about Gus. It had been easy enough to work into Gus's confidence, gain his trust, and get him involved. Gus was nothing if not greedy, and he, like Julia, had thought he'd been dealt a bad hand in life, was always looking for a quick buck. He'd not only helped with Megan's abduction; he'd willingly followed Charity to San Francisco, where he'd dealt with her.

How had everything gone so wrong?

For the first time since concocting this plan, Julia thought she might have to cut and run. Save her own skin.

What about Sophia?

Was she going to just let her rot in the tiny house? Die from starvation or dehydration or frostbite if she didn't keep paying that slime ball of a fuel driver who had come and delivered propane, no questions asked, skimming money off the top so that the owners of the fuel company wouldn't get suspicious? Julia had worked so hard for her plans to succeed, and now they were unraveling.

She should bail.

But the lure of the Cahill and Amhurst millions proved too great for her to give up now. She'd call Gus, offer him more money if she had to. And she'd find a way to deal with Phoebe. Certainly the old snoop might have to have another, more permanent accident. And though it hurt her, if she had to, Julia could kill Sophia as well, get rid of her body as she had Megan's. There was no way anyone could connect her to Willow Valente's death. If anyone had seen her, they would think Sophia had been the one who had followed her from James's house to her own sorry little apartment.

So she could cover her tracks.

If she worked at it.

She'd always been a clever girl, and now she was ready to put her intelligence to the test.

"Sophia?" James's voice startled her. She dropped the ornament, and it went tumbling, branch to branch until it shattered on the floor.

"Oh! Oh. I'm sorry."

"It's okay."

"You just surprised me. That's all."

"I think we need to talk," he said, and she started to panic all over again. He'd expect her to know what the fight with Sophia had been about. And she didn't. She'd have to follow his lead.

"Now?" she asked, stooping down to pick up the broken ornament. The wings had shattered, breaking off into tiny sharp shards of porcelain.

"Leave it for now." He glanced around the shop. It was nearly quitting time, and the store was empty. "I think we can shut this down. If someone really wants something, one of the waitresses in the café can come over." He offered her the slightest grin. "I'll put a good word in with the boss."

"Okay." Julia was nervous, but she decided to follow his lead; if she let him talk, just urging him to speak his mind, she might figure out why there had been a rift, why Sophia was "giving him some space."

"How 'bout in here?"

The café too was almost empty, the OPEN sign no longer lit, all of the tables with their red-and-white cloths cleaned, the salt and pepper shakers arranged around a glass-encased candle and small poinsettia, even the ever-present Christmas music no longer playing. A grandmother and child were finishing up cocoa and cookies at the only occupied table. As she attempted to get him into his jacket, he struggled against her, declaring firmly, "I do it!" But they were soon out the door, the lone waitress swooping in to pick up the tab and clear the table.

The kitchen was closing, the last busboy sweeping up.

"I've been doing a lot of thinking," James said after pulling out a chair for her at a table in one corner.

"Me too," she said, but had no idea what he was talking about.

"I overreacted," he said, and he was so damned sober as he sat across from her. Whatever had happened between Sophia and him was serious. Julia was starting to get a very bad feeling about what was coming.

The waitress started toward them, but he held up a hand, and she stopped in her tracks.

"Well, that happens," Julia said, trying to imagine what he was talking about.

"No, it wasn't good. It's just that you surprised me, coming into my room when I wasn't expecting it and then hitting me with that bombshell."

What bombshell? "I know," she said, but she didn't, and her heart was beginning to beat in dread. What the hell was he talking about?

His eyes found hers. "The truth is . . . ," he said, and she felt her pulse pound in her temples. "It's just that I've never even thought about being a father before. We never talked about it, and . . . it's just not been in my wheelhouse."

Wait! What? He was going to be a father? That's why he was upset with Sophia? Oh, holy Mother of God! Sophia was pregnant? No! This couldn't be happening. No, no, no! Julia felt the blood drain from her face. She forced her expression to remain frozen, to stop the shock from registering on her face.

"I've been an ass," he was saying, sadness touching the corners of his eyes. "I should never have said you couldn't work here, and—" He shoved a hand through his short hair. For a heart-stopping second, she thought he was going to propose to her, to do the right thing, to claim the baby that Sophia had told him she was carrying. Her throat went dry, and she felt the room spin, the floor beneath their table begin to buckle. "Hey—are you all right?" he asked suddenly, and she thought fast.

"My stomach," she said. "It's . . . nothing. I'm fine." But she wasn't. Not by a long shot. If Sophia was really pregnant . . . Oh, dear God . . . Did Sophia even know that Julia could never get pregnant, had been told by two doctors that the chances of her ever conceiving were pretty much zero?

For a second, she almost gave it all away, afraid she couldn't pull the masquerade off a second longer.

Buck up, Julia. Don't give up! Do not! You've worked too hard for this. You can handle it. You have to!

"You're sure you're all right?" Concern etched his face, deepening the crow's-feet near the corners of his eyes.

No! This is a disaster! "Yeah . . . yeah," she managed to get out. "Just a little queasy." She came up with a quick excuse and mentally crossed her fingers that he would buy it. "Morning sickness isn't always in the morning, you know."

"I didn't," he admitted.

"It sometimes hits at the oddest times." That sounded good, didn't it?

"Well, just so you know, I'm good with all this," he said, though he didn't look convincing. "There's still a lot of things to work through, of course."

"Of course."

"Still a lot going on that needs to be straightened out."

No shit. He was talking about Megan going missing and the murders. The cops had been everywhere and seemed to be zeroing in on Gus. Which was already a major worry. And now . . . on top of all that, she had to pretend to be pregnant?

"We'll find a way to get through it," he said as his phone rang and he looked at the screen. "I gotta run. Bobby's ready to close up the shop and needs me to check out some of the work."

"Okay." God, her voice sounded weak. Strangled.

For a second, she thought he would lean over and kiss her. Wouldn't that be the normal reaction after a conversation like this? He didn't. Instead, he walked out the back door, and Julia felt as if she really could be sick. But not yet. She had too much to do.

She screeched back her chair, hurried through the Christmas shop, and found her coat in the closet behind the counter. Her thoughts spinning a million miles a minute, she snapped out the lights and walked outside, where the air was cold and bracing, hoping her head would clear.

Pregnant. Sophia was pregnant.

And she didn't tell you!

That stung.

What else had Sophia kept from her?

Julia started walking to her car. Maybe there was a way she could make this work to her advantage, she thought. Could she press James for a quick marriage—maybe suggest eloping for the baby's sake—and then have a miscarriage right away? Would that work? Or should she hold him off and start wearing a baby-bump? But, no, he would expect sex . . .

Still thinking, Julia slid into her car and turned on the wipers, watching as they slapped the snow from the glass. She was so close to getting everything she'd ever wanted, being rich beyond her wildest dreams.

But one wrong step would spell disaster, and she'd end up in a prison cell for life.

Or she could run.

But just how far would she get?

As she drove away from the café, she imagined the cops chasing after her, relentlessly chasing her down, determined to destroy her.

Screw that!

She hadn't come this far to quit now.

No way. No how.

CHAPTER 49

December 22

"Let's just hope Jardine's as talkative as Porter," Rivers said as he slammed the door of his Jeep closed after parking on the street in front of a two-story Victorian blazing with Christmas lights, a fake Santa halfway down the chimney, only his rear end and a big sack of toys visible, a decorative sleigh and reindeer mounted along the roof's ridge.

Jardine lived behind the main house, in a garage that had been converted into an apartment.

"I wouldn't bet on it." Mendoza adjusted the hood of her thick jacket, faux fur framing her face, as they started walking down the long drive. She'd thawed a little toward him, and they were working as a team again. "We got lucky with Porter."

"We'll see." They had more to persuade Jardine with.

The lab reports had come in on the scrapings beneath Charity Spritz's fingernails; the skin had come back as male. They would have to compare DNA samples, of course, and Rivers doubted Jardine would give a sample of his spit voluntarily, but they had the bite marks, security footage, and Porter's statement.

A row of arborvitae, branches dusted with snow, separated the backyard of the main house from the little garage. On one side of the hedge, the colorful lights of the main house twinkled and shone, and on the far side, the area surrounding Jardine's home, the area was dark. Two vehicles, a truck and a small Honda, were squeezed into a small parking apron.

The garage was devoid of any Christmas decorations, but light filtered out from behind the blinds, and Rivers knew that Gus had been released from the hospital the day before.

He knocked, heard quick footsteps approaching, and the click of two locks before the door opened a crack, a security chain preventing it from swinging wide. A slice of Jennifer Korpi's face appeared. "Oh." She looked nervous. "Detectives." The one eye that was visible moved so that she could see both Rivers and Mendoza.

"We'd like to talk to Gus."

"Oh, well . . . he's resting now." She forced a smile, but the half of it Rivers could see trembled and fell. "I just came to take care of him for a few days until he can drive and get himself to physical therapy and appointments."

"Still, we need to talk to him."

She licked her lips. "I don't know . . ."

Rivers waited.

"Well, I suppose that would be all right." She closed the door for a second, the chain rattling as it was being released; then the door swung open.

Jennifer Korpi stood in a small vestibule, and she looked worried. "Come in . . . but please, don't stay long. He just got out of the hospital yesterday evening."

"And you're staying with him?" Rivers stepped inside and followed Korpi into a compact living room filled with worn furniture and smelling of smoke from a wood stove where a fire was burning, fir snapping as it was consumed by flames.

"Yes. For a few days. The school's closed for the holidays, and Harold is out of town on business until Christmas Day, so it only made sense that I help Gus out for a while . . ."

Nervously, she cast a glance at a plaid sofa that had seen better days, then at a worn leather La-Z-Boy, empty but still in the recline position. A cigarette was burning but forgotten in an ashtray on the coffee table. She frowned. "He was just here . . . Gus!" she called. And over her shoulder, to Rivers and Mendoza, "I think he might have—Oh! There you are."

Gus stuck his head from around a partial wall separating the kitchen from the living room. "Just grabbing a beer," he said, but didn't step into the open space.

Jennifer scowled at her brother. "You know the doctor said no alcohol until you're off the pain meds."

Jardine let out a disgusted huff. "What does he know?" His eyes were focused on the two cops, and Rivers was getting a bad feeling about this. He saw Jardine's right hand, wrapped in bandages, but the left, along with half of Jardine's body, was hidden by the wall.

Not good.

Korpi stood, unmoving, in the middle of the living area, right next to the coffee table and directly between Rivers and Jardine.

"Back away," Rivers said.

"What?" Korpi turned toward him.

Rivers didn't let his gaze move from Jardine. "I'd like to talk to Gus alone."

"Oh, well." She inched backward, unsure.

"This way!" Mendoza ordered.

"We need a word with you," Rivers said to Jardine. "Come on out." His cop sense went into overdrive. "Come on out." Rivers was already reaching for his pistol, but this closed space was no place to fire a gun, and Jennifer Korpi was still directly in the line of fire.

"I don't want to talk to you." Jardine's gaze shifted to his stepsister for an instant. "Didn't I tell you not to let them in?"

"It's okay, Gus," she said, but she was nervous now as well. Frozen to the spot. She swallowed hard and quickly sketched the sign of the cross over her chest.

"Get back!" Rivers ordered.

"It's not okay!" Gus stepped out from behind the wall, and damn it, he had a gun in his left hand.

"Don't shoot!" Rivers ordered.

Jennifer let out a mewling cry and scrambled past Rivers and Mendoza, whose weapon was already trained on Jardine.

"Drop the gun!" Mendoza ordered. "Now!"

"No way!" Jardine was backing toward the rear door.

"Drop it!" Rivers too had his pistol pointed at Jardine, who awkwardly swung it, aiming first at Rivers, then Mendoza, and back again.

"Put the gun down, Gus," Rivers said. "It's over. We know you were in San Francisco the night Charity Spritz was killed."

"No!" Korpi cried from the vestibule. "Oh, Gus! You couldn't. You didn't."

Jardine snapped, "Shut up, Jen. Just shut the fuck up."

"Oh. Dear. God. You told me you didn't do it!"

"I said, 'Shut the fuck up'!"

Sobbing, Jennifer opened the front door, letting in a rush of cold air carrying with it the sound of ever-approaching sirens.

Jardine was rattled. "You're bluffing," he said to Rivers. "I was here that night."

"No, you weren't. Your alibi doesn't hold up, and Charity Spritz scratched you, Jardine. Got some skin under her nails. DNA came back, and once we get a sample of yours . . ."

"Not happening!" Gus shook his head. "Nuh-uh!"

"We'll get a court order. Until then, we've got pictures of your hand before surgery, and guess what? Teeth marks match her bite."

"What? No!" He was wild-eyed now, moving slowly and steadily to the door, but with one hand in a bandage and the other holding the gun, he couldn't open it.

"Careful," Mendoza said, still aiming.

"This is all a lie!" Gus charged, but he was sweating. "I'm not goin' down for this. You set me up! You fuckin' cops set me up!"

"Drop the weapon," Mendoza ordered again.

"It's over, Gus," Rivers said and saw the reaction in Jardine's face.

"Shit!" Mendoza said, and three guns fired as Rivers threw himself behind the recliner, a bullet whizzing within inches of his head.

Jardine spun, dropped the gun, and went down hard, his head cracking against the back door as he fell, his gun flying out of his hand.

"Gus! No! Gus!" Jennifer Korpi screamed and attempted to run to her brother, but Mendoza restrained her.

"Stay back! Ambulance is on its way," Mendoza said. "I called. It'll be here in two minutes."

Jardine's eyes started to glaze over. "I'm gonna sue you," he swore as he stared up at Rivers as he approached.

Rivers kicked the gun into the living room, far from Jardine's reach.

But the injured man wasn't done with his invective. "I'm gonna sue the hell outta you, you miserable cocksucker, and I'm going to sue that shitty Sheriff's Department for all it's worth."

"No, Gus, that's not going to happen. You got it wrong." Rivers squatted just out of Jardine's reach, his gun still drawn. "I'll tell you what's going to happen. You're going down. For the murder of Charity Spritz and maybe a few more. If you don't want to spend the rest of your life behind bars, you'll tell us everything you know and cut a deal. Not just about the murder in San Francisco, but who killed Willow Valente and what the hell happened to Megan Travers."

"Not me," he said. Then, before the EMTs and two deputies burst through the door, his face contorted in pain, a stain of red showing through his shirt at his right shoulder, he said again, "I'm gonna sue your ass, Rivers. And you know what? I'm going to sue everybody else's fuckin' ass, too."

"Is that right?" Rivers said, spying the cigarette lighter Gus had dropped. He picked it up, slipped it quietly into his pocket, and said, "I don't fuckin' think so."

How many days had passed?

Five?

Six?

Ten?

Sophia had lost count. But from the loft, wrapped in a sleeping bag, the fire gently hissing in the gas fireplace below, she'd stared out the small windows, watching the day break and pass to become the never-ending night.

With each day that passed, she felt a little stronger, the vengeance growing in her heart, a beating, palpable thing. She'd find a way to best her sister.

If she didn't die first.

CHAPTER 50

December 29

Rebecca was no good at this.

She just wasn't cut out to be a detective, or a spy, or whatever.

As she sat in her rental car, huddled in a down jacket and scarf, cradling a cup of coffee in her gloved hands, she kept her eyes on Sophia Russo's apartment and felt like a stalker. And she was getting nowhere fast.

No activity in the apartment.

Again.

The clock on the dash of the little Ford Escape, a car she'd rented so that Sophia wouldn't recognize her, read 11:30. Rebecca took a sip of the now-tepid coffee and watched as the lights in Sophia's apartment were turned out, one by one. Just like they had been every other night.

Tonight, Sophia had been in her unit for hours, her car parked in the attached lot and becoming slowly buried by the ever-falling snow. Rebecca's rental too had collected an inch of the white stuff. She had to keep turning on the wipers to swipe the layer away and cranking up the defroster to keep the windows clear—in the process, she thought, probably drawing attention to herself.

Though it seemed no one noticed.

Certainly not Sophia.

"This is nuts," she told her reflection in the rearview mirror.

She'd watched people come and go, traffic becoming lighter as the hours had passed and night had deepened, the traffic light at the far end of the street turning from red to green, in mesmerizing slow motion. To pass the time, she'd listened to podcasts or music on her phone, which she'd recharge by turning on the car for a few minutes at a time.

Christmas had come and gone, and for the first time in her life, Rebecca had been totally alone. She'd avoided the lobby of the hotel and the attached restaurant, ordered in room service, and felt sorry for herself as she picked at her plate of turkey, stuffing, cranberry sauce, and sweet potatoes—a meal she assumed the hotel served at Thanksgiving as well, but she had swapped out the pumpkin pie for a mocha yule log decorated in red and green. She'd barely touched it, but had drunk two glasses of wine.

Her parents were wrapped in their own new lives, apart from hers, and though each had called and wished her a "Merry Christmas," with promises to get together soon and concern for Megan, they'd disconnected to plug in to the people they were now close to, while Rebecca had thought of Megan, wondering about her, wishing she could at least have a glass of wine and wish her sister the best. Despite everything, all the pain, all the betrayal, all the damned not trusting, Megan was, in the end, her sibling, as close to her as anyone.

She had thought of James and saw that he'd actually called, but Christmas itself wasn't a time to bring up that old pain, or the nostalgia that might come from connecting with him. There would have been a good chance she would have done something stupid—so it had been smarter not to fall into that emotional trap on a lonely night.

So it had been a lonely, empty Christmas, and Rebecca couldn't help but note the irony of the situation; she'd been bombarded with holiday lights, trees, songs, and smells ever since driving into Riggs Crossing.

But now it was over.

The new year loomed.

"Let's hope it's a better one," she muttered and wondered if she'd ever see her sister again.

For the past seven days, Rebecca had followed Sophia and discovered nothing remotely suggesting the blonde was doing anything the least bit sketchy.

Sophia went to work, ran errands, attended a yoga class, bought groceries and gas, used the drive-thru at a bank, and purchased espresso at a coffee kiosk located off Main Street. Then, every night, she would tuck into her apartment.

A boring, simple life.

Rebecca couldn't follow her 24/7, of course, but as far as she could tell, Sophia just seemed to be going about her life.

Outwardly, she was doing nothing that would cause the least bit of concern.

Except she didn't have a single friend and zero social life.

None of the women Sophia worked with hung out with her, nor did she linger after yoga to chat with the women who attended the same class. She did have a few social media accounts, but they had been inactive for a while. Rebecca had checked.

No girlfriends.

No boyfriends.

Nothing.

Even the sister whom Rebecca had seen a couple of times, the dark-haired woman with glasses, didn't seem to be around anymore. Rebecca wondered about that as the woman hadn't seemed to have her own wheels; she'd always driven Sophia's car. But when the two were together, Julia had always driven.

So what?

Not a big deal.

But a little odd.

Also odd was the fact that the landlady of the apartment building had been in the hospital, nearly died. Probably just a coincidence, but Rebecca made note of it.

She'd also started digging into Sophia Russo's life to find out exactly how Sophia had ended up here in Riggs Crossing, but so far had found nothing that would suggest anything other than that she'd found a job here.

Still, this little town in the middle of northern Washington was a long way from the Bay Area.

The only true reason Rebecca was following her was because of Megan, who was still missing. Sophia had been the source of the breakup between Megan and James, the cause of their violent fight that had sent James to the hospital and Megan driving over the mountains . . .

And then she'd disappeared.

No sign of her.

Until her car had been found in Harold Sinclaire's cabin.

Rebecca had hoped that the police would get a hit, some information from Megan's computer and phone, both found in her car—evidence, a fingerprint or whatever on the Toyota itself that would lead them to her sister.

So far that hadn't been the case.

She started her rental, intent on leaving for the night, but she took one last look at the Cascadia apartments and stopped.

She saw the door of Sophia's darkened apartment open. In a second, the blonde locked her door, hurried to her parked car, and backed out.

"So where are you going now?" Rebecca wondered aloud and then, heart pounding, started to follow.

"Hey, man, I fucked up," Rowdy said from the other end of the wireless connection.

"How?" James, after working long into the night, was just walking out of the shop, Ralph shooting past him to sniff around the fence in the fresh dusting of snow. He'd been too wired to sleep, so after driving into town and making sure Rebecca's Subaru was parked behind the hotel, he'd come back to the shop when it was quiet, no saws screaming, no nail guns tattooing, no workers milling, and no music pulsing through the building, to catch up on paperwork. The end of the month—make that end of the year—was fast approaching, and he was way behind.

Crocker was rarely wrong, at least the way he told it, and if he did mess up, he wasn't going to readily admit it. Mistakes, he'd once said, ruined his "cred."

He opened the door to his Explorer. Ralph bounded into the cab.

"It's about your unknown cousin," Crocker explained. "The kid given up for adoption by your nutcase of a relative?"

"Yeah?" James climbed behind the wheel and turned on the ignition. "So there wasn't a cousin?" That would be good news.

"Oh, no. Just the opposite. She didn't give up one baby for adoption. She had twins. Girls."

James's stomach dropped. This was bad news. Otherwise, Crocker wouldn't be calling. "Okay." He started the engine, turned on the wipers to swipe away two inches of fresh snow on the windshield.

"It's kind of the whole separated-at-birth thing; that's why I screwed up. I found one certificate of live birth and figured that was it. But on further digging, not only did I find another birth certificate, but two sets of adoption papers."

James still didn't see how it connected to him. "So I have two unknown cousins."

Oh. Shit.

"That's right, but here's the kicker. One is named Julia Harper, and she's a dead ringer for her twin."

"What?" James said, but his mind was spinning . . . "You're saying that . . . wait a sec . . . a twin of whom?"

"Sophia Russo."

"No." Bile rose up in his throat. No, no, no!

"Hell, yeah."

"You have to be wrong," he said, more emphatically. *Oh, God, NO!* "Distant relative" or not, he could not be related to Sophia, not in the least.

"I'm sorry, man, but you're being played. I think that Sophia chick might really be Julia Harper. The car she drives is registered to Julia."

What? This wasn't making any sense!

Crocker said, "I'm still checking, and I'll keep you posted, but I wanted to give you a heads-up ASAP."

The cop's question came back to haunt him as he stared out the window, his thoughts muddled. *"Is she related to you?"* they'd asked him. Because they knew. Damn it, the cops had known.

His throat closed as all the little questions that had been haunting him came to the fore. Hadn't he wondered about Sophia's rapid-fire changes in personality? How she could be almost saccharine-sweet one day and sarcastic, to the point of being brittle, the next? And there were the other discrepancies that he'd tried to ignore.

As the snow fell around his Explorer, he remembered her coming out of the shower, her hair pinned away from her face, freckles visible on her shoulder; yet another time, now that he thought about it, in a similar situation, when her hair had been swept up in a messy bun that same shoulder was flawless—no makeup. He knew. He'd kissed her bare skin. And then there were her toes. One had been broken and wouldn't fit easily into a boot, and yet another time when she was wearing those same knee-highs, he'd watched her dress and the foot had slipped easily inside.

His stomach roiled.

He hadn't been sleeping with one woman who was possibly related to him, but two. And one—God, he hoped only one—now claimed to be pregnant!

Saliva collected in his mouth, and he rolled down the window and spat.

Were Sophia and Julia somehow involved in the murders that had gone down? Did they have something to do with Megan going missing? Every muscle in his back and neck was tight, his fingers surrounding the steering wheel in a death grip.

"Look, I'm going to do some more checking, find out where Julia Harper is, and I'll get back to you." He disconnected before James could tell him that he already knew where Julia was.

Right here.

In Riggs Crossing.

Sophia had mentioned that James had caught a glimpse of her sister a couple of times when she'd dropped Sophia off at work. Always at a distance. Even so, he thought now that something was off. She was a heavy-set girl with dark hair and glasses.

No twin. At least not an identical twin. Or . . . a woman in a disguise.

His jaw clenched.

Crocker was right: He'd been played.

James tossed his phone onto the passenger seat. This was wrong. So very wrong. His thoughts spinning madly, his stomach turning over and over, the saliva forming in his mouth, a warning that had him fighting the bile that rose in his throat. He dug in the console and found the receiver for the GPS tracking device he'd bought in Seattle, then hidden on the underside of Sophia's car when she'd been working.

As soon as the screen came to life, the indicator light starting to blink, he hit the gas.

Gus Jardine must've had a come-to-Jesus epiphany on the way to Valley General, because as the EMTs were lowering him from the back of the ambulance, he demanded to see Rivers, who, with Mendoza, had followed the ambulance as it had raced, lights flashing, siren shrieking, to the hospital.

From his gurney under the portico of the ER, Jardine, pale and wan, stared up at the cop. "I want a deal," he choked out. "If I make it through this, I want a deal."

"For what?" Rivers asked. Mendoza was at his side, possibly recording the conversation, her phone in her hand.

One of the nurses who had run from the open doors of the hospital intervened. "We have to get him inside. STAT." Thin, no-nonsense, in charge, and shivering in the cold, she motioned for the EMTs to roll Jardine inside. "Get him into ER2."

"No!" Jardine croaked out. "A deal, Rivers! Immunity. No charges." He cleared his throat. "And . . . and I'll tell you where she is."

"Who?"

The nurse interjected, "Hey, I'm sorry, but we really have to roll!"

"The missing girl. Megan Travers," Gus said, his face pale as death in the flashing lights of the ambulance.

"This will have to wait." The nurse was getting angry.

"I mean it, Rivers." Gus looked like he might pass out at any second. His voice was the barest of whispers.

"Done." Rivers didn't have time to waste. "Where?"

"We're going inside. Now!" the nurse insisted, and Rivers leaned forward just as Gus said, "Land owned by Cahill. Area called Regret Mountain. Spur off of Johnson Road."

"But where—?"

Jardine's eyes closed.

"Let's go!" the nurse commanded and bustled into the hospital, leading the EMTs as they rolled Gus through the sliding-glass doors.

"Got it," Mendoza said, scrolling through information on the phone as they walked back to the Jeep. "James Cahill owns a whole tract of land. Up in the hills."

"Let's go."

Rivers didn't dare hope they'd find Megan Travers. Gus Jardine could have been bullshitting him. But maybe not. When he'd held onto Jardine's lighter for a few seconds, he'd had an image of Jardine driving Megan's car, then another one with Megan bound and gagged in the back seat.

And his accomplice?

A blond woman who scared him just a little, whom he thought might double-cross him, a woman he called, "Julia."

Where the hell was she going?

As Rebecca followed Sophia's little hatchback through town, she tried to lie back with her rental car, which was difficult as there was still traffic, though very light, not many vehicles providing a buffer, the falling snow providing a thin veil. And it got worse. As Sophia left Riggs Crossing behind, Rebecca lagged even farther back, just barely keeping the taillights of the hatchback in sight.

Few cars were driving in the opposite direction, those that did passing quickly in the snow. Fortunately, a truck pulled out from a farmhouse lane and right in front of Rebecca's rental car, offering cover. Though she worried she would lose Sophia, the truck drove fast and hard, so Rebecca could lag back a bit and hope the swirling flakes and the pickup's headlights would be blinding, not allowing Sophia to know that she was being followed.

As she squinted into the night, Rebecca's heart was thudding, anxiety twisting her insides. What was she getting herself into? She nearly called James, then thought better of it. After all, they were heading toward his property, and it occurred to Rebecca that Sophia might be meeting James at his house.

"Great."

If Sophia turned into the lane leading to James's place, so be it.

Rebecca would let it go.

This wasn't about James.

It wasn't about her.

It was about Megan.

Her gloved hands tightened over the wheel, and she felt sweat forming on her palms. For a split second, she considered phoning the cops, but what would she say? That she'd been staking out Sophia Russo's apartment and now she was driving out of town?

She'd look like a nutjob.

Nope.

Better to just keep driving.

Rebecca followed the truck over the bridge, and to her despair, she watched as the driver pulled into the oncoming lane, then roared past Sophia's little hatchback.

"Son of a—"

The pickup slid a little, and Rebecca held her breath and tapped her brakes. The driver was a maniac. Sophia's taillights flashed for a second, and Rebecca lagged back farther as the truck sped forward and careened in Sophia's path.

Now there was nothing between the cars, nothing but the falling snow to prevent Sophia from seeing her. She lagged back even more and was certain that Sophia was heading to James's home, when suddenly, at a crossroads, she slowed and turned, heading east toward the mountains.

"What the devil?" Rebecca shot past the turn rather than make it so obvious to Sophia that she was being tailed. Instead, she drove south for a quarter mile, until she saw a driveway, nosed in, reversed, and headed back, taking the turn she'd ignored two minutes earlier. She only hoped she hadn't lost Sophia, but saw no taillights, nothing but the ever-falling snow.

Crap!

She hit the accelerator. Speeding up, she crested a small rise in the road.

Nothing!

Just the wintry night and the whine of her rental car's engine.

Her throat tightened.

"Come on, come on," she said aloud, but wondered if she were on a wild goose chase. Sophia might not be doing anything nefarious, and here Rebecca was, trailing after her for what reason? A hunch? Because she'd stolen James from Megan? Well, if so, there was nothing to worry about; she was safe in her car, and if she lost Sophia, so what? The woman had a right to a private life.

Right?

Squinting into the distance, she saw no hint of the car.

So this whole damned heart-stopping, anxiety-riddled midnight ride was for nothing. She started to slow and look for a spot where she could turn around just as she spied a flicker of a red light ahead.

The road had dipped, but now Sophia's car was on the other side of the depression, steadily climbing, and Rebecca could see it again.

She took it as a sign and gave the car more gas.

Once again, she thought she should call someone, let them know what she was doing, but who? She'd already dismissed the police and James, which left no one.

Taking up her phone, she dialed 9-1-1, teeing up the emergency number. Now all she would have to do was hit one button and she'd be connected to the police.

And how long will it take for them to get up here? You're miles from civilization.

Tough. She'd come this far. She wasn't backing down.

Someone was on the road behind her!

Driving to the tiny house with a load of supplies, Julia saw the headlights in her rearview mirror as she passed through the thickets of evergreen trees, boughs heavy with their snowy mantles, the narrow road winding ever upward.

The flashes of light came and went, disappearing for a few minutes only to flash again.

Was she being followed?

What were the chances of someone else driving through these forested hills in the middle of the night?

Kids!

It could be kids.

Teenagers out of school, looking for somewhere private to party or make out or whatever.

But she'd had the feeling she was being tailed—well, of course, there had been the idiot truck that had nearly blinded her before passing, but she'd sensed another car as well. Lagging back. Acting sketchy. She'd told herself she was being paranoid, that no one knew about the tiny house, that no one suspected she wasn't Sophia.

But she couldn't be certain.

And there it was again, the faintest light flashing against the falling snow.

She wouldn't panic, not yet, but she'd keep her eye on whoever it was and, of course, if worse came to worst . . . she glanced at the passenger seat and spied her gun, winking in the barest of light from the dash.

Another glimmer in her rearview, and Julia set her jaw. Then she saw the turnoff, where she'd have to stop the car and open the gate. She wondered what the car behind her would do.

Didn't matter.

As long as Julia knew what was happening, she had the upper hand.

James's heart dropped as he followed the indicator on the map. Julia was driving into the mountains, specifically Johnson Road in the Regret Mountain area. He owned property up there, had received it in exchange for five tiny homes just last year; the final home had been delivered two months earlier.

Only a handful of people even knew where the acres of forest on Regret Mountain were or that they belonged to him.

But Sophia did.

She'd seen the transaction on one of the days she'd worked in the office, had even asked him about it.

His pulse pounded in his brain.

There was nothing up here; the land was completely undeveloped, no structure, not even a shed, just acres of trees.

But there was a reason she was heading there, and his heart thudded painfully in his chest as he turned off the county road and spied the taillights of her car winking ahead. He lagged back, not willing to give himself away, seeing a car drive straight through the open gate.

But there was something off about the scene.

Yes, the snow shrouded it, and he couldn't be certain, but the back end of the car, reflecting in the snow, didn't have the same shape as Sophia's little hatchback, yet his tracker was attached to the underside of her car's carriage.

Unless she'd discovered the tracker and had transferred it to another vehicle.

But no . . . No one else would come up here. Not on his property.

He glanced down at the GPS monitor. She was here. But . . . she wasn't moving. The indicator was pulsing, but staying at one point, and the car in front of him was definitely wending through the trees, moving . . .

Then it hit him.

Someone else was here. Had followed her.

Someone she planned to meet far from the prying eyes of anyone she knew?

As the car disappeared into the trees, he drove through the open gate, following the fresh ruts, his hands in a death grip over the steering wheel. Who was in front of him, and what were they doing?

For the first time since having it stolen, James wished to high heaven he had his Glock.

CHAPTER 51

The car ahead of her stopped, brake lights flashing.

Immediately, Rebecca cut her lights and shut down her engine. She was still tucked into the trees, hidden, she hoped, by the forest, but ahead of her, the lane opened to a clearing on a rise, where, through the falling snow, she saw that the other car had stopped in front of a frickin' tiny house.

Here?

In the middle of nowhere?

One of James's?

She licked her lips. Considered getting out of the Ford. But the car ahead was still idling, the headlights still casting twin beams across the side of the house.

Rebecca could barely breathe. She couldn't see through the windows of the hatchback, but she thought the driver was still inside. And in the dark little house?

Megan?

Oh. God.

Is this where she'd been taken?

If only! Please let her be alive!

She reached for her phone—

Her driver's door opened suddenly, a gust of cold wind rushing into the interior, the dome light blinking on.

She gasped. What the—?

"Get out!" a woman's voice snarled.

Rebecca's stomach dropped.

She looked up to see Sophia standing in the opening, with a gun aimed straight at Rebecca's head. "Get out. Now!"

Rebecca started to reach for her phone.

"Don't even think about it," Sophia warned, and in her eyes, there was a gleam as evil as the creases in Satan's heart. "Don't you think it's time you met Sister?"

"She's here? Megan?" Rebecca couldn't believe it. Had Megan been up here all the time? That didn't seem right. But why else would Sophia be coming here? No, no . . . this had to be a trap. But if Megan were alive. If she were—

"I said, 'Get out'!"

In a split second, she thought she might have a chance if she was out of the car. *And get how far on foot?*

The keys were still in the ignition—

As if she realized Rebecca's intention, Sophia took a step back. "Fine. Your choice." She fired.

Hot pain seared Rebecca's shoulder. She fell backward, then was yanked viciously, Sophia's thumb digging into the wound made by the bullet. Rebecca cried out as she tumbled out of the car, falling deep into the snow. "Get up!" Sophia yelled at her. "Get up!"

Rebecca tried to get her feet under her, stumbled for a second.

"I said—"

Rebecca charged!

Aimed straight for Sophia's legs. With all of her force, she propelled her body forward, rammed the blonde, and Sophia slipped, the gun flying from her hand, her shoulder banging against the open car door.

Rebecca dove for the gun.

"Stop!" Sophia, sputtering, was on top of her, grappling with her, reaching for the pistol and knocking it away, burying it in the drifts.

"Shit!" Sophia cried, as Rebecca threw her weight backward and Sophia landed on her back. "Ooof!"

The gun! Get the gun!

Pain screamed through Rebecca's shoulder as she scrambled, trying to dig frantically for the weapon, but Sophia flung herself onto Rebecca's back again, dragging her down.

No! Adrenaline fired Rebecca's blood as they fought, tooth and nail, hitting and gouging, pulling hair as their entangled bodies slid through the snow, slowly down the hillside, away from the clearing. They rolled and tumbled, the dark sky and white landscape windmilling behind her eyes as Rebecca strained against the other woman, who was smaller, but strong and uninjured, while Rebecca's left arm was useless.

Don't give up!

You can take her.

Together, swinging and kicking, they struggled, screaming and groaning, punching and clawing.

Sophia let go and struggled to her feet.

Rebecca threw herself at the other woman's legs, and they were snarled together again, fighting, sliding ever downward. Sophia's lips were pulled back in hatred, and Rebecca flung a hand up, grabbed Sophia's hat, taking hold of a hank of hair, ripping it by the roots as Sophia howled in agony.

Down, down, down they rolled, sliding over buried roots and rocks and ice. Kicking and punching, Rebecca's shoulder throbbing, her thoughts only on finding her sister as she slid.

"Stop! Just stop! It's over," Sophia said, then her words halted as her leg caught in a hidden root and she had to let go. Rebecca slid on her back, trying and failing to gain purchase, the boughs of the trees spinning overhead.

Bam! She crashed into the trunk of a fir, her head hitting hard against the gnarled bark; pain splintered behind her eyes, and for a second, the world went dark.

Don't pass out. You can't pass out. She'll kill you if you do.

Head whirling, she struggled to her feet and threw herself forward, intent on hiding in the forest, but her feet slid out from under her, and she fell again.

Hard.

Collapsing on a bundle of something—hard and frozen, and oh, God . . . She blinked, saw the edge of what seemed to be a piece of clothing. Something pink maybe. A jacket?

What?

She scrambled back, disturbing the snow from what was obviously a body. Staring in horror, her heart banging wildly in her chest, her brain screaming denial, she stared down at a body, lying face up.

"No!" she screamed, horror gripping her in a choke hold. "Oh, God, noooo!"

Brown hair poked out of a woolen cap; the legs were covered in denim leggings, a pink jacket zipped to the neck. And above that? The frozen face of her sister.

Rebecca tried to scuttle away from the image of Megan's blue eyes, open but sightless, her face pale and gray, her lips frozen.

"No!" Rebecca breathed again, all of her worst fears congealing. "Nooooo!"

Sophia.

She'd killed Megan.

"You did this," she charged, her own shoulder bleeding through her jacket, staining the snow, as she leveled her outraged gaze up the hill at Sophia.

The blonde was standing, breathing hard, her face twisted in hatred. She'd scraped away the snow and found her gun.

Incensed, Rebecca said in a low, measured voice, "You killed her."

"No shit, Sherlock." Sophia aimed straight at Rebecca. "And you, sister, are next!"

"No! Sophia, don't!"

At that, her attacker gave off a disgusted laugh. "Sophia?" she said and then in a snarky falsetto voice repeated Megan's desperate request. "No, Sophia, don't!" Another horrid laugh. "Are you fucking stupid? You really still think I'm Sophia?"

Rebecca didn't understand, and she was slowly sliding down the hill.

"I'm her damned twin. How about that. Julia. Without the wig and the fat suit."

What? There were two of them? What was this monster trying to tell her?

"Sophia, she could never pull this off. I probably shouldn't have brought her into it in the first place."

"Pulled what off?"

"Oh, you poor pathetic little moron," Julia said, still aiming straight at Rebecca. "Don't you get it. Sophia . . . well, no, I'm going to marry James!"

"Marry him?" Rebecca repeated, still stunned and trying to piece it all together.

"Of course."

"For his money."

"Why else?" She was shaking her head at how pathetic she thought Rebecca was, how dense. "That's why I had to get rid of Megan. She was in the way, and then that Charity woman started nosing around, and Willow too, always skulking through the hallways like a damned zombie."

"You killed them all," Rebecca said, a lump filling in her throat. "You didn't have to—"

"Of course I did!" Julia snapped. "Dead women tell no tales. Right?" Again she lined up her shot, the barrel of the gun sighted straight at Rebecca. "You're looking at the next Mrs. James Cahill."

"I'm looking at a murdering bitch," Rebecca said, horrified. She couldn't let Julia get away with it! But what could she do?

"Where's Sophia?"

"Here," Julia said with a knowing smile.

"You killed your own sister?"

"Not yet. But . . ." Julia gave a shrug. Her lips twisted in a malignant, self-satisfied grin that chilled Rebecca to the bone.

"You're a monster!" she yelled.

"And you're dead!" With that, Julia fired.

The sound of a gunshot echoed through the night.

"Fuck!" James pounded the steering wheel with his fist and trod hard on the accelerator.

Wheels spinning, his Explorer tore up the winding lane, its headlights burning bright against the white landscape. James's heart was in his throat. He was too late.

Who was shooting?

Sophia?

Or was she the victim?

What about the driver of the other car?

The trees went by in a blur as he followed the tracks. What would he find? Who would he find? Was someone injured? Or worse?

He skidded around a final corner and nearly rammed into a Ford Escape—the car he hadn't recognized—and stood on the brakes, stopping just inches short of the smaller car. Looking up the final feet to the clearing, he spied Sophia—or was it Julia?—aiming down the hillside, ready to pop off another.

Caught in the Explorer's headlights, she at first trained the gun at his windshield, then, thinking better of it, turned and ran to the tiny house perched in the clearing. "Wait!" he yelled as she frantically unlocked the door before throwing herself inside.

James resisted the urge to spring from the SUV. He called 9-1-1 and, as soon as the operator picked up, yelled, "This is James Cahill. I'm at my property, don't have an address, but off Johnson Road on Regret Mountain. I've heard gunshots. Call Detective Rivers."

"Sir, if you would state your location—"

"No time." He jammed the phone in his pocket and thanked God that Rebecca wasn't involved in this.

CHAPTER 52

The Isolated Cabin
That Same Night

At the cabin/tiny house, Sophia waited. She no longer had a weapon, but she wasn't finished yet and intended to fight back. She had removed all the light bulbs except one in the small bathroom.

Breathing hard, she went over her plan for the dozenth time:

When her snake of a sister finally arrived for another visit, she would be in for a surprise. Julia would step inside the cabin and hit the switch to turn on the light, but nothing would happen, the room would remain dark. That might worry her, give her pause, but she'd push her concerns aside. After all, she was Julia and, for the most part, fearless. Hopefully, then she would spy the bit of illumination showing from the crack beneath the bathroom door at the opposite end of the small building and be drawn to it. All the while, Sophia would stay quiet, hidden in the little niche to the right of the door. Surely, Julia would look in the direction of the light and, hopefully, believe that Sophia would be hiding in the bathroom or in the loft above. But she would be nervous and probably armed with that horrid stun gun. This time, though, Sophia would be ready!

But, she reminded herself, she would have to play it perfectly, to time her leap from above so that she would be able to knock Julia down, somehow turn the tables on her, steal her damned Taser, grab her keys, and lock her inside this prison.

All in the dark.

"God help me," she whispered, her palms sweaty at the thought of it.

But it was time for Julia to see what it felt like to rot up here in the mountains for a change! Let her be the one who couldn't escape, who would be dependent upon her own damned sister, who had to fear that Sophia might never return. Julia would see what it was like to feel as if she were slowly going out of her mind.

At that thought, Sophia actually smiled.

The trouble was, Sophia had no clue as to when—or if—Julia would deign to return. She gnawed on a fingernail, then realizing what she was doing, quit.

"Get it together," she whispered. She was never exactly sure when Julia would arrive, but so far it had been about every other day—but now, it had been several days longer, and Sophia was beginning to worry. Her stomach curdled at the thought that she was almost out of supplies. "Don't freak out."

Crap! There she was talking to herself again, having conversations not only with herself, but others as well. Not just with Julia but James as well . . .

As her mind wandered to James again, she caught herself and ignored the painful ache in her heart, the lump in her throat. She didn't have time to dwell on him right now.

"Oh, James," she whispered in a moment of weakness, then shoved thoughts of his handsome face from her mind. Right now, she had to concentrate.

Julia had to return soon. Even she couldn't be so cruel as to let her sister—her damned twin—die a slow, torturous death of dehydration or starvation.

But then, something could have happened to her. What if Julia were injured? Lost? Killed in some freak accident? Arrested?

Would anyone know Sophia was imprisoned here?

Gus Jardine? Well, maybe. But would he care?

Not at all. Gus only cared about himself.

So who would find her?

The answer was as bleak as the surrounding hills: no damned one.

Sophia's throat closed in fear again, and she had to force herself to back off the worries, to slow her suddenly panicked breathing.

Eventually, her parents would start to wonder, despite the fact that they'd been estranged.

Oh, what a fool she'd been to trust Julia.

She closed her eyes.

Waited.

In the dark.

Alone.

As she had been for days.

Time ticked slowly by, and Sophia could only keep her panic at bay for so long before the questions that had plagued her started repeating, over and over again, in a never-ending loop.

Would Julia ever know the angst of . . . ? Wait!

Sophia froze, her ears straining.

Had she imagined the noise, the whine of a struggling engine?

Her heart nearly stopped.

But there it was again.

The rumble getting ever louder.

She shifted on the ledge, stared out the windows as her lungs constricted.

Oh, please!

A flash of light caught in the surrounding firs, and the sound of the engine grew closer.

Julia!

Sophia licked her lips.

Come on, Sister! Let's do this!

The engine stopped.

Once again, the night was quiet.

Sophia swallowed against a dry throat.

A car door slammed.

Oh. God. Oh. God.

Her every muscle tensed. Her every nerve was strung tight as a bowstring.

And then, over footsteps, the faint growl of an engine—

What?

Had the car started again? Panicked, she strained to see out the small windows, but the engine was moving, coming closer, and sounded larger. Oh, crap, was there a second vehicle?

What?

Craning her neck to view more of the surrounding landscape through the window, she caught a glimpse of Julia, visible in the reflection of headlights on the snow, standing stock-still, facing the lane.

She brought someone with her? In another vehicle?

Why?

No good reason.

Julia took a step backward, more visible now. She reached into her pocket and withdrew a gun, aiming directly into the light.

A pistol? Not the stun gun? What was she doing? Holy shit, was she really going to shoot someone?

Sophia thought of Megan. "No!"

Bang!

Too late.

Julia fired, a flash showing in the muzzle of the gun just as Sophia caught a glimpse of Rebecca Travers, being hit, stepping backward, and then falling and running.

What in the world was Rebecca doing here?

This is wrong. So wrong!

Julia disappeared, moving quickly out of Sophia's field of vision through the small window, chasing Rebecca, intent on killing her.

Over the thudding of her own heart, Sophia heard screaming and shouting, but couldn't make out the words. Did Rebecca know Sophia was locked in the tiny house? Was she still alive?

She thought she might throw up, but climbed onto the ladder to get a different view through another small window. She saw no one. Should she bang on the door and yell for help? What would happen if . . .

Illumination washed up the hillside from the parked car.

Then Sophia saw someone running, heading toward the front door, avoiding being caught in the wash of light, her blond hair streaming behind her.

Julia.

Heart racing, Sophia scrambled back to her hiding place as she heard the rattle of keys in the lock. Julia was swearing, cursing under her breath, as she fumbled to unlock the door.

Oh, God, oh, God, oh, God. This is it!

The lock clicked, and the door swung open. "Sophia?" Julia called, panic audible in her voice.

Sophia fought the urge to say a word.

"Sophia?"

She heard Julia slap at the light switch. "What the hell?" Then, "Sophia! Oh, for God's sake, where are you? I know you're in here. Listen, we have a problem." She stepped inside, and Sophia held her breath, wouldn't be tricked. "I don't have time for games," Julia was saying, starting to sound frustrated. "Seriously. This is *not* the time!" She paused just inside the door, cold air sweeping and tugging at the hem of her coat.

Sophia felt her twin's fear, sensed her ever-mounting anxiety.

"Sophia?"

A beat. Julia was waiting for her eyes to adjust to the darkness; only faint light seeped in through the open door. Then she turned and finally seemed to notice the thin strip of illumination visible beneath the bathroom door. "Are you . . . Are you okay?"

Sophia's pulse thundered in her ears.

She didn't answer.

"What the hell is this?" Julia said, obviously not fooled. "Fine!" she called out. "Your choice, Sophia. You want to stay up here all alone, then I'll just leave, and I won't come back!"

Cruel, horrid woman. Sophia wanted to scream at her.

No! Not yet.

"Oh, for God's sake! Have it your way. Wait. Oh, crap! What the hell?" Julia said, her voice strangled, then, "Oh, shit! No . . . no! No! . . . this is no good!"

Sophia dared peek over the edge.

The front door was still open. Julia was caught in relief by some kind of weird moving light . . . light from another set of headlights?

Sophia's heart stopped.

She spied the gun in her sister's hand.

The gun that probably killed Rebecca. And will kill whoever followed her up here . . . and Sophia as well. She couldn't kid herself. The reason Julia arrived with a pistol was to kill Sophia, to get rid of the traitorous twin who had become a liability. She coiled all of her muscles and poised on the edge of the ledge, ready to spring.

"Crap!" Julia hesitated, then yanked the door shut. She reached up to throw the dead bolt before she realized that the cabin locked from the outside; there was no way to secure the door from within. Sophia knew. She'd checked over every square inch of this place

The room was nearly dark again, only faint light shimmering through the row of small windows. Julia took one step backward.

NOW!

Sophia pounced!

She flew across the open space and hit Julia square.

Julia shrieked in sheer terror but went down, Sophia clinging to her, tumbling to the floor as one. "What—what the fuck?" Julia growled as they fought, Sophia attacking, determined to wrest the gun from Julia's hand.

"Get off me! What're you doing? Stop!" Julia cried, twisting and writhing as Sophia clawed at her, trying to pin her down, wildly attempting to grab the damned pistol.

But Julia was fired on adrenaline and wriggled and swung her arms. "Are you crazy?" she spat out.

Probably. "Are you?"

"Stop this! For . . . for . . . God's sake, Sophia . . . You're going to get us both killed!" Julia charged, breathing with difficulty, trying to scoot across the floor, but Sophia wouldn't let her go and continued to scrabble for the gun. If she could just reach her sister's hand—

Thud! Craaack! The butt of the gun splintered Sophia's cheek. Pain screamed through her head. She blinked. Fought to stay conscious. Blood ran from her nose as, in desperation, she flung an arm wide, her fingers tangling in Julia's hair. She pulled, using all her weight.

"Stop! Oh, owww! You bitch!"

Bang!

The gun went off!

The noise deafening.

Sophia felt her body jerk.

Then a searing pain shot through her abdomen.

Noooooo!

The world spun. She collapsed as Julia slid out from under her. She began to spit, tasted blood, and heard her sister scream, but her voice was far away, sounding as if Julia were under water, gurgling her name . . . "Sophia . . . no . . . oh, no . . . Sophia . . . please . . ."

Another bang!

But not a gun, Sophia thought, trying to focus. More like the door being flung open and hitting the wall . . . but she couldn't be sure. Not of anything. She touched her side, felt the sticky warmth of her own blood.

So this is what it's like to die . . .

Someone was crying. Far away, though. Sobbing brokenly.

Julia? It sounded like her.

"Why did you do this? Why?" she demanded, her voice wet. "You ruined everything."

Ruined it all? Me? No, no . . . that isn't right.

"You should never have gotten pregnant. How could you have been so stupid?"

"I . . . I didn't." Sophia argued—the words were forming, but her lips—did they move? Had she actually said the words aloud? Or were they just echoing in her own mind? The world was spinning, but she forced a harsh, horrid whisper. "No baby," she said, sputtering.

"What?" Julia demanded, but her voice was so far away.

Still, she had to tell her sister, try to make her understand. "Mistake . . . to get James . . . to marry me . . . marry . . . us . . . we . . . we . . . were losing him . . . Had to force himmmm . . ." She couldn't stay awake. She was sooo cold, and the pain in her side throbbed and . . . and really . . . it didn't matter . . .

"You're not pregnant? This was all a lie?" Julia said, her faraway voice sounding distraught. "Wait . . . no . . . are you telling the truth?"

Sophia licked her lips. Forced air through her voice box and opened her eyes. "No . . . baby," she insisted and noticed a figure looming in the open doorway.

"You stupid bitch," Julia said brokenly, as she pushed her twin away and struggled to her feet. Glaring down at Sophia, she shook her head. "You are so messed up!" With a wobbling hand, she trained the gun on Sophia.

"No!" a man's voice boomed, and Sophia almost smiled.

James? The figure in the doorway was James? He's come to rescue me . . .

"Don't!" he ordered.

For the briefest of instants, Sophia's heart soared, and then everything in her tiny prison began to fade, the seductive darkness pulling her under . . .

She spied Julia, now on her feet, hair as wild as her eyes as she whirled, the gun leveled at James.

"*No!*" Sophia tried to scream, but her command was only the barest of whispers. *Please, no! Not James.*

"Stop. Julia! I know about you. About Sophia. About the baby."

"No baby," Sophia insisted, forcing out the words, her voice gurgling strangely. "Never . . . never a baby. Fake pregnancy . . . test."

"She's lying!" James stepped into the tiny house. "To save the child."

Julia said, "More like her own skin."

"But she's bleeding out." He pulled a phone from his pocket and started to dial; all the while, Julia, her hands trembling, aimed the pistol straight at his heart. No! She couldn't kill James!

Sophia blinked and tried to stay conscious. If she didn't, Julia would murder James, then turn the gun on her dying sister.

"Where's Megan?" James demanded, "What happened to her?"

"You didn't see her?" Julia taunted.

"Oh, God, is that who you were shooting at?" His voice was tinged with horror and disgust.

Julia snorted. "Megan's already dead, James."

"Then—?"

"Rebecca, of course."

"Rebecca?" He sounded stunned. Horrified. Oh, Lord, Sophia heard it in his voice, that he still cared for Megan's sister, that he probably had always cared for her, even loved her . . . "You sick—"

Sophia's heart cracked.

"Put down the phone," Julia ordered, backing up a step.

"It's over," he said, and there was a new, brutal quality to his words.

"No . . . not yet." Julia took one more step backward, and Sophia, despite everything, could almost hear the gears turning in her twin's mind. "We can work something out," Julia was saying, her voice softer. "Really, James, I just want a little bit."

"A little bit?"

"Yeah. You know. Just some of the money I should have inherited."

"What? How can you think of that now? For the love of God, Rebecca—Jesus, Rebecca's dead, and your sister's dying!" James said. "Put down the damned gun!"

Sophia heard a tinny voice squawking, and James cut it off, talking sharply into his phone. "This is James Cahill. I need to report—"

Julia said, "No! Stop it! I'm serious, James, and—" Julia was still inching backward, the heel of her boot brushing Sophia's side so that she was standing directly above her twin.

So close, Sophia thought.

Precious sister.

Just near enough.

"I'm warning you," Julia said to James.

Now!

With all of her strength, Sophia flung her torso up, flailing out with her arms, her fingers striking Julia's knee but sliding.

"What the—?"

Gritting her teeth, Sophia forced her fingers to clamp over Julia's ankle.

"Quit that!" Julia began to kick.

Still clinging to the boot, Sophia threw back her body, pulling Julia down as James leapt forward.

Blam!

The gun went off!

An earsplitting bang echoed through the small cabin.

Julia screamed, falling, toppling onto her twin, her weight mashing Sophia against the floor. "You . . . you bitch," she spat over the sound of a siren wailing distantly. "You goddamned . . . stupid . . . bitch—" Words failed her. She started to gurgle and gasp, to cough, her eyes wide. "No . . . oh . . ."

Pushing her away, Sophia looked up just in time to watch James sway in the doorway, blood sprouting on his chest.

Oh, no . . .

He fell forward, crumpling, his head striking the bottom rung of the ladder with a horrifying thud.

Tears filled Sophia's eyes. "No baby," she whispered, vaguely aware of the sirens as her consciousness threatened to fade. Eyes fluttering closed, she heard the thunder of footsteps and the shouted, frantic bark of orders.

"Three down!" A woman's voice. One she couldn't name, but it was familiar . . . or was it? Sophia couldn't concentrate, was losing touch.

"You heard me!" the woman barked again. "Three!" Her voice crackled with authority and concern. "I need EMTs. ASAP! . . . Yes, same address! Shit, just hurry!"

"Still unidentified?" Another voice. Male?

"Did you hear me? It's bad here!" the woman said again. "I'm losing two, possibly all three."

Sophia closed her eyes, felt a hand on her, heard the gentle commands from a distance. "Stay with me . . . can you hear me? Come on, now, lady, stay with me . . ."

But Sophia, fading, wasn't paying attention.

Another voice was rising over the din.

Julia was speaking to her.

While the emergency worker tried vainly to capture her attention, Sophia heard her sister's voice, as clear as the toll of a church bell. "We're sisters, Sophia. You and I. *Twins.* It's a miracle we found each other, and now we have a special, unbreakable bond. We're together, you and I. Nothing can destroy that. Nothing!"

She didn't have to say it. Sophia knew. But it was so hard to concentrate, to focus . . . she stopped trying.

"We'll always have each other," Julia whispered in a voice that broke with its sincerity, its truth. And as the blackness came for her, Sophia heard her sister's vow. "Always. We'll be together. I promise."

I promise too.

And then Sophia let go.

CHAPTER 53

James opened an eye.

His head hurt.

His shoulder hurt.

His whole damned body hurt.

The room was in semi-darkness, and he saw that he was in the hospital.

"*Déjà vu* all over again," he said through cracked lips. He barely recognized his own voice as he blinked and looked around the room to spy a man seated in a chair, wearing an overcoat, holding a hat between his knees. The detective. Of course.

"You got that right," Rivers said.

"How . . . how long . . . ?" He was trying to piece together how he got here and remembered in bits and pieces his frantic drive following Julia to the cabin—a tiny house, on his own damned property. Then there was the panic, the gunshot that propelled him into the cabin. Sophia was on the floor, and there was so much blood, so damned much blood . . .

"You've been here a week."

No!

"Surgery. And you hit your head, and it wasn't completely healed from the last time . . . oh, hell, it's not up to me to fill you in; the doctor will do that."

"Rebecca?" he asked, his first thoughts of her. She'd been hurt.

"Back in Seattle."

"But she was shot."

"Bullet went through and through. Upper arm. Didn't even nick a bone. Got some bruises and cuts, from the fight she had with Julia Harper, but, all in all, she's lucky. She'll be fine."

He felt relief that she was okay, but a little jab of disappointment that she'd left. And he didn't know how lucky she was—or he was, for that matter, all things considered. His mouth was dry, and he licked his parched lips. "Sophia?" he asked.

"She's alive. Behind bars. Looks like she'll make it. I can't speak to anything else."

"Julia?"

"Dead. Died that night. She was the connection to Gus Jardine, who's still angling for a plea deal. Jennifer Korpi and Harold Sinclaire are innocent. Gus played them both."

James felt nothing. Even as he listened to Rivers explain what he'd already figured out, that long-lost twins, daughters of his mother's half-sister's daughter and an unknown father, had finally found each other and cooked up a scheme to seduce James, marry him, probably kill him, and inherit a fortune. In the process, they'd hired Gus Jardine to kill Charity Spritz because she was close to unmasking them, and Willow Valente because she was getting suspicious that Sophia was really two people; and they'd nearly murdered Phoebe Matrix, the landlady who had been snooping around. Julia was the more deadly of the two, but Sophia was no angel. She would be prosecuted and sent to prison for a long time.

"Not long enough, though," Rivers admitted. "She's a piece of work."

"So it was all about the money," James said.

"Seems as if. And there's something else you missed while you were out."

"Yeah?"

"We found Megan Travers's remains. Rebecca actually stumbled on her—Julia didn't even bother burying her—well, maybe she couldn't, the ground being so hard. They left her body to freeze, buried in the snow. Sophia says the murder was Julia's doing, with the help of Gus Jardine. He's claiming innocence, of course. Sophia claimed that Julia had sworn she'd kidnapped Megan and was going to hold her captive in that cabin, but there was a fight, and Megan tried to escape, so she had to be killed. Julia didn't tell Sophia and then decided to imprison Sophia when she wasn't going along with the scheme."

"To fleece me."

"To marry you, fleece you, and, in my opinion, to ultimately kill you." Rivers pinned James in his glare. "Both of them."

James closed his eyes for a second.

He thought of the baby that had never existed and about the fact that he had been foolish enough to have been duped by them all. How his life had changed for a few weeks at the thought of becoming a father.

He thought of Rebecca again, and his heart squeezed.

Rivers stood. "By the way, we've still got your gun, but we'll need to hold onto it as evidence for a while."

"Keep it," James said. He wanted no reminders.

The cop's eyes seemed to glisten as he placed his hat on his head. "You sure?"

"Yeah." He was sure. "It's the department's. Or yours, if you want it."

Rivers actually cracked a smile. "Thanks." As he left, Rivers said, "A word of advice, Cahill."

"Yeah?"

"Lay off the women, okay? They're just too damned dangerous."

EPILOGUE

The next February
Riggs Crossing, Washington

James adjusted his tool belt over his hips and was about to climb up onto a trailer, where a tiny house was being built to look sleek and modern, with Scandinavian elements.

"Uh-oh." Bobby Knowlton, picking a bit of cat hair from his sleeve, was approaching from the rear of the building and was peering through the open barn door. He glanced down the lane. "Incoming."

Glancing over his shoulder, James spied a white Subaru fast approaching, splashing through puddles in the gravel.

Rebecca.

Despite the cop's advice, James had called her and texted several times.

She'd never responded.

Not once.

But here she was, and his pulse jumped, his heart racing.

As her Subaru stopped and she cut the engine, he felt every muscle in his back tighten.

"I'll be a minute," he said to Bobby.

Bareheaded, in jeans, a sweater, and a long coat, she waited at the side of her car.

"Don't tell me," he said, forcing a smile as he approached. "You missed me."

She rolled her eyes. "Oh, God, I knew this was a mistake," she said but cracked a bit of a smile, and he noticed that it was just starting to snow again, a few flakes drifting from gray skies and catching in her hair.

"What's a mistake?"

"Coming back, but since I am here . . ." She squared her shoulders. "I've been thinking."

"Always good."

"Yeah, well. I've been thinking *a lot.* I decided I owe you an apology. I got your texts—"

"And didn't respond."

"Right. And I didn't pick up your calls, because I just wasn't ready. I had a lot of things to work out . . . because of Megan and . . . well, everything that happened, but when I finally got my head together, I thought I should say I'm sorry for leaving as I did. I only stuck around long enough to be stitched up and to hear that you were out of the woods—going to be okay. And I didn't want to call or text. Not after everything that had happened. Even when you contacted me. Didn't seem right somehow. Didn't seem personal enough."

He eyed her. "So you drove all the way from Seattle?"

"Yeah." She was nodding.

"You don't owe me an—"

"Just let me do this, okay?" she said and gathered herself. "I blamed you for everything, from messing up my life, to messing up Megan's and somehow being involved in her disappearance. I just . . . I just wanted to make you out as the bad guy, and I did."

He waited.

"Then, you know, I came here, and I found out differently, but I just couldn't believe it. I didn't *want* to believe that you weren't involved. I needed you to be the bad guy, and I thought you needed to know that I was . . . I was wrong about you." She cleared her throat. "I was wrong."

"I think that makes two of us." His jaw slid to the side, and he glanced over at the dog for a second. "I wasn't exactly a white knight, or even a knight at all." He couldn't begin to explain all the guilt he'd suffered. He rubbed the back of his neck and, for once in his life, was tongue-tied around a woman. This woman.

A breeze skittered through the yard, and a few brittle leaves, left over from last autumn's shedding, danced and swirled.

From the corner of his eye, he spotted Ralph, who had been sleeping up in the office, hurrying down the stairs. The shepherd bounded out of the building to circle the tree and whine as if he could scare up a nonexistent squirrel in its bare branches.

Rebecca's gaze followed the dog's path, then returned to James. "Okay, well, I just thought you should know." She jangled the keys in her pocket.

"You're leaving?"

"Yeah. Job and life back in Seattle. A safer place, one where I'm less likely to get shot." She was teasing, a light shining in her eyes.

"But . . ." He eyed her. "A long way to come for a ten-minute conversation."

"Five," she corrected.

He laughed. "Fine. But let me buy you dinner."

"Not a good idea."

"Then a drink?"

"An even worse idea," she said, but at least she smiled.

"You know," he said, gauging her reaction, "maybe you and I, we should try again. I messed up the first time."

"Really messed up," she reminded him.

"Yeah. So . . . maybe I should give it another go."

She actually laughed. "Oh, James, no. I think that ship has sailed." And before he could say another word, she got into her car and started the engine. She didn't even wave as she drove off, but as he watched her leave, the little Subaru skimming down the rutted lane, he thought that sailing ships often come back to port. If he played his cards right, he could probably find a way to change her mind.

After all, James Cahill liked nothing better than a challenge.

And he was sure as hell that Rebecca Travers knew it.

Things might just be looking up. He walked back to the shop, where he found Bobby standing, arms over his chest, gaze moving from the now-empty lane to James.

"Don't even think about it," Bobby warned, adjusting his baseball cap on his head. "After what you've been through? No woman is worth it."

"That's where you're wrong," James told him as he walked inside and pulled his hammer from his tool belt, his thoughts on Rebecca's smile. "Some women are worth just about every damned thing."

The Otter Creek Women's Correctional Facility
February

Sophia lay on the examination table in the prison, a skinny female doctor with a graying Afro administering an ultrasound. The gel was cold against her bare skin, the wand moving slowly, the whooshing sound of the baby's heartbeat audible in this tiny, overheated room.

Sophia closed her eyes, thankful that the baby had survived, and trying to find something good to hang on to.

But how could she?

She thought of James, how she'd loved him, would have done anything for him, given her heart to him—and now? Now all she felt was a deep-seated rage, burning bright, feeding on the dreams she'd once clung to.

He was the reason she was locked inside these thick concrete walls.

He was the reason that she no longer had the sister she'd so recently found.

He was the reason she was so totally and utterly alone.

She had sacrificed everything for him, including Julia, and now she had nothing.

Nothing but the baby . . .

She'd lied to him, to all of them that night at the tiny house. Afraid the baby might be killed, or that James would try to claim it, she'd forced out the lie that she wasn't pregnant. And because of privacy laws, he still didn't know that he was soon to be a father.

As the doctor continued the ultrasound, Sophia thought of the money, all of the Amhurst fortune.

Not only did she deserve her share, but her baby should inherit it all.

She'd made certain James didn't know, that he wouldn't come with a bevy of lawyers demanding she give him the child or any sort of parental rights whatsoever.

Not now.

Not until the timing was right.

She wasn't certain exactly what her maternal rights were as she was in prison, but she was going to work the system to make certain she was a part of her baby's life.

Forever.

She opened her eyes, and lying on her back, Sophia watched a bug crawling across the ceiling tile and noticed a spiderweb directly in its path in the corner.

Stupid, wretched insect.

As the doctor stared at the ultrasound screen, Sophia noticed the bug reach the web, disturbing the intricate strands, and the spider quickly scuttle out of its hiding spot in the corner, pouncing, biting, and paralyzing its unsuspecting prey before wrapping it up for savoring later.

Sophia connected with the spider, intent on survival.

Suddenly, the wand over her belly stopped moving.

"Is something wrong?" Sophia asked, worried. She'd been told that the bullet that had hit her had gone through and through, nicking her spleen and her stomach, but sparing all other organs, including her uterus.

"No." The doctor shook her head, and the wand began moving slowly again and the doctor, glancing at the screen, began to smile. "Nothing at all. Except, hear that other noise, fainter, but steady?"

She did. Barely audible. An echoing, whooshing sound.

Oh. My.

"And look at this . . ." The doctor pointed to the screen, and Sophia looked at the monitor. "Two," the doctor said, nodding slowly. "You're carrying twins." A broad smile cracked her face. "How about that?"

"Twins?" Sophia whispered, hardly believing.

She thought to the future.

About James.

About the Cahill and Amhurst fortunes.

About not one, but two heirs.

The vengeful rage within her burned a little hotter as she thought of the twins, joined together for life. One would be named Amhurst, the other Cahill, or variations thereof.

"Amy" or "Hurst" and "Cassie" or "Cade." Depending on their sexes.

She glanced again at the spider on the ceiling and saw that it was now looming over the trapped insect and appeared to be feeding on the bug, sucking out its blood, while the insect could do nothing but accept its horrid, deadly fate.

She thought then of James, and the vengeance in her heart turned ice-cold.

She would have to be patient.

She would have to wait.

But here, within these thick prison walls, she had all the time in the world.

Eventually, she knew, running a hand over her slightly swollen belly and seeing her future crystalize before her eyes, she would get even.

Just you wait.